CW00631863

— AMONG THE THIN GHOSTS —

CONSTANTINE PHIPPS

BLOOMSBURY

First published 1989

Copyright © 1989 by Constantine Phipps

Bloomsbury Publishing Ltd, 2 Soho Square, London WIV 5DE

A CIP catalogue record for this book
is available from the British Library

ISBN 0-7475-0434-2

Typeset by Hewer Text Composition Services, Edinburgh
Printed in Great Britain by Butler & Tanner Ltd, Frome and London

Larry was not the only man to fall under the spell of Eva Clermont. Her restless wilfulness intoxicated everyone who knew her. 'Let's just be young and in love and then kill ourselves,' she told him as they swam in the lake at her parents' house, that first glorious summer. Nothing must ever degenerate into the ordinary for them.

But things just don't turn out like that. Somehow she ends up marrying Carlo Spinelli, an ageing charmer and prince of the *dolce farniente*, whom she doesn't even love. She descends into Hell. Spinelli draws her into a piece of property speculation which turns out to be more speculative than they'd imagined . . . Are their lives really in danger? And what failure of will is corroding that golden confidence which has so far protected Eva? These are the questions which Larry goes to Rome to answer. But is it possible to bring a lover back from the land of the dead?

When Constantine Phipps weaves a narrative of suspense, acute curiosity and emotional turmoil may bedevil the reader. His elegant story-telling compels new, sometimes startling, views of human behaviour, and the virtuosity of his craft is spellbinding.

FOR KATE

. . . nam nupta per herbas
dum nova naiadum turba comitata vagatur,
occidit in talum serpentis dente recepto.
quam satis ad superas postquam Rhodopeius auras
deflevit vates, ne non temptaret et umbras,
ad Styga Taenaria est ausus descendere porta
perque leves populos simulacraque functa sepulcro
Persephonen adiit inamoenaque regna tenentem
umbrarum dominum . . .

. . . for while the new bride was wandering in the meadows, with her
band of naiads, a serpent bit her ankle, and she sank lifeless to the
ground. The Thracian poet mourned her loss; when he had wept for
her to the full in the upper world, he made so bold as to descend
through the gate of Taenarus to the Styx, to try to rouse the sympathy
of the shades as well. There he passed among the thin ghosts, the
wraiths of the dead, till he reached Persephone and her lord, who
holds sway over these dismal regions . . .

Ovid, *Metamorphoses* x, 8–16
[English translation by Mary M. Innes]

— 1 —

Scrope said, 'I'm worried about Eva.'

They were in the first-floor sitting room of Scrope's North London house and it was evening. Scrope was slumped back on the sofa staring out of the window with his hands together as if in prayer, the tips of his fingers resting on his chin. He was a medium-sized man, rather overweight, with a fleshy, cleanshaven face, and brown eyes which had a way of looking a little sad. Although only 35 he looked older; recently his curly hair had begun to turn grey at the sides. He was wearing a white shirt open at the neck and a crumpled maroon suit. The shoulders of the suit sloped steeply down from his neck and his trousers went in at the ankles so that, with his portliness about the middle, he had a torpedo shape, reminiscent of one of his cigars. He was frowning. Eventually Larry said, 'Why? What's wrong with her?'

'She's very quiet these days. She doesn't strike me as her normal self. Sometimes when I speak to her on the phone I feel she's not really there at all. I suppose she's unhappy.'

'You said she was very upset by losing that baby.'

'Yes. But that was a long time ago now. And she seems to get worse. Do you know she said to me the other day that she didn't have any friends?'

Larry tried to imagine it. In the old days people had stuck to Eva like flies to paper. He said, 'What does she do with herself these days?'

'I don't know. She says she's taken up the piano again.'

'Is she acting?'

'Not that I know of.'

Larry said, 'Maybe it's a good thing if she doesn't see so many people.'

'But Larry, she's so subdued. And now, on top of it all, she suddenly wants large sums of money. But that reminds me – the key to Capilano Place. I'll get it for you.'

Larry contemplated the familiar disorder of Scrope's life which lay scattered about: busts and piles of books on the floor and tables, with more books in closely packed shelves; theatrical prints and pictures on the walls and others on the floor propped against the furniture; a confusion of in-trays spilling press-cuttings and photocopies on the desk. The only part of the room to give an air of cleanliness and order was the drinks tray, with its well-replenished decanters, its fresh bowl of nuts and its gleaming array of glasses. Larry picked some ice-cubes out of the bucket, dropped them in a long tumbler, and splashed them with whisky out of a decanter. He went and stood by the open fire, lit a cigarette and blew the smoke up into the face of one of Scrope's forebears, a sallow, undistinguished-looking fellow in a military uniform. There were one or two prints of other Clermont ancestors about, but mainly the room was cluttered with theatrical memorabilia: prints of Inigo Jones costume designs, two Bakst watercolours, innumerable *commedia dell'arte* characters. On the wall behind the desk was Zoffany's painting of Garrick playing Macbeth. Scrope was writing a book about the Italian Comedy in Paris. There were two tables beside the desk, covered in notes and papers, and on one of these lay a print of Pasquati as Pantaloon which Larry hadn't seen here before. In all this the keys to Scrope's affections were the three photos which stood on the mantelpiece: a studio portrait of his mother after her marriage, rather formal but looking very beautiful; a snapshot of Noël Dersofi, the actor, who had been Scrope's lover; and a picture of Eva in her school play as St Joan. She must have been 15, still too much of a child to look very soldier-like. On her head she wore a curious turban which, together with her oddly slanting eyes, gave her a slightly oriental look. Larry peered at the photo, trying to match it with the Eva he'd met a year or two later. Out of nowhere there sprang into his mind an incident he hadn't thought about in years. Eva had been caught with a flat battery, and when she asked a passer-by to help her he went across the road to Harrods and bought her a set of jump-leads. Gave them to her, too, when they'd started it. That was Eva all over, he thought. Everyone came under her spell.

When Scrope returned with the key they went to dinner. It was light outside, a chilly May evening. It had rained earlier and the streets were still wet, and although the plane trees had bright new leaves on them it felt as though spring would never come. They walked to the end of the block and turned south on the high street towards Costa's Kebab House, next to the railway bridge. Scrope was a regular here. Eva had been a favourite of Costa's too, in the old days. When she went off with Spinelli, Costa used to say to Larry, 'Why you let that Eva girl go? She's a beautiful girl, real lady, very good.' Tact had never been his strong suit. He had a painting of Winston Churchill on the wall, and posters of Cyprus, and fishing nets.

They ate crab and haloumi and chops. Scrope said, 'We ought to have champagne, really. I hear you won the Arbuckle Prize.' But fearing what Costa might give them, they drank Greek wine instead, perfumed and resiny. Larry said, 'It's a lottery.' He thought of the ceremony, only a week ago, the stuffy room at the Ostlers' Club, the bad food and too much wine. Potocki, for once out of the office, sweating in his heavy check sportscoat. The man from Yamasaki, sponsors of the prize. One or two publishers. Some publicity people from the papers, happy to get a free lunch without having to work over it, settling down to wineglasses of cheap brandy. He had wanted to say something about how unsatisfactory, even reprehensible, it felt to have photographed an event like that one. He shouldn't even have tried.

'All the same,' Scrope said. 'Congratulations.'

Larry tried to put it out of his mind: the smoke-filled club-room, the screwed-up paper napkins, the ashtrays and half-eaten bowls of lemon mousse. The journalists were bored. He was making a fool of himself. He said, 'Are you going to Polly's wedding on Saturday?'

'I think so. Are you?'

'She asked me to do the photos.'

'Really? That seems . . . I don't know, it seems strange.'

'Does it? Yes, I suppose it does. But then again, not.'

'Was she in love with you?'

'I think we both wanted to be, so we tried very hard. But what use is trying in such matters? No one is the master of his affections. Once Polly and I realized that, we got along much better. You see, I was still trying to get over the thing with Eva. And Polly was very upset about her Cambridge don going off with the P.E. coach. So we both hoped, I think, that by joining forces we could forget about them.'

'They say one nail drives out another.'

'They say it, but it isn't true. Only the passing of time makes any difference.'

'Does even that do any good? I wonder.'

'Oh yes,' Larry said. 'Definitely. He thought of the time when Eva left him. Often in those days he had come and dined here with Scrope, just for the sake of hearing something about her. He never brought her name up himself – his pride didn't allow it – but if Scrope mentioned her he would leap at the chance to question him more closely. In fact Scrope never had much news of Eva. Or perhaps he spared Larry it because he understood that particular craving. They had in common the solitude which follows rejection.

Scrope picked up the crudely cut carafe of water and poured a trickle into his glass of ouzo, turning it instantly milky. He said, 'Eva's buying Spinelli's house off him. In fact she's buying both of them – the house on the coast and the flat in Rome.'

'Why?'

'That's what I'm worried about. It sounds fishy to me. Of course there's one obvious reason for her to do it: so that she and Spinelli can get their hands on her trust money. You see, Ma and Pa never let her have it when she got married. They were empowered to, as her trustees, but they were scared that Carlo was after her money so they kept it all in trust and only gave her some income. So the only way for Carlo to get hold of a big capital sum would be for her to buy his houses. That way they still have their places to live, but also a large chunk of cash – actually it comes to pretty well everything she's got.'

'So why did your parents agree?'

'It would have been difficult not to, really. You see, all she was asking them to buy were the houses she lived in, which from the point of view of trustees is perfectly reasonable. You know my father's passion for fairness. He was acting as her trustee so he felt he must behave like one. Ergo, he wouldn't allow himself to object on the grounds that the vendor was her husband. But I'm pretty sure that's why my parents are selling Capilano Place. They're saying to Eva, "Look, you wanted to buy those houses. Now you've got to live in them. We're not going to keep a flat in London for you any more."'

'Will that make any difference? I mean, Eva never comes to London anyway, does she?'

'You're right. I think it's pointless. But I believe they're determined to make some gesture of disapproval. My mother has become violently anti-Carlo since they got married. I'm not sure why; she seemed to like him well enough at first. And of course Pa never liked him. In any case, for whatever reason, they're selling Capilano Place now. I just hope they're not making a terrible mistake.'

'Why should they be?'

'Like I said, I'm worried about Eva. And I suppose in the back of my mind I've always thought of Capilano Place as a somewhere she would go if anything went wrong. You can imagine how difficult she would find it to come to any of us. After all, we all told her not to marry him.'

'So you think her marriage has gone wrong.'

Scrope shrugged. He got out a cigar and picked up the candle in its little china holder. For a moment he looked as though he was going to say something, then he stuck the end of the cigar in the flame and began to puff, sending up thick bundles of smoke. When he sat back again he said, 'I'd no idea you still had things in Capilano Place. Otherwise I'd have given you the key ages ago.'

'I haven't missed it in years, whatever's there. It can't be so important.'

'All the same.'

Costa brought coffee, and a saucer of Turkish Delight. He said to Larry, 'Miss Polly, how's she?'

'She's fine, Costa. She's getting married on Saturday.'

'Eh, Miss Polly's a beautiful girl. Like her mother. That mother's a film star, very beautiful. These beautiful girls very expensive when you marry them. Lotta dress, lotta pretty clothes, plenty money. They spend it all, yeah.'

'You're quite right, Costa.'

'I know. This Polly, she's cost a lot of money. Her husband, he pay.'

'He hasn't a lot of money, Costa.'

'He's better find some now.'

When he'd gone Scrope said, 'The great thing about Costa is he's so encouraging.'

'But he's wrong about Polly. No one could be less grasping than Polly.'

'In any case she probably earns more than poor old Joe Dansk.'

Larry took a piece of loukhoum on the end of a toothpick and twiddled it in the air, loosing some of its fine powder sugar on to the table. His face bore a slightly puzzled expression as he observed it, as if he was undecided whether to put it in his mouth or not. He said, 'Talking of Rome, I gather there's going to be a conference on nuclear energy there in a couple of weeks' time.'

'Is there?'

'As a matter of fact I'm covering it.'

'I see. Do you think you'll see Eva while you're there?'

'I don't know.'

'I just thought you would have been able to tell . . . well, if she was all right.'

'Maybe. I don't usually have much time on this kind of job.'

'No, I suppose not. What is it exactly?'

'International thing. Big companies, governments. And a massive rally by the anti-nuclear people. That's what I'm there for, really.'

'They seem to have them everywhere at the moment,' Scrope said. 'I wish I felt it did any good.'

'Don't you think it does?'

'Some things have their own momentum and I'm afraid the arms race is one of them. The fact that we would like to stop it isn't enough. It's developed its own logic.'

'How depressing,' Larry said. If he had been deliberating whether or not to eat the loukhoum it seemed he had forgotten it now because he dropped it absent-mindedly back on the saucer. They finished the coffee and ouzo and said goodbye to Alexandra in the kitchen. She was very deaf. When you spoke to her she grinned and nodded, but she rarely understood unless Costa shouted in Greek. She said she'd tell their fortunes next time they came. She did it by reading the pattern of coffee grounds in your cup.

Outside in the street Scrope gave him the key to the flat in Capilano Place.

Larry still had his own key. He kept it in an old jam jar from Hediard on his bedroom mantelpiece, along with some notes and coins of foreign currency. But for some reason he had never mentioned this. He took the key and said goodbye to Scrope; and walked back towards his flat through the chilly darkness, past the lines of boarded-up shops with their rubbish left outside in black plastic sacks, thinking about the old days, and the jump-leads, and the flat in Capilano Place.

Larry Hudson's grandmother was opening a can of corned beef when Larry told her the news. Normally Mrs Gramercy was fond of gossip, but even the most casual observer would have seen that she did not like what Larry was telling her now. She left the can suspended in mid-air on the can-opener and, turning to face him, said, 'Capilano Place?'

'Yes,' Larry said. 'Her parents are selling it. Scrope rang to tell me. He wants me to go and get my things out before they put it on the market.'

'What things?'

'My things that I left there when I moved out. You look worried, Grandma.'

'I just don't understand, dear. I didn't realize the Clermonts still owned the flat in Capilano Place.'

'Why shouldn't they?'

'Because I thought Eva was living in Italy now.'

'Perhaps that's why they're selling it.'

'I see. You mean they kept it for her all this time?'

'I suppose so.'

His grandmother looked slightly panic-stricken, holding on to the edge of the sink behind her with both hands. She said, 'Why have they kept it if she lives in Italy?'

'I don't know, Grandma. Perhaps they thought it would be useful when she came to London.'

'I didn't realize she came to London so often.'

'She doesn't come often.'

'Then why can't she stay with her parents, if she only comes occasionally?'

'Maybe that's why they're selling the flat, Grandma.'

'Well,' said his grandmother, turning back to the can of beef, 'I don't know about that.'

The phrase was one his grandmother often used to close a discussion. It could simply mean, 'No'; or at times it could mean, 'I don't like the sound of it and I don't wish to discuss it either.' On this occasion it was the second interpretation which applied. Not that in the old days his grandmother had anything against Eva; in fact she liked her. She used to say to Larry, 'I always thought you'd drive some poor woman round the bend. But you and that girl are two of a kind.' It was only after Eva went off and married Spinelli that her name ceased to be mentioned, and that if it was Mrs Gramercy would look away, murmuring vaguely, 'I don't know about that.'

'What don't you know about, Grandma?'

'Nothing, dear.'

Mrs Gramercy had always had a protective attitude towards her grandson. Her daughter Chloe had abandoned Larry and his father when Larry was a child. The marriage, like everything Chloe did, had been hurried. She and Mrs Gramercy had gone out to visit relatives in Rhodesia. On the boat she met John Hudson, a South African-born sugar farmer, exactly twice her age. In the Suez Canal she seduced him; passing Zanzibar they became engaged. Getting off the boat at Beira she said, 'Great, where are the shops?' She was 17. The four years she spent on his farm in Rhodesia were by far the most settled period of her life. Then one day at the Salisbury Club she met Gunther Baumgarten, playboy, globe-trotter, inheritor of great wealth. Baumgarten lived nowhere. Pleasure-loving and rootless, he had just the right temperament for Chloe, and they set off immediately for Singapore and New York. Larry was left with his father on the farm.

The contrast between this life and the one he lived with his mother could not have been more acute. Baumgarten was a shallow man whose greatest passion was polo. He was dashing, slightly cruel, and exuded a magnetic confidence. His life with Larry's mother was lived under the bell-jar of his enormous wealth. They reminded Larry of ice-skaters, their beautiful dance caught in the spotlight, gracefully detached from the pace of ordinary life. Larry loved his mother very much but he wasn't close to her. He saw her rarely, and he always felt like an outsider in her world. For this reason he longed more than anything to be accepted in it. As he sat in the dust at home on the farm, he dreamed of swift horses and waiters carrying trays piled with food. Once or twice a year – and often with little warning – he would be put on the crowded, animal-laden bus to the capital and flown to a faraway land where a driver would meet him with a little placard bearing his name – LARRY HUDSON – and the driver would take him by limousine to a house which he might or might not have seen before and where his mother and Gunther Baumgarten were living at the time. They often lived in rented houses; but even the ones they owned felt as if they were rented because they spent so little time in them. In these houses, when he woke in the early hours of the morning, he would hear laughter and loud voices coming from a distant reception room, and when he peeped out of the bedroom window there would be dozens of cars parked in the driveway. Larry's mother was restless and her life with Baumgarten suited her well. She was beautiful and flirtatious, irresistible some said. Her similarity to Eva was too clear to be brushed aside: the seductions, the restlessness, the fascination with death. His mother was dead now, killed with Baumgarten when their plane crashed in a storm over Argentina. In a way, that made her harder to come to terms with, doing away with the reality so that he was left arguing with a phantom. And are not ghosts the most unnerving of adversaries? Like lovers who have rejected us they still hold us in thrall, yet without any promise of gratification. Larry frowned. His grandmother had striven hard to fill the gap left by his mother's disappearance. Every year out of her meagre funds she managed to send him a ticket to come to England; and occasionally she had come herself to stay with them in Africa.

But now it was Larry's grandmother who was frowning. Little vertical marks appeared on her forehead. Wisps of hair trailed distractedly from her chignon, her mouth trembled a little. There was something very beautiful about the combination of courage and fragility in her pale blue eyes, her wide mouth, her creased face.

'I didn't know you still had things in Capilano Place,' she said. 'I thought you'd moved out years ago.'

'Of course I moved out, Grandma,' he said with some exasperation. 'It's just that there are bound to be some old things lying about that I might as well go through. For instance, I know there are some undeveloped rolls of film there.'

'And what about Eva's things?'

'Well, what about them?'

'Who's going to go through them?'

'I don't know, Grandma. I'm not responsible for Eva, you know.'

'I know, dear, of course not. When are you going there?'

'Right away. Scrope gave me the key last night.'

'I see.'

Mrs Gramercy put the corned beef and the baked potatoes on the table beside a salad in a broad wooden bowl. 'I'm sorry it's so plain, dear,' she said. 'You should have warned me you were coming.'

'That's all right, Grandma. You shouldn't worry about me.' He put some butter on the potato, sprinkled on some salt and then mashed it in. His grandmother poured them each a glass of cider.

'Well,' she said. 'Here's to the winner of the Arbuckle Prize.'

Larry said, 'Did you see the photo in the paper?'

'Of course. I saw it when it came out. Such a dreadful thing. I don't know how you can bear it.'

'Nor do I. Of course, I didn't know it was going to happen, and it was all over in a moment. I think I did lose my balance a bit afterwards.'

'You never said a word about it at the time. You bottle things up inside you too much. Like your mother. She never talked about anything that was important to her.'

Larry thought about this. When he thought of his mother it was always as laughing and talking, radiant among her admirers. Somehow it hadn't occurred to him that she might be keeping her feelings to herself.

For a few moments they ate in a silence broken only by the rattle of cutlery and the ticking of the grandfather clock. At last Mrs Gramercy said, 'You're not going back there are you? I mean to Salvador?'

'I don't know, Grandma. It depends if anyone wants to send me.'

'I thought you were freelance now.'

'You know how it is. When you're freelance you can't afford to be choosy.'

'I must say I don't understand why you have to do wars at all. There are plenty of other things you could cover.'

'I know. In all honesty I don't want to go back either. Not because of the danger, but because there's something terrible about being a spectator. That's something I've learnt which I didn't understand when I started out. It makes one feel corrupt. On the other hand, it's still my job. I have to do it as well as I can. And I have a backlog of tax to pay.'

'Why's that, dear?'

'Because I didn't organize myself properly when I went freelance. And now I've got a book-keeper.'

'I see.'

'By the way, Grandma, did you know Polly's getting married on Saturday?'

'This Saturday?'

'That's right. In St Paul's, Covent Garden.'

'Ah yes. The actors' church. Did she ask you?'

'Of course. Why ever not?'

'I don't know. You young people nowadays seem to find that sort of thing quite easy. In my day we didn't. Still, I'm sure you know best.'

When they finished eating Mrs Gramercy washed up and Larry dried. By tradition this was the only part he was allowed to play in making lunch. It never took long when there were only two of them. As he was putting away the knives and forks in the drawer Larry said, 'I wonder how much they're selling it for?'

'Selling what?'

'Capilano Place. If it wasn't too much I could buy it myself. Now that I've won that prize the bank will probably cough up for a mortgage.'

'I'm sure it's very expensive, dear. Aren't you better off staying in Chalk Farm?'

'I don't know. After all, it's quite small really, and I could sell off the garage underneath: that is, if her parents aren't going to keep the garage. And it would make a lot of sense for me to have a place of my own with a mortgage: I could write off the payments against tax.'

'Well, dear,' said his grandmother. 'I really don't know about that.'

It annoyed Larry that she looked on the flat in Capilano Place with suspicion. He had been unhappy for a long time when Eva left him but he was not unhappy any longer. That was all a long time ago.

— 2 —

Capilano Place was a quiet cul-de-sac off the King's Road with a tall white-painted terrace on one side and a series of detached or semi-detached studios on the other. The black door in front of which Larry Hudson was standing bore the number 79, by coincidence the same as the year he had first lived here. This door stood beside two battered garage doors made of grey-painted metal, each of which bore the legend 'No Parking' in faded black letters. Eva's parents had bought the place after the war for the garages, which were handy for their house in Chelsea Square. The flat above them had stood empty for a number of years. Then for a while the gardener's son had it while he was studying at Guy's. Then Eva had it. The building was one of the detached ones on the studio side of the street. On the left side was an alley which separated it from the next house where they kept the dustbins; on the other side was the garden of the nursery school. Above the garage there were three sash windows with filthy white glazing bars, their panes so grimed up that a passer-by must have thought they enclosed some little-visited attic or perhaps even assumed that they were windows of the garages themselves. These were the windows of the flat, one for the kitchen and two for the sitting room. Larry had seen them often enough from the outside in the last three years, usually in the distance from the King's Road. The flat was near the end of the street, so there was no cause to pass it in the usual course of things. Sometimes people thought there was a way through, but when they got to the end they found it was blocked by three bollards, so they had to turn round and go back: at night their headlights would flare on the wall of the sitting room of the flat. The bollards didn't stop Eva, though. In the little yellow Renault she could just squeeze round to one side of them, with an inch to spare; and for a long time after she left there were yellow streaks on the wall.

Larry took the key out of his pocket. Eva would be certain to have lost hers by now, he reflected. She'd have to get one off Scrope if she wanted to go through her things. Probably she wouldn't even bother, and then they would all be packed into crates by the removal men and stored in the old brewery at Clermont. He wondered if at any time since they'd left the flat she had come back here, unknown to him, to look for anything, or even just out of curiosity. He unlocked the door and went in. It smelt of mould, like it always had, because of the garage next door. In front of him the stairs stretched away up to the flat. There was a pile of junk mail and fliers on the floor of the little entrance.

The flat was less dusty than he'd imagined it would be. In the sitting room he opened the window on to the nursery school garden and let in some fresh air. In spite of the dirty panes it was light in here, the sun coming through the open window together with the noise of the children playing. He could see the fig tree in the garden, just as it had always been, and the nursery school teachers smoking and gossiping on their bench as they watched the children play. The inside of the flat was tidier than he remembered it; but then, nowhere was tidy for long with Eva around. She had that sort of character which created chaos within minutes: if she sat down on a sofa she would straight away throw half the cushions on the floor and pile the other half up underneath her and then kick off her shoes and soon there would be an ashtray, the remains of a half-eaten biscuit – it could have been sluttish, but it was more childlike than anything. There were discarded tights and knickers all over the flat, in her car even, and the floor was always littered with magazines, hairbrushes, sunglasses, hats, cigarettes, half-drunk cans of Coke, Bic lighters, make-up pencils and so on. When she came in, instead of putting her keys in a particular place she would throw them down anywhere, in the kitchen, in the bathroom, on the floor, so that when they had to go out again she always spent five or ten minutes looking for them. But now everything was in its place. Perhaps Eva's mother had sent someone in to clean; it certainly didn't look as if Eva had set foot in here. The records were all stacked on the shelf, the phone directories piled up by the phone, the books and magazines put neatly away. On the walls there were still the old pictures: the prints of Clermont as it had been in the Regency; the prints which Scrope had given her of Inigo Jones's designs for *Midsummer Night's Dream*; on the back of the door the photo of Sid Vicious which he'd taken in the 100

Club. The floor had been stripped back to the boards and the walls painted white like the uneven, atticky ceiling. There was a white, uncovered sofa and two Louis XIV armchairs from Clermont. In the corner was a hammerite table and four Fifties' kitchen chairs. At the time they had both thought the flat rather smart, but now it all looked shabby and cheap, apart from the chairs from Clermont. Familiarity, far from breeding contempt, had given these objects an enhanced value which they no longer possessed; and it crossed his mind whether the same could apply to Eva and himself.

In the bedroom Larry opened the french windows and went out on to the fire-escape. From here you looked down on the gardens at the back of Flower Street, long thin strips divided by walls and wattle fences. The Clermont flat didn't have a garden: but you could get up the fire-escape on to the roof, and they had some old chairs up there. The bedroom itself was tidier than he'd ever remembered it, and it smelt musty. The blankets were all in a pile in the middle of the mattress, the pillows on top. The television, instead of being at the end of the bed, where they'd always kept it, was pushed into a corner, and the videos had all been put away on the shelf. The big chest of drawers with the mirror on it had always been strewn with odds and ends of Eva's, and now these were not so much tidied as gathered together in a dense mass. Beside the mirror the photo of Eva had been laid flat in its frame. He picked it up and took it to the window and wiped the dust off it with his sleeve. It was the first picture he'd ever taken of her, the night of Scrope's party down at Clermont. It wasn't the kind of party he usually got invited to, and indeed, he hadn't been invited to this one. In fact it was a whole world that was new to him, coming from Africa: a small world like a back-eddy of a river which he had gone round and round in because of one girl. But wasn't that how the world always worked? Every life was a kind of whirlpool, he thought. Perhaps all beautiful women were Lorelei.

Patrick Lynch took him along. 'We can go down there on your bike,' he said. 'It's only twenty minutes from Oxford. If you want we'll stop for a drink in the city. I know a good place.'

It was Saturday evening in mid-summer and the air was warm as they rolled through the streets. In the gardens of the colleges the leaves hung lifelessly, and outside the pubs there were crowds of students in shirtsleeves and the smell of beer in the air. Posters were up all over the city, some announcing last week's CND march and others which read:

MALVINO'S MARVELLOUS MIMES
Performing three days only.

They didn't stop for a drink here. Patrick said it would be less crowded where they were going, and Larry rode on, following his directions, into a series of lanes. It was balmy. Every now and then glimpses of a long sky with spires would flash up, diapositive-like in the distance. At length they came to a village and stopped at the pub. It was an old-fashioned place with two bars: one a 'saloon', with a carpet and brass ornaments on the mantelpiece; the other – in which they found themselves – with a dartboard where a match was going on. They ordered beers. Patrick, in his usual way, struck up a conversation with the man at the bar.

As a journalist, one of Patrick's most useful characteristics was his ability to get to know people quickly. He didn't seem like that sort of person when you first met him, perhaps because he had such a soft voice and such an undemonstrative, retiring manner; and yet people told him things. He never seemed to be encouraging them. That was what made him a marvellous listener. He was adored by women: quite apart from his charm, he was good-looking, with very pale skin, very blue eyes and a shock of black hair that waved around on his head. His plump cheeks gave him a boyish air, but he had a girl's lips. When he was trying to impress a girl he had a way of talking slightly above her head and then agreeing with anything she said: this gave an impression that they were both rather brilliant. He made it well known that his father was a philosophy professor, which added to the mystique.

They had finished their beers and were about to leave when a girl wearing a black cocktail dress came through the door, marched up to the bar, and announced, 'Sixty Benson's, please!' in a voice so loud and rasping that even had she not been dressed so strikingly she would have stopped the conversation. The barman, turning round, caught sight of her, shut off the tap of the beer he was drawing, crossed the bar and gave her the cigarettes. But something arrogant in the way she now asked for cigarette papers caused the man to turn surly, so that when he handed them to her he slapped down the change on the counter and turned sharply away.

The girl appeared to be oblivious of this. She put two packets of cigarettes in her bag, tore the wrapper off the third, and lit one, gazing distractedly at the darts game which had been resumed on that side of the bar. Her face made Larry think of a doll, partly because, although it was pretty, there appeared to be no bones in it, and partly because it was utterly devoid of expression. In an analogous way, her voice lacked any sort of variety or nuance. She was heavily made-up and her lipstick was a startling shade of pink. To the darts-players she was clearly extremely glamorous. Patrick, seizing the initiative as usual, asked her if she wanted a drink.

'Oh,' she said, as if trying to remember, 'I don't know you, do I? Yes, all right. I'll have a Bloody Mary. I promised Dog I'd stick on the same thing tonight but he started me off on wine. Still, what's the difference?'

She looked quite steady but she spoke so loudly Larry thought she must be tight in spite of what she said about wine. Just then the door of the pub opened again and a young man wearing a dinner jacket stepped in. He was well-built, with thick lips, brown curly hair and black-rimmed glasses. There was something about his mouth which hinted at coarseness.

'Hello, Dog,' said the girl.

'Come on, Maria, we're all sick of waiting.'

'I'm having a drink with these boys. Don't think you know them.'

'Are you going to Scrope's party too?' the man asked Larry. Larry said they were.

'Oh,' he said. 'Are you press or something?'

'As a matter of fact you're right,' Patrick cut in cheerfully, 'we are from the press, but not in an official capacity tonight. In fact we're here to relax. I'm Patrick Lynch. Will you have something to drink with us?'

His pleasant Irish manner overrode the other man's hostility. He said, 'Cyril Gracechurch, pleased to meet you. This is Maria Beckman.'

'Yes,' said the girl. 'Why don't we all have a drink for God's sake?'

'Maria, the others are waiting in the car.'

'Oh, Dog. They can wait a second. These boys are inviting us. Good friends of mine, met them a minute ago. Don't be boring. What's your name again?'

'Larry Hudson.'

'Where d'you come from, Larry?'

'Kenya. But I was born in Zimbabwe.'

'That's Rhodesia, isn't it? I thought you were from Australia by the accent. Are you two boys friends of Scrope's then?'

'He is,' Larry said, indicating Patrick. 'I'm just along with him.'

'Crashing, eh?'

'In a way, yes.'

'I love crashing parties,' the girl said. 'Absolutely love it. Trouble is, I'm always asked.'

Her friend said, 'Yes, and you're usually thrown out, too.'

'Belt up, Dog. He's such a bore when he's trying to be funny. Got no sense of bloody humour.'

Patrick said, 'Why d'you call him Dog?'

The girl looked mystified for a second. Then she said, 'Scrope's party, that's right. For a minute I couldn't remember why we were here.'

They left the pub and Dog and Maria got into a car which, in the fading light, was crammed with more heads than one could count. About a mile from the village the road began to follow a high wall, and a little further on they turned in at a lodge gate with sculpted lions on either side. The drive went between an avenue of lime trees for some way. They could see a large Queen Anne house beyond, and when they came clear of the trees, a lawn to its right, thronging with people. In the light of dusk, patches of red clothing flared up intensely. Beyond lay a stretch of open parkland, and a lake, shiny and reflecting the turquoise sky. The car they were following parked on the gravel in front of the house and Larry pulled the bike up beside it. Everyone got out. Maria still had her glass of Bloody Mary from the pub. At megaphone pitch she was braying something about finding herself a man at the party.

It seemed Malvino's Marvellous Mimes had been invited. Some were still in costume – a heterogeneous bunch which included Harlequin, Charlie Chaplin and Captain Marvel; others had changed out of their stage dress but still wore white, *enfarinés* faces. Apart from Dog and Maria's party there was hardly anyone in evening dress. Almost immediately they were hailed by Scrope, dressed in a dark suit and smoking one of his torpedo-shaped cigars. He was perspiring slightly and from time to time he mopped his face with a handkerchief. Maria said to him. 'Have we missed the performance?'

'I'm afraid you have.'

'Thank God for that.' She turned to Larry and said, 'Scrope's mad on this mime stuff. He's writing a book about it. Hey, Scrope, what about a drink?'

Scrope handed her glass to the waiter who ladled some punch into it.

'Pimms, is it?' said Maria, tasting the drink. 'Oh well, better than nothing I suppose.'

'Where's Dog?' Scrope said.

'Oh, he's around, worst luck. I'm so bored of him. He's lost his virility. Or perhaps I've burned him out. Have you got any new blood around here, Scrope?'

Soon Larry was able to slip away unnoticed. Already he rather regretted having come. This kind of occasion was all right for Patrick, who could get on with everyone, but Larry felt irritated by Maria and he knew from experience that if he stayed he would end up by becoming aggressive or depressed.

It was getting dark now, though the sky was still a pale turquoise colour with towering pinkish clouds like crumpled drapery. On the stone parapet at the end of the lawn someone had lit some lanterns and others hung from the branches of a tall beech tree. Larry could see Patrick talking to a mousy girl by the tree. He strolled away from the party and sat on the parapet, looking back at the house behind. At a window on the second floor a girl in a white dress was sitting astride the frame. She had one leg inside the room and the other dangling palely outside against the leaves of a Virginia Creeper which grew up the wall. In her hand she held a tennis racket which once or twice she spun with a flick of the wrist. She never looked out into the garden, but remained completely absorbed by the room within, and this imparted to her a sense of privacy and introspection.

Perhaps it was this which made her noticeable in the humdrum of the party; or perhaps it was the odd way she was illuminated by both the last daylight and the electric light from inside, giving her leg a ghostly look and her dress a faintly orange tinge; whatever it was, without even thinking about it he took a photo of her with the camera he always wore.

The children had gone inside and the garden of the nursery school was quiet once again. Larry turned the picture over and opened the little catch on the hinged back of the frame. He took out the photo and held it up to the light, free of reflections in the glass. It was black-and-white and slightly grainy because in the original she'd been too small a part of the picture and he'd had to enlarge it. Although her face was partially hidden, you couldn't have mistaken the easy way she sat, with the small of her back naturally held in and her flat chest forward, nor could you have mistaken her straight dark hair. She held the tennis racket in front of her, giving a slightly surreal impression, as if she'd been superimposed from a tennis court on to the façade of the house.

He got off the balustrade and started to thread his way back through the party. Scrope had disappeared, and Maria was talking to a bearded man with a trident. He gave them a wide berth and came to the front of the house. In the hall there was a huge tapestry of Cronos devouring his children. A group of people were standing about, wanting to leave and arguing about arrangements. As he went up the broad polished stairs he could hear a girl wailing, 'I don't want to go at all, the party's hardly begun. And anyway it's my car.' On the first floor a gallery ran above the stairwell. There were portraits here, and some views of Venice by Guardi, and a fine picture of Diana and her attendants in the French school. Larry went to the end of the gallery, where one leaf of a double door stood ajar, and peered into a long library overlooking the park and the lake. At the far end of the room stood a sofa on which a couple were lying in each other's arms, kissing. The boy was wearing leather and chains and the girl's long yellow hair spilled around them; at their side a bald and bespectacled young man was distractedly spinning a terrestrial globe. None of this oddly disconnected trio appeared to notice his presence. He left the library and, going back along the gallery, took the next flight of stairs and followed a crooked corridor to what he fancied must be the lake side of the house. He could hear voices from somewhere and he went down another passage towards them, till he came to a door.

In the centre of the room the girl he had seen at the window was having a nosebleed, a handkerchief pressed to her upturned face. There were bloodstains on her white dress. The other people in the room were spreadeagled across the bed and sofa, talking in loud voices.

'Come in,' the girl said, 'and shut the door. This damn bleeding will stop soon. Dog, you introduce everyone.'

'Well,' Dog said, 'if it isn't Larry.' He had taken off his jacket and the ends of his bow-tie hung from his open collar. He was propped up on a mound of pillows and a china bowl stood on his stomach into which every now and then he flicked the ash from his cigarette. He was elegant, self-assured, like a grown-up cherub with all his brown curly hair. It was really the thick, ugly mouth which stopped him from being good-looking. He wore a gold signet ring and gold links, and there was a wine-stain on the front of his shirt. He said, 'Maria Hugo Suki Eva.'

None of those present did more than nod at him when Dog said their names. Larry often felt like an outsider in England. But there was also something hostile about the way the people in the room ignored him: was it money or class? He could sense both, but more than this there was a feeling of clique, of a circle of intimate acquaintances warding off the outsider. He went to the window. Outside he could see Patrick Lynch talking to the mousy girl. In her hand she held a wine bottle by the neck, and from time to time she shifted to extract her high heels from the turf. She wasn't exactly pretty, Larry thought, but she had a nice figure. He wondered how Patrick could work up the enthusiasm for this sort of thing.

The girl in the white dress came over to the washbasin in the corner where Larry was. Her handkerchief was stained all over with blood and she threw it in the bowl. She scrubbed her face and hands under the tap, dried off on a towel and then went over to the low table by the sofa where there was a mirror lying flat with a rolled up note beside it. She picked it up.

'Thank God for that,' she said, glancing at her reflection and then putting the mirror down again. 'Someone give me a cigarette.'

'Here you are,' said Dog. He lit it for her with a thin gold lighter.

The girl stood for a moment, inhaling deeply. Larry noticed how her eyes slanted back slightly from her long nose. She blew out a stream of smoke and said, 'That's better.' Her voice was low and gravelly. She came over to Larry and said, 'I get these nosebleeds you know. Nobody knows why.' Her slanting eyes looked faintly amused. She held out her hand and he shook it.

'Larry Hudson.'

'Eva. Are you with Malvino?'

'No. Are you?'

'No. But I wish I was.'

'Why's that?'

'Didn't you see them?'

'I came too late.'

'You missed something. They were very good. I'm going to go down in a minute and ask Malvino for a job. I don't suppose he's got one, but it's worth a try, isn't it?'

'Are you an actress?'

'I want to be, but I don't have my card. I have to have some experience first, it doesn't matter what it is.'

She laughed, and he found himself laughing too. There was something boyish about the way she stood now, leaning against the wall with one foot crossed over the other; just as in her movements when she was washing her face and hands at the basin there had been something boyish. Her eyes were brown, the colour of the polished stairs of the house, and her brows were very fine. She had an unusual complexion. It was naturally dark, but with a rosiness in the cheeks as well. It had that freshness which is nine-tenths of the enchantment of youth.

He said, 'Being an actress is an awful life.'

'No. It's very wonderful. I'll tell you why. Look.' She took hold of his arm as she pointed out of the window. 'Do you see Harlequin down there? Now if you'd been here for the show you'd have seen how gay and innocent he was. Honestly, you felt you were in some painting of Watteau. In fact, looking at him from up here you can almost imagine it now, can't you? Of course, he's not like that in real life. None of us is. But on the stage he is able to show us a piece of heaven. Fragments of paradise, that's what they are. It's the distance between us and them, I think, which creates the effect. Look!' She leaned on the window-sill a moment looking down into the garden. The lanterns had something of the effect of spotlights in the dusk, illuminating a circle of faces around them. It was true that from up here there was a fairy-tale, elysian quality about the scene below – the branches of foliage, the costumes of the guests, the mythological mimes dotted among them.

He said, 'So you want to work for Malvino.'

'Yes. I want to be a star, you see,' she added, and gave a low laugh so he was unable to decide how serious she was.

He said, 'Stars have unhappy lives. Do you think it's worth it?'

She looked at him a little surprised and said, 'Of course. I know that it'll probably destroy me. I accept all that.'

In the park more torches had been lit beside the lake, and their reflections flapped about in synchrony underneath them. He said, 'D'you think anybody's going to swim down there?'

'They probably will in the pool.' She looked down at the white dress covered in bloodstains. 'Maybe I should go for a swim in it before it dries.' She tossed her head, a flattering gesture for her because it made her straight hair come alive and drew attention to her long, gracile neck.

'I'll come for a swim!' said the girl called Suki who overheard her. 'I will too!'

Everyone wanted to swim except for Dog. Even Larry, who a moment ago had wanted to get away from them all and even to leave the party, now found he wanted to join in the expedition. They all trooped downstairs through the hall and outside into the warm night. The air was charged with the smell of mown grass and the hubbub of voices. England! Mid-summer! He felt elated, as if something wonderful had happened. But nothing had happened, he told himself; nothing had happened at all.

Eva was inspecting his motorbike. 'I used to have a BSA,' she said. Larry got astride the bike. He kicked the motor into life and eased it off its stand.

'Get on,' he said. 'I'll give you a ride.'

Eva climbed on behind him. The beam of the headlamp splayed across the lawn, catching the figures of surprised party-goers at the door of the house.

'Hey! Where are you going?'

The shrieks died away as they sped down the drive. Before they got to the lodge he turned off down a path across the park which brought them to the lakeside where the torches threw out a wide ring of light on the bullrushes and the dark water. They circumscribed the lake and headed back towards the party. Some people on the parapet waved and shouted, but they kept on round the back of the house, and then climbed a terraced lawn to the garden. Here they stopped by a wrought-iron gate. Larry cut the engine but neither of them got off. Through the iron bars of the gate they could see the flare of the swimming pool lights and the bathing hut and the heads of the others bobbing around in the water. Dog was sitting on a deckchair at the door of the hut, smoking. His black dinner jacket was elegant and formal, at odds with the rest of the scene in a faintly sinister way, like a raven of ill-omen.

Larry said, 'Let's swim later.'

They rode downhill again and into a wood at the back of the house where a bumpy forest track brought them to a clearing with some sandy hillocks. There were pine trees dotted around here and their cones lay in the sand. Larry stopped the bike. He said, 'I want to jump some of those mounds. You'll have to get off for a minute.'

She dismounted. The angle of the headlamp meant he was jumping into the dark, and the bike slewed a bit on the soft sand when he landed, but he controlled it.

Eva said, 'Can I have a go?'

She took the bike and rode it around to get the feel of it. Then she turned and ran it at the jump. Larry whipped on the flash and took two pictures as she came over, and she sprang twice out of the night behind the headlamp, her neck muscles standing out and the blood in dark blotches on her dress. The bike went down, the lamp plunged and skidded across the ground. But Eva had been thrown clear. She sat up and said in that low, gravelly way, 'Twisted the damn wheel when I came down. Should have held it straight but I thought I was going over.'

'I shouldn't have used the flash like that. I must have blinded you.'

'It's OK. I couldn't see a damn thing anyway. Silly thing to do really. Had no idea what I was going to land on. Just thought I'd give it a go. Let's have a cigarette.' Her hand was trembling wildly as she took it. 'Dear God! That shook me up. Still, it's quite a thrill, isn't it? I mean, you get quite a bang when you shoot off like that into the dark.'

'You were very good. I didn't really think you'd do it.'

'D'you always take that camera around with you?'

'It's my job.'

'Photography?'

'News stuff. I've trained myself. I do it without thinking, whenever anything sudden or unexpected happens. It's a question of reflexes.'

'Will you give me a print of it?'

'Of course.'

He had that print somewhere, perhaps in the chest next door where he kept shoeboxes full of them. He thought it must be in black and white, because the other one had been, the one of Eva sitting at the window. And yet he seemed to recollect her eyes red in the flash and the red bloodstains on her dress. Had he changed the film? He went through into the sitting room and lifted the lid of the chest. The shoeboxes were all there. He wondered if Eva had taken anything from them. But what use were they to either of them now? He looked out of the window at the fig tree in the nursery school garden. There was a blue and orange climbing frame beneath it which hadn't been there in the old days. He was no longer resentful, not even sad. He reached into the chest and picked out one of the boxes and set it down on the table. There were scores of old photos here, stacked like index cards in a file, as well as postcards he had bought in various museums. He picked up one which the Ashmolean called, 'Relief of a lyre-player, possibly Orpheus, *circa* 150 BC.' For an instant the idea came into his head that he should send it to Eva, but he instantly dismissed it. What did he have to say to her now? On the other hand, if he was going to be in Rome to cover the demonstration . . . but why should he see her? He had humiliated himself enough in the past with his endless letters, all of them unanswered. Eva had never sent him a postcard in her life. He put the card down on the table and began to hunt through the photos in the box for the one of her straining at the handlebars as she jumped the bike. And he remembered her saying as she lay on the sandy floor of the woods, 'Oh hell. I forgot to ask Malvino for that damn job.'

— 3 —

His father sat on a chair with the book on his knees and the children sat crosslegged around him on the dirt floor of the chapel. The photograph could easily have been of a religious service except that there were no grown-ups present, so it was more likely just a story that his father was reading to the children.

The chapel was used for school as well as religious offices. It consisted of a grass roof supported by wooden pillars. There were no walls. The grass roof had to be repaired each year but his father said it was cooler than corrugated iron in that climate. In this photo you could see his long features quite clearly in its shade, with the result that beyond him the background was lost in a glare of sunlight. His face was at rest, his eyes looking down to the page through his half-moon spectacles. The children stared up at him from the floor. His father made all their lessons into stories if possible. Born into an oral tradition they could listen quietly for hours, and remember them perfectly afterwards.

Mr Hudson was doggedly hard-working and deeply religious. In Rhodesia he struggled year after year to make the farm pay; but the land was poor and the credit was dear and eventually he was forced out of business. He became a Methodist minister and moved to Kenya, starting a mission school in the North-West Frontier District. On the farm, they had led an existence remote from the rest of the world, but here they were even more out of touch. The further from the world they were and the less they had to do with city life the more Mr Hudson liked it. He was a lanky, wiry man, wizened by life out of doors in the sun. He drank tea unceasingly and smoked cigarettes which he rolled on an ancient machine shaped like a box. When the tobacco and paper were laid out in it he shut the box, licked the rim of gum and then ran his fingers over the mechanism so that the cigarette jumped out of the other end. The children at the mission loved to see him do it; some of them thought it was magic.

He had always loved Africa and the countryside, but after Larry's mother ran off with Baumgarten he developed a positive hatred for cities and towns. He disdained the developed world too, especially Europe, and although he never went there he seemed to hate it more and more as the years went by. He considered Europe decadent, a continent whose age had passed. To use a phrase of his own, it had 'lost its faith'. What did his father mean by this? Larry found it hard to understand. It seemed to him that what his father meant by faith must be really a kind of will-power; and yet it was more than this. It implied holiness as well: faith as a single-minded determination about what is holy. But what was holiness in a world without God? Were the same things holy that always had been? His father used to say, 'Faith is the strength of the Jews.' And yet he often spoke as if the Marxists had it too.

Whatever it was, his father thought that Europe had lost it. 'In any case, Europe is too crowded now,' he used to say. 'Faith comes from the open, from the desert. Look at Islam, look at the Christian hermits and saints. Didn't Christ go into the wilderness for forty days and forty nights? Don't the Saddhus take an oath to eschew the habited places of the earth? The desert has always been the high altar of God.' And he would look out across the brown dust of the District with satisfaction. He was happy in this hard, solitary place.

Like so many people who live far from society and intelligent discourse, he cherished books and ideas. There was only one kindred spirit in that country with whom he could discuss these things. This was Mr Wilson, the Gujarati autodidact who brought the mail once a week. Wilson always stayed the night at the mission. There was no official delivery to outposts such as theirs so he made it his last call of the week. When he arrived on Friday evening he gave the letters to Larry's father and went to the wash-house in the yard where he performed seemingly interminable ablutions. Larry was never sure how he managed to take so long; there was nothing in there except a few buckets of water and a tiny shaving mirror. When he came out he changed into fresh clothes and went on to the veranda where Larry's father was waiting. The sun was going down; it glowed a fiery red through the dust thrown up by the day's activity. Before dinner the two men played a game of chess.

After dinner they drank tea and talked about literature or religion. There were wicker chairs on the veranda of the mission house, and an oil lamp stood on a low table where the teapot and glasses were laid out. Larry's father and Wilson were illuminated from below, giving them a slightly ghoulish appearance. Mr Hudson smoked, tapping the home-made cigarettes down for a minute at a time on the gun-metal gin before he tilted the glass of the lantern and held the end into the flame to light them. Their political discussions were of the far-reaching, epoch-making kind. They talked of the rise and fall of great empires, of the domination of continents, and the movement of races and world trade. The future of Africa was always on their lips. Sometimes their conversation, having wandered far and wide on the surface of the earth, ventured into the heavens; and then they would get out the telescope and peer up into the glittering night. Wilson knew a good deal of traditional Indian village astrology, the kind which is used to determine auspicious and inauspicious days. Larry struggled to understand the grown-ups as they discussed planetary alignment and the Placidean house system. Then Wilson would explain that what looked like a single star in Andromeda was in fact Messier 31, the Great Galaxy; that at a distance of two million light years it was the most distant object the unaided human eye could see; and that its light shining now up in the sky had left that distant region before the appearance on earth of Homo Sapiens. Now Larry's father would recount the corresponding myth: how Andromeda was the daughter of King Cepheus of Ethiopia and his Queen Cassiopeia; how Cassiopeia was so vain about her beauty that she boasted she was fairer than the Nereids; and how in punishment for this the unfortunate Andromeda was chained to a rock wearing nothing but her jewellery, for a monster to prey on. 'So were the sins of the parents visited on their children, even in those days,' his father said. He believed that we all take our direction in life from the sins of our parents so that the same problems are passed on remorselessly from grandparents to parents to children. 'Original sin,' he would say, 'is the sin which comes from our parents. That is why men dreamed up the idea of an immaculate conception. For Mary to be without sin she had to be miraculously conceived.'

'Of course,' Wilson would say, leaning forward into the light of the lantern in his excitement. 'It's not quite the same as the Hindu and Buddhist idea because in Eastern philosophy you suffer for your own sins in a previous life, whereas in your scheme of things, David, the sins come to us from our parents, like genes. But it's the same notion of suffering which endlessly repeats itself generation after generation.'

Larry's father spoke in a quiet voice. 'The worst sufferings are always repetitive. Think of Sisyphus, Tantalus and Ixion. Hell has always been a place where the same tortures repeat themselves again and again.'

In these conversations it was his guilt over his own divorce which weighed unspoken on him. And Wilson, who understood this, would go silent for a moment, while Larry's father went on, 'But it's not necessarily so. If you have faith you can break out of the cycle. Nothing is predestined. Everything is chosen.' And his gaze would fall on Larry, curled up and half asleep already in his chair. Often when he had been brooding for a few days the same theme would emerge in his Sunday sermon: the torment of sin repeating itself from generation to generation, and the saving virtue of faith. He preached in Turkana under the grass roof of his chapel without walls. His text would always be Matthew 9:29 – 'According to your faith be it unto you.' The boys and girls sat crosslegged on the bare ground, the flies buzzing round their heads as they watched him with large intelligent eyes. He told them that all they needed was faith and they would build a new Africa to rival the civilizations of Europe and America. 'Great things are done from small beginnings,' he would say. 'Think of the Pilgrim fathers, think of Cortés.' The children at that school knew a lot about Cortés. His father used to read aloud from Prescott's *Conquest of Mexico* and *Conquest of Peru*. For him these histories represented everything that faith could achieve against all odds. Sometimes Wilson would argue that faith had little to do with these bloody campaigns, and that the whole European expansion into the Americas was prompted only by greed for gold and silver. When this happened Larry knew they were in for a long night of it. As a child he tried hard to understand the argument, which slowly became more and more complicated, as though in a chess game, instead of pieces being taken away, new ones were constantly being brought into the combat. Eventually he would fall asleep in his chair, waking in his father's arms as he was carried to bed. Later, as an adolescent, he contradicted his father eagerly, and when he finally went to bed lay awake and longed to go to Nairobi.

Unfortunately for Larry, his father became less and less able to cope with expeditions to the city. When he was a child they had gone every year to a Christmas party in Salisbury, and Larry had been struck by the agony of embarrassment and disgust which his father suffered on these occasions. As soon as possible he would retire to a corner and sit stiffly on his own, rolling cigarettes in his metal box and looking a little absurd in his paper hat. But as the years went by they went less and less to the capital, and when they moved up to Kenya the visits ceased altogether. Even when Mrs Gramercy came to visit he declined to go down to Nairobi, sending Larry to meet her in his stead. It seemed to Larry that all celebrations reminded his father of Chloe. And perhaps this was at the bottom of Larry's own ambivalent attitude towards this kind of occasion: at the same time disliking it, and feeling that he had to meet it on its own terms.

He had inherited a good deal from his father: his sincerity and his determination and capacity for work. He admired his father for the pride and fortitude with which he had confronted the loss of Chloe. He recognized that his father was a warmer and more sensitive person than his mother and that he possessed moral and spiritual qualities which she entirely lacked. Nevertheless, these hadn't been enough for his mother. And this made him want to be a success in the eyes of the world as well. At the boarding school where he was sent when he was 12 he was the most competitive and hardworking of the boys. He excelled at schoolwork. He started a rifle club and became a crack shot. He set up a dark room and taught himself photography. But in the holidays he was always on his own. He studied and argued with his father; and when he felt he would die of being cooped up on the mission he would take his motorbike into the bush and ride all day. It was a reflective and serious boyhood.

The mission was a success. The people loved Mr Hudson and Mr Hudson loved God. Probably he would have liked Larry to follow in his footsteps, if not on this particular mission at least in some mission, at least in Africa. But as is the way with fathers and sons, Larry had different ideas.

Not far from the mission on the shore of Lake Turkana (at least, not far in terms of that country – about three hours by jeep) there was a post of the Kenyan army. Its colonel was an Englishman named Stanley Llewellyn who had taken Kenyan citizenship at independence. Llewellyn had been brought up in Masai country and spoke their language. He was an expert on crocodiles, and had written several studies of the ones in the lake. Larry began to visit him when he got his motorbike. He was 14, and in the school holidays he used to ride over to the camp, spending several days at a time there. He went on patrols with Llewellyn in his jeep, and watched the crocodiles on the lake from a hide they constructed together. He learnt to shoot too, not just the .22 rifles they were taught with at school, but army weapons, and Llewellyn's .45 pistol.

As an adolescent Larry found in this life an antidote to the stern moral and religious atmosphere of the mission. His father was an idealist, and like many children of idealist parents Larry found it hard to grow up in close proximity to him. Fortunately his father knew Llewellyn and liked him. Not that the two men saw very much of each other; they were both too solitary for that.

Llewellyn was one of those people who believe that words are best used sparingly. Actions were what he believed in, and the less said about them the better. He became very sheepish when asked about something which reflected well on himself – his excellent military record, for example, or the high regard in which his studies of crocodiles were held. He had no belief in God. But he respected Larry's father because he had chosen an existence that was as tough and far-flung as his own.

Although he was taciturn by nature he could be persuaded to talk given the right context. Usually this was when they had eaten at night and were sitting over their coffee. At such times if Larry didn't interrupt him he would launch into stories about his life among the Masai where he had grown up. His hero was T. E. Lawrence and he had a collection of books about him, and seemed to know *The Seven Pillars of Wisdom* almost by heart. He was also an admirer of Spengler.

One day he and Larry were walking on Mount Poor when Llewellyn picked up a stone.

'Do you see this, Larry? This is Africa.'

Larry looked at the stone in his big, nailbitten hand. It contained a number of cube-shaped crystals, blue in colour, which glinted in the sunlight.

'It's a pseudomorph. You probably don't know what that is. Well, it happens like this. Let's say you have some crystals which are embedded in a rock stratum. As time goes by they are eroded, leaving holes of a particular shape. Then new geological activity causes other molten minerals to flow into these holes, and instead of crystallizing into their own natural forms they take the shape of the moulds which exist there already. So their form belies their true crystalline structure. Like this fellow, here. He's blue quartz, and normally quartz is six-sided with a pyramid top. But in this instance it's taken the cube-shape of some fluorite that's been there before. Spengler applied the idea to culture. He claimed that the Arabs had never been able to develop a proper culture of their own because the mould of Graeco-Roman civilization was already there to receive them. Same thing with Russia. And of course that is exactly the problem here in Africa. The Europeans came with a new culture and set it in place, completely artificial and foreign to the existing tribal life. So it was bound to be pseudomorphic, forced into ancient, already developed patterns.'

Word for word Larry repeated this back to his father, excited to find an argument which contradicted directly all his father's notions about Africa being the world of the future and Europe being nothing but a fossil.

His father just said, 'Been talking to Stanley have you? I thought so. Personally I'm unconvinced by Spengler, always have been. But remember it was Spengler above all people who believed the West was in decline. As for Africa, it's much too early to say. After all, we have consciousness to understand our situation, and with faith we can change it. Even old Spengler believed in the primal importance of faith. The battle is constantly being fought. There is nothing to say that it's over, and we have lost.' His father always enjoyed these arguments. Nothing was too radical or unorthodox for him to discuss, in spite of his own iron convictions.

When Larry was 17 he went out on a night patrol where he saw his first action. Perhaps 'saw' is the wrong word: it was so dark that he saw very little, but some shots were exchanged, though no one was hit, and the cattle raiders soon ran away. But to Larry at 17 the brush with death was terrifying beyond anything he could have imagined. If he was conscious of anything during the few minutes of that encounter it was that he wished profoundly that he hadn't come and that certainly if he ever got out of it alive he would never be such a fool as to do it again. But when it was over he felt exhilarated, more alive and confident than he'd ever felt, as though he had been a hero in some way, although he knew perfectly well that he had done nothing except sit in a jeep. He wanted to talk about it, he wanted to tell everyone what he'd done, but of course he had no audience here. So he tried hard to act as if the episode counted for nothing, the way Llewellyn did. And he began to go out regularly with the border patrol. Danger was thrilling to him and he courted it.

Llewellyn had a beautiful wife. She was called Mary-Jane, she had long blonde hair and she had been a model in America. At 28 she met Llewellyn while shooting a perfume commercial on the shores of the Lake. They were quickly married. For a year or two she lived on the army base with him, but gradually, despite the best will in the world, she became bored of living there all the time, took up magazine journalism, and began dividing her time between Kenya and New York. At 32 she was still beautiful; to Larry she was the most attractive woman he'd ever seen, and he was too naive to realize that she was attracted to him too.

Mary-Jane looked as alien as a lily in the prehistoric desert of the District. But what was even more alien in Larry's eyes was her love of big city life. In fact she was the first person he'd met who loved the outside world. He could listen for hours while she told him about Manhattan, and Tokyo, and things he'd never seen like theatre and restaurants and nightclubs. She told him about her experiences as a model, and how wonderful it had been to travel to so many places. And as she told it Larry was taken back to those hazy childhood memories of busy cities and beaches and polo fields where he visited his mother.

Mary-Jane was passionately fond of food and her visits were marked by special feasts which she prepared with ingredients purchased in New York. Larry used to help her prepare them in the canvas cook-house, and in this most unlikely and primitive of locations he began to appreciate good cooking and acquire some of its skills. And it seemed to him then that by assisting her in this luxurious and rather exotic task he was already partaking of the sophisticated and exciting outside world. Gradually he went out less with the men, and spent more and more time in the camp with Mary-Jane. He found he could confide in her completely because she loved the outside world as he did; for, somehow, he was sure he did love it, even though he had not been there since earliest childhood. And Mary-Jane listened. She seemed to take it for granted that he would leave and make a life in Europe or America, and this gave him confidence, because at that time it still seemed an impossible, almost sacrilegious achievement. On the last night of his vacation they sat outside the tent and talked till very late, and suddenly she leaned across and kissed him on the mouth. It was only then that he realized that he was completely in love with her.

Their relationship never went any further. She was away during his next holidays and after that she was less intimate with him than she had been, though still friendly. Her role was not as his initiator in love, but as pander to his affair with the outside world. The next summer when he left school he booked a flight to London.

Moving to England was simpler than he'd expected. Rather than being an act of rebellion it turned out to be a respected and well-worn path for young men in his position. With the help of his grandmother he established himself in lodgings and took a languages degree at King's. If he had been slow to recognize his attractions with Mary-Jane he was not long in being convinced of them here.

When he left the university his tutors as well as his grandmother had encouraged him to go in for something solid and remunerative, such as banking. After all, as his grandmother pointed out, he had no money of his own, and some day he would want to get married and raise a family. Photography seemed unsure, and too peripatetic. But Larry had other ideas. He managed to get himself sent to Rhodesia by the *Illustrated Weekly* and took pictures that chilled the blood of his grandmother. One or two other notable reportages followed and he became known in a small way as someone both efficient and fearless. Then the *World* took him on.

So at 24 Larry had made his way to the old continent, acquired a university degree, a job and a flat; and what with his more than average good looks and his reputation for being a bit of a daredevil, he had come to consider himself something of a Don Juan. His main henchman and competitor was Patrick Lynch, and together they cultivated a cynicism which they thought was worldly-wise. They both agreed that the best stage of an affair was always the initial anticipation. 'Consummation is the beginning of the end,' Patrick used to say; and also, 'The best cure for a beautiful girl is to talk to her.' It was rather in this frame of mind that Larry rang up Eva after the night of Scrope's party.

— 4 —

He had gone to some trouble to track her down. Not only had she left without giving him her number, she had not even said goodbye, but simply disappeared into the throng. He looked for her everywhere in the course of the night. The party dwindled and dawn arrived, overcast and without a breath of wind, so that the lake was like mercury and the leaves of the great oaks were lifeless across the park. Patrick Lynch and the girl had already left. Larry got on the bike and rode it back through the country lanes to the ring road. There was no traffic at this hour. When he got to London the streets were all deserted and the traffic lights ran the changes at empty junctions. He was tired now and he went to bed. But for a long time he couldn't sleep, intoxicated as he was by the girl with the slanting brown eyes, and by the sensation of her light body pressed against him as they rode on the motorcycle. And when finally he slept, he dreamed that she came in at the door and sat on the end of the bed.

Eva didn't seem surprised to hear from him. She suggested a day to meet up the following week and gave him the address of the flat at Capilano Place. Larry tried to imagine what her flat would be like – the bedroom with printed wallpaper, he thought, and most likely a one-and-a-half sized bed, the one favoured by single girls. Then there was the bathroom, with all those skin creams and beauty-promoting lotions which are so intimate and feminine, and the kitchen fridge which often contained nothing more than some cottage cheese or the odd apple, but might equally harbour a pro-fusion of delicious cakes and chocolaty things, usually half-eaten. Or would it be like none of this? Anticipation was everything.

He decided he would bring her as a surprise the pictures he had taken of her that night. Girls always liked to get pictures of themselves (it was the one real advantage he had over Patrick), and moreover the one of Eva jumping the bike was arresting, a picture he could be proud of.

He rang the bell. A vague shout from within was followed by the sound of footsteps coming downstairs. She opened the door, he kissed her on the cheek, they went up. In the sitting room the television was on. Eva cut the sound and poured them both Stolichnaya vodka. 'I'm afraid it's all I have,' she said. Larry sipped the cold syrupy drink as she lay down on the sofa and kicked off her shoes. She pushed some magazines on to the floor and stuffed a cushion beneath her. 'Did you bring the photos?' she said.

'Photos?'

'Yes, of Scrope's party. You took some of me that evening, didn't you?'

'Yes, of course. Yes.'

'That's good. Can I see them now?'

She looked at them for a moment, with that total absorption which she always had for pictures of herself, then dropped them on the floor and shook herself a cigarette. She said, 'I met a boy last week who was a photographer. He took a whole lot of pictures of me. Said it would be useful when I go up for a part in a play.' She jumped up and went next door for a moment, returning with a disordered heap of photos which she dumped on the floor and began sorting through.

'What do you think of them?' she asked.

The pictures were stylish but curiously impersonal. The boy who had taken them had avoided her crooked teeth and understated the unusually long nose. She was pretty. But the photos somehow missed the liveliness of the girl on her knees beside him now. They made her look sophisticated, which she wasn't. What they had caught best were the wide mouth and the brown slanting eyes. He said, 'Yes, they're good enough. You look very pretty.'

They talked for an hour or so as the long June evening grew stuffy, darkened, and then turned to a heavy shower. Through the open windows of the flat the rain hissed in Capilano Place and on the nursery school garden. The air became fresh. When it was over the sky cleared and turned pale and streaky. Eva chattered about herself. She told him her parents were very sweet but that they didn't understand about contemporary life. Larry nodded sagely. Coming from her it didn't seem like a commonplace; on the contrary, it sounded rather perceptive and almost original.

'They live completely in the past,' she said. 'In the eighteenth century to be exact. It drives me mad, I mean, why the eighteenth century? There were plenty of centuries before that.'

He laughed. 'Surely it's of some interest?'

'Maybe, but my parents really exaggerate. They spend the whole time thinking about what people would have done and then trying to copy them.'

'My upbringing was exactly the opposite. My father emigrated to Africa precisely to get away from the old world. He always told me that Europe was finished and the future lay with Africa. He believed that Europe had lost its faith and that nothing new could come out of it now. "Communism was Europe's last child," he used to say. "She died in parturition."'

'What's parturition?'

'Childbirth.'

'I see.'

'So he deliberately turned his back on all that when he emigrated. And he brought me up to think only of the future.'

'And do you?'

'I suppose I'm drawn to what he rejected. Otherwise I wouldn't be here now. In the old country.'

'I think it's wrong to be too concerned about the future.'

'Why's that?'

'Because it's cowardly to think ahead. People should do what they want to do and not be afraid of the future. Yes, even of dying. Once you're afraid of anything you live a coward's life.'

She said it as a child might have said it and he couldn't help smiling, and seeing this she smiled too and then burst out laughing. She seemed to move quite seamlessly between almost oppressive seriousness and gaiety.

The phone rang and she went and picked it up.

'Hullo?' She made a face as she sat down, tucking her legs under her, so close to Larry that he could hear the voice of her interlocutor without being able to distinguish what he was saying.

'No I *don't* want to,' she said into the phone. 'Why not? Because you're a bore.' She slammed the phone down and burst out laughing. Larry couldn't help laughing too, and seeing she was sitting so close to him he leaned over and kissed her. Then he kissed her again. Then she said, 'How funny that we're both the opposite of our parents.'

'And why not? There's no law that says we have to be the same.'
He took her hand in his. She had a ring on the middle finger with
a pale blue transparent stone not unlike the quartz pseudomorph
he had found with Llewellyn on Mount Poor.

'What's this?'

'It's a sapphire my father gave me. Actually it belonged to my
great-great-grandmother, or someone like that.' She withdrew her
hand from his. 'Would you do something for me?'

'What's that?'

'I'll have to show you. Come down to the garage.'

She had two farmhouse ducks there, hanging on a nail.

'I can't cook myself but I have a girlfriend who's brilliant. Only
she can't pluck. You don't mind do you? It's best if you do it inside
one of these dustbin liners, so all the feathers don't go everywhere.
Have you done it before?'

'Of course. I always used to do them at home.'

'You mean in Africa?'

'Yes.'

'Africa! It must be wonderful to live there!'

'Do you think so?'

'Why yes!' She said it as though it was impossible for anyone
not to relish the idea of living in Africa.

He said, 'It's very barren and remote, where my father lives.
There aren't many people. Most strangers find it rather spooky.
You come across the bones of prehistoric animals and fossilized
tree-trunks lying on the ground.'

'It sounds like what I've always dreamed of. Have you ever shot
a lion?'

'There aren't many lions in those parts. There are elephants,
though. I've spent a lot of time protecting those.'

'What do you mean protecting them?'

'From poachers. I used to go out with the army and chase
poachers coming over the border from Ethiopia and Uganda.
The colonel was a friend of ours. In fact he and his men were
our nearest neighbours.'

'Did you ever catch them?'

'Usually they ran away. Sometimes they were better organized,
and then there'd be a bit of a shoot-out; but usually they'd just
hop back over the border. We couldn't chase them there, you see.
Different country.'

'You had real shoot-outs?'

'Sometimes.'

'My God!' She hugged herself and spun round.

Kenya! They discussed it while he plucked the birds and it seemed that since his arrival in England he hadn't met anyone till now who was properly interested in his country. The curious truth was that they thought alike about everything – customs and people, tribalism and witch doctors, Rift Valley, Mau-Mau and Australopithecus.

When he had finished they went back up to the flat and Eva said, 'I have to go now.'

'But aren't we having dinner?'

'I can't. It was lovely to see you though. Thanks so much for plucking the birds.'

Of course, he wasn't in love with her. That would have been impossible, seeing they'd only met twice and hadn't even slept together. And in any case Larry had never been in love with anyone except possibly Mary-Jane Llewellyn. Nor did he much want to be. He enjoyed the reputation he had as a slayer of hearts, and by definition a heart-slayer soon gets bored of the girls he is with.

Nevertheless, he called her the next day and asked her to dinner.

'I'm going to the country,' she said.

'How about when you get back then?'

'OK. When I get back.'

'When do you get back?'

'I don't know. Next week.'

'Well how about Wednesday?'

'OK, Wednesday then.'

He was unusually happy that week. In the mornings he woke up feeling glad, and whenever he thought of plucking the ducks he found it unaccountably funny, and laughed out loud. He was impatient for Wednesday to come, and because he knew it would, he felt quite pleased with himself. He thought it was the best anticipation he'd ever experienced.

Wednesday came, and she was to arrive at eight o'clock. At a quarter to nine the phone rang.

'Larry? It's Eva. Listen, I don't think I'm going to come after all.'

'I see. What is it? Aren't you feeling well?'

'No, I'm fine. I just don't feel like it.'

'I see.'

'Goodbye then.'

'Goodbye.'

He put the phone down.

He didn't ring again. Sometimes he felt like doing it but then he remembered her telling the man on the phone he was a bore and bursting out laughing. He, Larry Hudson, wasn't going to be laughed at. And he wasn't going to be stood up either.

But for some reason the image of her kept returning to him, sitting on the sofa as she had that evening, looking up at him with her slanting eyes while the rain hissed outside on the pavement. He found himself imagining the most peculiar things: how, if they were having an affair, he and Eva would spend Sunday mornings; or else what they would do if they went to Africa. He thought of her in his father's chapel with its corrugated-iron roof, and then he thought of her lying in the narrow bed of a wagon-lit, first class, as it hurtled across Europe. All these imagined scenes were as vivid and illogical as dreams. And although he had determined not to call her, he couldn't help bringing her name up when he saw Patrick Lynch. Patrick said, 'Eva? She's a lovely girl all right, but a bit of a handful.'

Not long after this the Bajekhistan embassy was occupied by Islamic fundamentalists who held three Bajekhi officials and two British nationals hostage. Larry and thirty other photographers, together with fifty-odd journalists and a fair number of bystanders, formed a posse of observers across the street from the white porticoed building. The vigil went on day and night. Danny Potocki, Larry's boss at the *World*, had put him and another photographer on alternate twelve-hour shifts. Patrick Lynch was there a lot of the time. As the siege wore on, an ad-hoc village began to develop, with an almost festive atmosphere. The network crews put up towers to get them a better view. The French had their meals brought from a restaurant nearby. But after the initial novelty of the gathering there wasn't much for the journalists to do. It was a stage-managed affair on both sides, and Larry regarded this as a challenge to his ingenuity.

The room where the hostages were rumoured to be held was on the third floor of the building. Its windows were shuttered except for one at the end, where the terrorists sometimes appeared with their captives and spoke through megaphones. Larry worked out that from the roof of one of the nearby buildings he might be able to see through this window into the room itself and get pictures of the inside.

There were no holds on the roof. He worked his way along the ridge on the side away from the embassy and peered over. He could see one man inside. He was facing away. Larry got his camera up and started taking pictures. Two bullets smashed into the slates beside him, he ducked behind the ridge, lost hold, slithered and fell two floors on to a fire escape, breaking his left leg and his right arm.

In hospital they operated on some complications to the leg fracture and put both leg and arm in plaster. Next morning he saw the incident on TV. They showed the gunman who'd shot at him from a lower window, and then it showed him disappearing behind the ridge of the rooftop. His spectacular fall had been entirely hidden from view, but he did have the consolation that the announcer had called him a renowned daredevil. The police chief came on next and said this kind of stunt only made his job more difficult.

Danny Potocki called him and pretended to be annoyed, though in fact he was sympathetic. His grandmother came, more worried than ever but so happy to see him alive she could only kiss his hand again and again. Patrick Lynch brought him a bottle of champagne, and in the evening Eva came.

'I saw you on TV,' she said. 'They said you fell off the roof.'

'Like an idiot. I lost my hold and dropped down two storeys. Landed on the fire escape, luckily.'

'Are you terribly smashed up?'

'Just the arm and leg. It's nice of you to come by.'

'I was worried it might have been worse. It looked very high on telly.'

'I was lucky.'

'It must have been pretty scary up there.'

'It wasn't so bad. If I'd pulled it off it would have been a big scoop. Of course, everyone's furious with me now.'

'I thought you were terrific.'

'Thanks. Would you like some champagne?'

'I'd love some.'

'Will you open it? I'm a bit incapacitated with this arm.'

She twisted off the wire from around the cork and was starting to unscrew it when it flew off, narrowly missing Larry's head, and blasted into his toothmug over the sink. The foam surged out of the neck of the bottle and she automatically held it away from her, with the result that it spilled all over the end of the bed. They were both laughing too much to do anything, so it went on spewing out on to the bed and the floor of the room. When at last it subsided she sat down beside him where the bedclothes were still dry, and they shared a cigarette and drank out of the bottle. After a while a nurse came in and Eva hid it. She said to the nurse, 'How long does he have to be in here?'

'Just a day or two. It's for shock, and because of the operation.'

'Did you have an operation?'

The nurse smiled and said, 'That's why he's not allowed to drink.'

Now Eva wanted to see the plaster on his leg. One of the nurses had written her name on it and so Eva wrote hers too. She drew the three letters and then she drew a flag round them and then she drew a ship underneath and attached the flag to its mast. She wrote his name on the ship. When she had finished that he put his hand in her hair and she just went on staring at the plaster so he leant over and kissed her, and she put her arms around his neck and held on to him tightly.

It was not very difficult for her to spend the night in the hospital. Towards morning they decided they couldn't wait two more days so he got dressed and hobbled out of the hospital on her arm and they took a taxi to the flat in Capilano Place.

Danny Potocki. Among the photos in the shoebox Larry found one of him at his desk at the office. It was typical of Potocki, his arms on the desk, the phone tucked between his head and his shoulder, his striped shirtsleeves rolled up to his elbows and his tie loosened, a cigarette smoking in the ashtray. The photo, although it lay flat in the shoebox, had at one time been crumpled, and two heavy creases lay across it, one through the desk and the other across the top of his bald pate. Larry took it out. Black-and-white, taken without flash, the daylight from the window heightened the left side of his face and froze up the seaweed strands of the smoke beside him.

It was Potocki who gave Larry his assignments, and if Larry had an idea of his own, it was Potocki who had to authorize it. Potocki was 50, divorced from his wife, married to the paper. He was overweight, with sideburns, rubber lips, a tendency to sweat.

He was addicted to coffee. He had a bucket desk-chair which spun round as well as rolling about on wheels, and he moved about his office in it as if in a wheelchair. From the office next door where Larry had a desk you could hear the fitful mumble of his peregrinations from morning to night, an unsettling sound, like that of a thunderstorm still out of sight on a clear day. He wore towelling shirts with bright knitted ties and a heavy tweed jacket which hung on the back of his chair and flowed out behind when he moved. He had an idea that all the younger people who worked under him sat around with their feet on the desks gossiping, and his typical word of encouragement was, 'Come on, get your feet off that desk . . .'

Potocki regarded Larry as his protégé. He approved of his dedication to the job, which he saw as a reflection of his own. But more than this, he was impressed by Larry's knack of being everywhere at the right time, by the way he always caught the critical moment of the action, however unexpected it might be. And he noticed that when Larry suggested there might be a picture in something, there nearly always was.

'It's good, Larry,' he'd say. 'It's very good. But tell me: how do you know these things are going to happen? Have you a pact with the gentleman who organizes them?' He was always talking about the devil as if he had an office round the corner, and about God as if He was his uncle.

'I don't know these things are going to happen, Danny. It's just that I don't miss them when they do.'

'My boy,' Potocki would say, 'you have an instinct for disaster. You'll make a good reporter and a very bad marriage.'

There had been a cooling of relations when Larry had gone freelance. If in the past Potocki had always behaved as though the paper was his wife, now he acted as if it was his daughter whom Larry had abandoned. However, in time there was a thaw in the hostility and before long he was on the phone almost every month saying, 'Listen, why don't you get us something on Mugabe?' Or else, 'Get your feet off that desk and find us some kind of a picture!'

Larry dropped the photo back in the shoebox. When Potocki had asked him to cover the nuclear conference he had said, 'It's too quiet for me, Danny. You could send anyone there.'

'What d'you mean, too dull for you? Last week you were telling me you had a tax bill to pay.'

Down the phone Larry could hear a muffled drum-roll as Potocki shifted his chair across the office. He said, 'Well, do you want it or don't you?'

'I'll do it, Danny.'

But he wouldn't see Eva and Spinelli while he was there. Eva was no longer the girl he had lived with, the ghostly Eva who came back to him now, conjured by the garage fumes in the hall, by the sunlight falling across the boards of the sitting room floor, and the voices of the children playing in the garden of the nursery school. That was the Eva he had believed in. And without this fundamental act of faith everything else had changed its character, like the colours on a shell out of the water: her flightiness became mere vacuousness, her love of danger seemed self-destructive, her gaiety trivial. He thought of his father at the mission, preaching on Matthew 9:29: 'According to your faith be it unto you.' The children stared up at him with rapt faces, flies crawling at the corners of their eyes, the hens pecking round them in the dirt. His father had an African voice, deep and resonant.

— 5 —

She nursed him with infinite attentions during those first days. He was supposed to remain in bed, and she stayed with him day and night, bringing him – since she couldn't cook herself – sandwiches or takeaway meals from the Wok Long Chinese restaurant down the road. In the morning she went out first thing and bought flowers which she stood in pots and pans round the bedroom. Then she washed him all over with sponges and brought him coffee and breakfast. She stayed in bed with him most of the day, getting up only to play the upright piano at the top of the stairs. She could easily have played well, but she hated to practise, so she just improvised for hours at a time. Larry liked to hear her as he lay in bed with the window open on to the fire-escape and the sunshine coming into the room. Sometimes they listened to operas together, following the words in the libretto. She wrote bars of the music on his plasters.

That year the Sahara high made one of its occasional forays northwards, bringing an unaccustomed hot summer to the whole of North Europe. Larry put a mattress on the roof of the flat and they slept up there. They went barefoot in the flat, and the windows stayed open day and night. That summer! It was as though by falling in love they had abolished ordinary life. Larry was on sick leave, so there was no going in to work any more. Eva didn't work anyway. They cloistered themselves at the flat and unplugged the phone. They saw no one.

Every August Eva went with her parents to their house in Italy, but this year she abandoned the trip and stayed on at Capilano Place with Larry. She said, 'When your plasters come off we can drive down to Clermont and swim.'

Only the cook was there when they arrived. Larry's leg and arm were shrivelled up, no thicker than a child's. It was actually harder for him to move now than it had been with the plasters, because his joints and muscles had grown painful with disuse. But it felt marvellous to be free of them in this heat.

Clermont! The hot weather seemed to be going on forever. In front of the house the lawn turned to hay in the ground and the flowers in the walled garden had to be watered every day. The raspberries and peaches were sweeter than they'd ever been. Larry could swim more easily than he could walk in those first days, so they spent most of their time at the pool, and their skin smelt constantly of chlorine. There wasn't a soul in the place but themselves: the brick walls of the house, with their climbing roses, the pilastered façade looking towards the lake, the gardens with their statues and fountains, and circling it all the spreading park with its massive ancient trees – everything was deserted, giving the impression of an Eden made expressly for their use.

Unlike Eden, however, Clermont was not the work of six days or even six generations, but had grown up across hundreds of years. It was exactly what Europe had always meant to him: the pattern of the past lying like bones under the flesh of everyday life. It was what his father had gone to Africa to get away from, and what Larry, rejecting his father's view of life, had returned to find. It didn't seem rotten to him at all; on the contrary it was as flourishing as it ever had been.

Then the drought was officially declared, and the fountain with the statue of Neptune and the Nereids had to be turned off, together with the sprinklers for the vegetables and flowerbeds. They stopped using the pool, and went instead to the lake, which was quite warm after the weeks of heatwave. At the near end it was choked with weeds in the shallows, but from the boat-house onwards there was deeper water all the way to the other end where Eva's father had the sheds and pens for his flamingos. Sometimes Eva got them to feed from her hand, and to see her standing naked among them, the tall pink birds almost as high as she was, gave him even more the sensation of being arrived in Paradise. She had tiny, almost invisible breasts, and her thin legs tapered down to the knee in an unusual way. But in spite of her thinness she had a wiry strength. In the lake she was a strong swimmer.

The roses began to wilt. In the house the windows stood open all day long to take advantage of the slightest breeze, and when Eva was playing the piano in the drawing room he could hear her from as far away as the walled garden. His leg strengthened, and they began to go for walks across the dun-coloured park and through the limp woods. In the fields the combine harvesters were at work. There was dust in the air, and tar oozed on the roads.

In the dining room of the house there was a photograph of Eva's mother when she was first married. She stood with one hand on a chair, wearing a tightly fitted dress and a flower behind her ear. The likeness with Eva was very marked in the wide mouth and the long straight nose. But her mother had a more fleshy face, without Eva's high cheekbones, and a much fuller bosom which was well displayed by the evening gown she was wearing. Also, her eyes were smaller than Eva's, and not slanting.

He said to Eva, 'Your mother must have been a great beauty when she was young.'

'Didn't you know?'

'There's something about old photographs, isn't there? Maybe it's because the past is a little foreign to us, I don't know. To me they have a glamour that our generation lacks.'

'I dunno. Not my taste really.'

She took a cigarette out of a box on the table and lit it. Her eyes avoided his. He said, 'You don't get on with your mother, do you?'

'Not really.'

'Why not?'

She thought for a moment, her mouth half parted, showing her slightly crooked upper front teeth. If her face expressed anything at all it was vague puzzlement. Beside her the smoke from her cigarette went up in a slate-coloured thread which intermittently broke into a scribble. She said, 'I don't think she really likes me.'

There was little point in his trying to deny this. In any case it was as if she were talking more to herself than to him, staring straight ahead of her, out of the window. 'She doesn't like me,' she repeated, 'but it's not only that. I never told anyone about this, so you won't say anything, will you? You see, she used to beat me up. The first time it happened I was 16. It was my summer holidays and we were down at Castagna. I suppose I was being very difficult and adolescent at the time. The year before I still played with the children; but that year some of the local boys round about started to ask me over and I used to hang out with them down in the village at the café: they used to come and pick me up on their motorinos. My mother was always getting at me to make myself useful. She wanted me to help her in the garden and with the shopping and all that. I hated it, especially the shopping because there wasn't really anything for me to do. I just had to ride along with her like a child, and I was afraid my friends would see me from the café. One morning my mother came and woke me up and said we were going down to the village to buy the food. I got up and started to get dressed, but then I decided I'd much rather go swimming so I put on my bikini instead. After that I didn't quite dare go downstairs so I stayed in my room hoping she'd go off without me. I heard her shouting for me in the hall first; then she came upstairs. She took one look at me and said, "What are you doing in that bikini?"

' "Going swimming."

' "And what about the shopping?"

' "You do it," I said. "I can't be bothered."

'She flew at me. I didn't fight back at all. I suppose I was just too shocked or surprised, I don't know which. Afterwards she went off to the village on her own and I stayed up in my room. When she saw me again she was very nice to me, I guess because she was ashamed of what she'd done. But that didn't matter, because she'd won, you see. I should have fought back, but I didn't. I was scared of the way she went out of control and how angry she was. Since then I've always felt that I missed my chance to fight her. I let her dominate me. If I'd fought her then, she'd still have beaten me but she wouldn't have dominated me like she has. I would have got her off my back once and for all. But I didn't stand up to her and I've always regretted it.'

Larry could imagine the skinny child turning into a beautiful girl, the rattle of the boys' motorinos on the drive, their handsome faces outside her door. He thought of his own motorbike, leaning against the veranda at the mission, and his father and Wilson in the wicker chairs talking about the stars. The vanity of Cassiopeia, the fate of Andromeda.

'She did it again, the winter Alexei Menelov turned up. He was incredibly good-looking and he'd been my mother's lover – there were plenty of people around to tell me that. He was very nice to me. He came to lunch at Clermont and afterwards we played draughts in the library. Then in London he took me out to lunch a couple of times and gave me a diamond brooch. When my mother saw that she got mad and told me I was too young to be given jewellery and it was very silly of Alexei. She took the brooch away and I never saw it again so I guess she gave it back to him. Anyway, he never took me out to lunch again. After that she beat me up, too. That was when I ran away for the first time. I was only gone for a couple of days but I think it really scared her . . .' She broke off and began to fiddle with the cigarette in the ashtray.

Larry said, 'Maybe you have to get used to the idea that your mother regards you as a rival.'

'I know. But you mustn't think she was jealous because he gave me the brooch. You see, Alexei's my father. Of course they never told me that.'

'So how d'you know?'

'I know. I worked it out for myself, ages ago. Apparently he has a son in Paris who looks exactly like me. I've seen photos, of course – it's difficult to see yourself in someone else, but I can see it. That's where I get my slanting eyes – Russian, you see. I don't look anything like Daddy. I think that was why I ran away from school. I wanted to be independent of everything to do with them. I was at that place in Switzerland at the time. One day I'd had enough. I just walked out and hitch-hiked down to the South of France. I hung out there and found a job as a waitress. I was calling myself Giselle, no one knew who I was. It was quite fun for a month or so, but then it was the holidays and I began to miss home. So I sent Scrope a card. That did it. Daddy came down immediately. He didn't know where to look for me but I met him by chance in the town square. He was wonderful. He just said, "Hello Eva," and gave me a hug, and then he said did I want to go for a walk on the beach? I explained about working in the café and he said we could maybe go for a walk when I'd finished work. He didn't get mad at me or even say I had to leave the job or anything. Of course, it was him who came and found me. My mother couldn't be bothered.'

On their last night they walked down to the lake. The moon was so bright that the trees in the park cast clearly defined shadows, and on the still air the honking of frogs came to them where they stood at the boat-house. Not a ripple stirred on the lake. They undressed and waded out over the muddy bottom and swam right to the end where the flamingo house was. The birds shifted restlessly in their pens, grey and ill-defined. Eva said, 'Sometimes I think we should split up now.'

The moonlight gave him the impression he could see her quite clearly and yet, as in a dream, he couldn't make out the expression on her face, if she was frowning or sad or serene.

'We've had the perfect love affair, don't you see? And if we split up now it would remain perfect.'

'Eva, what are you afraid of?'

'I suppose I'm afraid of the future. Because nothing could be better than this, could it? So it would have to be less good. I'm afraid of it becoming more ordinary, degenerating.'

'What do you mean, degenerating?'

'Becoming mundane, like a married couple. The passion gradually ebbs out of it. Soon you are unfaithful. Then you begin to prefer your lovers to your husband or your wife. At best you have a sort of companionship. In the end you've built up a whole life of cars and houses and children – all around a love which no longer exists. So the whole structure of your life is empty inside, in a way a lie.'

'That's your parents, Eva, not you. I don't want to be unfaithful to you.'

'Nor do I. But if I ever did I'd leave you. I couldn't bear to be with you and feel more passionately about somebody else. Will you promise me you'd do the same?'

'Eva, you're mad!'

'No! I'm not! I know exactly what I'm saying and I've never been more in earnest. Promise!' Her voice was trembling as she spoke it.

Larry said, 'Yes, I promise. But I'm not going to love somebody else and nor are you.'

'No, my darling, we're not. Let's be different. Let's never become like all the rest.'

She put her arms round him and clung on to him tightly. He could feel her wet hair on his chest, as the water dripped round them. In front of them the flamingos stirred uneasily in the moonlight.

They left that night in the yellow car. Day broke as they came over the Chilterns. The suburbs of London were deserted, row upon row of semi-detached brick villas locked up, their inhabitants sleeping; line upon line of bow windows and double front doors. The little front yards were planted with cherry and laburnum and weeping willow. After the lawns of Clermont it looked like a toy town, empty and pristine in the pale light between dawn and sunrise. Eva said, 'This is what we must never arrive at.'

When they had gone a little further she said, 'Let's never get married. Let's never have children. Let's just be young and in love, and then kill ourselves.'

By mid-September his leg was fully healed and in his arm he felt only occasional twinges of pain. He was to return to work in October. Although neither of them could have said why, they both had a sense of impending doom about this date. Perhaps it was in order to counter this that they decided to spend the last ten days of his sick-leave in Greece. Through a friend of Patrick Lynch, Larry got hold of a small house on Crete. It was in the hills back from the coast, and to get to the sea they rented a motorbike off one of the men in the village. During most of their stay a strong wind blew, which cleared the air so you could see for miles and miles. At night the chimney muttered in the big room downstairs.

They found one cove which was always sheltered. It had a shingle beach and a piece of overhanging cliff where there was shade in the afternoon. Beyond the bounds of the cove itself the sea was choppy, a dark blue colour ribbed with white. But inside this the water was perfectly clear and green, and the shingle was too hot to stand on. In the morning they went for long swims, and in the afternoon they lazed about in the sun or slept under the cliff. Eva said she could live like this for ever, and Larry, knowing that he had to return to work in a week, felt he could too. On one such day she said, 'If we both really wish we could live like this for ever, then why don't we?'

'Eva darling, we'd be very bored if we stayed here any longer.'

'No, I don't mean literally here, on this beach. But why don't we live like we really want to? We could base ourselves in London and spend time here. Then you could stop work and we could travel. We wouldn't need much money. We could go to cheap places, like India. You can live for a year in India on what we'd get through in London in a month.'

They began to imagine how their ideal life would be. In the winter they would definitely travel, they decided, preferably to somewhere hot like Mexico or the Sahara. It wouldn't be the same place every year. There would be several different places which they would revisit from time to time. Then in the spring they would go to her parents' house in Italy. It was wonderfully fresh then, she said, and the leaves came out on the trees and everything was growing at breakneck speed. The hills were covered in flowers. Strawberries and apricots appeared in the markets.

Summer would find them in London. They would sleep on the roof at Capilano Place, and go to concerts, and in August when her parents were away they would move down to Clermont. It would be exactly like this summer had been. And for the autumn, back to Crete again, to their rented house in the village and the motorbike and the cove. At 21 and 24 they had no need of possessions. And above all they didn't need other people. 'It'll be just the two of us,' Larry said. 'Like this summer.'

'We can see our friends in London,' Eva said. 'So we won't need to see anyone here. Oh, darling, don't you see we can really do all this? All you have to do is give up your job.'

'And what would I do all day?'

'But what have you done this summer? And yet we've been happy, haven't we? Please say yes.'

'And what will we live on?'

'We don't need money!'

'We'll need some.'

'Don't be so cautious! We'll find some along the road. What does it matter if it doesn't work out? At least we'll have tried.'

Larry didn't reply. To himself he was thinking that it was hard for Eva to understand what that meant to him, coming from a family without money or position. She was so young and so privileged that she had never weighed what these things mean, and placed no value on them. He cast his mind back to his childhood on the farm, and to the dust and the stupefying heat of the mission. The sky was huge in that country. He remembered the laughter of the people and the familiar, nonchalant way they looked on death. His father's voice was friendly and informal when he read from the Bible in chapel. 'Lay not up for yourselves treasures upon earth where moth and rust corrupt, and where thieves break through and steal; but lay up for yourselves treasures in heaven . . . For where your treasure is, there will your heart be also . . . Is not the life more than meat, and the body more than raiment?' Mr Hudson had given up sugar-farming, moved to Kenya and started the mission.

When Larry asked Potocki for a sabbatical period he said he was intending to write a book; but the weeks went by and he hadn't even thought of a subject for it. The wonderful summer began to turn into autumn. The sky was a deeper blue and a freshness crept into the air. The leaves grew yellow and fell on the pavement like paper stars. Now that Larry's leg was healed they could use the motorbike again. Sometimes, not having any particular reason to go out, they simply rode about town. Their days were completely free.

He taught her how a camera worked and how to develop film and print it. He explained about the focal length of a lens and its speed, and the speed of a film, and how that affected the exposure. In the past Eva had always taken photography for granted as something boys did to flatter her, or as a pretext for getting to know her. But Larry had a different way of looking at her. He saw things in her which she herself was only vaguely aware of, and when he photographed her he would turn her this way and that, as though nothing of her surface gave him an exact view of what he was seeing. He had a very quick eye. Walking in the street he would point out a statue that looked like Patrick Lynch, or an interesting façade of a building, or a house which looked like a face with a moustache, and so on. He was always photographing unexpected movements in the way he'd taught himself to do.

He had a dark room at his flat in Chalk Farm where he taught her how to develop film and how to make prints of varying sizes. He showed her how, passing her hands over parts of the paper or covering pieces up, she could vary the tones of the composition. Side by side they watched the shapes of their own image emerge in the chemical baths, lit by the single red bulb which hung from the ceiling. At the beginning she watched like a child at a conjuring show; later, as she became accomplished, she took control herself, shifting the papers with sure, deft movements. She stuck the pictures of Larry up all over her bedroom. She said she was making it into a shrine.

They began to spend a lot of time in the kitchen. Until now cooking had always been a house-and-garden subject in her mind, interesting only if you led a sufficiently boring life, like her mother. But now Larry began to teach her the elements of cooking: different ways to prepare meats, fish, vegetables, how to thicken sauces, how to use egg white and herbs. When Larry did these things they no longer seemed trivial or feminine to her. He took her shopping and showed her how to choose food at the market, what to ask the merchants about the fruit and vegetables that day, how to select fish by the colour of their gills and the state of their eyes. She found she was interested, and became adept. Sometimes they spent all day preparing a special dinner.

Eating in restaurants also became interesting to her. They had to be careful about this. Larry had almost no money now that he wasn't working and Eva was always kept short by her parents, who believed it would encourage her to get a job. However, some of the best places in town gave a special price at lunch-time, and they visited these. In the evenings they restricted themselves to a handful of cheap places where the cooking was simple. First among these was the Isfahan in Kensington, where they did Persian stews and paper-thin bread from a clay oven.

They went to concerts, too, though here again they had to be careful about prices. They both derived a certain pride from the fact that they could live a life of discernment without spending a lot of money. The autumn was sunny, they loved one another, priceless music was cheap.

— 6 —

It was around November that the Indian summer finally broke. The clocks had gone back a week or two before and now the days were short and it turned cold and rainy, with a blustery wind which caught at your umbrella and rattled the raindrops against the window-panes.

Seeing neither of them had a job they still spent a good deal of time alone, but in the evenings they usually went out. Eva had a wide circle of acquaintance in London. She was forever meeting people on buses, especially men. But the core of her social life was her parents' circle, where Larry was slightly ill-at-ease. He didn't come from an important English family, he was poor – even poorer now – and unlike Eva he didn't have the knack of immediately getting on with everyone he met. Usually he was shy, and it made him gruff.

Another problem they had with these friends was that it was expensive to see them. Eva said, 'Oh, let them pay for us, it doesn't matter,' but Larry refused to be paid for. It was different for her because she was a girl, and anyway she belonged in that circle. But for Larry it would have been humiliating, and his small reserve of savings began to be depleted at an alarming rate. Sometimes they would spend more on cocktails and a plate of tortellini than they'd needed for the whole of their stay in Greece. This led to the first arguments between them.

The weeks before Christmas were one extended party. In London they went from house to house, and from club to club. They danced every night, and they were always the last to leave. Often the early traffic had already begun when they made their way home to Capilano Place in the yellow Renault. Sometimes it was already dark when they got out of bed. Eva was always the loveliest girl on the floor. He was intoxicated by her, by the pace of their life, and by the continual dancing and making love. He had given up hope of making his money last now. The only question was whether it would hold out until Christmas.

Christmas Day he had promised to his grandmother. After that he was going to Clermont to stay with Eva for New Year, to meet her parents. But on Boxing Day Eva rang up. 'I can't stand that cow a moment longer,' she said.

'What happened?'

'It's too boring to explain. I'm coming up to London. We can spend New Year at Capilano Place instead.'

It was always like that when they were meant to be meeting her parents. Eva invariably found some reason to cancel at the last minute. And if she didn't, her mother did. Lady Clermont rang Scrope several times a week, but she hardly ever spoke to Eva.

Larry was now penniless. He got his grandmother to lend him some money and he and Eva made a resolution not to go out any more, but of course they had to celebrate the New Year, and although the pace slowed after that there was always something that Eva would beg him to go to. She would start working on him the day before if necessary, sometimes even several days before. She had a way of being in a bad mood until he said yes, and it was maddening to have her sulking or pleading with him three-quarters of the day. In the end he told her that he couldn't stand it any longer and that he was going back to work.

'For God's sake, don't do that!' She had turned visibly pale at the idea.

'What else can I do?' he said. 'I have no more money.'

'But I'll pay for you.'

'I won't let you.'

'I don't care! I swear to God, money is nothing to me, nothing!'

'In any case, you don't really have any either.'

'We'll live cheaply!'

'But we don't, Eva. We thought we were going to but as it turns out we're living more expensively than we've ever lived.'

'We'll change all that. I swear we won't go out any more. We didn't go out in the summer, did we?'

'Not much.'

'Well, there you are! We don't have to go out. We've done it before. In fact it was the best time, wasn't it, the summer, when there were just the two of us and we were always alone?'

Suddenly she put her hands to her face, and started crying. He said, 'Eva, what is it?' but she went on crying and he sat down beside her and put his arm round her shoulders. She said, 'Don't you see what I just said? It's like it's gone already, we've lost it.'

'We haven't lost anything!' He started to laugh. 'Eva, are you mad? Look at us, we can do anything! Think of it!'

She wiped her eyes on his handkerchief and said, 'I'm sorry. I'm being silly. It's just that when you say you're going back to work I have a vision of us . . . but it won't be like that. We'll get back to living how we used to live without being extravagant. I don't mind. In fact I'd prefer it. Let's go abroad again and be alone, just the two of us somewhere. Please say you will.'

'When I get back I'll have to work.'

'No you won't. Because we'll have got back into the old way of living and it won't cost us a thing. Not a thing. You'll see. It'll be just like it was last summer.' And she began to cry once again.

They went to Mexico. On the Pacific coast south of Ixtapa they found a little resort with a run-down concrete hotel. The place didn't look much when you first saw it because of the debris of construction round the approach to the village and the general litter and shabbiness. Many of the buildings had roofs of corrugated-iron, the streets were dirt, there were chickens and pigs in them. But the sea was clear and warm, and there was a long sandy beach with a palm grove behind. The hotel had a bar down there with cold drinks. If you walked to the other end there was a settlement of a dozen or so houses, grass-roofed, owned or rented by American artists. Apart from these the beach was completely empty. Sometimes they swam across to the little peninsula, at the end of the bay. On the windward side driftwood had piled up and bleached in the sun, and on the leeward there were hundreds of tiny crabs on the beach, which disappeared into their holes as you approached. Eva went brown very fast. By day the dry sea-salt thickened her hair, and at night her skin smelled of tanning oil, and the sun. They lived more or less exclusively on red snapper and mangoes. Once they hired a fisherman to take them out after sailfish and marlin. They set their alarm the night before, getting up in the tepid darkness and walking along the beach to the village as the sky grew luminous. The fisherman had a small boat which heaved about a lot on the swell, and when Eva caught a sailfish it jumped clear out of the water and walked on its tail. The fish was too large to bring on board so they tied it alongside the boat to get it back to the shore.

Larry got up from the table and reopened the ottoman. From among the shoe-boxes inside he picked one after another, making a cursory inspection of their contents before replacing them, until he found the one he was looking for, of Eva and the fish.

In the picture the fish's tailfin was above her head, its straight bill pointing downwards was as long as her legs. She looked very pleased to have caught it, and with reason. To see her beside it now you would hardly have believed it possible, her bare arms looked so thin. But then Eva had always been stronger than she looked. The picture had a thumb-tack hole in the top where it had been stuck to the kitchen wall at one time. Larry turned it over and saw that she had written 'Mexico, Jan 1980' on the back. He remembered how they had walked back along the beach to their hotel and she had been so exhausted she had fallen straight to sleep on the bed. But that night at dinner she said, 'When we went out this morning early – when we were down on the pier loading the tackle on the boat – I could imagine that I'd only just met you, that we were completely new lovers, just starting our affair.' And later, she said, 'Darling, are you sure you want to go back to London?'

'You know I have to.'

'But didn't we agree right at the beginning not to compromise?'

'Eva, don't start on at me now. In any case, I owe my grandmother two thousand pounds.'

They returned to London and Larry went back to his job at the *World*. Their life seemed happier than it had been before. Eva had been very nervous about him going to work again – she regarded everything that took him away from her as a threat – but in time she became accustomed to it. In the day she used to see Maria Beckman and go to the cinema, or sometimes she would just stay in bed reading; and in the evenings Larry went out with her. She always insisted that he came, although she often ignored him and flirted with other men. He met a thousand people. After a year of living with Eva he realized that wherever they went he knew people now. Yet as luck would have it the only ones they seemed to see regularly were Dog Gracechurch and his friends. Larry had never got on with Dog and Maria. Right from the start, when they christened him 'son of a preacher man', they made it clear that they considered him an utter nobody. And they implied that he was after Eva's money, pointing out with enthusiasm that her brother was a homosexual and referring to her as an heiress. They were good at knowing what would make him feel uncomfortable. Part of the trouble with Dog and Maria was that they weren't stupid.

Maria had been at school with Eva. She was loud, self-obsessed, and could be very funny. She had met Dog at a party soon after they left school and they had been together ever since. But she was always saying she was bored with him and this invariably put Dog in a good humour – whether it was because he believed it or because he disbelieved it was difficult to tell. He was the most intelligent of them and the leader of the gang. However, under his confident and jovial manner lay a strong masochistic streak.

His father had made some money in the petrol pump business and Dog realized he wasn't living up to him. The old man had understood early on that Dog had more aptitude for spending money than making it, so he had put him into the law with the idea that he might at least put his gift of the gab to advantage. But Dog was a lazy lawyer in a languishing practice. His talent was for joking and devilry, not legal analysis. In another age he would have made a jester for a king.

Then there was Hugo, and inevitably after Hugo came Suki Brett. Suki was plump and in love with Hugo and she followed him round everywhere although he wasn't in love with her. He used to take out very thin, very pretty girls who were the opposite of Suki. He claimed to be bisexual but in reality he rarely had affairs with anyone, of whatever gender.

Then there was Polly. Larry remembered well enough the first time he met Polly. It was in the club called Angels in Paradise and he had gone there late. Eva and the others had all been at a dinner at Dog's place before, and Larry had deliberately avoided this part, having dinner with Potocki instead round the corner from the office. The first thing he saw when he got to the club was Eva, wearing her red dress, locked in a mouth-to-mouth kiss with a boy. He had the sensation of a man who, having been knocked unconscious, wakes from a painless sleep on the floor of a boxing ring. For a second he wondered if it was her. Then Maria Beckman appeared at his side, saying, 'Oh, look, there's Eva with Johnny Extraordinaire.' Eva and the boy broke apart, laughing hysterically.

Larry said, 'Who is he?'

'For goodness' sake, haven't you heard of him? He's a rock star. Let's try and meet him.' She waved, and Eva saw them and waved back and set off towards them, dragging Johnny with her. He was a dye-blond, with blue eyes and a thin, unattractive mouth. A little gold stud sat like a pimple on the side of his nose.

'Johnny,' Eva said. 'Larry, Maria.'

She tried to kiss Larry, but he turned away and took a swig of beer. Johnny Extraordinaire had an arm round Maria; he was shouting something at her, but with this racket you couldn't hear what. Eva was drunk. She was very pleased to see Larry and kept trying to kiss him.

'Why didn't you come to Dog's?' she said.

'I was working.'

'I'm so glad you've come, Lily!' It was a lover's name which they used only between them. He didn't reply. She hung on tightly to his arm. 'Have you been here long, darling?'

'I was just leaving.'

'Baby! I wanted to dance with you all evening.' She put her arms round his neck and started swaying from side to side. Her cheek was damp and hot and he could feel how hot she was even through her dress and his shirt. He pushed her away.

'You go and have a dance,' he said. 'Then we can go.'

'I don't want to go. I want to dance with you.'

'Then stay. I'm going anyway.'

'What's wrong, baby?'

'Nothing's wrong: I just said I'm leaving in a minute. If you want to dance, go ahead.'

At this point Dog showed up and took Eva to dance, leaving Larry with Maria.

Maria pulled a small bottle of Stolichnaya out of her handbag and offered it to Larry. He took a swig. She said, 'That was a great dinner at Dog's wasn't it?'

'I didn't go.'

'Didn't you? No, nor you did.' She raised one foot and wiggled her high heel which had come loose. 'Almost broke my neck coming downstairs. The trouble is, you can't take your shoes off here because of the glass.'

This was perfectly true. The floor was crunchy with pieces of broken bottle as well as drenched with beer. At the other end of the club he could see Dog and Eva dancing. Dog rolled about

— 59 —

unpredictably, as if he was on board ship in a rough sea; but Eva danced beautifully. When he saw Eva dance like that it made him feel terribly vulnerable.

Maria said, 'D'you want to join us?'

'Who's us?'

'That lot at the table.'

For the first time he saw the little group in one of the alcoves which abutted the main body of the floor: Hugo Cram, little Suki Brett, and another girl, with red hair, sitting with her back to him.

He said, 'I'm going to leave in a minute.'

'Well come anyway. Suki wants to talk to you. She thinks you're wonderful.'

'I'm not in the mood.'

'You don't really like us, do you?'

Her question took him a little by surprise. He said, 'Why do you say that?'

'Well, you always look . . . how shall I say? . . . sort of ill-at-ease with the fun. As if you disapproved of us all but were trying not to show it. I suppose you do disapprove.'

'No.'

'I know what it is you look like. You look like a trendy vicar at a party. Hey, just a moment. He's talking to Hugo.'

'Who?'

'Johnny Extraordinaire. Come on, let's go and investigate.'

She dragged him through the crush, stumbling a little on her broken heel, and they sat down at the table. But by now Johnny had got into conversation with the red-haired girl which, because of the way they were sitting and the general racket in the club, was difficult for Maria to break into.

Larry said, 'Who's the girl?'

'Polly Fort. Her mother's Rita Cookson. Did you see her in *Damn and Blast*?'

'Who?'

'Rita Cookson, silly! Don't tell me you've never heard of her.'

It did not surprise Larry that the girl Johnny was talking to was the daughter of a famous beauty. With her red hair and her pale skin she reminded him of a butterfly, fragile and glamorous in a way that only nature could have imagined. In a moment Johnny and she got up and went to dance. She had on a bright green dress with a big frilly bow at the back. She looked absurdly overdressed in the surroundings of this club; but Polly always dressed like a Knightsbridge girl. Dog and Eva had disappeared from the floor now. Larry caught sight of them at the bar, clutching bottles of beer and talking with another man Larry didn't know. Eva was leaning with one arm on the bar. The red dress made it stand out how skinny she was, but you could see she was vigorous too, from her movements – the way she took a pull from the beer bottle and the way she gesticulated when she spoke. Now she tossed her head prettily: it was just the movement required to make her hair come alive and show off her long neck. Once again he found himself wondering if she knew this or if she did it instinctively.

Eventually Dog and Eva left the bar and came to join them. Eva said, 'Hugo, who's your new friend?'

'She's called Polly,' said Hugo in his thin, effeminate voice. 'She's quite sexy don't you think? Her mother's Rita Cookson and her father's Richard Fort.'

'She looks like a parrot in that dress,' Eva said.

'You're right,' said Maria. 'God that bow looks ridiculous. D'you think she's a tart?'

'Don't be silly,' said Dog. 'She's got her own business. Buys antiques and so on. Bought a whole lot for the Connors. People don't know what to buy, Polly tells them. Makes a fortune at it. Very bright girl.'

'The Parrot? Bright? I can't believe it,' said Suki. 'Is she, Hugo?'

'Brilliant,' said Hugo.

'You men are all the same,' said Maria. 'Any girl's bright if she's pretty.'

'You admit she's pretty.'

'Pretty Polly,' said Eva. 'Pretty Polly, Pretty Polly. Does she talk?'

The girls all began to giggle.

Larry got up and went through into the bedroom. He himself had made the cupboard where she hung her clothes. At that point there had been a small alcove, and he had put two doors flush with the wall and a rail inside. All her old clothes were here, and her shoes. Eva rarely wore anything very feminine because it wouldn't have looked right on her boyish figure. She wore dresses which a teenager could have worn, or else punky stuff, and things made up by her friend Valerie. She had an extensive collection of vintage shoes which she had purchased at fleamarkets all over London. Typically these remained in the cupboard and she went around in sneakers. All this, he supposed, would go straight into cases and be stored away in the old brewery at Clermont. Who would ever get it out again, and when? Doubtless not Eva. Not Lord Clermont either. Would Scrope, perhaps? Or perhaps after they were all dead – himself, Eva Scrope, Lord and Lady Clermont – perhaps then some child of Eva's as yet unborn would go over from Italy, not even speaking English, and break open the crates and wonder where it all came from: shoes from the Thirties and Fifties, these Eighties' clothes and the videos of old zombie movies – *Night of the Living Dead, Death of a Planter, Revenge of the Voodoo Queen*. He might as well take any he wanted. He might as well take them all. But did he really want them? Did any of these objects – not just the videos but the furniture, the bed and blankets – did any of this have a place in his life after the years he'd spent getting it out of his system? No, if he was really going to take a mortgage on the place and live here it must be without any of these things. He'd even dismantle the cupboard he'd built. Everything would change: he'd put the kitchen where the bathroom was now so as to give it a view on the street; he'd often thought it was a bad layout. He didn't want anything to be the same. So why then did he want to come here at all? Perhaps because although he had said goodbye to that life for ever it remained a part of him which it was better to recognize – like those adventurers who sailed away to found a new world and ended up calling it New England, New Scotland, New Spain.

He took out the red dress on its hanger. The red dress! It seemed almost pathetically small. She wasn't a tiny girl at all, but the dress was ruched all the way up like an elasticated tube so that on the hanger it seemed hardly bigger than a large stocking. That had been Valerie's idea, the ruching. The dress was his birthday present to Eva, when she was 22. They came home that night and he went up on the roof of the flat with a bottle of champagne. It was clear and moonless and you could see the odd star in the orange sky. Across the road the street lamp nearest him swarmed with moths. Larry put the bottle and glasses down on the parapet which ran around the edge of the roof. He poured some wine into a tumbler and carried it over to the mattress and sat down. The tree in the garden of the nursery school was black, almost invisible in the shadow.

Eva came up, looking dejected. She went and leaned on the parapet wall, looking down into the street.

'Have some champagne,' he said. She didn't move, but just went on looking down into the street, one foot slightly behind the other, the toe of her sneaker resting on the ground. At the intersection the lights must have changed, for he could hear two or three cars accelerate away noisily, the sound of their engines dying away down the King's Road.

'Eva, come and sit with me.'

She didn't turn round. Slowly she filled the glass from the bottle, took a sip, and replaced it on the parapet. After a minute she said, 'I hate that fucking cow.' She picked up the glass and looked at it for a moment, then idly let it fall to the pavement below. The noise of its breaking seemed very loud in the quiet street. 'She didn't even ring me up on my fucking birthday.'

'She probably did. We've been out all day.'

'No, I've just listened to the machine.' She picked up the bottle and came and sat down on the mattress beside him. That must have been the first night she ever wore the red dress. But how many parties had she worn it at since! In his mind it symbolized the flirtatious Eva of those long nights when, not wanting to go home and leave her, he had sat up with all those people he hated so much to the very end. It was pointless to pretend to himself that he trusted her.

He picked up the red dress and hung it back on the rail. Eva's party clothes had been striking in the old days, somehow ahead of the game; but now they were only a few years old they already seemed quite ordinary, even out of date. Even if she did come back it was unlikely that she'd want them.

Eva appeared to need very little sleep. On nights when they stayed in she usually read novels long after he was asleep, or else watched videos of old zombie movies which she collected. Usually she watched with the sound turned off, listening through headphones so as not to keep him awake. But she was ruthless about waking him up if she wanted to. The fact that he had to work in the morning meant nothing to her. In Eva's chaotic existence all hours of the day were equal.

She also had a recurring dream which terrified her. This was what she called seeing her 'ghosts'. Soon after falling asleep she would dream she was lying in bed, a dream so like reality that she was never sure if she was awake or asleep. Gradually she would become aware of a presence in the room – not exactly a figure, but a darkish patch on the edge of her vision, something of indefinable shape which was never there when she looked at it. And simultaneously she felt a pressure being exerted on her chest, as though bands were tightening about her, making it more and more difficult to breathe. She always woke him when she dreamed of these 'ghosts'. They had a disproportionately terrifying effect on her: she would be trembling all over, almost in tears, and she clung to him like a child. It was almost impossible for her to get back to sleep.

He remembered one of those nights when she was so anguished she couldn't even lie still to watch TV. She kept getting up to change the video, and when he complained she went next door and talked for ages on the phone. Through the wall he could hear her chattering and laughing, without being able to distinguish what she was saying. The TV was still flickering away silently: he put the headphones on the floor and switched it off with the remote control. But just as he was dropping off to sleep Eva came back in and started banging around by the wardrobe. He sat up and put on the light. She had on a pair of panties and she was struggling into a T-shirt.

'Did I wake you? I'm sorry, but with the TV off I couldn't see what I was doing.'

'What *are* you doing?'

'I'm going over to see Polly. I can't sleep.'

'Polly who?'

'Polly Fort. You know.'

'I thought you hated her.'

'No, I think she's great! We're terrific friends.'

'Since when?'

'Just recently, silly. I've only known her a few weeks.' She pulled on her jeans and a black sweater. 'Bye Lily, darling, I promise not to wake you when I get back.'

He'd been sleeping for a few hours when he was woken by a commotion on the stairs. A moment later Eva burst in and put the light on.

'Look!' she said. 'Look what I've got!'

The next instant a dog bounded into the room and leapt about barking. Then a tall man with short blond hair appeared. He was pink-cheeked, with a small head and a long neck. He was wearing a plaid jacket and jeans. The dog was very friendly. It got up on the bed and started to lick Larry's hand.

'This is Ricky,' Eva said. 'I'm sorry, I've forgotten your other name.'

'Berlin. Like the city.'

Eva had traces of blood on her clothes. It was obvious she'd had another nosebleed. She said, 'Ricky's a racing driver. Damn good one. He drove me back from the Hindenberg. How do you like the dog?'

Nearly always it is unpleasant to be woken up in the night by dogs and strangers, but if you are in love it can be a pleasant surprise. He said, 'The dog's fine.'

'What shall we call him?' Eva said. 'What about Johnson?'

'Why on earth Johnson?'

'Oh! Don't you think it would suit him?'

'Well, yes, I suppose so.' Only now did it begin to dawn on Larry that the dog didn't belong to the young man, but had somehow been acquired during the course of the night.

'OK then, that's it. We'll call him Johnson. Johnson, come here!'

Larry put on a dressing gown and they went into the sitting room. It turned out that Ricky didn't drink because he was in training so he and Larry had apple juice and Eva had some vodka. Larry found himself wondering how she'd ended up at the Hindenberg. Had she gone on there from Polly's? Had she and Polly both gone or had she gone on her own? Perhaps Ricky had taken them. Perhaps he was a friend of Polly's. He said, 'Where did you get the dog?'

'We found him,' Eva said. 'On the way back from the Hindenberg. Ricky was showing me a few racing tricks and suddenly we saw him sitting in the middle of the road. Anyway, we stopped and I opened the door and he jumped in.'

'He probably belongs to somebody.'

'Hmm. Maybe.' Apparently this hadn't occurred to Eva until now.

'That's all right,' Ricky said cheerfully. 'We can call the police and tell them we want to keep him if nobody claims.' No sooner had he said this than he briskly set about putting it into action.

'Hello? Police? Which station? I don't mind which station. What have you got near Marble Arch?' His voice had a faint Australian intonation. 'Yes, I found a dog. Or at least a friend of mine has. Name? Eva . . . er . . .'

'Clermont.'

'Clermont.' He gave them the number and address.

'I'm sure there was no need to do that, Ricky,' Eva said when he'd finished. 'I mean, if he belongs to somebody he'll just run home. I shall be damned upset if somebody does want him. He's such a nice dog, don't you agree?'

'Terrific.'

'I admit he's not very beautiful but he's got a good nature, haven't you, Johnson? Oh, Larry, you can't imagine what a fast car Ricky's got. It's really a thrill. Listen, Ricky, why don't you take Larry out just to show him?'

'Of course,' Ricky said.

'Thank you, I won't tonight, Ricky. Maybe another day.'

'Any time.'

Before he left, Ricky invited them to come and watch him race and it was agreed that Larry would take some photos. When he had gone Eva said, 'Isn't he great?'

'Terrific. Where did you meet him?'

'At the Hindenberg.'

'Didn't you go to Polly's?'

'Of course. I went there first.'

'Did Polly go with you? To the Hindenberg, I mean?'

'Sure. Darling, what's wrong?'

'Nothing at all. I just wondered. Is Ricky a friend of hers?'

'Of Polly's? No, we just bumped into him there.'

She started playing with the dog, fondling his ears and hugging him to her. She seemed to have won his affections already, as she had won Ricky's and as she won everybody's. He thought, now that she's young she can do this without really trying, but when she's older what will it be like? Her mother wore décolleté dresses and had a way of standing very close and looking into your eyes. He had met her only once, at her house in Chelsea Square. It had been a slightly awkward occasion because Eva was supposed to be joining them but she didn't show up. Eva rarely spoke of her mother's love affairs. On one occasion when Larry asked her about it she said in a casual way, as if it meant nothing to her, 'Heavens above, yes. It was always quite obvious who she was screwing. I remember when I was a child walking into the library when she was actually

— 66 —

having it off on the sofa. I remember thinking how silly they looked, with her skirt round her waist and his trousers pulled down. His bottom was very white.'

He imagined the little girl at the library door, the two grown-ups half naked on the sofa beside the greeny-yellow globe and the tall bookshelves with their calf-bound volumes.

'She probably thought I'd forgotten about it. Then when I was about 19 I was going out with Roger Cross and she told me I shouldn't make love to him. I got so angry I told her I could remember seeing this. She denied it, but it gave her a tremendous shock, I could tell. And I think that was really why she threw me out of home and gave me this flat to live in, though ostensibly it was for a row we had about something else.'

'What was that?'

'It was all terribly silly really. What happened was this. We were in the house in Chelsea Square – I was living there then, of course – and she was going out to dinner. A cousin of ours called John Hoopoe who was also going was supposed to be picking her up in his car. Well it so happened he got to us rather early. Maman was still in her dressing room and I was chatting with her and she asked him to come up and join us. When he arrived she was putting on her lipstick at the mirror. She turned round and said, "Any wrinkles?"

'Slightly embarrassed, John peered into her face and said, "None whatever."

'"I mean the dress," she said. "It's made of linen."

'This incident sent me into a fit of uncontrollable laughter. They were both embarrassed by it and tried to ignore it but you know how much worse that makes it if you want to laugh. I kept bursting out again and again. Eventually John went downstairs and my mother told me I had to leave the house and go to live at Capilano Place. I didn't think she really would throw me out but as it happened the next day Daddy discovered about the carpet so that gave her a proper excuse.'

'What about the carpet?'

'It was one I found in the attic. I took it down to Christie's. I never thought anyone would notice it was gone. Then on the day of the sale Daddy came in to lunch in a really good mood. "Remember that Persian rug in the attic?" he said to Mummy. "Well, another one just like it came up at Christie's and I bought it. So now we have a pair." Of course I had to give back the money. But it gave her a proper excuse to get me out of the house.'

'And what did your father say?'

'He was terribly angry about the carpet. But I think he was sad when I moved out because that's when he gave me this ring.' And she held up the sapphire which had reminded Larry of the pseudomorph on Mount Poor. He remembered Llewellyn explaining how cultures, like minerals, could take on a pre-existing shape rather than the one that was natural to them. And at the same time there came into his mind the veranda of his father's house with his father and Wilson, their faces illuminated by the light of the lantern, and his father saying: 'Sin is passed on from grandparents to parents to children. Hell has always been a place where the same tortures repeat themselves.'

They went to see Ricky race and he won. That night he took them all to dinner in London. It was typical of many dinners at that time. Dog and Maria were there, and Polly, and dark little Suki Brett and Hugo Cram. In fact Ricky had only asked Polly, but the others showed up all the same. It was something you came to expect with Dog's crowd. The waiters did some reshuffling and in the end everyone was accommodated. There was also a boy from New York. He had an angular face, intelligent grey eyes, a closely cropped head and an accent which was mainly American but with undertones of a foreign language as well: it turned out that he was Czech by origin. Surprisingly in view of this, it seemed that his name was Gawain. He was quiet without being timid. His clothes were second-hand but carefully chosen, of good quality. He said he used a pendulum to find lost objects and help him take decisions: once he had located a lost child in Brooklyn which had caused a sensation in the press. At the moment he was using it to search for oil deposits, using a large-scale map of Kentucky. He said he had the pendulum in his pocket but he wouldn't demonstrate it to them because he believed it wouldn't work for him if he treated it lightly. Everyone was half impressed. Larry found himself wondering whose friend he was, where he fitted in. Most probably Eva had found him somewhere.

Maria ate only ice-cream. She told everyone she was going to have her bush removed by electrolysis because she couldn't bear having it waxed any longer. This immediately started Eva up on the subject. She said (and Larry knew she was making this up) that she had hers done at Harrods, which was by far the best service. She gave a detailed explanation. Suki pretended to be terribly impressed. She insisted on knowing how much it cost and how long it took. Larry knew this charade would go on for a long time now. They were hoping to shock someone but in fact everyone was bored.

Only Polly looked a little uncomfortable, or did she also find it tedious? Larry caught her eye once or twice. He thought he detected a feeling similar to his own, a longing to leave combined with a knowledge that it was still just too early to break up the party. After the coffee they would go. He found himself wondering why he wasn't having an affair with Polly instead of Eva. She was beautiful. He thought she rather liked him. He remembered how swiftly Eva had moved to become her friend.

Inevitably, by the end of the dinner Maria was throwing food. Larry started to go.

'What's the matter, darling?' Eva said. 'Aren't you having fun?'

'Not really. Let's go.'

'Well I'm having terrific fun. Talking with Ricky and Dog.'

'Come on, Larry,' said Dog. 'Don't be such a party poop.' He put his arms round Eva's shoulders and she sagged drunkenly against him, closing her eyes and opening them again. Larry went round behind her and said into her ear, 'Let's go now, Eva, you've already had enough.'

Eva sat up sharply.

'What did you say? Perfectly all right. Feeling terrific. Just getting bored waiting for the dancing, that's all.'

'There isn't any dancing.'

'What do you mean, no dancing?' She rose sharply to her feet, swayed heavily and steadied herself on the table. 'Darling, please take me dancing. I love dancing better than anything. Dance with Dog and Ricky. Dance with you.' She put her arms round his neck and they did a few steps.

'Darling,' Larry said. 'Come home with me.'

'But I want to dance!' Eva said. She broke away from him and twirled around, making her dress fly out.

'Brava!' said Ricky and clapped his hands.

'Hooray!' Dog was shouting. 'I'll dance with you!'

'I will!'

'I will!'

Everybody wanted to dance with Eva.

Anastasia's was generally held to be one of the smartest clubs and Larry supposed this was why Dog liked to come here. At any rate, there seemed to be no other good reason: it was crowded and the music was hell, and a round of drinks cost more than Larry usually spent on dinner. The clientele were old and loutish. A few sexy young things, tarts mostly, added the depressing feeling that beauty is cheap.

They sat round a long table which was so close to its neighbours that you practically had to clamber over them to sit down. Unless you could shout like Maria Beckman, there was little chance of making yourself heard to anyone but the person immediately next to you. Larry saw Dog order something from the waiter, but couldn't hear what. It was dark. In front of him a candle rose out of a glass bowl in which some rose petals and a cigarette butt were floating. He wondered if he should leave now, before, out of boredom, he had any more to drink. He had to go to Belgium the next day.

Champagne arrived in silver buckets. The waiters, maintaining an impossible decorum in the scrum, managed to set out the glasses round the table and serve it. Maria was shouting for cigarettes. Somebody else ordered smoked salmon and scrambled eggs. At the other end of the table a newcomer to the group had squeezed in next to Polly Fort and was polishing his glasses vigorously with a handkerchief as if he didn't believe what he was seeing. Certainly Polly was looking beautiful tonight. No wonder the girls said she wasn't clever. He kept his eye on Eva, tossing her head and laughing, leaning right across the table on her elbows and talking to the boy from New York, who was also leaning forwards, so their faces were quite close. In profile one was scarcely aware of the slant of her eyes. It was the long straight nose which stood out. She was animated, magnetic. The boy took a piece of cloth out of his pocket and began unwrapping it, extracting a lump of something on the end of a string. He held it so it hung straight down between them. They were both very still now, their heads almost touching. The pendulum swayed from side to side in little movements, then began to circle. The boy stopped it with his other hand. In a moment it began again. Larry got up and made his way to the back of the club. There were some sofas here and a fake log fire. It looked terribly unconvincing, like an English study in a film: spanking new leather sofas, sporting prints, brass fire-irons and fender, imitation antique side tables. He sat down on a wide armchair. On the sofa were three tarts with a vast dish of oysters in front of them, and on the other side of this three suited Japanese perched on chairs and conversed between themselves. It seemed that neither side had touched the oysters: possibly they had been ordered as a result of some linguistic misunderstanding. On their silver tray surrounded by gauze-wrapped lemons, they conferred an allegorical status on the little group.

On to the arm of his chair slid Polly Fort.

'Hello, Larry,' she said. For a moment he thought she might have come to tell him they were leaving, but she didn't offer any further conversation. She looked wistfully at the oysters.

He said, 'Hello.'

Her perfect stocking-clad legs lay beside him along the arm of the chair. She had simple black shoes with low heels. Everything about Polly was simplicity itself. She said, 'What are you doing here all on your own?'

'Nothing really. Just relaxing. Look, why don't you sit here?' He got up and moved to the opposite arm of the chair and Polly slid down on to the cushions. He noticed how slender her arms were, and her waist. She looked up at him. Both her parents were famous actors; Larry had sometimes wondered if she felt overshadowed by them.

'Do you want a drink, Polly?'

'No thanks, I don't.'

'What, never?'

'Never.'

'Polly, why don't you become an actress? I'm sure you'd be a star.'

She laughed. 'I don't like acting. And I don't want to be a star.'

'What do you want?'

She thought for a moment. 'I'd like to have children and live outside London.'

'Where outside London?'

'Somewhere like Cambridge.'

Larry remembered she was supposed to have a lover who was a don at Cambridge. But hadn't she split up with him or something? He couldn't remember exactly what he'd heard. He said, 'And apart from that, do you have any ambition?'

'Not ambition,' she said, 'because I'm not an ambitious person.

But I'd like to make a success of something. I've started buying antiques for people. But that's not really an ambition. It's just something I do, well . . . before I settle down.'

'Eva wants to be an actress. Do you think she'd be good?'

'Oh, I think she'd be marvellous.' When Polly made a remark like this, how genuine was it?

The Japanese businessmen were all looking at her now. Surprisingly, the tarts seemed a little irked; one of them leaned forward and tried to re-engage the men in conversation. Polly didn't notice any of this; or was it that she was so accustomed to it she paid it no attention? Here again Larry found himself wondering how naïve she was. Why had she come over here in the first place? Was it by accident or was it to find him?

Suki Brett and another girl appeared. Larry relinquished his chair to them and went back to the table. Eva had gone. He went to the dance floor but it was so dark that he could only make out the outlines of the dancing figures. Strings of minute lights set into the floor twinkled uselessly at their feet. He made his way back between the tables and took the stairway to the dining room. Two potted palm trees stood outside the door. After where he'd come from it seemed astonishingly quiet here; and the ceiling, though hardly tall by ordinary standards, was at least far enough away to give a sense of space to the room. It had been decorated in the art nouveau style with brass fittings, red plush and mirrors. Floral lamps glowed on the walls.

'Sir?' The head waiter stood in front of him and Larry suddenly had the feeling that he was trying to block his way, like a bouncer at a party.

'Looking for someone.' He peered over the man's shoulder. At the nearest table was a group of Arabs. A bottle of whisky stood on the table and some glasses of Coca-cola. Three of the men wore robes and kheffiyas, the other two were in business suits.

'Whose party, sir?'

'I don't know. Couldn't I just have a look?' The man stood aside – unwillingly it seemed – and Larry advanced into the dining room. About half the tables were occupied. He saw Dog and Maria Beckman in the corner and went over. A plate of half-melted ice-cream stood between them on the table. Dog had a drink that looked like whisky and soda. Maria had a Coke. She was smoking nervously.

'Hullo Dog, Maria.'

'Hullo, Larry. Have some ice-cream, won't you? Maria can't eat it.'

'Tiny bit jittery, that's all. I'm on a diet. Having a cigarette instead. I say, Larry, how much would you pay to fuck me?'

'. . .'

'Dog's just given me a hundred pounds. It's rather flattering isn't it? Look.' She pointed to a wad of notes that lay on the table. Dog grinned.

'You only get it if you pork,' he said.

'Larry disapproves, don't you, Larry?'

'No I don't,' Larry said irritably. How did she always manage to catch him off guard?

'Does that mean you'll do it? Come on, let's go to the loo now.'

Larry said, 'Cut it out, Maria.' Dog seemed to be enjoying the performance.

'He thinks I'm coarse,' Maria said. 'Don't you, Larry? Admit it.'

'Naturally, Maria. You are coarse.'

'You wouldn't mind if it was Polly though, would you? I bet you'd fuck Polly all right.'

'Have either of you two seen Eva?' Larry asked.

'She's probably gone dancing.'

'She's probably gone off with Ricky.'

He left. On his way out he was stopped again by the head waiter, as if he had been trying to get away without paying. Or perhaps he imagined it. He was still unused to this kind of place. It would never occur to the others that the waiter would suspect them of anything. Last week they had been here with Anastasia herself, and Maria Beckman had been caught stealing a bottle of wine. But nothing happened. Maria belonged here. He, Larry Hudson, could never be caught stealing wine. To hell with it, he thought.

He looked downstairs again but it was obvious Eva was not in the club so he rode back to Capilano Place on the bike.

When he saw the two windows unlit he knew for sure what he had known all along: that it must be Gawain she had gone off with. He unlocked the garage and put his bike inside. For a moment he wondered whether to go to his own flat and stay the night there. He supposed that was what he ought to do if Eva was being unfaithful to him. But he wanted to have it out with her. He went upstairs and lay down on the bed.

When she came back it was after dawn. She said, 'I've got something to show you. Get down, Johnson!' The dog was leaping around trying to lick her face.

'What is it? Where have you been, Eva?' She disappeared next door and came back with a shoebox. Inside there was something wrapped in a piece of cloth. She layed it on the bed and gingerly removed the cloth. It was a handgun. There was ammunition too, which she also unwrapped. He said, 'Where the hell did you get that?'

'Somewhere in the East End. Gawain took me.'

'Where in the East End?'

'I don't know. Some place on the other side of the City. It was very seedy. There were lots of Pakis.'

'How much did it cost?'

'Two hundred quid.'

'Two hundred quid? Where did you find that?'

'I went to the bank today. Don't you think it's great?'

Larry picked up the gun and opened the chamber. The magazine was empty. He said, 'How many does it hold?'

'Eight. It's a Two-two.'

Larry weighed it in his hand and then pointed it at the photo of himself by her bedside. He said, without turning round, 'Did you sleep with him?'

'Of course not. It took ages to get there and we got lost.'

Larry squeezed the trigger and the gun made a tiny click. He knew Eva hadn't been to the bank to cash two hundred pounds. He knew there were no Pakistanis in the East End at this time of night because at this time of night the East End was deserted like everywhere else. He said, 'Are you going to keep this?'

'Of course, it's mine. Shall we fire it now?'

'In the flat? Are you crazy?'

'No, out the window. We can shoot into the nursery school garden. There's nobody about.' She put some bullets into the clip and snapped it shut. Then she opened the window and fired three times into the garden. Johnson started barking madly.

Larry said, 'Shut the window and give it to me! Johnson, will you shut up!'

Eva shut the window. He said, 'Put it away, Eva. For God's sake, you don't even have a licence for that thing. And don't scream at the dog, you're encouraging him.' He meant her to hide it somewhere or at least stow it where the first comer wouldn't stumble across it, but this didn't even occur to Eva. She put the gun on the dressing table and started taking off her clothes. When she was undressed she went into the bathroom and he listened to the swish of the shower and imagined the bathroom flooding with water as it always did when she washed, and the toilet rolls sodden in their basket. When she came back she was wearing the towel around her head in a turban and her nipples had contracted to tiny buttons on her chest. She went over to the video and began to look for a tape.

Larry said, 'Eva, you didn't go to the East End, did you? Gawain gave it to you.'

'Yes.' She didn't turn round. For a second the strong back, the turban, the long legs all froze; and then she went on searching, rather frenziedly.

He said, 'I always know when you're lying, Eva, because you're such a bad liar. But I can't take that kind of thing. I'm telling you so you'll know for the future. If you're going to screw around it's over. Are you listening?'

She was fiddling with the tape deck, slotting in a cassette. She switched the TV on to the video channel and sat down on the end of the bed, and the titles of *Death of a Planter* began to go up on the screen. Larry put his foot against the screen and it crashed to the floor.

'What are you doing?' Eva was trying to be irritable but he could tell she was nervous. The television, lying at an angle on the floor, somehow went on playing, and the changing light from the screen was visible on her face as she stood beside it.

He said, 'No, we're not going to watch a video now. We're going to damn well make an agreement, you and me.'

'What agreement?'

'That you don't ever do that again, ever. Understand? Not only you don't screw around with anyone else, you don't even look at anyone else. Because I'm not going to stand for it. OK?'

He never imagined she would disagree. He supposed she would be sorry for what she'd done or at least frightened by the rage he was in. But she just said, 'Oh, really?' and laughed. He was so dumbfounded that for a moment he thought he'd misunderstood, that she wasn't really laughing at him and that perhaps he had unintentionally said something funny.

He was aware then for the first time of the absolute coldness in her nature. It wasn't cruelty but rather something that was missing, a blank part like one of those black holes in space which swallows up and abolishes matter. The more he gave, the more she would take from him. There was really no end to what she would demand.

He left her. It didn't last long, of course – little more than a week if you counted the days – but at the time it seemed long enough to both of them. In the end it was made up as such quarrels usually are: without resolving very much. Eva said she thought she had gone off with Gawain out of frustration with her own life. Certainly it wasn't because she didn't love Larry, or because she particularly wanted to be with Gawain. She kept saying she didn't know what she was doing and she cried a good deal. They had a long talk about her future, in the course of which it was agreed that she would go to acting lessons. And she did go for a month or so. But she was unhappy with them: because of the time of year she couldn't get into a proper drama school, and the evening classes she took instead were not very well taught, or very serious. Further than this, there was still a part of her which rejected the idea of work of any kind, as she rejected motherhood, and all the usual concerns of adult life. She was fond of insisting that she felt the same now as she had at 14. 'I suppose I'm just reluctant to face what's inevitable,' she said. 'But somehow being grown-up doesn't seem to have any advantages. I mean, you decay physically, you don't have fun any more, you become obsessed with things I don't value at all, like money, and house-and-garden and all that.'

'Surely not necessarily.'

'But you do! Whenever I look at people over thirty, over twenty-five even, I'm filled with horror at the idea of becoming like that. Physically they're decaying. Their skin has lost its freshness, their hair looks more and more as if it's been put in the wash and faded. Their flesh starts to sag and wrinkles appear. Pretty soon they look grotesque. Doesn't it ever strike you how *ugly* old people are? And then their lives: the men spend all their time working and the women just hand over their lives to their children. They get obsessed with material things. But why spend all year working just so you can afford to go away for three weeks? I mean, Jesus! It's all so predictable, so boring.'

'But Eva, we're all growing old. What do you propose to do about it?'

'Let's kill ourselves. Let's live like we want to live as long as we're young and then just die. I don't want to live like that, ever!'

Nothing in their lives changed very much. Eva went out a lot and Larry went on with his job. They still went to concerts. The best times were when they were outside London, especially in Germany or Italy, because then they were alone, and cut off from the world they knew. Like a prophet, their relationship seemed to fare better outside its own country. Bergamo, West Berlin, Ghent, Copenhagen, Cracow . . . there were postcards from all these places in the shoeboxes, and photos too, of Eva in pensione bedrooms. These were the times which Eva lived for. 'London is a compromise,' she used to say. 'I get depressed there. Why can't we always live abroad?' And Larry would reply, 'London is exactly what Berlin would become if we moved to Berlin.'
'Then why do we have to live anywhere at all? I'd rather move around all the time, like a nomad. Nomads aren't concerned with material things.'
'But we're not nomads.'
'Why not? Our best times are always when we go away together.'
But Larry began to go away more alone. On account of his reputation as a dare-devil he had always been asked to go to trouble spots from time to time. Now he began to suggest this himself to Potocki, and Potocki was usually happy to send him. Ordinary existence became an interval between moments of danger, and ordinary problems ceased to be serious. And because Eva was attracted by danger in a similar way – even at second-hand – neither of them paid much attention to their life together beyond the immediate passionate feeling it inspired. In this respect they were too alike to be of much help to each other.
Larry put the shoe-boxes away and shut the ottoman. He was hungry now, so he went out to the Wok Long and brought back a takeaway. He washed off a dusty plate at the kitchen sink and opened the drawer where the knives and forks were kept. God, how familiar it all was to him, the light green dining plates bought by Eva's mother for the flat, the forks and the knives with their bone handles! He picked out a pair of chopsticks, turned the food out of its foil containers and sat down to eat at the table next door in the sitting room. The postcard of the Orpheus figure was still

lying there. In the story, when his wife Eurydice died Orpheus went down into the land of the dead to get her back. It was about the death of love – or else its survival, depending on which way you looked at it. There was no Eurydice on this relief though, only the man with the lyre. Perhaps that was why they weren't sure if it was Orpheus or not, Larry thought. The strange part of it was that he couldn't remember ever having been with Eva to the Ashmolean.

— 7 —

'Don't get there before dark,' she said, 'or Daddy will make you carry wood for the fire or something. He's terrible about giving people jobs. But for heaven's sake don't be late either, because Guy Fawkes means a terrible lot to him, God only knows why. He spends months collecting the fireworks. Makes a lot of them himself. Personally I can't see the point of it.'

'I see. And what time will you arrive?'

'I'll probably be there before you. Actually, maybe later. I promised to drop in on Ricky Berlin. He's got a present for me.'

'He always seems to have a present for you.'

'Ricky loves giving presents.'

The conversation was taking place at two in the morning on the telephone. Larry was in Belfast covering an IRA funeral and demonstration. A neon sign was flashing through the flimsy curtain of his hotel causing the wardrobe in the corner to appear and disappear; down the telephone behind Eva's voice he could hear a confusion of loud voices. She said, 'Darling boy, I wish you were here.'

Larry had made the mistake, out of boredom, of drinking with some journalists in the bar of the hotel. The alcohol combined with the air-conditioning of his room made him feel brittle and dried up. He said, 'Me too. I wish I was there. Where are you?'

'In Smithfield. Chap called Eddie Brewer's house. I met him in Chelsea Books this morning, he's an explorer. Damn good one too, he's been to the Amazon any number of times. Says it's just like home to him now. Showed us all the pictures. Runs about starkers with the Indians. You'll like him no end.'

'I'm sure I will. I think I'll go to sleep now, though.'

He could tell Eva was drunk.

She said, 'Don't you want to talk?'

'Not feeling too good, my darling. Bad day, a few drinks, middle of the night.'

'Poor baby. I'll see you tomorrow. Maybe I'll bring Eddie.'

'Yes, bring Eddie.'

'Love you, darling.'

The next day he rode his bike from Heathrow down to Clermont. On the M40 there were some car side-lights on, but the thin winter light still bore up the red barns and tiled roofs, and the yellow of the last leaves. It was cold. Later, mists would form, and in the early morning they would settle in frost on the roads, making them dangerous for the bike. He left the motorway and then the Oxford ring road. As it grew dark his headlamp picked up the grass verges and hedges. When he came to the village the lights were on. Someone was burning leaves in an unseen garden and the smoke drifted across the road, giving edges to the beam of his headlamp. Its veil caused the pub with its hanging sign to appear insubstantial, like a ghostly memory of the night of Scrope's party. Maria had worn a black dress and the darts players all looked at her legs. He thought of Eva sitting at the window of the house with a tennis racket in her hand, her leg so pale against the creeper, the garden full of mimes. Fragments of Paradise, she had called them.

Larry drove slowly through the village and took the lane which led to the house. In summer it had been a tunnel of greenery, but now it was too dark to see anything except the black road spattered with yellow leaves under his headlamp. He ran beside the wall of the park until he came to the gateposts with the sculpted lions on top and the brick lodge. The cattle grid rattled underneath him. A low mist was forming. There were cowpats on the drive and on either side horned cattle turned their heads, their eyes reflecting in the headlamp. The tall iron gates loomed up ahead, the second grid rumbled, he felt the crunch of gravel under the wheels. Outside the house there were a lot of cars, a dozen maybe, but Eva's wasn't there yet. She was very nervous about the Guy Fawkes party. Twice she had told him she wanted to cancel going, but both times she had relented.

In the hall a certain confusion reigned. Dustsheets were spread over the floor in front of the tapestry of Cronos, where two women were struggling to stuff straw into a jacket and trousers. Half a bale stood beside them on a piece of sacking. On an oak table in the centre of the room wonderful lilies grew out of brass buckets, their smell pervading the room.

He had just got out of his biking gear when Lady Clermont appeared, followed by a Great Dane which snuffled round Larry and licked his hand.

'Hello, Larry!' she said. 'Here, Minty! Leave him alone!'

She was a good-looking woman of medium height with dark wiry hair swept back very tight against her head, a wide mouth like Eva's and a long thin nose. What she didn't have was Eva's eyes, nor her skinny figure. Characteristically, she was wearing a blouse cut so low that one couldn't help noticing her large bosom. The dog backed off and fawned about her legs.

In a shrill voice she continued. 'I'm so glad you found us all right, everybody gets lost in the village and ends up at Chadbury. Where did you come from? London? You should have come earlier really, it's a pretty drive in daylight. As it is, you probably missed the best bit. You've been before? Ah, to Scrope's party, of course. Unfortunately we had to be in the Amazon to look at a bird. My husband was, anyway. I visited some friends. Everything's in chaos here as you see, because of Cooper's silly old guy. Now come along and I'll get you a drink and introduce you to everyone. I'm afraid Eva's not arrived yet. She rang to say she was going to visit some young man who's a racing driver on the way down so I expect that's why.' She spoke in that high register which is common among French women, though there was barely a trace of French in her accent. She had a habit in conversation of asking questions and then not waiting for the answer.

They went upstairs to the library where a fire was burning. From among the visitors sitting round Scrope got up and fetched him a drink. Lady Clermont introduced Larry to Sir Thomas Kingston, the conductor of the London Symphony Orchestra, and Margaret Doe, whom Larry had heard of as the formidable head of John Doe Publishing, and hostess of the famous John Doe literary lunches. There was also a Sikh couple in late middle age, distinguished-looking, the man with rolled beard and turban and a tweed suit, the woman in trousers. They were introduced to him as the Raja and Ranee of Nagpur, though Lady Clermont called them Charlie and Tavleen. Finally there was Tom Newman, whom Larry had met in London. He had a gallery which exhibited some of the big stars of the contemporary art world. He was a great bon viveur and had a reputation for chasing women, usually without much success. Naturally he tried it with Eva too.

When everyone was introduced, Lady Clermont said, 'They're just finishing the guy, Scrope, darling. Do go and tell them whether it's all right.'

'Is it all right?'

'Darling, how should I know?'

'You've just seen it, Maman.'

'Darling, it's for you to say. You know very well I refuse to have anything to do with it.'

Wearily Scrope got to his feet and left the room.

The guests at Clermont were always a heterogeneous lot. Lady Clermont was the driving force behind all the entertaining and she was conscious of her reputation as a hostess. All her guests were what her generation called 'lions': that is, anyone rich, noble or famous. Her personal hobby had always been the arts, but in recent years she had begun to show something of a penchant for great wealth. She didn't care much for beautiful women; some said it was easier for a rich man to enter heaven than a beautiful girl the iron gates of Clermont – though a lioness could get in. She always made a lot of her guests and praised them to each other; and in return she liked them to show appreciation of herself, and, of course, her house. The house was really the centre of her life. Taking the arm of her most leonine visitor she would lead the little group to the new statue in the garden, or the rhododendron in the park, or the bed of daffodils beside the lake. It was the world-outlook to which Eva referred scornfully as house-and-garden.

'I hear you're a photographer,' Lady Clermont said. 'Do you have exhibitions? I saw the most wonderful exhibition the other day: a young man named Bonitzer. Do you know his work? It was really most impressive. I tried to get Tom to take him on but he's so stick-in-the-mud he won't take on any photographers.' She stood very close to Larry in a way which he found disconcerting. It made her voice seem uncomfortably shrill.

'I've never had an exhibition,' Larry said. 'You see, I'm not an artist, I'm a news photographer.'

'You mean you don't consider photography an art?'

'No,' Larry said. 'It's just that I don't know anything about that side of it. My job is to be there when something happens, and record it. I have to catch the crucial instant. That's what I've trained myself to be good at.'

'Is that why you wear the camera round your neck?'

'That's right. I like to think that if anything were to happen – if, say, that chandelier were to fall on to the table – I would have a photo of it.'

Lady Clermont looked unimpressed. She said, 'You must be a very good reporter then.'

'I hope so.' He felt he had made her uncomfortable by his seriousness. It had always been like this when he was with his mother and Baumgarten. Baumgarten wanted everything to be amusing. He became quite irritable if you tried to talk to him seriously. Almost in spite of himself, Larry went on, 'I've trained myself to react to unexpected movement. Sometimes I've taken the picture before I'm even aware of what's happened.'

'How fascinating,' said Lady Clermont. 'We shall put you to the test later on. Though not, I hope, with the chandelier.'

Everyone laughed at this, and at that moment Lord Clermont made his entrance. He was a tall man, stooping, with a large jaw and a nose hooked like a beak. He had grey eyes set rather close together and overhung by a very prominent brow. His face was angular and heavily creased. He had big hands, rather incongruously attached to skinny wrists in a way that reminded Larry of a scarecrow. The rest of him was lost in the folds of his baggy corduroy trousers and his shapeless brown pullover.

'Isn't Eva here yet?' he said as he shook hands with Larry.

'I knew she'd be late,' Lady Clermont said, 'because she's calling on some young man on the way. She's late even when she doesn't call on someone. She'll miss the fireworks. I knew it would happen. I do think it's terribly rude of her, don't you? I mean, Larry's already arrived and she's not even here.'

'I'm sure she'll be here very soon,' said Lord Clermont.

'Don't you mind her being late, Larry? I'm sure I would if I were a man.'

'I'm quite used to it. In any case, I'm a little late myself.'

'It doesn't matter at all,' Lord Clermont said. 'You're in time for the fireworks, that's the main thing. We gather in the hall around five to seven, fairly punctually, and walk down to the lakeside. The fireworks will be over by quarter past. Then we light the bonfire and come back to the house to change. Dinner at quarter past eight. Tavleen, why don't you watch from the library with Pauline? You'll be much warmer.'

'Oh, I'll be quite warm enough in a coat.'

'Nonsense!' said Lady Clermont. 'You'll catch your death of cold. In any case, I must have someone to keep me company.'

'In that case . . .' The Ranee made a gesture of assent. She had poise, in a rather cold, austere way. Her husband had been at Cambridge with Lord Clermont and like him was a passionate bird-lover. He was a retired major-general, a jovial and sociable person.

Left to his own devices, Lord Clermont would have been quite happy to spend his weekends alone, occupied with his work for the House of Lords and his birds. Yet he was prepared to indulge his wife's passion for house parties and entertainments. He himself appeared only at meals. In spite of his fierce appearance he had wonderful manners and charmed everyone by his simplicity. He spent most of the day closeted with his birds in the aviaries at the other end of the lake, or else in his study. A visitor to the house rarely came across him. In the early morning, perhaps, when one was getting dressed, one might get a glimpse of him on his way down to the aviaries, stopping where a yellow drift of leaves had gathered at the edge of the path to clear a drain with the end of his stick, or at the far end of the lake, up to his thighs in ground-mist so that he seemed to be wading, while at his side appeared and disappeared the periscopic heads of his flamingos.

Clermont House was the one interest Eva's parents had in common. They were so different it was hard to imagine how they had ever come together in the first place. The evil gossips said she seduced him and then pretended she was pregnant, which was probably untrue; but whatever the mysterious origin of the marriage, there was no doubt that the house held it together. With painstaking care they had restored it, stripping away the Edwardian wings, cultivating the old walled gardens once again and planting lawns in front of the house where the Victorian flowerbeds had been; uncovering old panelling and putting back windows bricked up for tax; finding and buying and hanging wallpapers of the period; tracking down and bidding for paintings which had been dispersed; unblocking the chimneys, replanting the orchard, relaying and polishing the floors until the house came to the lovely, old, elegant state in which it was today.

Neither Lord Clermont nor Lady Clermont was at all interested in the century we live in. Nor was the Enlightenment an accidental moment to have stripped the house back to. Particularly in Lord

Clermont's mind it was a zenith towards which civilization had developed and from which it had ever since degenerated. Year after year, in his tall cluttered study abutting the library, he went through the papers of his family during this era, indexing and cross-indexing, pondering on little conundrums, pencilling notes into the margins of his catalogue, checking accounts, ordering and reordering bills and deeds and titles. The papers were kept in tin trunks with painted numbers on top and at a given moment one or two of these trunks would always be found in Lord Clermont's study, the lids hanging open, the bundles inside tied up in withered ribbon. It was in one of these that Lord Clermont had stumbled on the drawings for an aviary commissioned by his ancestor from William Kent. The rest of the room was cluttered, table and floor, with stacks of papers – works on sewage were especially prevalent (at one time he had sat on the Parliamentary commission on sewage); and then there were the ornithological periodicals, and the books on country houses and their gardens, architecture, landscape, forestry, agriculture, painting through the ages. Eva always referred to her ancestors as 'relations' and pretended to know nothing about them. 'Darling,' she said, when Larry first asked her, 'I hate all my relations. They were all terrible bores, usually in the army.'

Scrope came back into the library with the news that the guy was finished and satisfactory. 'I must say I have always abhorred this burning in effigy,' said Lady Clermont. 'It reminds me of *les Khomeinistes*. In any case, as a papist myself, I rather sympathize with Mr Fawkes.'

'Fawkes was set up,' said Scrope. 'Everyone knows the whole show was organized by the anti-Spanish faction.'

'Good gracious,' said Charlie Nagpur. 'Is nothing sacred any more?'

'In any case,' Lady Clermont went on, 'if you've ever dined at the House you'll admit it's worth blowing up for gastronomic reasons alone. Don't you agree with me, Tommy?'

The little conductor was perched very erect on the edge of the sofa. He had his legs tucked under him in such a way that his knees were practically on the floor. He said, 'I've only eaten there once, but I adored every minute of it.'

'But the food, Tommy!'

'Especially the food. It was all so Parliamentary: the leathery old chops and the puddings and so on. It was quite perfect!'

The talk moved on to people in Parliament. Larry tried to imagine Eva as a little girl at the door, and Lady Clermont on the sofa at the far end of the room, her legs around a strange man. He remembered coming in during Scrope's party and seeing the girl with the long yellow hair spreadeagled with the boy in leathers, and the bespectacled figure beside them, spinning the globe. He got up and walked over. Laying his hands on it now he noticed it was not of the earth at all, but of the heavens, with the stars and constellations marked in Latin around its surface. Cepheus, Cassiopeia, Andromeda chained to her rock. Everyone was punished for the sins of their parents, and the punishment was to commit the same sins all over again. He could hear his father's voice talking about repetitive hells on the veranda with Wilson. Would Lady Clermont, he wondered, have been a friend of Baumgarten's? Behind the sofa was a shelf of Diderot's works which must have certainly looked down on her antics and who knew what other scenes of family life. He took out *Jacques le Fataliste* and looked inside: Buisson, 1796. It had seen a few generations of Clermonts go by. He remembered the exchange:

JACQUES: *Mais si vous êtes et si vous avez toujours été le maître de vouloir, que ne voulez-vous à présent aimer une guenon; et que n'avez-vous cessé d'aimer Agathe toutes les fois que vous l'avez voulu? Mon maître, on passe les trois quarts de sa vie à vouloir, sans faire.*
LE MAÎTRE: *Il est vrai.*
JACQUES: *Et à faire sans vouloir.*[1]

But although he looked for it he couldn't remember where it came. He put the book back in the shelf and span the celestial globe gently. Sisyphus, Tantalus, Ixion . . . the heavens themselves went round and round. Small wonder men had tried to read their destiny in the stars. He thought of the Baumgarten plane spinning in the glittering night as it plummeted earthwards over the pampas . . .

---

[1] Jacques: But if you are and always have been master of your will, why don't you go and fall in love with a shrew; and why haven't you stopped loving Agatha all the times you've wanted to? My master, we pass three-quarters of our existence in wanting what we can't have.
His Master: It's true.
Jacques: And getting what we don't want.

When someone says 'around five to seven fairly punctually' you know you have to be on time. Larry went upstairs to his room. A change of clothes was laid out on the chair at the end of his bed. He lay down and lit a cigarette and tried to think about the pictures he had taken that morning. There had been nothing sudden or dramatic to capture. The Minister had flown over because of the riots: not to do anything in particular, but to put in an appearance. There had been a huge amount of security. There was always an element of danger for these people, but less on an impromptu visit such as this: real terrorist attacks require a lot of planning; sometimes it took months for them to set something up. In fact the Minister probably lived less dangerously than someone like Ricky. Ricky had plenty of pluck. It was important not to start trying to detract from Ricky in his mind. He turned to the books on the bedside table. A biography, a few thrillers, a book on country houses, an abridged edition of Prescott's *Conquest of Mexico*. How his father had loved that book! It was not only Cortés and the Pizarros who had inspired his father, but also blind Prescott himself, labouring away at his epic in the blackness. His father said Prescott was the greatest American stylist. He would read this later on if he couldn't sleep.

In the hall Lord Clermont was fitting Margaret Doe with a pair of boots. Everyone was struggling into scarves and hats and pullovers except for Lady Clermont and the Ranee. 'Scrope!' Lady Clermont's cry shilled above the noise of all the preparations. 'Scrope! The guy is *affreux*! You haven't even got a nose on him!'

'I didn't really think it mattered, Maman.'

'For goodness' sake, I told you to make sure it was all right!'

'But it is all right. It's perfectly all right. Why should it have a nose?'

'Really, Scrope, you are hopeless! Come on, Tavleen, let's go into the library. Nose or no nose this thing gives me the creeps.'

The two women went upstairs.

Lord Clermont lit four carriage lanterns and handed them round.

'The best thing on a blowy night,' he said. 'I found them in an attic over the stables and had them polished up. They're Regency, I think.' He looked at his watch.

'Right. Everybody ready?'

They set off across the park towards the lake. Over the years a ritual had grown up around Lord Clermont's fireworks. People from the village came to watch, but because they were home-made they sometimes went terribly wrong, and for this reason the spectators were kept well back behind a rope which was put up in the park, a little way from the lake. Lord Clermont himself lit the fireworks down by the lakeside.

The first rocket rushed into the sky and exploded like a heavy gun. A girl screamed and a curtain of silver and gold rain trickled harmlessly out of the sky, its smoke drifting away on the wind. Blackness returned. At the tall window of the library Larry could make out the figures of Lady Clermont and the Ranee standing like shadow puppets against the yellow lamplight.

A burning taper shielded between a pair of hands was moving about in the blackness. Once or twice its feeble illumination caught the jutting features of Lord Clermont huddled above it. Then a whole line of rockets whizzed upwards and burst without a sound, shooting out trails of glitter in all directions so that they looked like the heads of silver palm trees tossed in the wind. People round Larry made cooing noises and some of them clapped.

Next there were rockets which exploded with a great flash and a clap of thunder – one, two, three, four – and the flashes lit the house one after the other so that it seemed to jump to the sound of each explosion. In the window of the library Lady Clermont and the Ranee came and went, and the cars out in front skipped and flickered. For a moment Larry thought he could see Eva's car among them; but now down by the lake Lord Clermont switched to catherine wheels, plunging the gravel circle in front of the house once more into the gloom, so that the parked cars were distinguishable only in outline.

The display was not long but it was noisy. At the end Lord Clermont filled the sky with rocketed flares which floated earthwards like a massive airborne invasion and then suddenly blew themselves into smithereens.

Everything went dark and silent for a moment. Then a spark fizzed along the fuses of the set-piece which was the finale of the show: two iridescent birds blazed like phoenixes, face to face, lighting all that part of the park, and the assembly of spectators. The figure of Lord Clermont came scurrying across to join his guests.

'Bravo! Hooray!'

Everybody was shouting their appreciation.

'I say! Cooper! That's really splendid! Where do you find these things?'

'He makes them all himself!'

'He has them sent from China!'

'That's the best I've ever seen, Cooper. My goodness! What are they?'

'Tragopans,' said Lord Clermont. 'I'm trying to breed a pair at the moment.' By the light they threw off you could see he was tremendously excited by the success of the display; but all he said was, 'They look all right, don't they?'

The bonfire was lit and everyone stood around and warmed their hands at the blaze till the guy fell off, and then the house party trooped back across the park with their lanterns. As they approached the house Larry looked once again in the direction of the parked cars, but there was no sign of the yellow Renault.

He sat on Lady Clermont's left at dinner. Among such distinguished company he supposed he derived this honour from his relationship with Eva; though from the questions both her parents had asked him he didn't have the impression she'd told them very much about him. On his other side Eva's place was empty.

'What *does* Eva do in London?' Lady Clermont asked him. 'Personally, I can never make it out. Sometimes she says she goes to auditions but that can't take up much of her time. Frankly I think it's high time she forgot about becoming an actress and tried something else. What's the point of banging your head against a brick wall? If she was going to be a star it would have happened by now, don't you think? Look at Polly Fort's mother: she was a star in her first film. In any case, acting is the worst profession in the world if you're not extremely successful at it, don't you agree? Not that I'm pressing her to have a career: just something to keep her occupied – I mean, it must be so *depressing* hanging round all day with time on your hands. She doesn't seem to be able to make the most of her opportunities. Why doesn't she want to travel, for instance? There are such marvellous places to go to. I've offered to pay for her. Or else she could do a course in something. At her age one can do these things, it's a marvellous opportunity. Later on it all becomes more difficult.'

'Maybe she should get married,' said Newman. He had been drinking heavily all evening.

'Do you think so?' asked Lady Clermont. 'I had almost given

up hope. In my day if you weren't married by the time you were twenty-one you were almost an old maid, and Eva's twenty-two. I mean, in a couple of years *elle va coiffer la Sainte Catherine* as we say in France. I was only eighteen when I was married. Of course, it's not the same nowadays. Personally, I've never tried to put pressure on her. I think you miss out on a lot of things if you marry young.' She paused to let this point sink home, and then went on. 'I do think it's rude of her not to be here for Cooper's display.'

'What's that, Pauline?' Lord Clermont cut in, hearing his name in a lull in the conversation.

'I was just saying it was rude of Eva not to come.'

'Eva always misses the fireworks if she can.'

'You're talking nonsense, Cooper.'

'I'm not. It's a mystery to me why, but she doesn't like Guy Fawkes Night any more than you do, my dear. Like mother, like daughter.'

'You know very well that it's only the guy I object to. I adore your displays. I always watch from the library window. We enjoyed it hugely, didn't we, Tavleen?'

'It was marvellous,' said the Ranee. 'Like everything at Clermont, it was quite magical. You are so clever, Cooper. But then Clermont is always like that: everything always seems perfect, it's like a little Paradise.'

'Yes, yes!' the Raja joined in. 'Clermont is a Paradise!'

Half-way through the dinner Lady Clermont embarked on a long conversation with Newman about the painter Henry Goetz. It was clear that she was manoeuvring to become acquainted with Goetz, but unlike many of Tom's artists Goetz was scarcely interested in meeting rich and influential collectors. He went out rarely, and when he did it was to bars and clubs where he could meet young working-class boys. So Lady Clermont's best chance to get to know him was through the Newman gallery. Larry was abandoned to the empty chair on his left.

He wasn't hungry, but the courses kept coming. Savoury after the dessert, and then white grapes, satsumas and figs. He wanted desperately to smoke. He thought of Ricky on the chicane at Silverstone. Ricky had a certain glamour, it had to be admitted. After all, it wasn't everyone who could drive like that. He, Larry, was prepared to risk his neck sometimes. His job made that necessary. But Eva got a special kick out of danger. It excited her and made her amorous.

Ricky had looked very vulnerable when he climbed out of the car, a little bit proud and a little bit shaken, his straw-coloured hair rumpled and sticking to his head from the sweat under his helmet. The crowd cheered him. He was a pretty modest guy. To hell with Ricky, Larry thought. He wasn't going to think about it any more. If Eva didn't show up this time he would read a few chapters of Prescott and then he'd go to sleep and in the morning he'd ride back to London.

The next morning when he drew the curtains in his bathroom Eva's yellow Renault was parked on the gravel outside. He shaved, dressed, and went downstairs to the dining room. Margaret Doe was there, and Lady Clermont.

'Help yourself to some coffee,' she said. 'There are some papers over there. Do you like anything cooked?'

'I saw Eva's car at the front of the house.'

'Yes. She arrived at six o'clock this morning. Cooper told me, he's always about at the crack of dawn. Apparently there was something wrong with her car and by the time Ricky what's-his-name fixed it she was too late to come here. We have the alarms on at night you see. So she stayed there and drove over early. I do think it's pretty rude of her. How you young men put up with it I can't think.'

He found her in the walled garden. At one end there was a raised terrace edged by a parapet which formed a viewing-point; from here one could look down across the lawns and box hedges, and the beds for vegetables and summer fruit.

Eva said, 'I was looking for you.'

He made no reply, and she turned to look down at the fountain playing beneath them. It stood in the middle of a circular lawn and had a ring of flagstones around its bowl. In the middle was the figure of Neptune to which clung three spouting Nereids. The splashing of the water seemed to fill the whole garden.

Eva shouted, 'Johnson! Come here!' She let out the high-pitched scream which she used instead of a whistle. 'Johnson!' Her voice echoed off the brick walls. At the end of the garden, between some rose bushes, Johnson's brown form appeared and disappeared. Eva screamed again.

'Johnson!'

The dog bounded towards her through the flowerbeds, across the lawns and the vegetable-patches, and came up panting, wagging his tail. 'Bad dog, Johnson!' Eva said. She got down on her knees and put her face down close to the dog, stroking and pulling his ears.

'Bad dog! He attacked Minty as soon as we arrived. He hates Minty. Don't you, boy? Daddy said I have to keep him in the garden till we go. Bad boy!'

Larry leaned on the parapet. Below him the winter vegetables alternated with bands of earth dug over and replanted for next year, and above them ran strings with little pieces of silver paper attached, to keep the birds away from the seeds.

He said, 'Did you sleep with him?'

'Who?'

'Ricky Berlin!' he shouted at her, and his voice echoed round the walls. 'Who the hell d'you think?'

Johnson started barking. Eva said, 'What are you shouting at? Shut up, Johnson! Why do you ask that?'

'Because I want to know!'

'Of course not.'

'So why did you stay the night?'

'I had something wrong with the car. It wouldn't start.'

Larry looked down at Neptune and the vegetable-beds strung with silver paper. He noticed that one of the twists of silver foil had been blown on to the soil where it lay like a metal flower. He said, 'It's no good, Eva, I'm going to move my things out.'

'But I haven't done anything.'

'You just don't have the will to make it work.'

'What are you talking about?'

'Fidelity. Belief in it. Whatever you call it, you don't have it.'

He walked away from her down the steps and between the box hedges until he came to the door which led into the next garden, where the swimming pool was. There was no water in it now. Some leaves lay on the bottom and its turquoise walls were stained by dribbles of rust beneath the portholes which covered the lights. The bathing-house was shut. He crossed the lawn to the iron gate where he and Eva had stopped the bike and peered through the bars at the heads bobbing in the water. He remembered Dog Gracechurch sitting in his black dinner suit in front of the hut. It was hard to imagine that summer night in this cold season.

The gate creaked on its hinge. Below him lay the weathered,

brick house with its smooth lawns, and beyond it the huge park dotted with ancient pollard oaks. The lake was as dark as iron, the copper leaves of the young beeches reflected in its farther end. Beyond them, among the denuded branches of the mature trees, he could make out the classical rotunda of the aviary. The whole scene, constructed and lovingly tended by generations of Eva's family to reflect a certain idea of Arcadia, filled him with nothing but an oppressive sense of sterility. He stuck his hands in his pockets and began to walk down the terraced slope, skirting the house and the circle of gravel where Eva's car was parked. Crossing the lawn he jumped the ha-ha and tramped on across the park, past the ashes where the bonfire had been the night before, past the charred bodies of the spent catherine wheels, past the bullrushes and the landing stage at the edge of the lake. At last he came to the end of the lake where the flamingo sheds were and here he met Lord Clermont coming out carrying a bucket. He was wearing a sack-like tweed jacket and an old cap. 'Let me show you the tragopans,' he said. 'Melanocephalus – very interesting and rather rare.'

There was a plantation nearby with a well-worn track leading into it, and this brought them to a clearing in which the aviary stood. In front of it there was a small wooden shelter with sacks of feed and a dozen or so cans of the kind used for watering birds. The floor of the clearing was grassy, with patches of bracken here and there. The aviary was very big and very elegant. Lord Clermont let them in by a metal gate in the front. There were some gorse bushes in there, and elder shrubs and bracken. Lord Clermont peered around. 'No sign of them so far,' he said. 'We'd better give them something to eat and see if that will entice them out. They have a habit of getting into the bracken.' He emptied some corn from his bucket into the feeding-pan.

In the end they found the tragopans pecking about in the far corner. 'They've refused to breed for me so far,' Lord Clermont said. 'The trouble is, they don't like captivity. Not that I blame them. In fact I can understand it only too well. Captivity's a miserable condition for a free spirit. If they don't breed next spring I think I'll take them back. Otherwise I'm worried they won't be able to cope any more with life in the wild. They were quite young when they came to me, you see.' He made some cooing noises in his throat, like a pigeon. 'I have a relief at the house from ancient Egypt,' he went on. 'It portrays the sons of Isis and Seth making their way to the underworld in the form of birds. Very like these two, they look. The Egyptians thought the soul took the form of a bird when you died.'

They went back to the huts by the lake and Lord Clermont showed him the flamingos. He had some rare ducks there too, and some doves. They were looking at the incubators when they heard the bike draw up outside. Eva came in. She said, 'Papa, is it OK if I use the range?'

'Yes, all right. Which rifle are you going to take?'

'Just the Two-two. D'you want to come, Larry?'

Larry thought for a moment, then said rather deliberately, 'Yes, I'd like that very much.'

From the pocket of his voluminous corduroys Lord Clermont took the key to the gun-room, and they went out to the bike. Larry said, 'I'll drive.'

She gave him the keys. Neither of them looked at the other. They got on the bike and rode up to the gun-room. Eva got the little ·22 out of the glass-fronted cupboard and took a box of bullets from the drawer. There were some paper targets in there and she took some of these too.

'I'll take it,' Larry said. She gave him the gun. He checked the bolt, and slung it across his back and put the bullets in his jacket pocket. They got back on the bike with Larry driving and the gun between them and the box of bullets weighing down the pocket of his jacket on one side. They drove into the woods. The range was the place they had come to on the night of Scrope's party, to jump the bike. At one end of the clearing was a sandy bank where you lay to shoot. At the other there were some wooden posts to which you attached the targets. They walked down there and Eva began to put them up. Larry said, 'Take that target off and hold it like this. I'll shoot.'

It took her a moment to realize what he meant, but there was that same recklessness in both of them which made it impossible, once this had been suggested, not to go through with it. Larry walked back to the firing point at an even pace, lengthened the sling so it was comfortable and slipped a single round into the breach. Eva was standing with her left arm out and the white square of paper in her hand. She was wearing jeans and a black sweater and her skin was pale underneath the grey baseball cap. He aimed slightly to the right of the bull, about half-way between it and the edge of the target, and fired off. She looked at the paper. 'Only five,' she shouted. He got up and walked towards the targets and she met him half-way. He said, 'Now it's your turn.'

He walked down to where the posts were and waited, fingering the square of paper. When she was ready he held the target up so that the bottom edge was just above his head. It now looked as though she was aiming straight at him. He shut his eyes. His bones seemed to have liquefied and to be running out of him in sweat. The camera, hanging around his neck, weighed like lead. He heard the bullet go in the sand behind him, and the shot. The hole was in the centre, just clipping the edge of the bull. He reached for a cigarette and lit it. Eva was running towards him. They were both terribly excited now. It was as if they hadn't quarrelled. She put her arms around him and kissed him all over his face and neck.

At lunch the talk was mainly of mushrooms. They were home-grown, like everything that was eaten at Clermont: Eva's mother took a particular pride in this. She always said that in England you couldn't buy anything good and if you wanted to eat well you had to grow it. She had converted an old farm building into a mushroom house and grew half a dozen varieties. Everyone praised the soup enthusiastically. Newman, who'd had a few drinks already, became quite over-excited about it, and a discussion of mushroom cults was launched. Eva was animated and laughed at everything. Larry was no longer oppressed by Clermont. He decided it was an ideal place to come for the weekend, in fact they should come here more often. The other guests were not half as bad as he'd thought at first. Newman was a bit of a buffoon, but he was a likeable enough fellow. Margaret Doe, far from being the ogre she was made out to be, was quite human: she told a funny story about how she'd been turned away from one of her own lunches by the doorman. And when all was said and done Lady Clermont was really very witty and lively; it was only Eva's particular problems with her which made her appear in such a poor light. Even the Ranee relaxed a little and laughed loudly with all the rest of them.

After lunch Lady Clermont took Sir Thomas's arm and led them all to visit the mushroom house. But Eva and Larry had already seen it. They went up to the garden to collect Johnson and it was there that they became engaged.

─ 8 ─

When the train stopped at Genoa a small Franciscan friar got in and sat down opposite Larry. He had a newspaper parcel tied with string which he unwrapped on his knee, laying bare some slices of bread and ham and an apple. He carefully wound the string into a skein on his fingers and stowed it in the recesses of his habit. This done, he laid slices of ham on the bread and held the parcel out to Larry.

'Thank you. I've already eaten.'

'You speak Italian.' The friar seemed pleased by this.

'A little.'

'You have been here before?'

'Once before. I have studied as well in England.'

'You are English?'

'From Zimbabwe.'

'Ah. You studied at university?'

'No, on my own. At university I studied French and Spanish.'

'I see. I myself have studied only Latin and Greek.' The friar laid out the parcel on his lap and ate the slices of bread and ham one after the other. Then, from the pocket of his habit, he took out a small penknife and began to peel the apple, and its fresh smell was released into the stale smoky air of the carriage. He had eyes like black olives, completely opaque so that they were devoid of any depth. But he had a kindly face. He sat very straight with his feet resting beside each other in their sandals, and he gave the air of a man who was comfortable in spartan surroundings. They began to talk. Larry told him that his father was a minister and the friar said that he had known some Protestant priests in the war who had families.

'For us that is not permitted.' He gave a little smile and added, 'That is the most difficult part of the job, especially when one is young.'

Larry said, 'There are people in your Church who think that a priest should be allowed to marry.'

'Certainly. They think that because when you are forbidden women it is difficult to keep your mind off them. This is undoubtedly true. But marriage is even more difficult. Because if you are married it is not just a temptation but a duty. When a priest has a lovely wife and some children, like your father, mustn't he always be thinking of them? Perhaps your father is thinking about you now and that will be taking his attention away from God. And you – are you married?'

'Engaged.'

'I hope you will be happy.'

Larry wondered what the friar would make of Eva, so unreflecting, so prone to rash, impulsive acts. He thought of the way she'd gone off with Gawain, and then he decided not to think about it because that was all over now and he was going to join her and they had three weeks ahead of them without anyone else except Scrope and Henry Goetz and her parents. He was pleased that his Italian had held up in conversation with the friar and he thought if he worked every day for an hour with the dictionary he could probably read the whole *Divina Commedia* while he was here. Out of the window of the train the sea was very blue and ribbed a long way out with white-capped waves. You could see it intermittently between long reaches of holiday bungalows and woods of umbrella pine. Sometimes vineyards rushed by in shaggy green files and sometimes the coast indented, opening up a long meniscus of sand covered in holiday-makers like a melon teeming with fruit-flies. There were striped umbrellas on the beach and painted paddleboats among the bathers and the sunshine on their colours gave an irresistible gaiety to these shabby little resorts. The stations shot by before you had time to read their names: for a moment there was an empty platform with a couple of oleanders or a kiosk displaying brightly coloured 'windmills', and then you were back among the fields or the concrete villas with the sea out there beyond. There was a fair breeze blowing. Across the ruffled water white triangles marked the yachts like flags stuck into a map.

Among her holiday photos Eva had one of a sailboat lying to anchor in a tiny turquoise bay. She told him this boat belonged to friends of her parents and they could borrow it, and take it out just the two of them and sail it to deserted coves where the water was so clear you could see the bottom. She said they would take it to the islands – Elba, Pianosa, Giglio and Montecristo – and he tried to imagine the boat lying at anchor beneath the sheer cliffs and the silence of there being just the two of them, and the shadow of the boat fifty yards down beside the anchor. The other picture which had caught his imagination was one of Eva as a little girl, sitting beside a haystoop with her parents. She was looking straight at you with a laughing expression while her parents behind her smiled dutifully at the camera. He was fascinated by that picture of her. Her hair was in two plaits which came down in front of her shoulders. Her nose was a little less defined, a tiny bit rounder, perhaps not quite so long. The slanting eyes were the same, only completely innocent: it was Eva before the complications of sexuality. Behind the little family group you could make out the edge of a wood, with pure blue flowers in the shadows of trees, and the beginning of an old cart-track leading out of the picture. Down this path, Eva told him, if you followed it for several miles through the woods, you came to the ruin of a fortress from which you could see the islands and the mountains of Corsica, and the Ligurian Sea.

At Pisa he said goodbye to the friar and changed to the local train. It was only four carriages long, with cramped, upright seats, crowded with families dressed for the beach. He got off with a party of schoolchildren at Ronciglio. Eva was on the platform, wearing a red swimsuit and a straw hat and looking very tanned.

'Oh, Lily!' she said. 'I'm so pleased you're here at last. I thought that lousy paper would find some reason to call you back at the last moment. I've been terrified of getting a telegram all day and then at lunch-time one did arrive and I thought it was from you and I nearly died. Oh, Lily!'

Her face, turned a deeper brown by the sun, had lost the rosy flush it had in England, and the whites of her slanting eyes stood out more strongly. He kissed her and they went out to the car and set off across the railway lines, over the plain with its fields of tomatoes, along small roads lined with plane trees painted white at the bottom. From here, the lower reaches of the hills looked scrubby, with one or two square villas which stood out in clearings near the hilltops. The far distance was indistinct, on account of the dust mixed in the heat-haze. He was thinking that it would be cooler in the hills, where Castagna must lie. He said, 'Eva, what was the telegram that came this morning?'

'Oh, it was just Dog and Maria. They're coming to Italy and said they might drop in on their way.'

'On their way where?'

'Oh, I don't know. Rome, the South, I suppose.'

'You mean they're coming to stay at Castagna?'

'I don't know. They said they might look in. Darling, you don't mind do you? I mean, they are my friends. I could hardly tell them not to come. And even if I wanted to I don't know where I could contact them. The telegram came from Paris. Darling, it's all right, isn't it?'

'Of course it's all right. It's absolutely fine.'

'Why are you so cross then?'

'I'm not cross.'

'You look furious.'

'Well I'm not.'

'I didn't invite them. They asked themselves.'

'All right! Let's just drop it, OK?'

He knew she didn't mind at all if they came, in fact she would be rather pleased; but worse than that, he had a feeling that she had planned it all along. They drove on in silence.

They began to climb through a series of twisted valleys where the old villages clung to the sides of the hills and the road signs were pitted with rusted bullet-holes. From a side turning, a leprous dirt road led them into shady woodland, smelling of soil and greenery. Behind them a cloud of dust boiled up and whenever they came to a clearing they could see it hanging over the road below them. Then on one side the woods gave way to a gently sloping upland pasture, and by the road there were small fields of stubble. Once again they entered the wood, but only for a few hundred yards, coming out on the other side of the ridge where a long vista of agricultural valley fell away on one side, and ahead of them stood the house, a small villa built square with a raised attic floor and two small towers.

For Eva's father, Castagna was Clermont writ small. Instead of the sizeable estate which surrounded his home in Oxfordshire he had a small peasant holding consisting of three meadows and an olive grove. In addition to these, he had re-established a tiny vineyard with the help of their neighbour Maurizio, who had one of his own a little further down the hillside. The idea had come when Eva discovered the remains of some old terraces in the rough scrubland between the drive and the woods several years ago. The land in question was an impenetrable mass of gorse and brambles but inspection confirmed that indeed a vineyard had been worked there, probably abandoned after the phylloxera epidemic of the 1880s. Lord Clermont set about it with leather gloves and a machete. He took an almost obsessive interest in the vineyard. Perhaps, though he would never have admitted it, he felt that the modern agriculture at Clermont had lost touch with the soil, or perhaps his love of classical poetry made him conceive his role as that of farmer in the day of the Georgics; at any rate he spent most of his time pottering about the vineyard weeding or tying up grapes. But in addition to his own enthusiasm, he had an idea that his guests would also enjoy agricultural tasks, and when Eva and Larry went to the woods they used to avoid the path which led past the vineyard and instead go round by the back way; otherwise they were almost sure to be hailed by Lord Clermont toiling in his shirtsleeves, and dragooned into coming to help with the work.

Eva would say, 'Daddy, why don't you get Maurizio to do it?'

'He does come in the evenings, but he has his own land to work.'

'Well, why don't you get a gardener?'

'Far too extravagant. And anyway, we have plenty of able hands already.'

He worked all day like a peasant, except in the siesta hour, when he read and wrote letters in his study.

His other abiding interest, besides the vineyard, was his doves. Originally he had kept tumbling pigeons, but they had not thrived; they bred unwillingly, and dashed out their own brains tumbling on the stony hillside. Next he tried mookees. Supposed to be the original doves of Venus, these birds were much hardier than the tumblers; in fact they were aggressive, bad-tempered things in spite of their association with the goddess. As with the tumblers, Lord Clermont had trouble getting them to breed: apparently unaffected by the snowy beauty of their own species, they copulated wildly with the local wood pigeons with the result that their offspring were blotchy and mongrel. That year, when Larry arrived, Lord Clermont was experimenting with fantails. These were less rare than tumblers or mookees, but he hoped they would be less difficult to establish. One batch had been released in the old dovecot at the back of the house and a second batch was waiting to be housed in a new dovecot, which hadn't yet arrived. Lord Clermont kept them in their cages in the sitting room. This was the prettiest room in the house. It had medallions of the four winds by a local artist on the ceiling and windows on to the garden. Lady Clermont was not pleased. Unlike her husband, she didn't relish the eccentricity of receiving guests amid the purring, cooing pigeons. She protested vigorously that there was nowhere to sit and it was impossible to ask anyone to lunch, but this had no effect on Lord Clermont. As Eva said, 'That's the thing about Papa. You think he doesn't have his own way in anything because he's always so polite and because he loves giving things up. But whenever he wants something, he gets it.'

Lady Clermont entertained frequently. Often down the side of the dirt-track road which led to the house there were cars parked as far as the woods, from which elegant women were escorted as though over an obstacle course between ruts and pot-holes. The men wore their jackets draped over their shoulders and kissed the hands of the women. Lord Clermont was the odd man out. At lunch-time he would arrive straight from the vineyard wearing a collarless shirt and an aged pair of khaki shorts, very long in the thigh and bulging at the pockets, making his pale wiry legs seem pathetically thin. Sometimes, if he came from the dovecot, little pieces of down adhered to his clothes, their tiny plumes wafting this way and that as he moved, and once he came with a sick bird which lay inside his shirt throughout the meal.

Lady Clermont's other grievance that summer was the wine. The wine from the vineyard was almost undrinkable, but her husband refused to have any other. He believed that you should always drink the wine of the place you were in, so if you actually grew wine yourself you were mad to drink anything else. This had the paradoxical effect that he could drink good wine only in England where no wine is grown, and therefore he was free to choose any wine he wanted.

'Nobody's dared break it to him that they've started making wine in England too,' Eva said. 'If he ever got to hear of that it would be goodbye *premier cru classé*.'

Eva's mother objected daily to the wine he grew at Castagna, with the tacit support of Scrope and Goetz. One evening when there were guests for dinner, Lady Clermont told Derna not to put any wine on the table at all. At the beginning of the meal, just after she had told everybody where to sit, she said, 'I'm not giving you any wine to drink tonight because we have nothing drinkable in the house.'

The guests looked at each other uncomfortably. But Lord Clermont was very hard to beat. After the first course had been served he shuffled off and returned unobtrusively with a carafe of his red wine, poured himself a glass and offered it to his neighbour. Needless to say, most people preferred bad wine to no wine (Goetz in particular preferred a good deal of it) so that in the end it was Lady Clermont alone who went without.

They used to have dinner in the garden at the back of the house. Here a flat piece of ground, roughly semicircular in shape, formed a natural basin from which woods of Spanish chestnut rose on banks like an amphitheatre. The table was laid around dusk, when the light here was very soft: only the raised attic of the house with its two towers was still sometimes struck by the sun so that it seemed to glow like a neon sign; and the fantails on top would fly away looking like pink cut-outs on the evening sky, suddenly turning into real, startlingly white birds as they crossed the invisible boundary into shadow. Gradually the neon attic of the house narrowed and shut up like a penknife. Derna moved about under the fig tree, setting the table according to the ebb and flow of a special kind of tide: low water was when there was only a handful of people bunched around Lord Clermont at one end – at such times the table was like a long white beach, on which the stains left in the marble by the figs in autumn made bluish seaweed patches. And its high tides were the dinners for twenty people, where the carafes of Lord Clermont's wine stood like red marker buoys down the length of it, and the plates with their locked napkins stood in ranks opposite each other like model men o'war about to engage in battle.

When Larry arrived there were only six of them: the four Clermonts, the painter Henry Goetz, and himself. Lady Clermont had finally succeeded in getting to know Goetz through Tom Newman, and now she was hoping his considerable charm and intelligence would win her husband over to the idea of buying one of his pictures.

In Italy as in England, the Clermonts' table conversation reverted constantly to the subject of their houses. On Larry's first evening the conversation revolved mostly round ideas for changing the garden. Eva's father suggested a long artificial pond, in which the house would be reflected.

'Ah, yes!' said Lady Clermont. 'A reflection! But it wouldn't be visible from here because of the fig tree. We'd have to move the table over there and that would really be too much.'

'If you're going to re-do the whole garden,' Eva said, 'it can't be such a big deal to move the table across it.'

'But then I wouldn't be eating under my fig tree,' Lady Clermont went on enthusiastically. 'And I couldn't bear that. Do you know, Henry, this is the best fig tree in the whole of Tuscany? It gives more figs than you would believe. Derna makes them into cakes and sends them to me in England: they really are the most exquisite things. No, the table must remain here at all costs. In any case, a pond so close to the house – would it really be in period?'

'I don't see why not,' said Lord Clermont. 'They did it at Gaspari and Monticiglia.'

'Why do you have to make everything like it would have been?' Eva said. 'Why don't you just do it like you want it now?'

'Really, Eva!' said Lady Clermont.

'Eva does have a point, though,' Larry said. 'Isn't it something unhealthy in modern Europe, this respect for everthing that's of the past?'

'Surely,' said Lord Clermont, 'you wouldn't have us knock it all down like Bramante and Julius II did for St Peter's?'

'Exactly,' said Lady Clermont, misunderstanding her husband. 'We can preserve the Bramantes and Vaticans *and* create something new.'

'But the point is that we haven't created anything,' said Larry. 'What are the buildings of Paris and Berlin compared to those of Chicago and New York? I am thinking of post-war buildings, of course, the ones our own generation is accountable for. We've allowed our energies and resources to be absorbed by our past. It devours us, like Cronos eating his children.'

'The past is a completely safe country,' Goetz said, 'a kind of Paradise without the serpent. We are all survivors of it, otherwise we wouldn't be here. The golden age is always in the past, after all. The heroes always died a long time ago.'

'But in Europe we can't get free of it,' said Larry. 'Who builds a modern house when they can buy one like Clermont or Castagna?'

'On this hillside,' Lord Clermont said, 'it would be illegal to build. People who want a house here have to find a ruin, and build it up.'

'But in Europe it would be pointless anyway to build a new house, when there are so many lovely old ones. Even slightly vulgar. Our difficulty is that we have this past – tinged with perfection as Henry says – in such abundance. It precludes the need to do these things again, for our generation, and in consequence we lack a viable modern culture.'

He was surprised at how naturally there came to his lips exactly the sort of argument which his father used, and which he had come all the way to Europe in rebellion against.

'What nonsense, Larry,' Lady Clermont said. 'We have a perfectly good modern culture. Look at Henry here, an excellent modern artist as you well know. In fact I believe our century is one of the greatest moments in the history of art. What do you think, Henry?'

Goetz had finished his noodles and lit a cigarette. He drew on it and held the smoke in, possibly because he expected Lady Clermont to carry on talking, as she usually did, without waiting for a reply. But this time she held her peace. Goetz exhaled into the flames of the candelabra, causing the illumination to falter on his walnut-wrinkled face. He said, 'I think I'd like to do a painting of Eva for you.'

'Wonderful,' said Lady Clermont, 'or perhaps you should do my fig tree. I think it would be a marvellous subject for one of your still-lives – quite apart from its appearance, I mean – because it's rather a legend, this tree. You see, all the other trees in this region are its children. It happened like this: in sixty-three, when we had a terrible winter, all the fig trees died except mine. The olives as well, actually, but they grew back of their own accord. So everyone who lost their fig trees came and took cuttings from mine to grow new ones. And now – can you imagine? – everyone says their figs are better than they ever were before. You can see why I couldn't bear to move the table away from it even to see a reflection in the water.'

As the light faded, two pools of light had appeared round the lamps on the table and grew until they merged. Potted tobacco plants released their scent into the air, and at the corners of the terrace vertical cobalt bars sputtered quietly as they incinerated invisible insects. In the dark sky the bats were out hunting. Goetz drank. Lord Clermont's face looked even hollower. Derna brought out huge plates, piled high with meat and potatoes and salad. Larry began to think he had misjudged Eva. After all, it would be just like Dog and Maria to show up uninvited: he was surprised they had even bothered to send a telegram. And sitting in this garden, in the balmy night air, even Dog and Maria were beginning to seem quite inoffensive.

They didn't come the next day. Nor did they arrive the following day or the day after. There was no further telegram or phone call. After breakfast Larry and Eva went to the pool which stood a little way off from the villa. The pool was rectangular, surrounded by a wide border of grass and then a thick box hedge behind which huge dark cypresses stood like sentries. The only break in the geometry of the place were three large bougainvillaeas planted on one side which had grown up the hedge. When they were alone here it felt very private, but usually in the mornings they would find Scrope and Henry Goetz, Scrope sprawled out on a blue lounger, his plump, torpedo-shaped body looking very pale in the sun, and Goetz fully dressed and wearing a dirty panama hat, sitting under a huge white umbrella. He drew pen and ink sketches, usually of Eva. Larry and Eva swam, often racing each other. He had seen her swim once at Clermont, but she was even more impressive than he remembered, keeping a fast pace easily, and maintaining her rhythm over twenty or thirty lengths. She would emerge panting and a little shaky, and dry off in the sun for hours. She was turning an astonishingly dark colour. 'I want to be Larry's Ethiopian slave and concubine,' she used to say.

Papers were read, Italian and English. Crosswords. Intermittent conversation. The heat began to weigh. At some stage between midday and one Derna would appear with a jug of iced fruit juice, and a bottle of rum or vodka to mix with it. Goetz drank it strong, hogging the ice. A little life seeped into his face, smoothing out some of the puffiness, making it cohere. Scrope lit his first torpedo-shaped cigar. Sometimes Lady Clermont appeared and sat with them and discussed the programme for that evening or the guests of the night before. Then, after lunch, they all took a siesta. Because Eva's mother had put her and Larry at opposite ends of the house it was difficult for them to slip into each other's rooms; for this reason they often read together in the garden, Larry working at a snail's pace through his Dante. In the evening when it got cooler they went for walks in the woods along the forest roads which linked the outlying hamlets in those parts, walking slowly at first as the sleepiness of the siesta wore off, but then increasing their pace as they got into their stride. They were both proud of their athleticism and they went at a tremendous pace up the steep hills. The open hillside was hot so they kept in the shade of the trees as much as they could.

Several times they went to bathe at the old mill pond. The water was very cold here, but it had the advantage of being always deserted. They took the car or walked to a point about four kilometres down the forest road from the house, where the stream ran under a bridge of planks. From here there was a path which ran alongside the stream and after a few kilometres you came to the place: some huge black rocks choked off the little valley and a waterfall ran over them into the pool below, a surprisingly large one for such a little stream, bounded on one side by a small cliff with pine trees. There were some more big rocks on the near side of the pool where you could lie in the sun and dry off. Eva used to lie here getting endlessly browner. She didn't put on suncream any more. Larry usually read in the shade by the waterfall. The rocks were smooth, with comfortable hollows, and the continuous drumming of the water next to him made it easy to concentrate, like silence. Tall blue flowers grew in the crevices between the stones and by the waterline some mosses crept up the surface of the rock. At the far side of the pool there was a piece of shallow over some submerged boulders where he used to put bottles of wine to cool.

One day when they were lying side by side on the flat rocks, Eva said to him, 'Lily, do you think I'll ever make it as an actress?'

'Of course you will.'

'I don't even have an Equity card.'

'You'll get it.'

'Do you think so?'

'If you can manage to get up in time for your auditions.'

'But that's just it, isn't it? I never do. Every time I get a break I always screw it up for myself. Maybe I just don't have the self-discipline. What do you think?'

'Maybe. Maybe you should try doing something else, more like a regular job.' Eva made no reply to this. She was lying on her front with her face turned the other way. Her back and legs were a dark, even tan, her buttocks bore the pale triangular mark of a bikini. On an eddy in the middle of the pool he could see the white rectangle from the label on the wine bottle making little circles. He stubbed out his cigarette and dove into the middle of the pool where the wine label was, clenched it in a ball and threw it at Eva. It hit the rock just below her foot and rolled back into the water. He swam over to the submerged boulder and slithered across it to where the wine bottle lay. Under the water the rock was slimy against his front. He got hold of the neck of the bottle and tested the cork and then let the current push him slowly back across the table of stone into the deep part of the pool.

He got out beside Eva, his skin tensed by the cold, and pulled out the cork with his teeth. He dried his right hand on his shirt and got a cigarette out of the packet and lit it. Eva sat up. She had lines across her shallow breasts and her stomach from the way she had been lying on the rock. He passed her the bottle and she drank. The wine was very cold. She was looking out across the pool and she said, 'You don't believe I have the discipline, do you?'

'What discipline?'

'The discipline to be an actress.'

'No, it was you that said it. I only said you might be right.'

'But you think so. You don't really believe in me. I've known that all along.'

'I do believe in you. I believe in you whether you're an actress or not.'

'Exactly, you think it doesn't matter what a girl does because after all's said and done she's only a girl, and a girl isn't really meant to do anything anyway. Is that what it is?'

'A girl can do anything she likes.'

'Then why can't I do anything I like?'

'Stop blaming me. It's you that skips the auditions.'

Eva stared down into the pool She was sitting with her feet planted on the rock and her elbows on her knees and her face plunged into her hands. After a while she said, 'I know. It isn't your fault and anyway it's true. I do screw it up for myself. Oh God, I hate myself!' She picked up the bottle and took a long pull at it. Larry had never heard her talk like this before. In fact he was surprised to hear her talking so seriously about acting at all, considering how little effort she put into it. Perhaps she was beginning to reconsider a few things.

The black wet splashes he had made on the rock dwindled to nothing. They got dressed, and instead of setting off back downstream, they took the path leading up the side of the waterfall to where the ruins of the old mill-house stood. The roof had gone long ago and the first floor had caved in too at one corner, the fallen beams and rafters crossing each other cat's-cradle-like on the ground. Most of the windows were mere holes in the walls, but one near the front door remained partially intact, though it had lost all its glass and the ancient glazing bars were pitted with woodworm and eaten away by decay. It struck him how imperceptibly slow the action of rot was, and yet how completely destructive over a period of time.

Suddenly Eva's face appeared on the other side.

'Careful how you go,' he said. 'Those boards look fine, but they'll be completely rotten.'

'This is a terrific house, Lily. We could do it up and move in here when we get married. What do you think?'

'Sounds like a great idea.'

He uncorked the remains of the wine and went inside and kissed her, and they both drank out of the bottle. She said, 'We'll live here on our own and we won't have anyone to stay ever, especially not Dog or Maria.'

'Especially not them!' They both laughed. In the corner a piece of plaster fell from the wreckage of the ceiling above them with a dry rattle.

Eva said, 'A few minor alterations, perhaps, but there's already a swimming pool so we won't need to build that. Of course, this little lot will have to go' – she pointed to the fallen beams in the corner – 'and over here we could put a pair of french windows going out into the garden.' She giggled. 'Do I begin to sound like my mother? Oh well, let's inspect the dining room anyway.'

'Don't go in there, Eva. It looks rotten as hell.'

'Does it?' She smiled mischievously as she crossed the threshold. 'In that case we shall just have to . . .'

Suddenly she sank to half her height as the floor gave way beneath her. In the jolt of the fall she must have dislodged something because almost immediately the ceiling fell in on top of her and she disappeared in a cloud of dust. He rushed across and found her lying trapped under a huge beam, covered in blood.

'Eva!'

She turned weakly towards him. 'I think I'm all right,' she said.

'Don't struggle or something else is going to fall down!'

He began to lift the beam off her, as carefully as he could. To his surprise she stood up of her own accord. The blood which was all over her seemed to be from a nosebleed rather than any wound inflicted in the fall.

When they got outside she started kissing him and pulling off his clothes. She was crazy to make love then, though she was still trembling from what had just happened as well as bleeding at the nose.

Back at Castagna they found Dog's baby-blue Bentley parked outside in the drive with two wheels in the ditch and a sticker on the back saying 'Divers do it in rubber suits'.

'They've come,' said Eva. But Dog and Maria were not at the house. In one of the rooms upstairs they found a large suitcase of men's clothes on the bed and another marked 'C.G.' on the floor beside it. There was no sign of Maria's luggage except for a bunch of magazines on the bed in the next-door room which couldn't have been put there by the Clermonts: *Over 21*, *Tatler* and *Blitz*.

'You see,' Eva said, 'the old cow's put them next door to each other.'

When she had changed her clothes they went to the pool and found Goetz and Scrope with Lady Clermont.

'Where's Dog?' said Eva.

'What dog?' said Lady Clermont.

'Not a real dog,' Eva said petulantly. 'You know – Cyril. And Maria.'

'Have they arrived?'

'We saw Dog's Bentley in the drive.'

'Are you sure?'

'Of course I'm sure. His cases are upstairs too.'

'I'd better come and have a look.'

They found them at the top end of the vineyard, Dog in shirt-sleeves doubled up under the indicating finger of Lord Clermont, Maria sitting on his jacket under the chestnut tree. Lord Clermont was wearing a little newspaper hat of the type Italian workmen wear.

'Sickles in the shed,' he said. 'We're cleaning up here for a new terrace.'

'Hullo, Dog,' Eva said. 'I see Daddy's kidnapped you. Come in and have a drink.' She noticed Dog was a very grey colour. Sweat poured off his face. Maria was shaking hands with Lady Clermont.

'I practically amputated Dog's leg,' she said. 'I swung it like your husband showed me and it flew out of my hand. Then I tried

— 109 —

the scythe, but I couldn't lift it. Eva! Darling! Thank God we got here! I've had the worst holiday of my life. Dog left my suitcase in Paris and we didn't realize till we got to Cannes. I don't have anything to wear. I'm literally starkers underneath this and I don't have a stitch of clothes to change into. I've lived in it for days.'

The little yellow mini-dress did look rather the worse for wear: there were some dark stains down the front and it had a tired baggy look which reminded Larry of her and Dog's faces. But more worn even than the dress was her voice, so that although she tried to speak with her usual gusto she was scarcely audible.

Dinner that night was subdued. Maria came down wearing a white cotton dress of Eva's and said she couldn't eat anything. She sat by Lord Clermont and refused the wine, drinking Bloody Marys while the others ate. Dog gave an account of their journey from London, and Lady Clermont was irritated by Maria's saying she didn't like French food. 'My dear,' said Lord Clermont, taking Maria's side out of politeness, 'the sauces can be very rich – and perhaps since Maria hasn't been feeling well . . .'

'Nonsense, Cooper. You know as well as I do that in France you can eat as simply as you want. At Archimède, for instance. Did you go to Archimède?'

'We went to Cartier,' Maria said hoarsely, 'to get me a ring. What do you think?' She brandished it round the table so that everyone could see. A heavy growth of diamonds clogged her finger. Nobody was sure whether they were real or fake, it was so vulgar. 'Dog bought it for twenty grand. We're meant to be getting married, you see.' Everyone clamoured excitedly to know the details, but Maria seemed to have lost interest. She yawned and scratched herself. 'I've simply no idea when it's going to be. I want Dog to organize it all but my mother insists on doing it, so I just keep putting it off as long as possible.' Before long she fell asleep in her chair, a little double chin appearing where her head hung forward against her chest. From the way she was slumped Larry could see how pathetically thin her legs were.

'Perhaps,' Dog said to Lady Clermont, 'I'd better put Maria to bed.'

'Yes, do. *La pauvre. Elle est extenuée.*'

When they had gone the conversation reverted to the usual topic that summer: the proposed rearrangement of the garden to incorporate a pond. Goetz suggested that it should be positioned so as to reflect the woods when one was sitting at the table; Scrope said it should reflect nothing but pure sky.

'You see!' exclaimed Lady Clermont. 'It all comes down to nationality in the end. Henry with his English or German nature would rather reflect nature, whereas Scrope, who has his French blood from me, prefers geometric abstraction.' She could never resist a platitude on the subject of national characteristics.

Scrope said, 'It's a myth that the English invented the English garden. Its originator was Dufresny, one of the *commedia dell'arte* players at the Italian Theatre in Paris. It was typical of his luck though, that he's never been recognized for it. Poor old Dufresny. His jokes were stolen by Regnard and even his book was done better by Montesquieu.'

'I seem to remember,' said Lord Clermont, 'that Dufresny was so hopelessly improvident that he was eventually obliged to marry his laundrywoman because he couldn't pay her bills. His luck being what it was, even she wasn't faithful to him. The story goes,' and he glanced at Lady Clermont before turning to address Henry Goetz, 'the story goes that when he found one of her lovers in bed with her he merely remarked to the man, "*Et vous, qui n'êtes même pas obligé!*"'

Dog returned from putting Maria to bed. He said to Goetz, 'I think we have a friend in common. A man by the name of Carlo Spinelli.'

'Spinelli? I believe I've met him. He said he was going to buy one of my paintings but nothing came of it, if I remember.'

'That name says something to me,' Lady Clermont said tentatively.

'He's a famous prince of the Dolce Vita,' Goetz explained, 'or perhaps I should say infamous. They say he was imprisoned for smuggling opium into Italy.'

'He's the lover of Martina Mondi.'

'He's supposed to have been involved in black magic.'

'Heavens above!' said Lady Clermont. 'He sounds very Byronic. Do we dare have him to lunch, or will he start saying a Black Mass or something?'

'He's actually a very charming man,' Dog said. 'I once went to dinner with him in Rome. The flat was incredible, full of Eastern statuary which he'd brought back from India and places. Apparently he lived in India for a long time. He claims to be descended from the

Scipios and he has a pair of slippers which the Pope gave to one of his ancestors when he made them princes.'

'I adore these Italians,' Lady Clermont said, 'they're so excessive. Do let's invite him over. Will you promise to call tomorrow, Cyril?'

'Of course,' said Dog. 'If I can track him down.'

The next day Dog and Maria didn't appear from their siesta so Larry and Eva went alone to walk in the woods. This time they took the cart-track to the fort, passing through the field where Eva sat with her parents in the photograph. There were no stoops now, because Maurizio had baled the hay and taken it all away, but the wood was just as it had been, and there were blue flowers at the foot of the trees. The fort was very ancient. The stones were pitted and scarred by centuries of rain and frost; its towers were all down, though you could see their round bases protruding at intervals. They climbed up on to it and found it was covered in nettle-beds. But an opaque haze of dust and heat obscured the spectacular vista she'd told him about. They sat on the edge of the wall and looked out anyway.

Larry said, 'Do you think Dog and Maria will stay long?'

'No idea.'

'Dog told me they were going on south. To Capri.'

'Oh yes.'

'Did your mother ask how long they were staying?'

'No.'

Larry clasped his knees to his chest. Below them somewhere along the valley he could hear the distant crepitation of goat-bells.

'Maria seems in a pretty bad way,' he said.

'Just a bit tired after the drive.'

'Oh, come off it, Eva. You know damn well it isn't only the drive.'

Eva gave a kind of grunt that could have been agreement or not, and said, 'It's a funny thing, that way they have of announcing themselves and then not turning up, I've noticed it before. You're perfectly happy without them and then they announce they're coming and you begin by cursing them; but then when they don't show up you've somehow got used to the idea of them coming and you start wishing they would.'

'Why do you suppose that is?'

'I don't know. It's some kind of psychological trick they play on us.'

'Don't be obtuse, Eva.'

'I'm not being obtuse. And why are you so bad-tempered all of a sudden?'

'Because I don't like you taking that stuff with them, that's why.'

'What are you talking about? I only took it twice in my life.'

'Well don't take it again.'

'I'm not going to.'

'Good.'

'And stop being so damn bossy. If I felt like taking it I would.'

They took another route home. The path went through the thick woods down the side of the valley and after a couple of kilometres it came out on the road which went up to Castagna. The road did an omega-curve here around an old church with its campanile beside it. It was called Santa Maria dell'Orto, although the garden, if there had ever been one, had long since disappeared. Its doors were locked and its small windows, set high up, had been covered with wire mesh. It was obviously a medieval building: when it had last been used was harder to say. At the west end there was a vestry door and a low window beside it, and somehow Eva managed to get this open and climb in. She gave a scream like the one she used to call Johnson. He thought she must have discovered something.

'Come in here, Lily!'

Larry heaved himself in. The place was being used as a woodman's hut. It was cool inside and smelled strongly of sawdust and creosote. There was hardly room for them to stand between the equipment and the piles of stakes which occupied most of the floor.

'What is it?' he said. She grabbed hold of his face and kissed him.

'Do you love me?'

'Of course I love you.'

'Are you going to marry me?'

'Yes. You know I am.'

'Good, say it once more.'

'I love you. Eva, what's on your mind?'

'It's nothing. I suddenly had a feeling you didn't want to marry me after all.' Having said this, she immediately climbed back out of the window.

He followed her out into the sunlight. She was standing at the east end of the building, looking out over the woods below. There was no sound except the cicadas. In front of the apse a pair of yellow butterflies were dancing round each other.

'It's enchanting,' she said. 'Why don't we get married here?'

Spinelli came to dinner. They were having drinks at the front of the house when he arrived; it was their custom to sit here in the evening, when the sun was going down behind the trees and the house. You could see the opposite bank of the upper valley with its farms and its two villages with their campanili, and down the other end in the valley bottom, the small textile factory. There was no woodland on that opposite side: where the terraced fields ended a dense scrub took over, which was almost impenetrable.

There had been a lot of talk in the house as to whether Spinelli would bring Martina Mondi with him. Maria, who read the gossip columns every day, said they were rumoured to have split up. 'She had a breast-lift in Rio apparently,' she said. 'And I bet she's had her face stitched a few times too. The way she hits the bottle.'

'I didn't think she drank,' Dog said.

'Like a hole in the ground.'

'Not that I remember.'

'Goodness, have you met her?' Everyone wanted to know. It was exciting to have first-hand information about a world-famous actress, even if Dog was making it up. 'Is she as beautiful in real life?'

'Even more beautiful.'

'Was she wearing all the jewels?'

'She was in a bathing suit, actually. She had her make-up on too and she lay in the shade.'

'When? Where?'

'At Porto Ercole, last summer. She and Spinelli were there, staying at Reitman's villa. Did you know he used to keep a pet iguana in Rome? Dressed it in a bolero and took it for walks in the Villa Borghese gardens. Even took it to the opera. It was always quite quiet, you see. The music sent it to sleep.'

Spinelli arrived late. Instead of Martina Mondi he had with him an American called Don Tremoille. After all the talk they had expected somebody flamboyant, whereas in fact he was conventionally dressed, conventionally well-mannered. He wore a check tweed jacket and flannels, and a silk necktie. He must have been in his fifties, but he was so energetic he seemed younger. Larry wondered if he rather than Martina Mondi had had the face-lift: he had hollow cheeks, with salient bones and a rather protrusive mouth, reminiscent of certain snouted animals. His eyes were brown, as was the little hair which remained to him. There was something unhealthy about his skin. It was a yellow-grey colour, as if it had been smeared with ashes. When he smiled he showed a set of perfect teeth, but at such moments, with the skin stretched across his bones and his eyes seeming to recede a little, his head looked suddenly like a skull. Yet he was as active as a bird, and it was his darting, graceful movements which above all gave the impression of a much younger man.

Don Tremoille was plump without being fat, in the way little boys sometimes are; and in a man of 35 it gave him a molly-coddled appearance, enhanced no doubt by his very fine blond hair parted at the side. He had violet eyes without any wrinkles on the side, and his forehead was also completely smooth. He wore a shirt with a deep collar and a cashmere cardigan and suede shoes. He was incessantly pushing his hair back from his forehead. He gave Larry the impression that he had driven all his life in cars with air-conditioning and deeply-piled carpets, and that his body had corrupted from lack of use like a battery chicken's.

Because they had arrived rather late Lady Clermont took them almost immediately through to the garden where dinner was laid. She had Derna bring another place for Don and they all sat down. Although the Clermonts usually spoke Italian for their guests, Spinelli insisted on the conversation being in English. It was indicative of his charm that although he had arrived very late with an uninvited friend, he captivated Lady Clermont from the start by his enthusiasm. Some instinct of flattery made him begin by praising the fig tree, and after that he went on to the house, the garden, the food. He had passed some pigeons in the living room, fantails weren't they? He adored pigeons ever since as a child he used to receive messages in the country from carriers released by his mother in Rome.

'In fact,' he said, 'when I was a boy they were really my only friends. I have no brothers or sisters and my father used to keep me like a prisoner in the country with a governess and a tutor who hated each other.'

'What a monster!'

'It was quite normal for him because he'd been brought up that way himself. What I couldn't forgive him so easily was that he kept my mother prisoner in Rome. She was extremely beautiful and he was afraid that if he let anyone near her she'd run off with them. And in the end that's what happened; but that's another story.' He folded his hands on the table as though he had no wish to go on, but naturally everyone pressed him and he relented with a smile. 'My father's greatest friend was my godfather, Carlos Herrera, the Argentinian mining tycoon. The two men had tastes in common, mainly women and horses. They spent most of the racing season together and my father often went and stayed with Herrera in Argentina on his many ranches. Herrera bred literally hundreds of horses. Even more than my father he was consumed with a passion for the animals. Stocky, bandy-legged, tough as a gaucho, he prided himself on his skill at breaking them in, and it was said that on long journeys in the pampas he could sleep in the saddle, riding along quite automatically.'

'I went to sleep on a horse last year,' Maria said, 'but I fell off and broke my arm.'

'Maria, it was this year,' said Dog.

'Was it? So it was. And it was your fault too. He was being such a bore I just nodded off.' Everyone tittered.

'Let Carlo go on with his story,' Lady Clermont said.

'Even though they were such good friends,' Spinelli continued, 'my father never had Herrera in the house. When he came to Rome he used to rent the top floor of the Hassler for his entourage, though he himself often spent the night in some low bawdy-house. He used to tease my father about his jealous mania and tried every way to get himself invited. I think he genuinely felt that as my father's best friend he should be accorded a privilege which was denied everyone else. Then one night in Argentina they were playing poker and Herrera began to raise the stake to impossible heights, putting on all his mines in Peru. He insisted my father should put on a stake of equal enormity, namely, that he should have dinner at our house in Rome with my mother and myself. Of course, they were playing half as a joke, not in a casino, but in some wretched hut for gauchos on one of Herrera's vast estates in the south of the country – but my father accepted and lost. Immediately he fell into a profound depression. The next day Herrera, realizing what the trouble was, went to him and tried to call the whole thing off. What was the sense, he said, in allowing a bet to come between friends?

'"You would have given me the mines," my father replied.

'"But my dear fellow, the whole thing was a joke."

'"And what's so serious about having one's compadre to dinner?"

'During the next weeks Herrera did everything he could to get out of the dinner, but now my father was adamant. In fact he begged Herrera to come on his way to Newmarket that spring, especially to have dinner, and seeing there would be no peace until he went, Herrera accepted. I remember the dinner well enough. I had met Herrera before, when he came to shoot in the country, and I remember thinking it rather exciting that someone outside the family should sit down to dinner with us. The reality was disappointing. I don't remember what they talked about, only that Herrera tucked his napkin in over his collar and wiped his moustache obsessively, between each mouthful. After dinner my mother and I went upstairs and the two men sat up drinking brandy until after I was asleep. The next day everything seemed to be as usual: they got the train to Paris, my mother remained in Rome and I was sent back to the country. But alas, everything had changed. It seemed that Herrera had fallen in love with my mother. My father, who since the dinner trusted Herrera completely, showered invitations on him to stay in Rome and even asked him to travel with them to Como and Maggiore in the summer. At first Herrera refused, but my father insisted so often that he began to dine with us regularly in Rome that autumn. One day he called at the house when my father was out. My mother received him in the sitting room and it seems he lost control of himself, began kissing her and ended up ravishing her on the big sofa by the fireplace. Two days later she ran off with him.'

'She ran off with a man who raped her?' said Lady Clermont incredulously.

'That's right.'

'How extraordinary!'

'I don't think it's extraordinary,' said Eva. 'I mean, after being cooped up for so many years like a prisoner she must have been longing to get out.'

'But *chérie*, a man who raped her! How could she have done it, Carlo?'

'I suppose she changed her mind – like the Sabines.'

'I don't think it's the kind of thing a woman would take lightly,' said Lady Clermont.

'Nor did my father,' said Spinelli. 'He traced them to Madrid and demanded an interview with my mother. You see, I don't think he ever believed she would have gone with Herrera willingly and he wanted to restore the marriage, or what there was left of it; that was the old way of doing things. But when my mother saw him she told him she wasn't coming back.'

'And what did he do?'

'He went back to his hotel room and shot himself through the head.'

'Mon dieu!' said Lady Clermont. 'How dramatic. It's like an opera. Poor you! What a childhood!'

Spinelli smiled modestly. 'So that was the end of the carrier pigeons,' he said. 'My mother went off to Argentina and I stayed in the castle. But did you know' – he turned to Lord Clermont – 'that in India they attach a special type of whistle to the pigeon's wings which makes a fluting sound when it flies? I have some which I bought in Udaipur. You can have them if you like – I have no use for them myself.'

Spinelli seemed to have something for everyone. He invited the whole party to sail on his yacht, which was moored further down the coast at Porto Ercole. And he had a way of putting everyone at their ease. Even Don was a case in point. At one stage of the evening Don was a little left out of the conversation, possibly from shyness, so he appeared slightly morose. Spinelli skilfully drew him to everyone's attention, pointing out – in a way that was not in the least vulgar – how clever he was at business and how he'd quite recently made a fortune with scarcely any effort at all.

'The marvellous thing is that he scarcely has to work at it. He just enjoys himself until the right moment comes, and then the affair falls quite naturally into his lap like a ripe fruit. In fact he's just like those wonderful people you see in the East, sitting all day under a mango tree talking with their friends and watching the world go by. In the evening they pick two mangoes, eat one, sell the other, and go home to bed.'

'How marvellous,' said Lady Clermont. 'Do tell us your secret.'

'I really don't have one,' Don said. 'It's like Carlo says, I simply buy a property which is going to go up in value, wait till it does and then sell it. It's not all that difficult. At the moment I have an abattoir which is going to be worth a fortune quite soon. It stands in an outlying part of town so I bought it for almost nothing. But the city is planning to link up that district with the main road to the airport. When that happens, it'll be worth millions overnight.'

Lord Clermont was the last person to be interested in his real-estate deals; but as if he was perversely unable to see this, it was precisely to Lord Clermont that he kept turning as he explained the details of this stupendous affair, pushing his blond hair back from his forehead as he spoke. Lord Clermont had a way of saying nothing at all when he didn't agree with something. The effect of this on Don was to make him keep talking when he had said quite enough, and he might have gone on even longer had not Spinelli interrupted him and brought the conversation back to more general topics.

After coffee, the two visitors immediately took their leave.

'But we must have a photograph,' Lady Clermont insisted. 'Larry, you take it. Can you use my Polaroid? I'm so impatient I can never wait to have those things developed.' She had them all huddle into a group and then she wanted one of Spinelli on his own. She always got a picture of an important guest for her album. Eva called it 'The Zoo'.

When they had gone, Lady Clermont said, 'What an unusual man, Cyril, I'm so glad you introduced us.'

'Is he gay?' asked Maria, now quite drunk. After its initial debility, her voice had recovered its usual trumpet pitch.

'On the contrary. He's had quite a succession of girlfriends and wives.'

'I'm not at all surprised,' said Lady Clermont. 'I thought he was terribly attractive. And I loved the story about his parents – can you imagine? The mother locked up, the father gambling away the invitation to dinner and the elopement – it's like an opera! I do love Italy.'

'I think he made it all up,' said Eva.

'Do you really? I'm sure I believed every word. What do you think, Cyril?'

'I think it's true,' Dog said. 'At least, I've heard people say it before. The tragic thing was that Herrera never liked Carlo, which is why he never brought him to Argentina. It must have been tough on the kid to lose both his parents overnight like that. Herrera never gave him a penny either, even though he had no children of his own, which was a bit stingy to say the least.'

'Still,' said Lady Clermont, 'he can't be that badly off with a palace in Rome and a castle in the country.'

'I'm not so sure about the castle,' Dog said. 'I heard he had a small house on the coast at Fernia.'

'I'm sure he said it was a castle,' Lady Clermont said.

'Would you do that if I ran off, Dog?' said Maria. 'Shoot yourself in the head and all that?' But Dog ignored her in an uneasy way which suggested the occasion might have arisen already.

Larry watched the Polaroids develop on the table, first into swirls of green fog, then with muddy colours like the reflections on spilt oil, and finally resolving themselves into the form and features of Spinelli: erect, almost bald, his tight skin, his skull-like grin, the lively, intelligent eyes.

Before the arrival of Dog and Maria, Larry and Eva used to go to the swimming pool with Scrope and Henry Goetz to talk and drink wine when the Clermonts went to bed. This was because if they stayed in the house the sound of their voices could be heard from the Clermonts' bedroom. But tonight Larry was tired of Dog and Maria and he went up to his room to read. Even from his bedroom he could sometimes hear the rasping sound of Maria's voice up at the pool.

At about two o'clock he was still reading when Eva came in and sat down on the sofa. Her face had that greenish tinge which dark-skinned people get when they are sickly. She said, 'Ugh, I hate moths. They're so stubborn.' Although he was burning one of those little green spirals called *zampironi* to keep away mosquitoes, a number of moths had gathered around his lamp and were battering themselves against it, their huge shadows hurtling across the walls and ceiling. Larry understood what she meant. There was something rather repulsive about these creatures, the way they compulsively threw themselves at light whether it was beneficent or mortal.

'What did you think of Carlo?'

'Not much.'

'Didn't you think he was sweet?'

'He's too charming for me. I never like people who have that much charm.'

'Mummy took to him in a big way. D'you think she wants to seduce him?'

'I doubt it. Do you think he's sexy?'

'Not really. Something of a little boy about him, might appeal to some people. Damn creepy friend with him. What was he called?'

'Don.'

'That's him. I bet he rakes it in though. Those creepy types always do. Incredible really, isn't it? Hardly has to lift a finger and it rolls in. Not like you and me, huh?' Her head was on the sofa back and her eyes were shut. There was a long silence. He wondered if she'd nodded off. Then she said, 'Damn kind of Carlo to take us all out on his yacht, even if it isn't his.'

'Isn't it his?'

'Dog says it's Reitman's. All the same, not bad of him.'

Larry got off the bed and went to the window and opened the shutters. In front of him in the blackness were the scarce street-lamps of the villages, and further to the left the square barrage of light at the textile factory, much more imposing now than it was in the day-time. The air was full of crickets. Eva said, 'I think I'm going to be sick.'

She went across the passage to the lavatory. Through the open doors he could see her kneel over the bowl and begin to vomit, her slender body hunching down as the spasms took hold of her. He heard the sick go into the water and the little moans she let out as she caught her breath. Then she stiffened again, her hands grabbing at the side of the bowl as the paroxysm overcame her. Little by little the rhythm of her contractions slowed and came to an end. He thought of Cronos, vomiting up his children.

Eva wiped her face on the hand towel and came back and laid her head on his shoulder. He said, 'You smell of sick. Go and clean your teeth.' She went into the bathroom obediently, like a scolded child, and washed her teeth and blew her nose on some lavatory paper. She dabbed some aftershave on her neck. The drug gave her a racked, bruised appearance. She was shivering from throwing up. There would be no point in trying to talk to her now. Her big shiny eyes looked beautiful and vacant, like the eyes of a zombie, he thought. He said, 'You'd better go to bed now.' He led her downstairs, through the sitting room with its blanketed birdcages to her bedroom at the other end of the house. She got into bed in her shirt and shut her eyes.

At siesta-time the next day Eva came to his room. She was unusually amorous; her skin was flushed and her slanting eyes shone. They made love. Afterwards Larry said, 'It's like you're not there.'

'What do you mean?'

'You know what I mean. I can tell by the way your skin looks, and your eyes.'

'What about them?'

'And by the way you make love.'

'Listen, Larry, I promise I've not had anything, OK? Last night, yes, but not again. And I'm not going to either. I promise, promise, promise.' She was lying. What had changed, he thought, was that he wouldn't have known from the way she said it.

They didn't go out after their siesta the next day or the following one. Eva slept in her room and Larry read by the pool; but the pool began to wear on him, and its concentric rectangles of water, grass and hedge seemed to resemble nothing so much as a vast geometric playpen where the children were bored.

Dog and Maria were sleepy and subdued. In the past they had nearly always got restless quickly and Larry expected they would suggest visiting other people they knew who lived in Tuscany, or joining Goetz on his visits to Pisa and Florence; but instead Maria would lie in the sun, trying to dry out her spots and complaining of the heat, while Gracechurch sweated in the shade. Eva dozed on a blue lounger, her slender arms turned underside to the sun. As always when Dog and Maria were there the conversation had to be of people they knew, and after a while this made Larry irritable. Naturally Maria wasn't slow to pick up on this. 'I suppose anyone except Dante's too frivolous for you, Larry,' she said.

Unfortunately for Larry, Dog and Maria didn't seem to be in a hurry to get to Capri, and as the new routine became established at Castagna, he felt increasingly isolated. He didn't want to sleep with Eva any more. He began to think of the time, not so distant now, when he would have to go back to Fleet Street.

There was no word from Spinelli and his invitation had been more or less forgotten when one night he rang up, saying he had the yacht ready and wanted to take them out from Porto Ercole the next day. That was a Friday, and since Larry had to fly back to London on Sunday, he hoped Dog and Maria would go with Spinelli and he and Eva might have the day to themselves here at

Castagna. But when he suggested this to her she said, 'But Lil, we always wanted to go out on the boat together and now we've got the chance. What's wrong?'

Larry said he would stay at Castagna with Lord Clermont. The others were to drive to Porto Ercole after breakfast the next day.

That morning Larry helped Lord Clermont to clear a new terrace above the vineyard. From a page of *Corriere della sera* Lord Clermont showed him how to make a workman's paper hat to keep off the sun. He had a toughness and resilience which took Larry by surprise. He could go on for hour after hour under the hot sun, without seeming to tire. The slowness of the work made Larry impatient at the beginning. If they'd had some decent tools – a couple of power saws for instance – they could probably have got through the mass of undergrowth in about a week. Then the ground could have been broken up with a mechanical digger. But such practicalities were quite alien to Lord Clermont's way of thinking. He used an old machete and gave Larry a rather blunt sickle. It didn't really matter to him whether it took him a week or a month. He put a high value on agricultural work, which he believed was good in itself. 'Mao was right,' he said, 'when he sent everyone to work in the country for a month each year.'

Larry was soon exhausted and he was relieved when just before lunch the dovecot arrived and they broke off to oversee the operation of putting it up. Once this was done they fetched the fantails in their cages from the house. The release did not go smoothly. In the course of their long seclusion in the sitting room the pigeons seemed to have undergone some sort of schizophrenic trauma, as a result of which they spent all day flying backwards and forwards between this dovecot and the other one at the back of the house.

By evening the yacht party still hadn't returned. Larry found Lord Clermont reading in the sitting room; now that the pigeons were gone it was back in use again for the first time.

'Help yourself to a drink,' he said. 'I'm catching up with some Parliamentary work. Very interesting report this. On dam sluices.'

Larry got himself a drink. He read Dog's copy of *Time* magazine and smoked a couple of cigarettes. It seemed very silent in here without the purring of the pigeons. You would certainly have heard a car on the drive outside. Eventually Lord Clermont put down his report.

'Got any plans for tomorrow?' he said.

By this time Larry knew Lord Clermont well enough to know this was likely to prelude a suggestion of further work in the vineyard. He said, 'Eva and I were planning a walk to the fort. Apparently you can see the whole Tuscan archipelago and even Corsica.' It was more of an excuse than a genuine plan; but now he'd said it, it seemed like a good idea, seeing as Maria and Dog certainly wouldn't want to walk all that way.

'You'll be lucky if you see much,' Lord Clermont said. 'At this time of year there's not usually enough visibility. As a matter of fact I think the weather's about to break. My shark-oil barometer has clouded up. It's an uncanny thing – I got it in Bermuda.' He pulled out his watch and flicked it open. 'Nine o'clock,' he said. 'Looks like they're going to be late. I'll go and tell Derna to hold dinner.'

Larry read *Time* again. This time he also read the bits he'd left out, like the baseball. Finally he got up and walked outside. The light was dying. Round the pool the cypresses were solidifying against the pale sky and the bougainvillaea seemed to have caught fire.

As he sat down on a deckchair he noticed there were spent matches in the grass around the table and a piece of silver foil, and he thought of the strings of silver paper over the lettuce beds at Clermont and Eva on her knees saying that she hadn't slept with Ricky and pulling the dog's ears. And then his heart was heavy because he knew that whatever he did to bring her back she would always slip away from him without a word, that he need only turn round and she would vanish, like Eurydice into the land of the dead. He mustn't begin to believe that. They had to think about the future now. Perhaps they could come and live in Italy when they were married; he could get a job in Milan and they would spend the weekends at Castagna, just the two of them. Perhaps then they really would convert the old mill-house together.

It was dark when he and Lord Clermont began dinner. The others arrived as they were half-way through, all except for Eva.

'She stayed to meet a film director,' Lady Clermont said. 'My dear! Can you imagine, Carlo says she's certain to be given a part in a new play! I can hardly believe it myself.'

'What's the name of the director?' Larry asked.

'I can't remember. Some woman who's meant to be absolutely marvellous – who is it, Scrope?'

'Rosa Agambo.'

'That's right. I mean, there's no reason why she should want to have Eva, is there? But somehow Carlo makes one think it's all going to be terribly easy. Sometimes people who have that kind of attitude actually do make things happen terribly easily, don't you think? It's a kind of talent for confidence – typically Italian, when you think of it. In any case, Carlo certainly has it.'

'He's certainly got a talent for borrowing,' Dog said, 'seeing as it wasn't his yacht.'

'I thought it was a filthy little boat,' said Maria. 'Not nearly as good as Bobby Doulandropoulos's.'

'But Maria, it was charming. You were seasick, that's all. Your health's too frail for boating.'

Eva was supposed to come back in time for lunch the next day. In the morning Larry went to the pool with Dog and Maria. The weather had broken; it was cloudy and extremely sultry. Larry tried to read but the sticky heat made it difficult to concentrate and the flies wouldn't leave him alone.

Maria said, 'My God, you're studious, Larry. How can you really enjoy that stuff when it takes you so long to read it?'

However much he didn't want to hear it, she was determined to tell him about the outing on the yacht.

'I was all right when we were on deck,' she said, 'but as soon as we went downstairs I felt dreadful. It was Dog's fault because he wanted me to play backgammon down there. I threw up all over the board, it was perfectly filthy. But even then I didn't feel any better. I just lay on the deck groaning all the way till we arrived. Carlo was sweet about the board, though.' She scratched herself, leaving long, white lines on her forearms. 'He was dead keen on Eva, I thought – didn't you, Dog?'

'I thought he was meant to be having an affair with Martina Mondi,' Larry said.

'They split up.'

Dog said, 'He struck me as the sort of guy who porks just about every woman around. Of course, with a place on the coast like he's got and a yacht to take them out on it's not surprising if they go for it.'

'Why don't you get a house and a yacht, Dog? It might be good for our sex life. We hardly ever do it,' she explained to Larry.

'God knows how we'll manage to make babies. I suppose once we're married we'll just have to.'

Eva didn't come. At lunch everyone was bored. The air was heavy, the pigeons flew maddeningly to and fro above their heads.

'Cooper, dear,' said Lady Clermont, 'if they don't settle down soon I'm going to insist that you shoot them. They're driving me mad.'

'They'll settle down, don't worry. It's only being shut up so long in those cages which has made them restless. They have a nature of their own to contend with, like the rest of us. You mustn't expect them to be perfect. Speaking of which reminds me: did Spinelli say anything about those pigeon whistles?'

'He had them there,' Dog said, 'and he was going to give them to us to bring back. But we only remembered at the last minute and he didn't have time to look them out. He's going to give them to Eva to bring over.'

During the siesta the wind got up and began to buffet the windows and bang loose shutters round the house. The day was still hot, but there was no sun, and for the first time they all stayed indoors. It was the kind of gusty wind that blew your papers on the floor and slammed the door in your face, and it made everyone irritable. In the sitting room he found Dog and Maria bickering over a game of Snap.

'Dog and I are going on to Capri tomorrow,' Maria said.

'I'm leaving tomorrow too.'

'Are you? But aren't you going to see Eva before you go?'

'Of course,' he said rather shortly. 'She's coming back today isn't she?'

'That's what she said.'

'Then I'll see her before I go.'

Dog and Maria went on with their game of Snap. 'You can play the winner, Larry,' Maria said.

'Thanks, I don't like cards.'

'God, you're so serious! Do you like anything frivolous at all? I suppose that's why you don't like me. You don't like me, do you? Why not? Why don't you like me?'

'Oh shut up, Maria, your nerves are on edge. You should eat more or something, you're too thin.'

He read the baseball column again. Dog and Maria went on with their game till Maria lost her temper over a call. She got so excited about it that Dog had to stop the game.

'My God,' said Maria. 'I'm sick to hell of you. I want to get out of here. Let's go for a drink to the village.'

'The café won't be open yet.'

'Well let's go when it is open. Will you come, Larry?'

'Sure, I'll come.'

Dog said, 'Don't you want to be here in case Eva arrives?'

'Why should I? She can arrive without a reception committee, can't she?'

'Why don't you stay, Dog?' Maria said. 'It'll give me a break from you. I think we're beginning to get on one another's nerves.'

Dog stayed. Larry took Maria down to the village in the jeep. In the piazza the wind blew dust in their faces and some got behind Maria's contact lenses. He couldn't think why she'd wanted him to come down here with her or why he'd come. Deprived of an audience, Maria seemed to have no desire even to needle him. They had nothing whatever to say to each other.

Eva didn't come back that evening. On account of the wind they had dinner in the dining room for the first time since Larry had been there. It blew even harder now, and from time to time grains of soot fell down the chimney and rattled on the paper in the grate.

Lord Clermont talked about a firework enthusiast who'd written to him from Illinois. The man wanted to visit him for Guy Fawkes day that year.

'I can't help being rather flattered that someone's heard of my displays in Illinois,' he said. 'He doesn't say how he knows about me. I wonder who he knows that's been to Clermont?'

'I'm not at all surprised, Cooper,' his wife said. 'Everyone knows about your fireworks by now. And quite rightly too. Heavens, they're miles better than anyone else's. You were there last year, Larry, don't you agree?'

'I remember very well,' Larry said. In his mind's eye he saw the cars parked in front of the house jump out of the darkness and then return to it again. He couldn't understand why she hadn't at least rung him, if only to say goodbye.

Towards the end of dinner Dog said, 'It's incredible that just through meeting the right person Eva might be working with a name director. In England she couldn't even get an Equity card.'

'That's Italy for you,' said Lady Clermont.

'I wonder why she hasn't rung,' said Maria. 'What do you think, Larry?'

'Oh, I forgot to say, she did ring earlier on,' Lady Clermont said. 'To say she wouldn't be back tonight.'

After dinner Larry drank whisky and played backgammon with Dog while Maria dozed off on the sofa. He kept his mind on the game as much as he could. The luck seemed to be slightly against him, but Dog was so sloppy that by midnight he was 100,000 lire up. Fortunately Dog wasn't anxious to go to bed. They played some more and it came out about evens, and then they went for a swim in the pool. Dog wasn't such a bad drinking companion. He was brighter than most of his friends and the grossness was mainly affectation. They stayed up talking until they were too tired to talk any more. Then Dog woke up Maria and they all went to bed.

The next morning Larry collected his bags and said goodbye to everyone. He had called a taxi to forestall any offers to take him down to the station. Now that he was going he felt a certain sense of relief. At the station he paid the taxi and bought himself a ticket from the booth at the entrance. The station was deserted except for a lone couple sitting on a bench. It was obviously the end of their affair. The man was in tears, the woman clearly impatient for the train to arrive. Every so often the man would sink his head into his hands and his shoulders shook. The woman looked at her wrist watch. She spoke to him in soothing tones and arranged his hair and his shirt collar fussily. The rather maternal gestures went uneasily with her hard, heavily made-up face and her stiffly lacquered hair. How was it possible to be in love with such a woman? At her feet a poodle on a lead sat looking up at her as if awaiting an instruction. After a while the woman got up and walked the poodle to the other end of the platform. She waited when it wanted to stop, but it just sniffed the ground. Her high heels made a clacking sound on the concrete. The man blew his nose and sat up straighter.

'Hullo, Lily.'

He turned round and Eva was standing right behind him. She put her arms round his neck and kissed him several times on the face.

He said, 'How did you get here?'

'I took a cab.'

'All the way from Fernia?'

'Yes. I wanted to say goodbye before you went.' Her slanting eyes looked at him shyly, slightly askance.

He said, 'What happened?'

'I think I got the part.'

'Why didn't you come back last night?'

'I stayed to meet the producer. Woman called Rosa Agambo. Didn't my mother tell you?'

'She just said you rang.'

'The old cow. I rang to tell you. You didn't mind, did you, Lily?'

'I thought you were seducing Spinelli.'

'Ha!' She burst out laughing, so infectiously that he couldn't help laughing too. 'That old Yorrick-head!'

The train appeared in the distance.

'Lily, shall I come with you to the airport? On the train?'

'No, there's no need. I'm just glad I saw you before I go. Here it is.'

'Oh, shall I come, Lily, darling?'

'No. I'll see you when you get back.' He suddenly realized she would be staying much longer if she had got the part. He kissed her.

'Thank you for coming.'

'I love you Lily darling.'

It was the last time he saw her.

— 9 —

'The gunman shot him in front of the class. Then they ordered all the students, among them Tommaso Bioni, nephew of the President of FBQ Italia, to go into the corridor and lie down. Here they shot them in the legs with a Kalishnikov automatic pistol. The attack was claimed this morning by Fazione 22, an extreme-left group taking its name from the twenty-second of October raid on the Boeing aircraft hijacked on the Fiumicino runway in which eight terrorists lost their lives . . .'

Eva, trying to open her eyes against a combined pain of news bulletin, headache and sharp white daylight, fumbled for the black grooved knob of the radio, knocking the carafe of water over, found it and turned the volume down low. With a mixture of blessed relief, and a dull pain located in the crown of her head but throbbing vaguely in her temples too, she sank back into the pillows and began to slip deliciously, as if on the fur-wrapped sleigh of sticky opium, back towards sleep. She was woken an hour later by cold pee in the bed against her warm skin, the spreading feeling of urine across her back and down her left ribcage, wet, clinging and unfriendly, only it wasn't urine, she realized, as she sat up suddenly, but the water from the carafe she had spilt only a moment before.

'. . . not to speak at the conference on nuclear power in Rome which begins next week. The bishop said that the conference was designed to serve the interests of world communism. It is understood that the Secretary-General has protested to the Vatican . . .'

Eva slipped out of bed and went into the bathroom. When she put the shower on the sound of the radio was drowned out by the hiss of water and the dull hum of the booster motor which Carlo had installed to compensate for the lack of water pressure in the top floor apartment. From time to time the motor choked momentarily and the water checked its flow; one of these days the damn thing would surely seize up altogether. She opened her mouth and let the droplets of water prickle inside, as refreshing as an effervescent drink. Then, stepping aside from the shower, she shampooed her hair and soaped her body all over. The soap was an English one made of coal-tar and she bought it because it reminded her of her childhood at Clermont where all the bathrooms were stocked with coal-tar blocks, yellow and sweet-smelling. How far away it seemed! For a minute she stopped soaping herself as she remembered the big cupboard let into the passage wall where the soap had been kept. The housekeeper opened it with a key from her bunch and the smell of concentrated soap, almost nauseating to a grown-up, had seemed incredibly sweet to her as a child. The passage was paved with flagstones, deformed by the endless wear of feet until it sagged like an old bed. Further along there was the larder, where there were wooden baskets of apples and potatoes from the garden and other more exotic provisions which were kept behind cupboards fronted with wire gauze. Of particular interest to Eva as a child were the chocolate bars – red packets with gold paper foil showing at the ends. The cupboards were locked, but she often came here just to look at them. The apples smelled sweet in the winter and in the summer there was the even more intoxicating perfume of strawberries.

Eva stepped back under the shower and the water bit into the foam on her head with a quiet roar, like the sound in a seashell. She lifted her arms and pushed her hair back from her forehead with both hands until it squeaked on her fingers. Then she dried herself on the big towel and tied it in a huge turban around her head. She cleared a piece of the mirror with her hand. Her reflection stared back from behind the lingering spots of water on the surface of the glass: the dark brown eyes with their slanting eyebrows, the high cheekbones, the wide mouth. In what did this girl differ from the one who ran the stairs and passages at Clermont? In some ways she had aged hardly at all; and yet there was something about her which spoke of suffering. For a moment she studied herself, unsure if this suffering came from within or if it was written on the surface of the mirror, on which beads of water were beginning to run down, leaving little tracks across her face like blood on the image of Christ in a medieval retable.

She put on a red silk dressing-gown and, still wearing the turban, made her way through the bedroom to the sitting room where a grill of sunlight lay in a rhombus on the carpet. As she approached the window the bars of yellow sun leapt from the floor on to her legs and stomach; she turned the stiff espagnolette handle of the window and opened it, letting in the sound of pianos, a trumpet, a violin, practising unrelated fragments in the music school at the end of the impasse. The Persian shutters were made of steel. In order to open them she had to throw a lock whose four-way mechanism sunk rods into the walls and the floor and the roof of the frame. She swung each shutter back in turn, till it caught on its stopper with a heavy clunk, and stepped out into the sunshine. The sun was high, the tiles of the balcony hot beneath her feet. She filled the watering-can at the tap and went along the stone parapet watering the geraniums. Across the alley a little way down was another balcony where a woman was stretched out on a garden chair, reading a magazine. The woman was about 40, slender and very brown with blond hair cut short and parted down one side like a boy's. The hair looked as if it was artificially lightened but it might have been bleached by the sun. The apartment – the only one on the same level as Carlo's – had been deserted until this year when the first warm days came and the woman appeared. She brought out a lounger and read magazines or sunbathed through most of the day. She appeared to have nothing to do. In the old days Eva herself used sometimes to read on the terrace under a big umbrella. But now the woman was there she felt inadequate to be doing it.

Eva finished the geraniums. The terrace was marked with wet patches, and dribbles of water from the flower pots rattled on the street down below. Round the hinges of the shutters there were fresh concrete scars left from their recent installation. She had meant to have the painter come and make them good but now she wondered if the jasmine wouldn't grow over them and make it unnecessary. She filled the pot of the jasmine to the brim and watched the little bubbles spring up as the level fell.

In the hall, the awful headline was staring up at her from the newspaper lying on the floor.

'NAPOLI DISTRUTTA.'

Naples destroyed! Into her mind sprang a vision of Naples in ruins, blackened by fire, flattened like Hiroshima. But it was only a football match. 'TRIONFANO I GIALLOROSSI' she read, when she unfolded it. The red and yellow win. She picked up the rest of the mail and went into the kitchen. There was a pain in her chest.

She had never worried about her health in the old days. But this pain came so regularly now that she thought she must have developed a cancer. It seemed not only possible, but horribly probable, that the 'ghosts' which used to press on her chest were premonitions of the disease. And once you stopped to think about it, there were many confirming signs – for example, that her ascendant sign of the zodiac was Cancer. The sight of any crustacean filled her with dread now. At the market she walked round the block so as not to go past the fish stalls.

Often when she got to her feet she blacked out, one time losing consciousness completely and coming round on the floor. Sometimes she was seized by uncontrollable fits of shaking which she could do nothing to control and which were assuaged only by opium. This was the real reason she was terrified of being without the drug. She went almost mad with fear when Carlo allowed the supply to run out.

She had been prone to hallucinations of late. Usually they came when she switched on the light in a darkened room: yesterday night, for example, when she got up to go to the bathroom, there had been an old woman with serpents coiling round her head sitting in the chair. Eva had stared at her for a few seconds until she disappeared. The hallucinations always disappeared if you stared at them. At first they had frightened her, but she was used to them now. What was much more terrifying were her simple premonitions of death. Yesterday it had happened again, in the garden of the Villa Borghese. There was a fun-fair set up in the field where the riding school is and she stopped for a moment to watch the big wheel and the roundabouts. There was something grotesque about the blaring music and the relentless circular movement of the machines, the big mechanical horses chasing their tails. Then, just at that moment, a cloud of dust blew up off the path and suddenly it happened. Her heart began to race and the blood pricked in her legs. She was certain that a war was going to come.

When these moments arrived she was too afraid to think rationally; and later, when she tried to reconsider, she couldn't shake off the feeling: if there was no basis for her premonition, from what had it come? So that her fear became a reason for fear. And sometimes a slightly different idea took hold of her: that because she was the only person who had these premonitions, only she was going to die.

Eva sifted through the letters, mainly business ones for Carlo, and found one addressed to herself, in Larry's handwriting. She held it in her hand for a moment as though weighing it, and then put it with the other letters and the paper on the kitchen table. It was several years now since she'd had a letter from Larry. She filled the bottom half of the coffee maker and put it on the stove. Then she took a handful of coffee beans out of the big Russian tin and let them run from her cupped palm into the plastic grinder. She was meant to be giving up coffee, but she decided she would have just one cup this morning while she read his letter. The stamp was English – she could see the little outline of the Queen from where she stood. She filled a glass at the tap, dropped two aspirins in, and watched them slowly disintegrate. Once or twice she had received postcards since her marriage. One had been of the church of Santa Maria dell'Orto near Castagna. She herself was too ashamed to write: not just because of leaving him for Carlo, but because of the way she'd done it, not telling him at all until he rang up, and never answering his letters.

When the coffee was made she went and sat down at the table. She picked up the envelope again. It felt stiff, as though there was a card inside. Could it be an invitation? But to what? Suddenly it occurred to her that it might be to his wedding. She opened the envelope. Inside was a postcard of a Greek marble relief, on the back of which was written, in Larry's small, neat hand:

I may be in Rome next week to cover a conference on nuclear energy. I'll call you when I arrive. Best love. Larry.

She looked at the date, written in lower-case Roman numerals at the top. Then she went into the bedroom and took off the yellow turban in front of the mirror. She brushed her hair back flat against her head. It was shorter now than in the days when she knew Larry. She thought that it suited her better short because it showed off her neck. She peered closer at the mirror. Her skin was a little pallid, but no less smooth and fine. In any case, it suited her to be pale with her dark hair and her brown eyes. In the corner of the mirror she caught sight of the magot chinois and a wave of mixed pain and pleasure washed across her. Forgetting her reflection, she stood up and walked over to where it stood in a lacquered niche by the bed: she reached out her hand and then hesitated, as if trying to make up her mind about something.

The whole room had been decorated in an 'oriental' style with a mishmash of objects Carlo had picked up on his Eastern travels. Tibetan tankas and Balinese paintings hung on the walls, and the chairs and sofas were spread with Kashmiri shawls and embroidered Chinese silks. Above the bed an awning hung from the ceiling, from the underside of which an embroidered image of the Buddha looked down on the bed. And beside this was the niche, and the magot chinois which had been converted to electricity and bore a shallow lampshade like a halo, just above its head.

Whatever Eva had been considering she now put it out of her head, because she turned smartly away from the magot and made her way through the flat to the box room off the hallway. It was months since she'd set foot in here. Dustsheets lay on everything, as anonymous and tempting as Christmas parcels. Once, when she had first moved in with Carlo, she had gone through all this and found the photos of Martina Mondi. She threw them away. She never admitted it to Carlo, even though he went almost berserk a year later when he discovered they were gone. If the truth were known she was not really jealous of Martina Mondi. She threw them away because she had never brought herself to throw away the others which he stuck up on the cupboard doors in the lavatory, both here and at Fernia: all those photos of beautiful girls he'd had affairs with. She despised this little gallery and she hoped that other people would secretly find it vulgar and laughable too. But she never took them down. It was simpler to leave things as they were, seeing she was going to divorce him in the end anyway. She could never imagine staying with him for very long.

The grip lay in the far corner of the room. She wiped it with a corner of dustsheet and its colours sprang back where the dust came away: green canvas, brown leather, looking unnaturally new. She unzipped the top and took out the plastic bag she was looking for. There were several letters in there, all from Larry.

'My darling girl,' she read:

You have no idea how much I miss you since you are gone. I long to abandon what I'm doing and come and join you at Castagna right away – but alas, without the money for this job I won't be able to afford it. So I must live out seven more dreary days in London. I don't blame you for wanting to get out of this city. The windy wet weather which seems to have been going on since Christmas has suddenly given way to a muggy heat full of exhaust fumes. At the end of the day I feel more dead than alive – my darkroom is like a sauna.

Darling, I could never stop being in love with you. When I was a boy I was frightened by the idea that you couldn't love someone for ever; but now the contrary seems almost more terrible. Do you remember the night we swam across the lake to the flamingos? I knew already then that I would never be more in love with anyone. So that for me you exclude all other possibilities: whatever I might feel for someone else in the future could only be an echo of what I feel for you now. I know this makes me want to hold something back, and I think it is also the reason for your unfaithfulness with Gawain, and Ricky. But, my darling, don't you see that it's madness to behave like this? I'm not reproaching you about it – I promised I wouldn't – I'm just trying to explain that these reactions are both essentially cowardly. Have we so little courage? For God's sake think about us, that's all I ask; otherwise I think your impulsiveness will be the end of both of us . . .

She remembered that night. She was standing in the lobby of Anastasia's night-club with her coat over her arm, her eyes on the door of the men's toilet. She was impatient to go now. It all rather depended on whether this boy whose name had sounded like Gawain but might have been Garwin would come out of the toilets before anyone she knew appeared. The coat-check attendant eyed her legs. She stared at him insolently for a few moments and then turned away, taking her lipstick out of her bag, and began to paint her lips in the small circular mirror on the wall behind her. She could see the attendant looking at her and then the door to the bar swinging open and a couple of businessmen coming out and collecting their coats. Eva looked at the framed 'Spy' cartoons on the wall: one was of her grandfather, the Foreign Secretary, something she'd noticed before and made a mental note to mention to her father. But then, as now, she had certainly been too drunk to remember this sort of thing the next day.

At length Gawain appeared. He was wearing a raincoat and he carried a brown trilby. They left the club and went out into the night. It had been raining. The air was warm and the square smelt of earth and new leaves. They began to walk across Mayfair, up Park Lane, along the north side of the park towards Lancaster Gate. Taxis and fast shiny cars shot round Marble Arch, their lights reflecting on the wet tarmac. Eva's high-heeled shoes were making her feet ache. She could feel the wet beginning to seep through the leather around the balls of her feet and her toes. She liked not knowing where they were going, not being taken in a taxi, not knowing quite what his name was. On the other side of the park railings a drift of red blossom was beginning to spill off a thorn tree, and some of it lay trodden across the wet pavement. As they walked over it (her white shoes, the red petals, the black pavement) she caught the mild smell of the flowers, fresh after the cigarettes she had smoked in the club. She took the boy by the arm. She wanted to say, 'Let's stay up all night,' but the greater excitement of doing whatever he wanted forced her to remain silent.

She had never wanted to sleep with him. That had been his idea and she had refused at first but he had been so insistent that somehow they'd ended up on the bed. It had been nothing. Even Larry realized that. She picked up the letter again, and read:

You are constantly in my mind. I keep thinking that I see you in the street, but of course it is always someone else. God how I long to take you in my arms and kiss your lovely eyes and fuck you and sleep with you and hold you all the time! Even the thought of it makes me feel quite intoxicated. Now that you're not here I think I must have been mad to let you out of my sight for a minute. Never again! I love you my darling girl . . .

Eva broke off as she heard the buzzer in the hall. She went out to answer and it was Carlo. His voice said, 'I forgot my keys.' She pushed the button and went into the spare bedroom and put the plastic bag with Larry's letters in the bottom left-hand drawer of the desk. When she got back to the kitchen Carlo was just coming in. He said, 'The money's arrived!'

Eva said, 'Oh, yes?' She was pleased about this, but she was irritated by his excitement, by the way he couldn't stand still, by the way his eyes shone and his head kept moving up and down like a bird's. When he was happy he wore a fixed smile that was boyish and winning if you didn't know him, but when you saw him all the time it began to be tiresome.

'Well?' he said. 'Shall we go and collect?'

Eva looked at the clock. She said, 'It's half past one, Carlo.'

'We can get there before two.'

'Let's go in the afternoon.'

Spinelli put down his briefcase on a chair and picked up the mail on the table. Eva said, 'I had a card from Larry. He's coming here next week.'

'Marvellous!' Spinelli didn't look up.

'He's covering the conference on nuclear energy.'

'Ah yes, it's really terrifying, isn't it? Do you know what Marina della Garratrea told me? Apparently nuclear energy is destroying the ozone layer and then we will be bombarded with all kinds of rays and it will finish humanity and all that will be left is ants. Can you imagine? It's terrifying!' Eva felt a wave of gloom come over her. Wasn't this just the kind of thing she had forebodings of? From where she stood she could see the headline 'NAPOLI DISTRUTTA' on the newspaper. She couldn't understand how people like Carlo and Marina della Garratrea seemed to treat it like almost any other piece of social tittle-tattle . . .

'Shall we go to the Pera for lunch?' Carlo was saying. 'I saw Anna and Toni this morning and they suggested we might all get together. Otherwise we could make something here and have them over.'

'I don't feel too great, Carlo, I don't want to have lunch,' Eva said. 'In fact I think I might go and lie down for a while.'

'Just as you like, my precious. I'll tell the others. Shall I make you a sandwich?'

'I told you I'm not feeling well.'

'Don't be annoyed. I just thought you might want a sandwich.'

'Why would I want a sandwich if I'm not feeling well?'

Eva went into the bedroom and lay down on the bed. In reality her headache had gone now, but she wanted to be alone and undisturbed. The fact that the money from her trustees had finally come ought to have put her in a good mood, because all their difficulties were resolved now; but she only felt depressed and irritable. She was always irritable with Carlo these days, even in public. And he was so polite, tactful, reasonable. It seemed he was always trying to please her. That was where he defeated her. His manners were so perfect he made her appear spoilt and difficult.

The door opened and he came in and lay down on the bed beside her. She was facing the other way and she didn't turn over. After a minute she felt his hand slip under her dressing-gown and start to move up her leg. She pushed it away vigorously. He said, 'Let me hold you!'

'Carlo, I'm not in the mood. I told you, I'm not feeling well.'

'I won't try to make love, I promise. I just want to stay close to you.' He put his arm round her and they lay quite still, but she couldn't bear the feeling of his arm against her stomach. She got off the bed and opened a little drawer at the base of the magot chinois. Inside there was a box with a picture of Adam and Eve inlaid in the lid. She got the brass tray which stood against the wall and sat down on the bed with the tray and the little box. Carlo said, 'Not now, Eva.'

'But I've got a headache.'

'You drink too much.'

'I hardly had anything last night. It's the coffee that makes my head ache. I had one when I got up.'

'Poor darling.'

Eva opened the box and took out the black sticky lump and began to make up a pipe. Spinelli said nothing. When the pipe was full he held the taper over it and she smoked in silence. Afterwards she lay back on the bed. The agitation had gone. The hangover had gone. Carlo undid her dressing-gown and she felt his lips and his skin, slightly rough, moving here and there across her stomach. She relaxed. Like the tentative beginnings of a breeze, a vague sensuality began to stir in her. She kept her eyes on the ceiling where the Buddha looked down with infinite compassion. One day soon she would leave Carlo. Very soon now, because the money had arrived. Really, once they had collected it from the bank there would be no reason not to tell him she was leaving. All her trials would soon be over and she would make a fresh start. How marvellous it would be to start all over again! How rich she would feel to be absolutely free! She could see it all now with perfect clarity. Of course it wasn't going to be easy, she had no illusions about that. He was bound to make tremendous objections and they would both be terribly upset. But that would only last a month or two. After that there would probably be awful moments: the details of the divorce, the signing of it; his letters and phone calls. But it couldn't last long: in her heart she knew that he would soon get over her and find somebody new, equally young, equally attractive. She would become to him like Martina Mondi was, another glorious episode, a photo on the cupboard door in the bathroom. Carlo was demonstrative and excitable and affectionate, but his soul was like a circus which could always be moved on. She would leave him, and he would find somebody else. It was all going to come out right in the end.

— 10 —

Polly's wedding was at St Paul's, Covent Garden. Because Polly had asked him to take the photos Larry had to be early, but even so he found Joe Dansk and his best man already there when he arrived, sitting on one of the benches outside and smoking nervously. Larry took their picture. He went into the church and looked at the memorial plaques for actors – Flora Robson, Charlie Chaplin, Noël Coward, and so on. They all seemed to have been knighted. He wondered if Polly's parents would be. Polly had told him no flash in the church so he took some light-readings. A florist was fussing with huge banks of magnolias by the altar. He saw Dog Gracechurch come into the church in a black morning suit. He had a top hat in one hand and a pile of service sheets in the other, which he deposited on a small table by the door. Larry took a picture of Dog. Mentally he compared it to the ones at Capilano Place: the curly hair had receded slightly, the face looked as though it had been taken off, boiled, and set back on his shoulders. He said, 'Well, well, if it isn't Larry.' Larry put the camera down. He took another light-reading beside Dog's head and said, 'You an usher, Dog?'

'That's right. Doing the honours for Polly. They all go in the end, don't they?'

'I suppose so. Except for you and me, Dog.'

'You just missed this one, didn't you? I mean you were her last one before Joe, weren't you? Lucky man. I never even got that far. What is it the girls see in you, Larry? You're not even rich.'

'No. Nor is Joe.'

'Do you have any regrets now?'

'No.'

'None at all? You're a cold fish, aren't you? I bet you do when you see her today.'

Larry went outside into the garden. The first guests started to arrive and he photographed some of them coming up the path towards the church door; others he posed beside the gates of the churchyard with the Inigo Jones façade in the background. They were all here, the people he hadn't seen since he split up with Polly, many of whom he had known with Eva as well: Maria Beckman, quite plump now and wearing a yellow hat with a veil, Suki Brett, Eddie Brewer, Ricky Berlin. Rita Cookson came in a limousine and posed elegantly several times on her way up the path to the church. Polly's nanny shuffled in, a little overawed by the occasion, and was shown to a place in the front row. Finally it was eleven o'clock and everyone was waiting for the bride. Larry was at the gate to catch her getting out of the car. She was five minutes late. She took her father's arm and said, 'Hello, Larry.' She was wearing a traditional white dress and a long veil which muted the red colour of her hair. They went into the church and Larry waited behind while she went up the aisle before slipping into his place. The service began.

'Who giveth this woman to be married to this man? . . .'

As a child Polly had lived with her Irish nanny in her parents' house in Knightsbridge while her parents furthered their careers abroad. Probably it was the marvellous love and warmth of this old lady which made her feel cared for; at any rate, Polly suffered none of the anxieties you might expect to find in one who had been so consistently neglected by her parents. Her mother and father kept in touch by picture postcards which she stuck up all over her bedroom. When she came down to breakfast her nanny would say, 'Look what's arrived for you today, my darling,' and hand her the brightly coloured card. 'Soon you'll have finished the whole cupboard and then, God help us, I suppose we'll have to begin on the wall by your bed.' And Polly would look at the picture to see if there were any of the little crosses which sometimes showed where they were staying before she turned it over to read what they had to say. If it was from her father there was usually a story about an animal he had met or a bird which came and sat on the table of his balcony, and if it was from her mother it asked about school and her cat. Often there were parcels waiting for her when she got back from school: a watch, a radio, a dress, a camera – marvellous presents which made her the envy of all her friends.

'. . . with all my worldly goods I thee endow . . .'

Polly had always been given everything: a car, the best schools, tickets to the theatre and opera, parties, anything that a girl might desire. Never for Polly was there cleaning to do in the house, or ironing, or cooking. Her nanny took care of all that, her mother and father paid for it. All was clean linen, airy rooms and regular meal-times at the white house in Rutland Gate. She had a little Volkswagen, sky-blue, to drive around in. If she wanted friends to dinner she only had to pick up the phone and invite them; if she wanted a new dress she had only to go out and choose it. But in spite of this she was not spoiled. Polly was good-natured, of a quiet disposition.

It never entered her head that she was particularly lucky or privileged. She had been brought up to find it natural that she should be surrounded by comforts and that life should be agreeable. In this way her upbringing was much more straightforward than Eva's. Polly's father had none of that perverse love of discomfort and that yearning for a vanished world which pervaded every act and thought of Lord Clermont. Unlike Eva's father the Forts found the modern world wholly acceptable.

Because Polly lived with her nanny it was impossible for Larry to spend the night at Rutland Gate. They used to sleep together at his flat in Chalk Farm and Polly would get up in the night and drive back to Knightsbridge. She never made a fuss about it: she said she woke up and went back to sleep easily. Often Larry didn't even wake up when she left.

She had started off by doing a course in furniture and picture appreciation at the Victoria and Albert Museum. Then a decorator friend of her mother's took her on as an assistant. Polly was competent, and quick to grasp the way the decorator resolved problems, and what his taste was. Larry could never make out if she had taste of her own. She had adapted her mind to think like her employer, so that before long he was able to send her instead of him to make certain purchases, or check on soft furnishings that were being made up. After a year or so he gave her time off to buy antiques for his clients, splitting the percentage with her. Polly found she could do this quite easily. When she added up all the money she'd made in a year she was amazed to see it came to thirty thousand pounds. She had no idea what to do with the money – she had never needed it herself – so she put it in the bank with the idea that one day it might come in useful. Larry couldn't make out if she enjoyed the work. She had the same attitude towards it as she had to everything in life: it was all quite natural and there was no reason things should be done any other way. You were tempted to say Polly enjoyed everything, liked everyone; but equally well it was possible to doubt whether she really liked anything or anyone at all. For example, did Polly really like the theatre or did she just go because her parents were actors and she had been brought up with it? Larry felt the same ambiguity about her attitude towards him. Did she really like him or did she just like him because he took her out and they went to bed together? She was not very intimate. In bed she had the same tone of voice, the same conversation as she had always.

'. . . *with my body I thee worship* . . .'

God knows he tried hard enough to love her and he pretended to himself and everyone else that he was mad about her. But when people said how beautiful she was, and how much more reliable and well-balanced than Eva, and that all in all he couldn't hope to find a more suitable girl, then his heart despaired because he knew he wasn't in love with her. How he wished he had been! He remembered going to see Eva's film with her at the Curzon. He remembered her tight black velvet dress and how people looked at her in the foyer. The softness of the velvet, the softness of her skin; the blackness of the velvet; her red hair like a spill of maple leaves. Nobody had more lovely hair than Polly. Nobody's eyes were prettier, nobody had more perfect gleaming teeth. But to Larry there was something lacklustre about her straight eyes, and her voluptuous figure appeared matronly. He longed to hold Eva's skinny body, to touch her straight dark hair and her tiny breasts. *On passe les trois quarts de sa vie à vouloir sans faire . . . et à faire sans vouloir.*

For a long time he had dreamt of Eva every night. Sometimes these encounters were fraught with difficulty: she would pace about the flat at Capilano Place avoiding his eyes, and he wasn't allowed to embrace her because Spinelli sat outside in the car. 'There's nothing I can do,' she told him. She was sad, her spirit was broken. The car horn sounded insistently in the street below, and he begged her to stay. He went to the window and looked for Spinelli's Jaguar but he couldn't see it anywhere though the horn went on sounding and sounding and in the end he would wake up and lie on his back waiting for some anti-theft alarm to finish. Other nights Spinelli wasn't there, but there was an indefinable sense of unease between them, an atmosphere akin to that mugginess in summer which may or may not presage a storm. But sometimes it was like in the old days before she was married, and nothing stood between them. Then he would press her to him and his whole being filled with an ecstasy of relief. But these moments of bliss were paid by the anguish of waking from them, of feeling her slip away from him even as he clasped her in his arms. Desperately he struggled to return to sleep, but it was no use; and her name echoed in his head like Orpheus' cries as he returned to consciousness in the arms of Polly, beautiful as the day.

'So ought men to love their wives as their own bodies. He that loveth his wife loveth himself: for no man ever yet hated his own flesh . . .'

The reception was at Rutland Gate. An awning had been put up over the garden, but because the day was warm and sunny it was rolled back and they stood outside under the open sky. There was no need for flash. He stayed mainly near Polly, making occasional forays in the direction of Joe, Richard Fort and Rita Cookson. There were a number of well-known actors there, and a lot of people he'd not seen before, probably friends of the parents. When everyone sat down to lunch he went from table to table making sure he got everyone. Scrope was there. The Northeans were at a table with Lord and Lady Clermont. Dog Gracechurch sat by Johnny Milne. Maria and Suki were at another table loaded with green Perrier bottles and coffee cups; since they had been dried out they kept their distance from Dog and Johnny. They were older and fatter and more subdued.

'I saw the article about you,' Suki said. 'Did you see it, Maria?'

'What article?'

'The one about the photo competition. Larry won it.'

'Did you, Larry?'

'Yes, and his photo was in the colour supplement, of the Lebanon. Wasn't it Lebanon, Larry?'

'Salvador.'

'That's right. Well, congratulations, anyway.'

'Gosh,' Maria said. 'Are you a famous photographer now, Larry?'

'Of course he is. He won the award. It was the best photo of the year or something. Wasn't it, Larry?'

'It was a promotion for the paper. It wasn't a big deal.'

'Gosh,' said Maria. 'Now you're famous do you still know us?'

She had lost a lot of her bite since drying out. This sort of remark was meant to be an offer of friendship. But Larry found it hard to take it up. There was something fastidious in him which rejected sudden changes of attitude.

Scrope came up and took him into the house. He looked tired and his morning suit was crushed. He said, 'Larry, I want to ask you a favour.'

'What's that?'

'It's about Eva. You see, Spinelli's been arrested.'

'Drugs?'

'Currency. Apparently he tried to drive through the Swiss frontier with a caseful of banknotes. The money we paid him for the house, I imagine.'

'What a cretin. Is he bailed?'

'His lawyer wants us to put it up. Naturally Ma and Pa are in a terrible state. What I wanted to ask you was: will you go and see her while you're down there?'

'Eva? What for?'

Scrope took out one of his torpedo-shaped cigars and sat down on the arm of the sofa.

'I don't know what to make of her,' he said. 'First she asked me to get Ma and Pa to pay the bail. She seemed desperate for it. But then at the end of the conversation she said maybe it's better if they don't pay it, maybe he's safer inside, because Spinelli and she were both in danger; and when I asked her what from she said the end of the world. To be quite honest I think the strain of it has been too much for her. But I'm frightened too that there may really be some danger, something she's not telling us about. I'd like to know what you think. It's very difficult to make head or tail of it from over here; and as you know she doesn't really speak to Ma and Pa since her marriage, so they're even more in the dark than I am.'

'Are they going to pay his bail?'

'I think they will, yes. My mother's convinced that if they do he'll skip; but my pa wants to, and he always gets his way on these things, in the end. Look, you don't mind doing this for us, do you?'

'Not at all. I was hoping to look in on her anyway.'

'Were you? That's all the better. And Larry . . .'

'Yes?'

'If you think I should come you'll phone me, won't you? I'll be there right away.'

'Don't worry.'

Scrope seemed to have no energy for the party. Larry left him there on the sofa and went outside to go on with his job. At Lady Clermont's table they all congratulated him on winning the prize. Lady Clermont said, 'I always knew you were going to be someone, Larry. Now come with me for a moment, I want to have a word in your ear.' She took him by the wrist and led him away from the table. There was a certain forced gaiety in her manner which she let drop as soon as they were alone. She looked a wreck. More than what Scrope said, this convinced him there was something seriously wrong. Eva had always told him her mother hadn't cared at all when she disappeared to the South of France, but he saw now this couldn't be true. She said, 'Did Scrope speak to you?'

'Yes. I'm going down to cover a conference on nuclear power. So it'll be easy for me to look in on her.'

'Thank God for that. The little Italian seems to have wanted to make off with all he could get. I always suspected he was crooked but it didn't occur to me he would be incompetent too. By the way, did you go to Capilano Place?'

'Yes, thank you. I had a look over the place but there wasn't anything there that I wanted to keep. I imagine Eva will want some of her things, though. It didn't look as though she'd moved anything out.'

'I know. But *entre nous* I think it might not be a bad thing if we held on to that flat after all. I mean, now the Italian's in prison she might want to come back here, at any rate for a while.'

'Have you spoken to her about it?'

'She says we should go ahead and sell, and that anyway the money is needed more than ever now for his bail. Personally, I should have preferred not to pay it. You know he asked Cooper for her money when he went down to see them in Italy? What a nerve! It makes my blood boil to give him twopence after that. But Eva is almost beside herself. One is honestly concerned about her stability.'

'I know. Scrope told me.'

'Larry, you are wonderful. Why she had to go off and marry the little crook I shall never know. One knew immediately that he was a bad lot.'

— 11 —

That morning Eva woke early. When she opened the shutters the outlines of the roofs and cupolas were very clear and the air was dry and fresh and hung with that faint smell of early morning which is reminiscent of woodsmoke. She watered the plants on the balcony. Across the street the blonde woman's shutters were still closed but the music school was already alive with discordant instruments. Today Larry would arrive. In the kitchen the dishes of the last few days lay piled up in the sink and on the tables. It was always like that since Graziella the maid had gone to her mother in the South. She must clean this place up before Larry got here. There weren't even any clean glasses. She picked one out of the sink and washed it under the hot tap. Then she washed the juicer and squeezed herself a grapefruit.

Perhaps, she thought, in view of the circumstances, she should allow herself coffee at the moment. But she dismissed the thought. She had resolved to give up coffee, which was doing her nerves no good. She must be firm with herself now, if she wasn't to lose her grip completely in the face of the dangers confronting her.

Today was her acting class. She only had to leave the flat four times in the week, twice for her acting class and twice for her piano lesson. The piano lesson was at four so she always made it to that, but the acting class was in the morning and she had a tendency not to wake up in time. She was meant to be the star of the class, the only one who had played a major film role, but because she had skipped it so often she had fallen behind the others and it made her feel uncomfortable. The bad reviews hadn't helped either.

That morning on the way to class she met Lorenzo Zacchi in the street. Lorenzo always had time for everyone. Charming, handsome, scion of an old and illustrious family, he hadn't a penny to his name and worked in a leisurely sort of way for the socialist TV channel which was partly owned by his wealthy brother. Eva took his arm and together they walked to the Caffè Greco, where they sat at a table. Lorenzo had coffee, Eva a Bloody Mary. He said, 'I hear Carlo's been arrested.'

'They've let him out on bail.'

'Thank heavens for that.'

'I know. It's a big relief to have him out. He'll certainly get off when it comes to trial. It was planted on him, you see.'

'Currency, wasn't it?' The question was tactfully phrased but she could see that Carlo's reputation for drugs had done him no good.

'Yes, currency.'

'He's back in Rome?'

'Milan. Seeing lawyers. He's coming back tomorrow.'

'If you're alone this evening come over and have dinner.'

'Thanks. It's very sweet of you. But I think a friend from England is arriving.'

'Well, if you want to come over, just ring me, OK?'

'All right, Lorenzo. And thanks.'

He put a note on the bill and rose. She said, 'I'll wait here a minute. I'm early for my class.'

She looked at her watch. Why had she said that? In fact it was ten-thirty already and the class would be beginning. For a moment she wondered if she should skip it (she had missed so many recently in any case) and go back and clean the flat for when Larry arrived. Perhaps she should ask him to stay. She could make up the bed in the spare room and put him in there. But she decided she would not allow herself to skip another class. In any case it was better Larry stayed at a hotel.

She went out in the street. The Spanish Steps were decked with pink geraniums, and more geraniums hung in clusters of pots down the Via Condotti. She began to walk in the direction of the Corso when suddenly she found herself standing in front of Settimio's bar. How early it opened! Inside she could see Settimio himself putting out the tiny snacks and sandwiches under the glass counter. He looked up and saw her.

'*Buongiorno* Signora Principessa!' The greeting was deadpan, like Settimio's face; possibly through being so many years with drinkers he had come to mistrust effusiveness. Eva stepped into the bar and shook his hand. It was a tiny place, a little enclave barely wider than the doorway which stood like a landing-stage off the busy stream of the Via Condotti. In the evening an overspill of people clustered round its green awning on the shady side of the street, while inside a crush of people massed round the tiny zinc bar clutching brightly coloured drinks and popping exquisite little canapés and talking, talking, talking. At this hour of the morning, it was cool and deserted. Eva sat on a stool. She had always liked the painting over the bar, a queer racehorse scene painted in an awkward way which gave the horses a wooden, rocking-horse appearance. It was darkened by cigarette smoke so that the jockeys' caps and shirts, once gaily painted in racing colours, now looked as though they had been put in a hot wash where the green had run.

'Vodka Martini, Settimio, and toast me a pizza.'

The barman put the minuscule piece of pizza between the leaves of a wire envelope and slotted it into a toaster at the back of the bar. The machine clicked away as he pulled down the bottles of vermouth and vodka from the shelf and shovelled ice-cubes into the shaker. He had the same woodeny colouring as the jockeys in the picture, and big jowels as smooth as wineskins. His bearing was impassive as he threw away the vermouth and upended the bottle of vodka over the ice-cubes. Eva had noticed before that where exactitude was called for in mixing up a drink, he gave the appearance of being slapdash: the quantity of vodka which he put in looked totally arbitrary. On the other hand, when no precision was required, as in the act of squeezing a piece of lemon peel over a drink, he did it with an exactness that could be envied by a surgeon; and when he came to pour the drink it would exactly fill to the brim the little conical glass. When the cocktail was made he set it down carefully on the bar and handed Eva the tiny pizza in a piece of paper.

'I've been hearing bad news,' he said.

'It's all right now. He's been released.'

'*Meno male.* It's just as well.'

Eva sniffed the drink and put it to her lips. Down her throat and inside her it burned with a fresh, oxygenating glow, which made her feel cleaner, like the stinging droplets of the morning shower in her mouth. Slowly, the hollow pain in her chest began to ease off a little.

'Yes,' she said. 'He's coming back tomorrow. It's just as well.'

By the time she left the bar it was too late to go to the class. The sun was up and it was hot already. For a moment she thought of taking her little yellow car and driving out to Fernia: the last piece of opium was there in the dressing-table drawer. But what was she thinking? She wasn't going all the way out to Fernia just for the sake of that. On the other hand it would be agreeable to spend the day in the garden, under the shady trellis, and bathe in the pool. She could drive back to Rome in the evening and still have dinner with Larry . . . No. There was no reason to go to Fernia, and moreover, she might miss Larry's call when he arrived.

She went back to the flat to practise the piano. The sun was streaming into the sitting room so she closed the shutters to keep it cool and sat down to play. She did some scales and opened a piece of Chopin which she was supposed to prepare for her lesson. But she had hardly begun this when she broke off and, getting up from the piano, went into the spare room and opened the shutters there. If Larry wanted to stay the night here it was quite ready for him. She herself would have preferred him to stay because it would have made her feel safer. She was frightened at night, not so much by her own hallucinations as by the idea that people might break into the flat. She had special steel shutters now, and a burglar alarm, but even so she was frightened. She remembered how her mother had slept here the time they all came to Rome for the gallery opening, after Larry had gone back to England. How glamorous Rome had seemed then, in the days before her affair with Carlo! The room hadn't changed at all. There were still the prints of historic Rome on the wall, the bed with its pale blue cover, the view over the rooftops. Eva sat down beside the desk on the chair with the bird's-head arms. Carlo had told her the chair had been made for his great grandfather and the bird's heads copied from a tomb at Luxor. She wondered if it was true: certainly they were not unlike the ones on the Egyptian relief which her father had at Clermont.

Then her mother and Scrope went back to England and she herself had moved in here. She had so few clothes in those days that she kept them all in the green canvas grip behind the door . . . what days those had been! Everything she did was touched with success, everyone in Rome seemed to be talking about her. How easy it had been, how little she had to try! She remembered taking Carlo's Jaguar through every red light on the Via Flaminia and driving on through the Piazza del Popolo and the Corso which were closed to traffic, and being stopped by the policeman at the far end. But in those days the policemen smiled and waved her on. She drove on through the balmy city, out into the fragrant suburbs, and she had the feeling she was being borne along by events, that it was her moment, her city. The phone rang incessantly. In the day she rehearsed with Rosa Agambo; the show was to open in two weeks. Eva was terrified, but Rosa said she was good.

Carlo became her personal attendant: he organized dinners at the flat, drove her places in the car, accompanied her to night-clubs, laid out her phone messages in lines on the credenza in the sitting room. Because she had no clothes, Carlo got all the Roman designers to lend her dresses. She was stylish and glamorous. Suddenly she felt she was grown-up and for the first time in her life that seemed desirable. But however inseparable from her Carlo became, she never for a moment thought of him as a possible lover. She always knew she was going back to Larry after the show. She was simply taking advantage of a God-sent opportunity: in London she had let her acting drop for too long.

Rosa Agambo was her new friend. She was slight, of medium height with brown hair and big, vulnerable, blue eyes. She was shy in company in a way that made her quiet most of the time, with occasional rather aggressive outbursts. She had a loud, infectious laugh. In spite of her frail appearance she had an iron will when it came to work. She taught Eva to concentrate and how to control herself on stage so that emotion had something to show its strength against; and how to ask questions of the text and then look for clues in it to get the answers. She said, 'It's not a difficult part. But if you do it well it will attract a lot of attention. It's all in the role. Let the role work for you. If we get good notices we'll make it into a film and the role will be bigger in the film. That's because I'll have to re-balance the story. Don't be distracted if people make a fuss of you here. Remember, this is a profession.'

One Saturday they were at Carlo's flat after the show and Eva offered her some opium. She refused and, to Eva's surprise, when she and Carlo started smoking it she got up and left. Carlo said, 'She had a boyfriend once who died of a heroin overdose. It upsets her to see any kind of drugs. She won't even drink.'

Nevertheless it made Eva feel uneasy. She herself had only smoked once or twice with Carlo, though she suspected he did it more often: his pupils were nearly always tiny in the evening, and when she asked him about it, he said it was his eyedrops.

He said, 'I only take opium occasionally. If you want to smoke some with me, that's fine, but I'd rather you didn't invite other people to join us. As a matter of fact I'd rather you didn't tell anyone about it at all. It's better if nobody knows these things, otherwise a lot of gossip starts to get around.' He grinned and nodded enthusiastically. He put it in such a friendly, polite way that Eva was immediately won over.

When she next saw Rosa Agambo she said, 'Carlo doesn't smoke opium any more really. It's my fault. I got it for him.'

And Rosa said, 'Eva, please believe this: don't ever let me hear you've been taking that stuff if you want to work with me again. I know Carlo pretends he doesn't smoke opium any more, but only fools believe that. Remember, you can carry on many things in the normal way when you take drugs, but all the time it eats into your will like rot. And that is the only thing that matters in the end. And Eva, one other thing, remember: all Carlo's girlfriends get messed up on opium sooner or later.'

'But I'm not Carlo's girlfriend.'

'OK then, that's OK.'

Secretly, Eva thought opium might be good for her work. When she smoked it she found she could watch herself from a distance as one might see an actor on stage. At the time it seemed to give her superhuman powers of understanding and portrayal; but when the drug wore off she was unsure how much she had learned. In the end she decided it was an illusion, and resolved to follow Rosa's advice and not take it again.

The curious thing was that they did tend to be looked on as a couple, she and Carlo. It was something that happened of its own accord: they lived together, they went out together, they were seen together. She liked Carlo because he never acted as though he owned her and he never tried to be anything more than a friend. As he himself said, 'Because I've had one or two affairs with beautiful women the paparazzi have made me out to be some kind of seducer. But I'm not that sort at all. I never in my life chased after women, or tried to seduce anyone. For me, either I get on with a girl or I don't. If something clicks, then it clicks. I never force it.' She liked this about him. It was civilized, un-macho. And so she didn't mind if people sometimes wrongly thought they were having an affair.

Every city has its cliché, and the Dolce Vita is Rome's. The clichés are usually circulated by foreigners who have a superficial acquaintance with the place, but sometimes there is a kernel of truth in them. In Rome, Spinelli was the kernel, the person who exemplified the Dolce Vita life, though he himself frankly admitted he was never quite sure what it was. However, he did know a lot of foreigners, particularly actors, and when they came to Rome he entertained them. As for the Romans, conservative and traditionalist, they knew he was one of them in virtue of his family, but looked on him with vague suspicion as a maverick and black sheep. There were all kinds of stories about him: apart from the one about the iguana (in some versions of this it had been a lobster), it was said he had three wives in India, that he had been to prison there, that he had been involved with black magic in the Vatican. All of this he denied vigorously. 'It's really incredible what the newspapers make up,' he used to say. 'The worst thing is that if they go on saying the same thing enough times, even your friends start to believe it. Even people who were there and know it isn't true. When I was in Orissa, for instance, I was living with my second wife, Gloria. But after the papers made up the stories about me having Indian wives, even the Maharaja of Patmore started to believe it. Yet he of all people should have known I was in love with Gloria: we went to dinner with him at the palace every day!' And he would smile and nod encouragingly and everyone would laugh. Eva admired the way he could get things going. Whenever a dinner was slightly flagging, if ever a party was burning a little low, Carlo would pour his enthusiasm on it like petrol. His stories were never coarse, but he had a way of being risqué which dissipated formality and shyness. His enthusiasm for society was innocent, like a child's; and like a child he could draw the grown-ups into the pleasures of the game. Yet he was not vindictive as children who give the lead often are. He was always a perfect gentleman. He could never let a woman approach without getting to his feet; he could never see her pick up an overcoat without helping her into it; he would never go through a door with a beautiful actress while a shy and rather plain girl came along behind. His thoughtfulness was inbred. Eva thought he had the best manners of anyone she knew. And she particularly admired the way he was polite to everyone regardless of who they were, unlike her mother who only cared about rich people and artists. Eva, as usual, made acquaintances everywhere, and Spinelli was always delighted to receive them at the flat, whoever they were. And of course everybody adored him. He was invited everywhere. If he didn't want to see someone he always made it sound as if he did, but that circumstances had prevented their meeting up. He loved to speak on the phone.

Between six and eight o'clock he had his 'quiet period'. She discovered now that, as she'd always suspected, he smoked opium at this time of day. 'I spend all day and most of the night with other people, and I need this period on my own, or I would lose my soul. Sometimes people say to me, "You're over fifty, but you stay up all night and behave like you were twenty – how do you do it?" Well, it's this period of meditation that restores my spirit. I use opium to meditate because it allows me to go straight into Paradise, and then I am afraid of nothing in this world. I don't use artificial drugs like heroin – they are things made by the devil which in the end only lead us astray. But opium is a natural thing. It comes from a plant without being manufactured. God provided it for us.' He showed her the drawer in the magot chinois and the box with the picture of Adam and Eve in which he kept the opium. Eva didn't join in these evening 'meditations' because of what Rosa had said and because at that time of day she was always getting ready for the show.

Only at odd moments did you suddenly get a glimpse of his real age. The first time Eva saw it was when he took her out on the borrowed yacht with her mother and Scrope and Dog and Maria, the day Larry sulked and stayed behind at Castagna. The yacht had an inflatable dinghy with a fast outboard engine, and after lunch she asked if she could go water-skiing. All sports exhilarated her and made her feel confident. Spinelli watched from the deck as the speedboat throttled up and she rose out of the water – like Venus, as it seemed to him – her legs tensed, the rope swinging in her hands. Easily she slid across the hard green water, leaning into her traverse so that the monoski raced faster and faster until she was almost level with the boat, way out to one side, in water so still she could see ribbed sand and algae on the sea bed; and there she seemed to hang for a moment, lifting the wooden bar above her head to keep the rope taut, as upright and brown as a Polynesian wood sculpture; and then her arms came down, she leant back and shot off across the wake once again, her back straight, her hips as slender as a boy's. Spinelli waved as she approached, and catching sight of him she set a new course and dashed straight at the boat, veering at the last moment so that a sheet of water opened at her heels like a fan and fell across the deck. And when she saw Spinelli stumbling backwards to avoid it there was something in this action which was the movement of an old man, and suddenly she felt sorry for him.

If his age sometimes made him seem pitiable it was partly because he tried so hard to forget it. Perhaps that was why he always had such young girlfriends. Once when they were having dinner at a restaurant a middle-aged woman came up and greeted him, fat and jolly. Carlo kissed her on both cheeks and exclaimed how delighted he was to see her again. But Eva could tell that the woman made him uneasy. When she had gone he said, 'I knew her years ago in St Tropez. You wouldn't believe how beautiful she was then. My God, she's aged! She used to be the craziest of all the girls – once during a heatwave she took off all her clothes and rode around the village on a motorino. The local people worshipped her.' Despite his enthusiasm Eva could see he was really a little embarrassed about her because of how old she seemed to him. He went on, 'It really was another life-time when I used to see all those people. I've died and been reborn since then, several times.' And he drummed with the rings of his fingers on the table. He had a habit of drumming with his rings when he was nervous.

Because of his age, and because she never found him sexy, it was a bit of a surprise to her when they did go to bed together. It happened at Fernia. Carlo had a small house there on the coast, a short way north of Rome. It was a Saturday night, and because she had no show the next day they drove up on an impulse after dinner. They swam in the pool and sat up talking in the sitting room. The vodka they were drinking dispelled sleepiness. They watched a video. At some stage, she didn't quite remember when, they must have gone upstairs and got into bed together.

In the morning, she woke to find him asleep on his front with his face turned to one side. His arms were stretched out around his head towards the bedhead. Something about his long thin back and his unusually thick forearms reminded Eva of a lobster. She noticed he had hairs on his back and shoulders. She hadn't enjoyed making love with him that night; but then she had never particularly supposed she would. Certainly, it was not something she was going to do again.

She went into the bathroom, put the shower on and began to

shampoo her hair. On the wall there was a picture of Annette Natusha, Spinelli's first wife and one of the most famous film-stars in the world: a big bust, wonderful cheekbones, a Sixties' hair-do, hands clasped behind her head. Eva noticed the way it was lit so that one side of her arms was in shadow, making them look thinner, and the way her breasts would have sagged if she hadn't had her arms in the air. Some men went for big hips and Annette had them. She must have to work damn hard to keep them down to size now . . . Eva stepped under the shower and the water bit into the shampoo with a sea-shell roar in her ear. She pushed her hands across her head, rubbed her tiny breasts. It seemed as though she had years before she got to Annette's age, almost a life-time in which to make her own career. And she was already on her way!

The bathroom shutters were open and beyond them the garden was still half in shadow. Beside the pool she could see where they had sat the night before, a red wine goblet and a black cigarette packet left on the table like two last chessmen. Between the umbrella pines beyond she caught glimpses of the dazzling blue Mediterranean. The sea, the sun, Italy!

Carlo used green homoeopathic toothpaste. She squeezed some on to his toothbrush and began to brush her teeth when in the mirror she saw him come through the door. He put his arms around her from behind and said, 'Eva, will you marry me?'

She began to laugh and stopped herself, catching sight of his face in the mirror, and said, 'No, I won't!' but her mouth was too full and it came out as a series of grunts. She went on brushing her teeth, spat, rinsed her mouth. Spinelli took his turn at the basin. He splashed his face with water, dabbled his shaving brush in a wooden bowl and began to lather his beard. In the mirror she could see him suck in his lips to keep the soap off them and then release them again, and the gesture reminded her of a woman putting on lipstick. He cocked his head and began to draw the razor down his cheek in little strokes, rinsing it every now and then under the hot tap. In the middle of this, his face still half covered in lather, he said, 'Well?' and turned to face her, holding the razor in the air to one side in the way a witness holds the Bible when he takes the oath. 'What do you say? Will you be my wife?'

'No,' she said. 'I have a boyfriend who I love very much.'

'That's all right,' he said. 'You don't have to marry me now. I'll wait for you. You can say no to me a hundred times as long as you say yes in the end.'

He made a kissing shape with his lips, still surrounded with foam, which made Eva giggle nervously. Spinelli laughed too. It was hard to tell whether his proposal was serious or in jest. Looking back on it she decided it had been funny and frightening all at the same time, in a way that reminded her absurdly of her schoolday 'dares'.

Downstairs in the sitting room there was a stench of ash and stale smoke. As though by a process of sedimentation everything had found its way on to the floor: cushions, bottles, glasses, a sponge which they had used to mop up spilt wine; videos and records and a spilt ashtray; her own panama; Spinelli's shoes; an atlas open at a map of South India. Eva picked up her hat and walked out into the garden. On the table by the pool she found her watch beside the glass and cigarette packet. It was an old one with an enamel face decorated in a cornflower pattern. She was fond of it because the black roman numerals reminded her of the clock in the nursery when she was a child, and because Larry had given it to her. Fortunately in the hot Italian night there had been no dew. She put it on and walked down the hedged path which led to the end of the garden where there was a wall with an iron gate set in it. The gate was locked so she looked through the bars. In front of her there was a field of tomatoes and on the other side of this a row of pine trees ran along the beach in both directions. Above the trees a jet, bright silver in the early sun, described a broad arc out over the bay, its peach-coloured tail spewing out behind it in apparent silence; and behind the black pine trunks long bands of white moved on the sea with gravelly sighs. The sea, Italy, morning . . .

In Rome Eva continued to occupy the little guest room. Nothing had changed except that she now disliked people associating Carlo and herself. They were not lovers; she didn't want them to be taken for lovers. Carlo was as submissive and excitable as a spaniel. He amused her and if she was tired she told him she wanted to be on her own.

The play closed. Rosa had found some backers to make it into a film and asked Eva to stay in Rome for screen tests. After that there would be a break before rehearsals began while locations and other production details were determined. Eva told Larry she would be home in a few weeks. But she was enjoying her Roman life. How could she not enjoy it? Mapplethorpe came to stay and took her picture for *Interview*. Peter Weir came to dinner and was interested by the idea of the film she was hoping to do with Rosa. It seemed inevitable that she was soon to be famous.

Don Tremoille used to drop in from time to time. Eva still found him physically repellent with his battery-hen physique and violet eyes, but he seemed to have taken a special liking to her, and she found she got used to him. One day he told Carlo that he had a cash problem which might mean he'd soon be taking on a partner in the abattoir project.

'I wondered if you or Eva would be interested,' he said. 'If someone's going to make a lot of money, I'd rather it was a friend than a bank or someone I don't know.'

Carlo was wild with excitement and Don said, 'I'm not promising, mind you. I still have some decisions to make before I'll know if I definitely want to take somebody on. But I'll bear you in mind anyway, now I know you're warm to the idea.'

And Eva thought, yes, even money is going to be easy to come by from now on . . .

When Don went he left a film canister with a piece of black opium wrapped in silver foil inside. 'The underworld was always thought to contain both heaven and hell within itself,' Carlo said as he packed the little silver bowl of the opium pipe. 'Heroin is Tartarus. This is the Elysian fields. Here, let me light it for you.'

Outside the window it was getting dark. The music school had shut and some pigeons cooed on the eaves above them, as peacefully as if they were in some monastery out in the country. Eva thought, yes, everything is going to be easy now . . .

She had always felt amorous after taking heroin, and now she found that opium wasn't very different. After smoking it was always easy to sleep.

The screen test was rescheduled for a few weeks later. She spent time on the coast at Fernia, swimming and staying brown. Summer was dying, but it was still hot in the middle of the day, and the sea was warm; though early in the mornings it was fresher than it had been, and once for two days the wind got up and blew the sea into great green waves which roared all day down on the beach. In Rome they entertained a lot. People came through from France and England and the States. Everyone said that she had cheered Carlo up after his depression from being left by Martina Mondi. Then one night they were having dinner as usual with a large group of friends when somebody called her Carlo's girlfriend. It was a society woman with red hair, a very distant cousin of Carlo's whom he had known all his life. Carlo put his hand on her arm and said, 'But Chiara, Eva isn't my girlfriend, the more's the pity,' and the woman, who must have been a little drunk by then, winked and said, 'I know she isn't meant to be. But *caro mio*, we are not all so credulous that we believe everything you tell us.'

Eva left the table. She went out to the Jaguar, got in and drove out all the way down Via del Corso, out through the suburbs where the villas were all locked up and the lights were going out. She cried as she drove, wiping the tears away with her sleeve until she found herself on the road to Fernia. When she got there she found she didn't have the key to the house, and she was frightened to go down on the beach on her own at night. So there was nowhere to go except back to Rome. It was late by this time and she was hoping Carlo would be asleep when she got back to the flat. Then she could go to the spare room without any fuss. But when she arrived he was not there. The light was on in the sitting room and the bedroom door was ajar. Perhaps he was out looking for her. She went into the spare room and got under the blue bedspread and turned out the light. But she couldn't get to sleep so she went and took the bottle of whisky from the cabinet in the sitting room and sat by the window in the chair with the bird's-head arms, drinking and smoking cigarettes until she heard Carlo come in and go to bed next door. Early the next day she woke with a headache and threw up in the toilet. *Cinghiale alla cacciatora, acciughe, olive, salsiccie.* The drinking and the emotion must have upset her stomach. Her head throbbed and the vomit stung her nostrils and her throat . . . Did she have to live this way? Surely it wasn't necessary for her to keep being unfaithful to Larry. It wasn't even as though she enjoyed it. She thought of Castagna, of the path leading up to the mill pool and the church of Santa Maria dell'Orto, its vestry stacked with wood and smelling of creosote. All this had been marvellous, sacred, something given to a man and woman by the gods, not to be trampled on but tilled and trained up like her father's vines, nourished carefully in the breast like he had nourished his sick pigeon. And then she thought, maybe it's not a hangover or anything I ate or being upset about what the red-headed woman said . . . and she started to throw up again. From that time on she had morning sickness daily.

Eva sat down on the bird's-head chair. She opened the bottom left-hand drawer of the desk and took out the plastic bag containing Larry's letters. It was better not to put him in the spare room, she thought, the place was infected with sadness and with her own failure. It was far better that he should stay in his hotel, wherever that was.

'My sweetest darling,' she read:

I will never call you that again, but I call you it now because that is what you are and what you will always be. How can I think of you as anything else? My darling, darling love. I will never be able to write you what I feel again: in fact I can only do it now because I am so stunned by the news of your engagement that I can hardly believe in it. I am like one of those accident victims who can't feel their wounds, who don't even know where they're wounded. My darling, what happened? Am I mad? I believed we were in love, and even happily in love. I cannot understand now how such disaster can come so quickly out of the blue. It's as if you had been killed in a plane crash, it is as if you were dead. I do not want to complain. You must determine your life as you wish. I feel very clear-headed about that. What I find so hard to understand is that I could be so wrong about what you felt. Tell me I am right, my darling, I beg you . . .

Eva stopped reading and folded the letter and put it back in its envelope. She picked up another and started to read it and then folded that too and put it in her bag. It was definitely better that Larry stayed in the hotel.

— 12 —

The door opened a crack. Inside it was so dark that he could hardly see but her voice was unmistakable: low, matter-of-fact, it came out of the doorway like a ghost into a seance.

'Oh, hullo, Larry, come in.'

Her hair was cut short. It was tousled and stuck up spikily in places. She was wearing a man's suit and tennis shoes. Larry followed her through into the sitting room. He still couldn't see her face because it was as dark as the hall in here, the shutters all being closed. Eva said, 'Something to drink?'

She poured him a beer and took some vodka for herself. While she went into the kitchen to get some ice he opened the shutters and stepped out on to the balcony. He noticed how heavy the shutters were, and that although they looked like ordinary wooden ones they were made out of metal. This side of the house was in shade now, but it was pleasantly warm. A small vine was growing up the wall at one end and some pots of geraniums stood along the parapet. He looked over the edge. There was no sign of life in the cul-de-sac. On a balcony across the street there was an empty lounger with a big umbrella over it to keep off the sun.

Eva returned with her iced drink. They clinked glasses and Eva took a swig of the vodka. Now she was in the daylight he noticed how pale she was. He said, 'You don't look as if you've done much sunbathing.'

'That's the trouble with living down here. You get sick to death of the sun after a while.'

'I suppose so. I remember how brown you got that summer we were at Castagna.'

Eva wrinkled her nose. 'I got disgusted seeing people on the beach at Fernia. Rows of them, covered in oil, lying side by side.

Like ducks in the window of a Chinese restaurant. Like the Wok Long – do you remember? I suppose it's still going.'

'Still going. I don't go there much any more.'

'And the Isfahan?'

'Nor the Isfahan. I never seem to have time.'

'You're doing well these days aren't you? Haven't you gone freelance or something?'

'And now my agent works me even harder than the paper. Still, I make a living.'

'Scrope said you won a prize.'

'Something I took in Salvador.' He fell silent. Across the street in the music school someone was practising Beethoven's first piano concerto. He said, 'Do you have lessons over there?'

'Don't change the subject. I want to hear about the prize you won.'

'You didn't see the photo?'

'No. Tell me about it.'

Larry sighed. He was obviously reluctant to speak of it, she had sensed that immediately. He said, 'I was drinking a beer in a café at the end of a village street. It was a sleepy, one-horse sort of place, crawling with flies. Suddenly these men appear, roped together. The militia made them lie down in the forecourt. Then they shot them. The guys were looking at me as they lay down on the ground. They were saying things to me that I couldn't understand. Maybe they thought I could help them, maybe they were telling me messages to pass on to their families. I don't know. The militia guys must have wanted me to take the photos. In those places everybody knows who you are.'

'Didn't you try to do something? I mean to stop them?'

'What can you do? I'm a reporter.'

'It sounds horrid. I don't think I could bear just to sit there and watch them being shot.'

'Let's talk about something else. Let's talk about you.'

'Me? There's nothing to tell.'

'What d'you get up to these days?'

'Get up to?'

'Yes, are you acting, or what?'

'Not much any more. I'm having piano lessons.'

'Can I hear you play?'

'Maybe later.'

'What are you playing?'

'Bach, Chopin. But don't let's talk about that, it's so boring.'

She took off her jacket and put on a pair of wrap-around sunglasses. She was wearing a striped man's shirt without a collar. She said, 'Have you seen Dog and Maria?'

'I saw them at Polly's wedding.'

'How were they?'

'Dog's much the same. Maria's become a bit of a bore since she got out of the clinic. Proselyte, you know.'

'I know, I saw her in Venice earlier this year.'

'Of course you did. I forgot.'

'Do you think she'll get back together with Dog?'

'She's not meant to, but everyone says she will. She says she wants to clean him out first.'

'Somehow it doesn't seem so much fun any more.'

'What?'

'Well, you know, the things that used to be fun in the old days.'

'I never thought Maria and Dog were that much fun.'

'No, you didn't, did you? Poor Larry! You always had to put up with them, though. Don't you think looking back on it that we had more fun in those days? Or do you have a much better time now?'

'We had a wonderful time.'

'Perhaps we're getting older.'

'You don't look it.'

'Don't I?'

'You haven't changed at all. It's uncanny. You must have a pact with the devil. Take off those glasses a minute.'

Eva took them off. It was true, her face was just the same, her dark slanting eyes and the long nose and wide mouth. Only she was paler than he remembered her and there was a certain tension about her eyes. Not wrinkles, but something in her gaze, that reminded him of Scrope. She said, 'You had an affair with her, didn't you? Polly Fort, I mean.'

He nodded. He thought of Polly's white skin and her perfect body, her masses of red curls falling on her shoulders. When he held her naked in bed, how he had longed for this defiant and rather fragile little figure in front of him now, with her crooked teeth and her sonorous, grating voice. Eva said, 'What's he like, the guy she married?'

'Tall, thin, little moustache. Used to be a conceptual artist. Now he sells bonds.'

'Are you jealous?'

'Who wouldn't be? Polly's a lovely girl.'

'Polly wasn't intelligent enough for you.'

'Who said I was looking for someone intellectual? Anyway, Polly's a perfectly bright girl.'

'Don't get mad. I just wondered what you and she had to talk about.'

'Oh,' Larry said, 'we had plenty.' He looked down into the cul-de-sac. He was thinking what a happy life Polly would have. He stubbed the end of his cigarette out and flicked it away and it spun down through the warm lifeless air on to the cobbles below. He said, 'Let's go out.'

'Where d'you want to go?'

'Anywhere. Stretch my legs and see Rome. What about the Villa Borghese?'

'There's a good cocktail bar nearby. We could go there.'

'Can you sit outside?'

'Not really.'

'Let's go somewhere we can sit outside.'

They took the lift down. In the hall, as they were about to go out, Eva remembered that she'd forgotten to put on the new burglar alarm. Suddenly she felt appallingly insecure. She paused, unable to make up her mind whether to go back or not.

Larry was watching her from the doorway. At her feet, the six rocks of St Peter were laid into the floor in mosaic: one of the marble pieces had come out and Eva appeared to be trying to disengage a cigarette butt that was caught in the indentation. He looked on in surprise as she poked at it with her toe. It seemed she had forgotten about everything else while she was occupied in this pointless task.

'Eva, what are you doing?'

'Nothing.' The burglar alarm would just have to stay off. She took Larry's arm and they went into the cul-de-sac. They walked through the narrow, shady streets until they came to the Piazza della Rotonda, where they took a table and sat. Larry ordered a beer for Eva and a fruit juice for himself. He wondered if Eva was all right. She seemed jumpy and her pallor made her look slightly green. He said, 'Do you still play tennis?'

'Hardly ever.'

'You should take it up again. It's not good for you to have no exercise.'

'I've no one to play with.'

'What about Carlo?'

'I can beat him too easily.' She took a packet of MS out of her pocket and gave him one. The orange juice arrived, and the beer. The ticket stuck to the bottom of the bottle and he peeled it off and tucked it under his saucer. On the glasses little beads of condensation had formed. Larry sipped the juice. He was beginning to feel more at ease with her. It was uncanny how they were already slipping back into their old intimacy, and he realized it was because he had got over her leaving. There had been a time when he had spent all evening trying to dial her number, but he had put that behind him now. He said, 'Scrope told me about Carlo's arrest.'

'So you know all about that.'

'Only what Scrope told me.'

'Did it make the papers in England?'

'No.'

'Thank God for that. You know he's been released?'

'I knew he was going to be, because Scrope had to persuade your mother to put up the bail.'

'I know. She didn't want to. Surprise, surprise.'

'She asked me what I thought, whether she ought to or not. Naturally I said there was no reason not to, as far as I could see.'

'She seems to have asked everybody's opinion about it. Except mine.'

'So he's here in Rome?'

'Not yet. He's seeing lawyers today in Milan and tomorrow in Florence. He's going to try and get here tomorrow night. Sends his regards, by the way.'

'Eva, does he have any chance? Of being found innocent, I mean?'

'Of course. It was a plant.'

'How do you mean, it was a plant?'

'I know it was. He told me.'

'But why?'

'We have enemies, you know the sort of thing.'

'What do you mean? Who are these enemies?'

'One can't really tell.'

It was difficult to know what the problem really was. Sometimes she thought it was simply time, and the fact that they were getting older; she thought how exciting it would have been in the old days to sit and flirt with Larry, or with anyone for that matter, wondering what sort of a scrape it would get her into. The sunshine lit up the portico of the Pantheon and the red and yellow façades of the houses, giving the square something of an atmosphere of *festa*, something bright and hopeful. Yet in some way it looked artificial to her, like an opera set, as though the attractive façades were cardboard flats, the obelisk papier mâché; and this insubstantiality made her uneasy. She said, 'I've drifted into hell. It's my own fault and it's probably too late to do anything about it. Of course, I've tried to patch up the security arrangements with shutters and burglar alarms and so on, but that can't put it right. It's just a first line of defence. Quite useless, ultimately.

'I should never have married Carlo. I'm not just saying that by way of apology. The truth is I never wanted to marry him and I did it by default, without meaning to.' Had she said that or only thought it? Larry was looking straight ahead of him into the piazza where a street performer had set up a little cardboard guillotine. Eva felt herself flush. The man put his head in the guillotine and taking the rope in his hand began to count down, conducting with his other arm the chanting bystanders.

'*Venti, diciannove, diciotto, diciassette . . .*'

There had been very few people at the wedding. Lady Clermont wanted to have an enormous party but Lord Clermont refused to give one, on the grounds that simple 'country' weddings were infinitely preferable. So the wedding was held in the chapel at Clermont, with only a handful of people present. Seldom could a marriage have been celebrated with so much acrimony on all sides. The day was cold. A strong wind from the park blew rain showers against the windows of the house. Umbrellas were blown inside out on the short walk to the chapel. Across the lake the young beeches tossed their dead leaves in the wind. Lord Clermont slipped and fell on the steps of the house and limped up the aisle. He was barely speaking to Spinelli since a conversation they'd had about Eva's money in the course of which he had lost his temper and told Spinelli she'd never get a penny more than she already had, and that was in trust and could only be got at with the permission of the trustees.

Not that the two men were likely to have got on in any case. Lord

Clermont was always suspicious of people without an occupation, especially those who, like Spinelli, did no voluntary or charitable work either. Civic responsibility stood as high among his priorities as it was low among Spinelli's. It would be putting it mildly to say that between the two men there was an essential difference of style. For Spinelli, appearances were of the utmost importance, even if reality couldn't quite measure up to them. He liked the story to be dramatic, if there was only a core of truth in it, and the party to be spectacular, even if it couldn't quite be paid for. He was not so vulgar as to brag, or make things up; he simply gave an impression that was more flamboyant than true. Though he usually denied the extravagant stories which were told everywhere about him, he must have rather enjoyed them, because he was constantly referring to them and bringing them into the conversation. It was hardly surprising that he had little success with Lord Clermont, who was almost obsessively private, modest, understated. Lord Clermont was a countryman, and at heart he distrusted people with no connection to the country. On this score, too, Spinelli was suspect; and although for a long time Lady Clermont was under the impression that he owned the castle in the country to which his mother had sent messages by carrier pigeon, it turned out that it had been sold when his father died. Lord Clermont, who had an instinct for hard realities, muttered that he had guessed as much all along. He was equally disbelieving about the pigeon whistles. In the beginning he always asked about them when he spoke to Eva or Spinelli; later the enquiry was transmuted to an ironical reference.

Lady Clermont was more favourable to Spinelli at the start. She didn't share her husband's compunctions about luxuries, nor did she care that Spinelli had no real occupation. And she liked his affable manner and the way he paid her compliments, and his stylishness. He promised to introduce her to the fashion designer Giorgio Monicelli whose clothes she admired more than anyone's. In fact, in the beginning, she had flirted with him, and it was really this which caused her to turn against him later on.

It happened when they visited Rome that first summer. Lady Clermont, Eva and Scrope were staying at the Palazzo Spinelli, Larry having returned to London and Lord Clermont remaining at Castagna. There was only one guest room at the flat, so Scrope was to sleep on the sofa in the sitting room and Eva on a truckle bed in Spinelli's study. That night, Reitman gave a dinner for Henry Goetz and afterwards there was a party at someone's house. It was late when they returned and they went straight to bed. Spinelli had taken off his tie and was sitting in front of the mirror thinking about Eva. She had troubled him from the start. It was on her account that he had asked them all on to his yacht in the first place, and while she was there he had become even more fascinated by her. She gave one the impression of being completely happy with herself and also – which is rare among happy people – of being completely unpredictable. He remembered her leaning on the rail of the boat looking down into the water, her poise, the exceptional slenderness of her knees and calves which gave her legs an unusual tapered look; and he recalled the athletic ease with which she ripped across the water on the end of that rope, the way she unpredictably leaned into a turn and drenched them. He was just wondering whether or not this was a good moment to pay her a visit in the study when there was a knock at the door. He experienced a sudden rush of exhilaration that events might have anticipated his plans, stood up, checked himself in the mirror and flung open the door. It was Lady Clermont in her dressing-gown.

'I just wanted to ask you . . .' she said, slipping past him into the room, 'Ah, but what an attractive bedroom you have! *On dirait une fumerie!*'

'I hope not,' he replied. 'The only opium dens I've ever been in have been very sordid, dirty places.'

The bedroom wasn't dirty, but it certainly gave an impression of the Orient. Lady Clermont looked about her, taking it all in.

'*Mon dieu,*' she said. '*Qu'est que c'est que ça?*'

'It's a vaporizer for producing steam. I use it every night for my lungs.'

'*Ça ressemble à une bouche d'enfer.*'

The machine stood on a low intaglio table. It had sides of orange transparent plastic, cushioned at the top so you could rest your face over the rising vapours. A faint hiss was audible.

'*Ça sent quelque chose,*' she said, sitting down beside it on the sofa.

'Yes. It's eucalyptus. I put in two or three drops. Try it if you like.'

Lady Clermont leaned forward and inhaled, then fell back on the sofa.

'I feel dizzy,' she said. 'Is it a drug?'

'You must be imagining it.'

Her dressing-gown had fallen open, whether by intention he couldn't tell, and he saw she was wearing a silk slip underneath it. But something else caught his attention, namely that her legs, remarkably well-preserved in a woman of her age, had exactly the same shape which he had noticed in Eva when they went out on the yacht, very narrow at the knee so that her thighs had a tapered appearance. The similarity was so striking that he blurted out, *'Vous avez des jambes . . .'* He was going to say *'comme celles d'Eva'*, but checked himself just in time and, desperately casting around for a way to finish the phrase, in the end simply added rather lamely, *'très belles.'*

There was no reason why he shouldn't have said she had legs like Eva; but because he had just been thinking about Eva's legs, and the possibility of sleeping with her tonight, he felt as guilty as if he'd been caught in the act; and so he said *'Vous avez des jambes très belles'* instead. Which was much worse. Lady Clermont came over and ran her hand through his hair. He tried to extricate himself and somehow his hand got caught in her dressing-gown. The next minute she was standing in her slip.

Having reached this stage, it was almost impossible for Spinelli to extricate himself without giving offence. Lady Clermont had obviously come here to seduce him and now, quite tipsy and almost naked, she fell into his arms.

Profuse apologies on his part could not undo what had happened. From that moment she was cool with Spinelli and after his engagement to Eva she began to disparage him behind his back. Speaking 'in confidence' she would say, 'Cooper and I are frightened to death that the little Italian's after Eva's money.' And whereas before she had been enthusiastic about his being a prince, now it seemed that all Italians were princes. 'Or waiters,' she would sometimes add.

She wasn't at all pleased that Eva didn't try to hide the fact that she was pregnant.

'If you hadn't gone round telling everyone we would have been able to give you a proper wedding and party. As it is, how can we?'

'Maman, I don't want a big wedding or a party. Let's have it as small as possible.'

'You're very ungrateful, Eva. As for Carlo, I wonder he dares show his face in your father's house after what he's done.'

'He hasn't done anything I haven't done.'

'He'll be after your money in no time.'

'Maman! You've no right to say that!'

'Well you can tell him right now that he's never going to get it. Your father and I are your trustees and we'll both see to that.'

'That's all right. We can make our own money.' She was thinking of Don Tremoille, and the way he dealt with it all so easily.

'It's not so simple, you'll soon find out. Oh Lord in heaven help me, this is all going to end in disaster. Eva, darling, why do you do this to your poor mother?'

The reception was in the library at Clermont. There were very few people. Of Eva's friends, Dog and Maria came, looking like real junkies now. Eva was surprised how much they had gone downhill and even Lady Clermont said they were looking under the weather. Polly Fort was there, looking cute in a blue dress and hat. For some reason Don showed up, although Eva couldn't remember having asked him. He said he was on his way to the States on business and made a lot of rather clumsy advances to Polly. Polly said, 'Who's that creep?'

'Some friend of Carlo's,' Eva replied. Later she noticed him taking Dog and Maria's phone number.

Eva didn't drink because of the baby. She told everybody a story of how the air hostess had thought Spinelli was her father on the way over. She noticed with relief that Carlo couldn't read the signs in her father's behaviour which betrayed his dislike of him.

They didn't go on a proper honeymoon because of her pregnancy. Initially they had thought of a trip to India but the doctor in Rome advised against long journeys and they stopped in Vienna for a few days instead, on the way back. Eva didn't feel well. It was snowing and they stayed most of the time in their room at the Sacher. Eva lay on a red plush sofa beside a big, grey-painted radiator, looking at videos on TV and making calls to her friends in England. It was warm in the hotel. If she put her hand on the window pane it was icy to touch, but in the room she could sit naked under her dressing-gown, drinking hot chocolate and watching the big snowflakes outside, as unreal as if they were in one of those glass blizzards given to children which, when you shake them, fill with tiny snowflakes that go swirling round a miniature Alpine village inside. And in fact, all the events of the last month had this feeling about them, since all she had done was agree to marry Carlo, and a whole flurry of events was set in motion, a storm which she was unable to stop and which completely transformed her world, so that although she knew Clermont and her parents were still there if she were to go back to them, in some inexpressible way they had been definitively taken away from her; a storm from which, like the one in the little glass hemisphere, she felt excluded, because her inner self was untouched in that she didn't love Carlo.

When she first realized she was pregnant she never thought of getting married. She was excited and serene at the same time: she knew she would have the baby, though it was unfortunate that Spinelli of all people should be the father. Still, he was sensitive and understanding. She was fond of him. Yet she was nervous to tell him about it. She realized that by constantly forgetting her pill she was responsible for what had happened and that he might be upset. So for a week she didn't say anything. She used to go to the park on her own and walk around trying to get used to the idea. It was February but the weather had been unusually mild and sunny all week and the mimosas were already in flower, wonderfully fresh and yellow. It seemed that in this country it was spring even in winter. She was happy. When she did tell Carlo about her pregnancy he was wild with excitement. He insisted they should get married immediately. 'Why not? Why not?' he kept saying. And she told him: because I'm not in love with you, I don't even love you.

Spinelli sat on the sofa with his head in his hands. She didn't want to know if he was crying. She went down in the lift and took the car for a drive. She stayed at Fernia that night, on her own. When she returned Carlo was cheerful, anxious to please her. He said he'd been thinking, and that he had no right to insist that she marry him, and he was sorry for what he'd said. It was very hard, she must understand, to hear that someone doesn't love you. Nevertheless, he wanted the baby to be born in wedlock, with his name. He had no other child, and he had always wanted one. If she would agree to this he would agree to divorce her afterwards, without making any problems for her. As a Catholic, he said, this was a very serious step for him. As to her not loving him, he said he was happy the way things were. He hoped she would stay with him till the child was born, but he didn't insist on it – how could he? Love could not be commanded, he said, nodding enthusiastically.

He was so tactful and rational after yesterday's scene that she let herself be convinced. She wanted to be married secretly somewhere like Reno where there would be no problem to get divorced afterwards. He agreed to all this, but somehow the secret soon came out, and once everybody knew a whole train of events, unstoppable in their momentum, had led to the chilly wedding at Clermont and the dismal reception in the library.

And so she sat by the window in the Philharmoniker Strasse watching the heavy flakes trying to blot out the dark figures huddling and shuffling below, sipping her chocolate, flicking the tissue-thin pages of her Pléiade Balzac and slipping her wedding ring backwards and forwards across her unaccustomed knuckle. Carlo had wanted to buy her an engagement ring too but she had told him it was pointless seeing as they were going to get divorced as soon as the baby was born. Instead, next to the wedding ring she wore her great-great-grandmother Laura's sapphire. When she was 18 Laura had fallen in love with a French officer, Eva's father had told her. But she had been married instead to their ancestor, presumably for reasons of what used to be called 'convenience'.

'I don't know how you can read those things,' Spinelli said. 'I'd need a magnifying glass for the chapter headings.'

He used to read the Italian newspapers in the morning and then go out for a walk, or to a gallery. Once, when it stopped snowing, Eva went with him, to the Kunsthistorisches and a coffee-house; but they always had dinner in the hotel, either downstairs in the formal dining room surrounded by elderly couples and little groups of businessmen, or in their room, in front of the TV. On the day after her excursion out of doors Eva had a little fever. Spinelli called in a doctor who felt her forehead and advised aspirin and antibiotics.

Spinelli said the man was a fool. Like any hypochondriac he had his own theories and pet remedies which he adored distributing to his friends and talking about at dinner parties. Eva took little notice of his suggestions and the pills she had from the doctor soon brought her fever down. To keep Carlo happy she took the vitamins and homoeopathic pills he gave her as well. But she refused to use his vaporizer because the eucalyptus made her feel queasy and she forbade him to use it either because it made the room smell. Secretly she was amused that he'd actually brought it on honeymoon with him. Of tablets and bathsalts he had a regular apothecary's shop, and he put Fuller's earth on his face because he thought it was good for his skin. He had a skullish look about him anyway, but with the green clay blotchy and half dried on his face he looked like a Hallowe'en ghoul.

It was still snowing when they left. Their plane was delayed three times on account of the weather and when they finally took off she was exhausted. Over the Alps a little turbulence made her feel sick. She could feel her temperature rising but she didn't say anything until they landed. That evening she was sick when they got back to the flat. She went straight to bed and shivered under a pile of blankets. A doctor came, took her temperature, and told her to stay in bed. The next day she felt a little better.

'But,' she said, 'what about the baby? Is the baby going to be all right?'

Her gynaecologist came and said it would be, but she was on no account to get up.

'What?' said Eva. 'Not until the baby is born?'

'Perhaps not. At any rate not for a couple of weeks.'

And so Eva began her married life as an invalid. She was meant to stay in bed all the time, but of course it was no more in her character to sit still than it was to obey doctors' orders, so she was up and about the apartment half the day. Carlo was furious if he caught her out of bed, but his busy social life kept him away for much of the time. When they were together they were curiously distant, as though they were lodgers sharing accommodation rather than husband and wife. Which in a way was true. One of the doctors had told them they could make love and another had said they shouldn't, so they did it occasionally.

Eva had to give up the part in the film. But she no longer minded about that: acting was something she could take up again later.

One day Carlo came to her with a will to sign. 'You'd better read it through,' he said, 'but take your time. Tacchella's not coming till next week, so there's no hurry.' Tacchella was his lawyer.

Eva put the document aside. She didn't look at it or give it a moment's thought until Carlo reminded her again. Reading it, she was outraged. The will left everything she had to Carlo. How did he have the effrontery to draw up such a document in favour of himself?

'But Eva, darling, what's extraordinary about it? I am your husband aren't I?'

'You are at the moment, yes, but only for the moment. It's outrageous to think that gives you a claim on everything I have. It wasn't part of our agreement.'

'But I don't want a thing from you. It isn't for me, it's for the baby. I thought you'd want your estate to benefit the child.'

'I do.'

'So why are you angry with me? If you die I'll be responsible for the child.'

Eva hadn't thought of this. Perhaps he was right. She said, 'What if I'd rather leave everything to the child?'

'You can't leave anything to someone who isn't born. Also, our child would be taxed on it, whereas I wouldn't. There's no death duty between husband and wife. I'm doing the same thing for you, so that if I die you'll have the flat and the house at Fernia and everything else.'

'But Carlo, I don't want your houses or your money.'

'Eva, my precious, it's only a formality really. If you die intestate everything you own goes to your spouse in any case. So it doesn't really make any difference.'

Eva knew nothing about the law, but she didn't doubt that he was right. What made her uncomfortable was that the law recognized they were married, when it was supposed to be something very temporary, between themselves. She said, 'Couldn't we leave it till the baby's born?'

'It's such a little thing,' he said. 'We might as well get it out of the way. Remember, in your will you can only leave what you own. None of your trust money will fall into your estate.' He smiled and nodded encouragingly.

She signed. Her parents had never made it clear what belonged to her trusts and what was her own. They had always made it seem that she herself had very little money, though she suspected this was partly to encourage her to get a job. In any case, Carlo was obviously right. It made sense to leave everything to him, at least until the child was born and they got divorced. Then she would see. But she was glad her parents didn't have to know about the new will. She had a feeling that in their eyes it would have looked bad.

'*Cinque, quattro, tre, due, uno . . .*'

The man jerked the cord of the guillotine but the mechanism failed to respond. He said something and the crowd burst into laughter. Doubtless it was all part of the act, but it made Eva's flesh creep to see the way they all treated human execution as a joke, the way Carlo and Marina della Garratrea treated nuclear war, when in fact it was threatening them with extinction at any minute. Any lunatic or even an accident could blow the whole planet to Kingdom come. And cancer . . . The man started the countdown again and the noise of the chant put up a score of pigeons which took off and flew over so low that people ducked.

'*Dieci, nove, otto, sette, sei* . . .'

Eva shivered. She felt her heart race and the blood prickle in her legs. 'Let's go,' she said. They stood up, and Eva stared emptily at the ground.

'Eva, what is it?'

She was gazing blankly, as if at nothing, and made no reply. The man at the guillotine loosed the cardboard blade and pulled a papier mâché head out of the basket, covered in gore. The crowd laughed, but Eva didn't appear to have noticed. She said, 'It's nothing. I sometimes black out when I stand up. It's gone now; let me take your arm. My health has been poor since I lost the baby.' She realized she hadn't spoken the last sentence. Yet she wanted to tell him about that, too, because it was a part of everything that was wrong. There was nothing she wanted to be a secret. She said, 'Shall we go to Fernia?'

'To Fernia? What on earth for?'

'I usually have a rest at this time of day. I meditate, it keeps me young. I suppose you would say it's my pact with the devil.' She smiled to herself. 'It's quiet out there.'

'You want to go all the way out to Fernia just to have a rest?'

'We could have dinner there, too. There's a little seafood place just up the coast, and we can drive back after.'

'How far is it?'

'Forty minutes. Half an hour.'

'I think I'd rather stay in town. Can't you meditate here?'

'I suppose so. I just thought it would be nice to eat there, at the house. You haven't seen it.'

'But Eva, I thought you said we would go to a restaurant up the coast.'

She realized he was right. It must be the blackout playing tricks with her memory. That time it had felt like she was going to faint away completely.

13

At the flat Eva tried to calm herself. She lay down on her bed and shut her eyes, but she couldn't keep them closed so she got up and opened the drawer in the magot chinois. It had a faint mustiness inside but it was quite empty. Why had she allowed Larry to persuade her not to go to Fernia? When she was with him she had felt confident, but the minute he was out of the room she became uneasy again. She flung herself down on the bed. It was mysterious that he had arrived just now when her life was in danger. Was it possible that he had realized this instinctively? Could it be that his visit was a sign that her time had come? She jumped up and looked at her face in the mirror. Her heart was racing. The nagging pain in her chest had started again.

Larry was reading in the sitting room. He was surprised at her lack of confidence, so unlike the old Eva. At times her voice trailed off and she seemed to forget what she was saying. And her exaggerated fear of people breaking into the flat, her jumpiness . . . he listened to her moving around the bedroom restlessly. It didn't sound as though much meditating was being done. When Scrope had told him she was lonely he had found it hard to believe. Now he could see that she might easily be. What was he to tell her parents? That she appeared frightened and distracted. That she was unhappily married.

Eventually Eva emerged and said she was going to cook dinner. But the kitchen was so cluttered with dirty dishes that he said they should go out. Eva said, 'I don't want to go out.'

'But Eva, look at the state of this place.' A feathery crop of mould had settled on the unwashed dishes like the fairies' handkerchiefs which lay on the lawns of Clermont in the early morning. It looked like a real junkie's kitchen, Larry thought. He remembered Maria Beckman, telling him she believed in a 'being greater than ourselves'. There was a roll of kitchen foil on the fridge, though that didn't necessarily mean anything.

'I'll clear it up,' Eva said. 'Honestly, I don't like leaving the house, Larry. It makes me nervous.'

'It makes you nervous?'

'In case of a break-in.'

'In case of a break-in?' Larry looked at her uncomprehendingly. She fidgeted, avoiding his eye. 'It'll do you good to go out, Eva. And me too. I'm only here for a couple of days.'

In the end she agreed to take him to the Meridiana. She insisted on showing him Settimio's bar on the way and they both had a vodka martini there, and then Eva had another. They were strong, but they had a calming effect on Eva. When they left she slipped her arm through Larry's and they walked through the ochre streets in the last daylight to the Piazza Matusalemme with the cinquecento sundial on the wall. The restaurant had put a lamp over this and its pool of yellow illumination was just becoming visible. Eva and Carlo always ate here on Sunday nights when the Pera was closed. She associated the place with coming back to Rome from Fernia: sometimes in summer she would come in tennis shoes and a T-shirt, straight from the beach, and find herself in Roman society once again with a suddenness which made her feel out of place; and by a reverse process, if they came in mid-week she had a sensation of proximity to the seaside, of the sand under her feet and the quiet sound of the waves filling the garden. That feeling would reassure her tonight.

The people here knew her. The head waiter who seated them put a tiny vase with three carnations on their table.

'He must have heard about Carlo being arrested,' Eva said. 'He's always been sweet to me, that Piero. An angel. Before I lost the baby he used to send food over to the apartment. It was a hellish time. I was always feeling lousy and getting a fever. It started as soon as we were married, on our honeymoon in Vienna, in fact. Then when we got down here the doctor said I had to stay in bed all the time, till the baby was born. It was not due till September. I was bleeding quite often. In May we had some kind of a heatwave and it was unbearable, like lying around in an oven.'

She remembered the long afternoons with the shutters all closed and the electric fans turning their faces this way and that. After lunch Carlo slept on the bed beside her, his mouth open and a little wet patch of saliva on the pillow. Eva could never sleep. She read more and more Balzac novels in the Pléiade edition, longing for the day to end and the burning sun to disappear from the sky. Then she would open the shutters and Carlo would take a shower and go out leaving her in peace. He did his best to lift her spirits. When she told him she was depressed by the oriental hangings in the bedroom he took them down. He brought people in to see her. He told her stories about people he'd seen, or gossip he'd heard. His head nodded enthusiastically, he was so attentive she felt bound to make an effort, for his sake; but all the time she was longing for the moment when he would go away and she would be on her own. When he returned at night she pretended to be asleep.

'In the end,' she said, 'it grew so hot that the doctors began to talk about a move to Fernia, in spite of the difficulties of moving me. It's always a bit cooler there, being right on the sea, and often there's a breeze. Carlo was against it. He swore that it never really got hot in the Palazzo Spinelli because the walls were so thick; and that even if his flat was too warm I could move down to his aunt's flat on the first floor which would be empty all summer when she went to a hideous and uncomfortable house in the Abruzzi. I said that was the last thing I wanted: her whole apartment stank, God knows what of; I don't think she ever opened a window in there. Restless and bored with my interminable confinement, I took the side of the doctors. After all, if it was like this in May what would it be like in July? I said to Carlo, "Look, I know you've got things to do in Rome and you won't be able to take care of me. But you don't have to. I'll go on my own and I'll be perfectly all right."

' "But who's going to look after you?"

' "Good heavens, Carlo, there's Gemma isn't there? Why d'you make everything sound so difficult?"

'In the end he agreed, and drove me out there one evening. The next day my temperature was up. I took it myself while he was downstairs because I didn't want him fussing. He always got so hysterical about illness. Luckily the temperature wasn't very high. Carlo went back to Rome that afternoon. It didn't seem any cooler here than it had been in Rome, but I was pleased to be on my own. Carlo said he'd come out and see me at the weekend.'

Why was she telling Larry all this? The story came out in a rush, as though it had been stored up inside her. She was aware of the waiter at her side, waiting to take their order.

'*Vodka con ghiaccio.*'

'And to eat?' the waiter said.

'*Fettucine.* But we'll have the drink first.' She waited while the waiter took Larry's order and then went on.

'My temperature went on going up. I didn't want to worry Carlo so I called the doctor myself, and when he came he said the move hadn't been good for me and I was to stay as still as I could. I told Gemma to make up the bed in the spare room so I could spend the afternoons in there when the sun was on the bedroom side of the house. I was sick of lying in a shuttered room all day. Each time I moved from one bed to the other Gemma changed the sheets. They were always wringing. On Gemma's day off the doctor said he would look in and make sure I was all right.'

Eva remembered little of that day. When she fell asleep, it felt as if she was fainting, except that her dreams were as real as being awake. It was hot, but the windows wouldn't open. She found a bolt at the top and pulled it back, but still it wouldn't open. She twisted the handle both ways and thumped the frame with her fist. Outside she could see the setting sun blazing on the lake, blood-coloured, and flames dancing in the leaves of the young beech trees. She could see that the wooden pens and sheds where her father kept his birds would catch fire next, and the birds would be burnt alive inside them. The great oak tree in the park shimmered in the heat. She must get the window open somehow or she would suffocate. The bolt at the top of the window was shut and she pulled it back. The window opened, but it was as hot outside as it was in the house, unbearably hot, it seemed to make no difference if the window was open or shut . . . Her father was calling her from the drawing room. With a spasm so violent it left her whole body trembling, she jerked awake. Dear God, it was hot. What was she doing in the bedroom with the shutters open and the sun shining straight in through the window? She must have been asleep for hours. And why did a bitter smell of burning penetrate the air, like a black odour left behind by her dream? Shakily she got out of bed and went to the bathroom. She ran the basin full of cold water and plunged her hands in it, splashing some on her face, and then putting her face right in. She remembered her mother telling her fortune by the lines in her hand. This is your lifeline, and this is your loveline. The left hand is your character and the right hand's what you make of yourself. All through your life the lines can develop but when you die all the lines disappear. Her father said he'd seen the lines on his hand disappear when he nearly died in hospital during the war. Eva looked at her hands. Whenever she tried to concentrate her vision on a particular pattern the lines started to shift like a pot of worms. It was the same with the hairline cracks in the paint on the ceiling, which grew under her gaze like runnels of water from a burst main.

She went through to the spare room and lay down on the bed. The sheets were crumpled and disordered: had she already slept in them? It was frightening not to be able to remember these things. She looked out of the window. To her surprise she saw that there was something burning on the low hills behind the road. She wondered if it was a controlled fire, or accidental. She imagined it coming down the brown fields of corn, across the road, sweeping into the wood and round the house. In the *Puranas* it was written that the horizon would be set alight, and multiple suns would appear in the sky, drying the sea and burning the whole earth in a universal fire. Her heart raced. It was impossible to imagine a clearer prophesy of nuclear holocaust. The *Samvartaka*, it was called. Carlo had told her. The afternoon was so hot that the air shimmered slightly in front of the corn, but the smoke was coming from a definite point in the near distance. The remains of an old rick being burnt off, perhaps. Whatever it was, it was burning with gusto, the great heat forcing up huge black billows at a tremendous rate. She wondered if she should ring the doctor, but she remembered he had said he would come anyway. She dreamt that she got out of bed and ran downstairs and out on to the lawn. In the park the oak tree had gone up like a huge torch and when she ran past she had to give it a wide berth so as not to catch fire herself. Beyond the lake she could see the sheds ablaze, and her father like a salamander in the middle of it, loosing bird after bird into the sky. The birds were all aflame, and they rose into the red evening and flew off across the lake. Her father was shouting to her . . . Suddenly a fire engine was there, its bells ringing quietly, a regular double chime, and the firemen got out and started pulling hoses out and shooting jets of water on to the flames. The flames were out, she walked over the lawn towards the house but the smell of the fire was over everything and soot flakes came down out of the air and settled like huge black moths on the lake. With a start she awoke, and the soft chime seemed to ring on inside her head. She sat up. The smoke from the fire had drifted across the valley to the house and hung in the hot summer air, almost blotting out the sun. It was acrid, almost choking. And the chime: the chime was exactly like the doorbell. Had somebody really been at the door? She got out of bed and went to the window and saw a car turning out of the end of their drive. Had it been the doctor? He had said he would call. She shut the window and remained rooted to the spot. A scalding cramp seized hold of her insides, so strong it was as though the fire had leapt straight across the valley and exploded like a bullet inside her. For a second she was unable to move, struggling for breath that wouldn't come, unable to understand where the blow had come from. Then the pain ebbed slowly and she understood. She went downstairs for the phone book and called the surgery.

She had already lost the child when Carlo arrived. They had given her a sedative which made her very drowsy. Aware of a vague commotion at her bedside, she opened her eyes, and there was Carlo, with Don standing at his elbow. Carlo stroked her hair.

'My poor precious,' he said.

She thought he looked rather sweet in his double-breasted suit with that solemn expression on his face, like a little boy in church. She was puzzled by the presence of Don. What was he doing here?

'The doctor tried to ring me when he couldn't get into the house,' Carlo said. 'But I was out at meetings all day. When they eventually did get hold of me I came straight out here.'

'I'm really sorry about what's happened,' Don said. 'If there's anything I can do for you, any errands I can run . . .' Eva shook her head. 'We were fixing up something really wonderful for you. Carlo's going to tell you about it when you're better.'

The waiter came with their *fettucine*. Eva ordered another Russian vodka. The drinks were having a good effect on the pain in her chest. It had retreated to a sensation which was not painful and which from time to time she could forget about altogether. She picked up her fork and toyed with the pasta in her bowl.

'I went back to Fernia for a few days when I got out of the hospital. Carlo stayed with me. Don had gone back to Rome, thank God. There was something about him which gave me the creeps, something I couldn't quite put my finger on, but which had to do with his violet eyes and that fat, fleshy face. He had plump hands too, smooth and hairless. When I shook hands with him I always held him at a distance in case he started kissing me hullo. I dreaded him kissing me.

'Anyway, after we'd been a few days in the country Carlo drove me back to Rome. He was incredibly solicitous about me. He kept saying how he didn't mind staying a bit longer at the coast if I wanted to so I could rest, and that he'd look after me. But there was no reason to stay out at Fernia now. The heatwave had passed and it would soon be boring out there on our own with nothing to do. I said we should go back to Rome right away.

'I remember in the car on the way back he said he had a surprise for me. I could recall Don saying something about this too and I was hoping it would be a cat. Carlo knew that I wanted one but so far he had held out against it because he said it would make the flat smell. But when we got back to the flat Carlo said, "It's not here. It's outside. We have to go there in the car."

'"Oh, for heaven's sake, Carlo, we've just been in the damn car!"

'I went and lay down in the bedroom. He had already put back the gloomy wall hangings. In fact the whole flat depressed me, because I realized that aside from the excitement of having a baby, our life was incredibly dull. I had nothing to do and I didn't even like the people we knew. And Carlo was getting on my nerves. I knew he was trying to help but it only made me more impatient. When he came into the bedroom I knew he would try to cheer me up so I pretended to be asleep. I could hear him fussing around clumsily, knocking something over on the table, banging the loo-seat in the bathroom, peeing, flushing the loo. Dear God, if I had really been asleep he would have woken me a hundred times by now! I waited till he had gone back into the living room before I uncurled and opened my eyes. I was always pretending to be asleep in those days.'

She pushed the plate of pasta away. It was almost cold now, but she wasn't hungry. She lit a cigarette and sipped the vodka. It had always been easy to talk to Larry. He understood everything you said, there was never any need to explain in laborious detail as she so often had to do with Carlo. They had great reserves of understanding from having loved each other for so long; or was it a shared view of existence, a common understanding of the world? Yet it seemed to be more than that, something she was aware of without being able to name. Suddenly she was seized by a conviction of having wasted her life: dear God, she had stayed too long in this damned marriage, in this God-forsaken town!

She remembered how she had lain on the bed that afternoon thinking, I must tell him I want to divorce him now that we've lost the baby. He agreed, and now I must hold him to it. She dreaded him giving her anything under these circumstances, even a cat. What would she do with the cat when she went back to England? Leave it with Carlo? He wouldn't want it. If she took it with her she'd have to leave it in quarantine for goodness knows how long to comply with the silly rules about animals they had over there.

'Eva, are you awake?'

Eva shut her eyes and stirred in the bed, giving a little groan.

'No, I was asleep.'

'Then sleep, little girl.'

'Well, you've woken me now, haven't you?' No, that wasn't right. She must be more patient with him. And she hadn't been sleeping anyway, so what was she trying to blame him for? She said, 'It doesn't matter, Carlo. I'm ready to go. I only wanted a nap.'

But Carlo hadn't been offended. He was in a mood where nothing could go wrong.

'You get into the car,' he said when they got down to the courtyard. 'I'll see to the doors myself.' He jumped in and out of the Jaguar like a young boy, and tooted the horn at the corner. '*Avanti!* Now, try and guess what it is! I'll give you ten questions. You have to get it before we arrive!'

'How far is it?'

Carlo mistook her weariness for enthusiasm.

'Ah-ha!' He took his hands off the wheel and rubbed them together. 'Not far at all! Only a few kilometres as the crow flies, perhaps half an hour depending on the traffic. That gives you a clue already. Next question.' And his rings rattled like a marching drum on the steering wheel. Eva slipped off her espadrilles and put her foot up on the dashboard. The sunlight burned through the windshield on her bare skin. She tried to think what the surprise was going to be. What did she want? She wanted nothing.

They were getting into the outer suburbs now and the road was pitted and almost empty except for occasional trucks. There were a lot of warehouses looking very dilapidated and blocks of flats built of stained, pinkish concrete with green metal blinds pulled down low against the sun. Carlo turned into a stretch of open concrete with weeds growing out of its cracks. There was a stunted hillside on the left with a row of shacks built into it, a chaotic huddle of planks and corrugated iron and plastic sheeting. Beside one of these a car stood with its bonnet open, and the legs of a man disappearing underneath. A dog, asleep on a chain in the shade, got to its feet and barked as they rolled by. On their right stood a low wall, with a metal gate over which, rather incongruously, a triangular pediment was perched. Carlo stopped the car. The gate was secured by a heavy padlock which he opened. He put his shoulder to it, and with a squeal it eased back a few feet. Carlo stood off and dusted the shoulder of his jacket, then held out an arm and inclined himself in a little bow. Eva went in. In front of her, on a huge expanse of rubble, scores of cats scarpered in all directions like maggots from an upturned log.

'Well?' Carlo said. 'What do you think?'

Eva looked at them. Having run out of immediate danger they were moving around more slowly but still warily a little distance away. She turned to Carlo. He was grinning as though something wonderful had happened.

'All this can be ours!' he said. 'For nothing! But don't say anything yet! Wait till you come over here.'

All this can be ours! The phrase with its Luciferan overtones seemed to her the very pinnacle of madness. All this rubble and dead weeds, all this broken cement and rusted cans, all this for what? They picked their way across the enclosure, Carlo taking her by the arm to help her over the difficult bits. A ginger cat slunk around them and then followed behind, backing away warily when Eva tried to pick it up. At the far side of the enclosure was a wall with a ladder propped against it, the kind which has a wide base and a narrow top.

'You first,' said Carlo.

Eva climbed to the top.

'Am I meant to get over, Carlo?'

'Wait there!'

The ladder gave a little under his weight. Beneath her, his bald crown rose by stages till he was standing on the rung below her, with his ringed hands beside hers on the wall.

'Look, Eva. D'you see that?'

When he spoke the feeling of his breath on her bare neck was almost more than she could bear. His arms were on either side of her so that she was trapped between him and the ladder.

'Do I see what?'

'Do you see that road?'

How could she not see it? Only a few hundred yards away the cars whizzed into a long banked curve and then cut away to their left behind some apartment buildings, like frenetic corpuscles of the prosperous and busy city being pumped urgently across a dying piece of its body.

'It's the airport road, little girl!'

'Carlo, I want to get down!'

She almost kicked him off the ladder in her irritation.

'Eva. What's the matter with you? All right. All right. I'm going as fast as I can.'

When they were down she hardly knew herself what had come over her – it seemed to have been a combination of irritation at his excitement and physical repulsion at feeling him so close, pinning her like that against the wall. She said, 'I'm sorry I kicked you. I had an attack of vertigo.'

'Poor baby. I didn't know you got vertigo. But did you see the road?'

'Yes.'

'Well, can you imagine? Next year they're going to complete a junction right here. And this space will all be designated for mixed development: factory, office, warehouse.' His head was nodding up and down like a puppet's. She had a sudden desire to take it between her hands and hold it still. 'There'll be a direct link-up with the airport. Everybody's been waiting for space like this to come on the market. As soon as the zoning decision goes through, the price of this land is going to go through the roof. And it's all going to belong to us!'

'But doesn't it belong to Don?'

'I'm afraid poor old Don's going to have to pull out of it altogether. It seems that his cash crisis is so severe that he can't even hang on till next year. He's offered it all to us!'

'And what are we going to buy it with?'

'We'll manage. Where there's a will there's a way.'

'It sounds a wonderful idea, Carlo,' she said.

But it all seemed dead to her, unutterably dull and ugly. They walked back across the uneven, weed-strewn expanse. At the far end there was a wide reticulation of brick remains, like the vestigial walls of an excavated town.

'That was where the slaughterhouses used to be in the old days.

All the rest was used for the gathering pens and so on. The meat market was on the other side, over there. You can see the floor. A wall used to run between the two. It's a huge area altogether. The commercial possibility is stupendous.'

They reached the front gate again. 'We'd better shut it,' said Carlo. 'Otherwise the couples come in their cars to make love.' He heaved and the big gate clanged shut. Slipping the key into his pocket, he said, 'Oh look. It's followed us to the car.'

The ginger cat had got out without their noticing and was miaowing before the door of the Jaguar. Eva took it in her arms.

'It seems to want to come with us,' she said.

'Yes,' Spinelli said. 'I suppose we might as well take this one as another.'

They got in and he started the motor. Across the way a horse and cart rumbled into sight, seeming to make straight for them. As it drew closer they saw it was one of the tourist buggies that you see on the Piazza di Spagna waiting to take people on a drive around the city.

'Good heavens!' said Carlo. 'What's that doing out here?'

But even as he spoke they saw that it was heading for a long shed where there were three other horses with their heads sticking out over the half-doors; and beside it, two unhitched carts with their shafts in the air.

'So this is where they keep them!' Carlo said. 'How exciting! Do you realize we're seeing a piece of living history? Because when this area is developed, it will be almost unimaginable that only three, four, five years ago it was so cheap and out of the way that they used to stable horses here! That's how history gets made! D'you know, it's not long since there were shepherds with their flocks at the Porta del Popolo? Recently enough for there to be photos of it? Photographs! That's how fast it happens!'

The car bumped out of the yard and back through the streets with Carlo's fingers rattling on the wheel. On Eva's lap the cat trembled as though it had a fever.

'Perhaps it would rather have stayed there,' she said.

'I thought you wanted a cat, Eva.'

'I do. But it seems odd just to go and take one. Like a kidnap, almost. I suppose she doesn't mind.'

'Why on earth should she mind? You're giving her a home, aren't you?'

Eva thought of Johnson on the pavement of Park Lane in the powerful beam of the headlamps. Ricky stopped the car, she opened the door, and Johnson bounded in, licking and panting. Ricky had been really surprised to find Larry in bed at the flat. She had so much confidence in those days.

Carlo said, 'What are you going to call it?'

'I think I'll call her Lady Macbeth.'

'Ah! A red-headed Scot!'

They rolled through the tenement district into the vast grid of crawling tailback which is Rome at five o'clock in the afternoon. Exhaust fumes rose into the air like the street was burning, but everyone had their windows all the way down. Scooters threaded past between the cars, working their way laboriously down the lines. For a long while nothing at all was said: Eva could tell he was thinking about the slaughterhouse and she felt she had hurt his feelings by not being enthusiastic about it. Before she lost the child she had thought Don's projects sounded exciting enough; now it was all wearyingly pointless. She tried to think of something encouraging to say to Carlo, and couldn't. In the end she said, 'How are we going to pay for it?'

His face lit up. 'I don't know,' he said. 'That's the thing about any really imaginative idea. You don't know how it's going to be done. You just know it's gotta be done.' From the way he said it she could tell he was repeating something Don had told him.

The waiter brought their sea-bass and began deftly to separate the flesh from the bones, laying the strips of white flesh on their plates. They each had a bowl of green salad with *rughetta* and Larry was drinking yellow wine from a carafe. The waiter had taken it to heart that Eva had barely touched the pasta. When he handed her the plate with the sea-bass on it he said encouragingly, 'Now here's a lovely piece of fish.'

Eva tried it. The fish was well cooked, not too dry and with a touch of basil, but she didn't have any appetite. She felt good talking to Larry. He was listening to her with an intelligent, attentive expression, and she longed more than anything that he should understand her, and why she was in such a mess, and so unhappy, because she didn't understand it herself. She wasn't even sure when it had begun. Had it been when she left him for Carlo? Not that, looking back on it, she had ever really intended to leave him. In fact her affair with Carlo had been more of a drift than a decision. And leaving Larry had been the absence of a decision, a failure of the will to hold on to a single relationship and make it important. She wanted to talk about this, but the extreme coldness and detachment with which she had behaved when she left him made it hard for her even to allude to it now. She had only written him one letter when she got engaged to Carlo, a silly letter thanking him for 'everything' but not talking about why she had done it or about anything important. Perhaps it would have been no good to discuss it anyway, perhaps once it was over between them there was nothing more to say and any explanation would have been superfluous. So at any rate she had told herself; but in her heart she knew it wasn't true and that a whole matrix of her deepest and most important feelings had been swept aside. The trouble was that as every week went by it became more difficult to imagine what to write. Difficult to imagine! With such difficulties are the most important things in life lost!

She took a swig from her vodka and said, 'I might as well admit my marriage is a failure. Perhaps because of that I've taken against this city as well. I feel as if I'm desiccating here, like those mimosa blooms which look as if they're going on for ever when in fact they're already dead.'

Larry said nothing. There was nothing for him to say. Her words, which at one time would have thrown so much into question, meant nothing to him now. He didn't want her any more. She went on. 'After I lost the child it got even worse. Rosa Agambo's film had been delayed again, till November this time, so she gave me my part back. I was pleased because it gave me something to look forward to. I didn't have the confidence to go out any more: people unnerved me. Without my being aware of it my life began to revolve more and more around meals. It's lucky I never get fat, or I would have become grotesque. We used to go out to restaurants a lot – trattorias and so on, always quite simple and homey. Grand places are never any good in this city. We came here often, and also the Pera . . .'

The Pera! It seemed half her marriage had been spent in the Pera. There was something about that place, just round the corner from where they lived, that was completely satisfying. It was not patronized by Roman society. There were no waiters: you were served by the family from the Abruzzi who did the cooking as well. They were a moody lot. On a bad day the two sons gave the impression of being deaf men and the pock-marked daughter stared at you as if she was dumb. At such times only Carlo seemed to have the knack of always getting their attention, of somehow coaxing from them a little sunburst of efficiency which made the delicious food arrive in an orderly fashion. He used to say the Pera was the only place outside India where you could eat lentils well cooked.

'Look how creamy they are! Do you know what the secret is? They cook them in a sealed pot for three days. It's incredible!'

The meat and the fish were always cooked very simply, without sauce. The portions were small, like an afterthought to the richly oiled bowls of pasta.

Married life! When she first moved in with Carlo she used to cook for him like she'd done with Larry, and she even taught him to cook a little too. But it soon came to seem too much effort and they began to go out more and more to the Pera and other restaurants. The endless meals! Sometimes it seemed they were killing days with lunches and dinners, and the time between them seemed nothing more than a useless and boring interval. She drank more heavily now, because it helped her to sleep in the afternoon.

She began to realize also that her acting success had been a fluke, and that she wasn't very good because she'd never worked at it or had any training. If she'd really wanted to succeed she should have been in drama school, or fringe, or repertory, like all the other young actors in London. She had had the incredible good fortune to land a part without any of this but she knew that did not make her a good actress. And in a way it was the same with her social success, and her feeling of being suddenly grown-up. All this had come on the back of Carlo and she had done nothing for it.

In this life her daydreams were always of Castagna. How often, in the oppressive oriental bedroom at Palazzo Spinelli, did she visit the old house above Lucca in her imagination! Or from the garden at Fernia, prostrate beside the turquoise cube of the swimming pool, how often did she in her mind follow the road north along the coast, through the conurbations of Grosseto, Livorno and Pisa, and, turning her back on the coast, set out on the quiet road into the hills, with its white-painted plane trees and its rusty, shot-pitted signs. In the summer there would be the path to the mill pond, and the exhausting heat of the day when you could eat nothing and see nothing beyond the other side of the valley on account of the haze. And when winter came the dun hillside went green under clouds so dark and solid that they seemed to be wrought out of slate, or else so impossibly rococo that they looked like frozen explosions, with billows and towering chimneys of smoke bursting outwards on all sides, dwarfing the gentle contours of the hills beneath them. There was no one on the roads then. The leaves drifted across the asphalt and lay until the rain washed them away, and you kicked through them with your boots when you were out walking. In the woods the dirt road turned to mud and little rivulets ran across it and on the corners it was easy to skid. Before the big storms the seagulls gathered round the house and Lord Clermont's shark-oil barometer clouded over. Sometimes a wind heralded these storms too, whipping the trees above the house and whistling eerily in the telephone wire on the drive. Other times they burst without warning in the night, rattling the windows like cannon fire and flashing the barred shadow of the persian shutters on to the floor of the bedroom. And in the morning there was a smell of earth and you could see for miles and the seagulls had left their white feathers on the meadow below the house. On such a day she imagined arriving, the air washed clean by the rain of the night before, puddles drying, oaks and spanish chestnuts all yellow and gold like the flounces of a ballgown; and the dark green-uniformed cypresses standing to attention beside the church of Santa Maria dell'Orto; and the old church itself, looking towards Lucca like a bride. Here was her father's vineyard, cut back in reticulate brown lines, and here the place where Maurizio had been cutting logs, the wood chips still white as confetti on the ground. Inside the house she could already see quite clearly the hall with its old bakelite telephone, and the sitting room with its medallions of the four winds by an unknown artist and its doors on to the garden. She had never taken Carlo there. When he suggested they drive over she told him her parents wouldn't let her go, but the truth was she had never asked them.

The first summer of her marriage her parents didn't come to Castagna. They went to the Himalayas instead, ostensibly to watch birds with the Nagpurs, though Eva often wondered if this was an excuse. Only once before in her memory had they failed to come to Italy in the summer. But her father came on his own, early the next April.

Maurizio met him at the airport and drove him up to Castagna, where Derna had lunch ready for him. It wasn't warm enough to eat outside under the fig tree that day, so he ate in the dining room of the villa. The sun shone through the south-facing windows on to the green-painted table and the old red tiles. Derna had put wisteria blooms in a vase. Lord Clermont told Maurizio to sit with him while he ate. He began to ask Maurizio about the crops and about how the vines had survived the frost which had been quite severe for three days in January.

'At the bottom of the front field I thought it had killed them,' Maurizio said, 'but I went down there yesterday and I found some live buds. The others are all in leaf. Three days is all right if it doesn't get down to the roots. Do you remember sixty-three when we lost every vine except the ones at the front of the house?'

'And yet they all came back in the end.'

'In the end.'

'And this year, you put water for the pigeons?'

'Every day. And I put straw, and I blocked up some of the holes like you said, so the wind wouldn't blow through the dovecots. But I'm afraid they're pairing up with the wild ones again.'

'We shall take a look after lunch. Tomorrow I need you to drive me. I'm going to lunch with Eva.'

'Ah, Eva!' Maurizio's face brightened. 'That's good. Derna and I were a little concerned when she came over in the autumn.'

'Eva came over?'

'Yes. One afternoon. Derna made dinner for her and then she said she wanted to stay the night and so Derna made up the bed in her room and I lit the fire. But she went in the night. We didn't hear her go. In the morning the car had gone. She hadn't slept in the bed.'

'I see.'

'We were concerned because she seemed very preoccupied.'

'In what way?'

'Very preoccupied. Not like she usually is at all. Perhaps she was sad because the Principe was away.'

'He was away?'

'Well, he wasn't with her. Doubtless he had business affairs to look after. Ah, she's well taken care of, that Eva!'

Maurizio and Derna were aware that there was a rift between Eva and her parents and that it was to do with Spinelli, but they didn't understand why. He arrived in a Jaguar; he had a palazzo in Rome; he was a prince and his breeding was apparent in his courteousness. He was grand without being rude or looking down on people like them. How was it then that Lord and Lady Clermont weren't content with him as a son-in-law? It must be that as foreigners they somehow failed to apprehend these virtues; for this reason Maurizio and Derna were always eager to point out Spinelli's excellent qualities to them.

Eva and Carlo were staying at Fernia when her father came. From the window she saw Maurizio drive up to the door, and her father got out, looking a little frail and stooping. He was wearing a baggy tweed jacket, extremely high-buttoned above, and bulging at the pockets below. About his shoulders he was carrying a fishing bag and a pair of binoculars. He looked very English and out of place here, yet his appearance made her feel more confident, happier than she'd felt for months. She ran downstairs into his arms like a little girl.

The waiter came and took away their plates. Eva had not even touched the sea-bass, but she ordered an ice-cream all the same. Larry couldn't remember how many vodkas she'd had by now. Four, five, six? She was very voluble and from time to time she broke off suddenly, as if she had lost track of what she was saying. Apart from this, which was more like vagueness than intoxication, she showed no sign whatever of being drunk.

'I had told Carlo I wanted to talk to Papa alone,' she was saying, 'so after they'd said hullo I took him to the far end of the garden where the door is which goes down to the beach. There's a big pine tree there with shade, and some chairs. We sat down and began to talk. But we scarcely had time to say anything before Carlo arrived, bearing a bottle of champagne in a cooler and glasses. I was furious.

'I suppose it was meant to be a nice surprise, but it didn't succeed at all. You know how Daddy is about champagne; he considers it suspect enough in England but he particularly doesn't like it in Italy because he considers it uncountrified not to drink the local muck. Anyway, Carlo sat down with us and poured out three glasses.

'"I thought we should celebrate," he said. "I would like to say how delighted Eva and I both are to have the honour at last of entertaining you under our roof – or, should I say, under our sky." He raised his glass to the sky: it was all very formal and pompous and unlike his normal self. Then he said something like, "Families should always resolve their differences." Daddy mumbled and pretended to take a minute sip from his glass.

Because he and Mummy never openly admitted to quarrelling with Carlo and me, he found this overt reference to it distasteful and embarrassing. You know what he's like.'

Eva smiled at the recollection and lit a cigarette. It was so easy to explain these things to Larry, they suddenly seemed laughable.

'All this was mildly comic and wouldn't have mattered at all if I hadn't wanted to talk to Daddy on my own so much. It's a funny thing about Carlo – he's the most helpful and kind person in the world but he is incapable of knowing when you want to be left alone. Well, we struggled through lunch. It was heavy going at first. Daddy asked Carlo about local agriculture and trees and things he knew nothing about, and Carlo asked Daddy about people in London whom he didn't know, or else was pretending he didn't know. It was all rather heavy going and slightly ludicrous at the same time. It struck me very forcibly that we were all three of completely different generations. Daddy was interested in all the little things of my life – my yellow car, my piano lessons, and so on. He was keen to get on with Carlo for my sake. I was touched. Carlo was really very sweet to him and made him laugh and got him to tell one or two stories about birds.

'By the end of lunch things seemed to be going quite well. Then suddenly, out of the blue, Carlo said, "Eva was asking me if it would be possible for her trustees to bring her trust to an end and give her control of her money." I was struck dumb, not so much by the directness and suddenness of the question as by its shameless untruth: at no time had I even suggested such a thing. But to my surprise Daddy didn't seem the least bit thrown, and replied immediately, "Eva's trustees, although possessed of such a power, would only exercise it if they were convinced that it would be in her best interests for them to do so. At present they are not convinced of it and there is no likelihood that they will change their minds in the future."

'This reply was so exact, and followed so swiftly on the question, that for a moment Carlo seemed stupefied. Then he said, "I see." There was a further silence. Then Daddy said, "I wonder if I could take a cutting from your clematis. I think it would grow very well against the dovecot at Castagna." And that was that.'

14

'As soon as Papa had gone I turned on Carlo.

'"Why did you ask him that? You know damn well how suspicious they are about you and my money. You must be out of your mind! Look what happened at the wedding when you asked about it. They haven't spoken to us for two years."

'"Oh," he said, "I thought you'd want me to. So that we could buy the abattoir and make lots of money. If you didn't want it why didn't you say so?"

'Carlo's so childish really. I suppose it's part of his charm. Anyway, I tried to explain to him that you couldn't say that kind of thing to Daddy. "Of course we want the money," I said, "but if you just say it straight out to Daddy without explaining why, he thinks you're trying to take my money away from me."

'"But that's ridiculous, Eva. I wouldn't take anything from you – on the contrary, you would be making a fortune."

'He seemed so hurt that I rather regretted saying anything. Still, I thought it was best that he should be aware of what my parents would think of that kind of thing.

'After that he spent a week or two fretting about the abattoir. Don had told him he couldn't hold out for ever and he would have to sell it to somebody else if we couldn't raise the money. Then one evening Don came into the Pera when we were having dinner and sat down at our table.

'"I think I've found someone who'll lend you the money," he said, "without your having to put up any security."

'"That's incredible, Don! That's stupendous! Who is it?"

'Because Carlo could be enthusiastic about practically anything I had developed a sixth sense for what really excited him, and in this case something told me that he had reservations. Perhaps he had anticipated what the answer to his question was going to be. Don leaned forward on his plump elbows. He said, "These people are *uomini d'onore*. That means the Mafia. But they're completely trustworthy. To do business with, they're much more trustworthy than straight businessmen. They're not petty crooks. It's an organization."

'Carlo looked unhappy. He said, "I don't know. It makes me uncomfortable to deal with these kind of men. What do you think, Eva?" I said I didn't know. To tell the truth I found the whole thing scary. I'd never met any Mafia guys before and naturally I was intrigued. I said, "How come they don't want any security?"

'Don made a calming gesture with his hand to make me speak less loudly. "You have to give them your word. These are men of honour, they work in an old-fashioned way. No written agreements, nothing official, no taxes either. It has a lot of advantages. They give you the money. After a year you pay it back, with some interest. There are no questions. And in the meantime you will have made a fortune."

'"And what if something goes wrong and we don't make a fortune? Do they have us murdered?"

'"If something goes wrong you simply sell the abattoir and get your money back. You won't have made a fortune, but you won't have lost anything either. That's the beauty of real estate development: the value of the site is always there when you want it."

'Carlo and I talked it over and in the end we couldn't resist it. We called Don and told him we were on. Carlo was scared to death. He kept saying how these people would kill you if you crossed them. But I could tell he wanted to go ahead anyhow.'

The truth was that Carlo didn't have enough money to live on. He had needed her money, the income which she had from her trust, ever since they were married. How he had managed before she didn't know; but the fact that he relied on her now made her feel, illogically, guilty about divorcing him. She wanted him to be rich, and independent of her. The abattoir would make him rich and that would make it easier for her to leave him.

'Don arranged for us to meet the people he knew at a country house he had been lent by a friend who was an opera singer. He came to the apartment one Saturday morning and we all drove out there together in the Jaguar. Don sat in the back and leaned forward with his arms on the backs of our seats to talk to us. It made my flesh creep to feel the sleeve of his cashmere cardigan beside my neck. He told us we weren't to say anything about the abattoir to the mob, otherwise they might cut us out of it and take it for themselves. "You don't have to tell them what it's for,' he said. "You just have to give them your word that you're going to pay it back." Carlo drummed on the wheel with his rings. He was unusually quiet, probably because he was nervous. In fact, we were all nervous.

'The villa was near a lake in the hills. We went in and Don took us round it, opening the shutters as he went. On the first floor there was a loggia which had been glassed in and frescoed with modern paintings. There were lots of leather chairs and opera posters, and a huge fireplace and panels of mirror everywhere. I started playing the piano in the big sitting room. It was a beautiful day. Although the air was quite fresh up there in the hills, the sun was hot. It came in through the big plate window on to a red Moroccan rug at the far end of the room. Downstairs, Don and Carlo were sitting out on the terrace.

'Eventually a car came up the drive and stopped outside. I shut the piano and went down on to the terrace to join them. There were three of them: a boy in his twenties who was the driver, with dark eyes and straight features, obviously the protection. The other two were much older: one was in his forties, bald, and dressed in a dark business suit; the other was older, and scruffier. He looked like a peasant, with baggy corduroy trousers like Maurizio wears and a small felt hat on his head. It turned out that he was the boss, although I initially thought the guy in the suit was. Don gave everyone a glass of something, and then asked them if they wanted to step inside to talk business. The two older men followed him, but the young guy went and sat in the car. Carlo said, "Aren't you coming too, Eva?" but I told him to go ahead and settle it between the men. The real reason was I wanted to talk to the driver. I could see a mile off that he was armed. So as soon as the others had gone I went down to the car and asked him if I could have a look. He was called Giulio. The gun was a Forty-five. He said to me, "How did you know I had a gun anyway?" I told him I'd done a bit of shooting and that I had a gun of my own. I don't think he really believed me. He must have been pretty dumb. I took aim at an old can that was lying by the garage and fired two shots. This brought the others down straight away. The smart guy tore a terrific strip off Giulio and told him to get back in the car. But when they realized it was me who fired it they all just laughed.

'Eventually the three of them left. Don and Carlo were both in fine spirits now and we had lunch outside. There was a barbecue on which we grilled steaks and we had salad and cheese and some light red wine we found in the cellar. After lunch we had coffee and a brandy each. The freshness of the morning had given way to a balmy afternoon. Carlo brought down the case of money and Don produced some cigars. It was hilarious sitting up there smoking those Havanas with the case of money open on the table: a million dollars, and all in Swiss francs, like some gangster film. We all felt terrific. It seemed very easy, just like Don had said it would be.'

She didn't know if it was using a gun again after so long, or seeing all that money on the table, or the brandy and cigars or what: Eva felt more confident than she had in a long time. In front of her, flocks of waterfowl were moving around on the lake and you could see the wooded hills on the other side reflected in the water. She would talk to Carlo about the divorce as soon as Don left. The chapter was closing. Things were starting to go her way again. She was so sure of this that she made the mistake of telling Don and Carlo that she had arranged to go and shoot targets in the hills the next day with Giulio. Carlo was appalled. 'But Eva,' he kept saying, 'don't you understand these people are criminals? That old man like a peasant, Tuccio – he can have people disappear like that!' and he snapped his fingers in the air.

'Giulio's only a kid, Carlo.'

'You're not to have anything to do with them – any of them.'

'Are you mad? We've just taken a million dollars off them.'

'I forbid you to see him, Eva.' He made Don get in touch with Tuccio and cancel the arrangement.

Eva didn't tell this part of the story to Larry. On the face of it she could have told it, but the boy Giulio had been so good-looking that she preferred not to. All the time she had been with Carlo she had never gone off with anyone like she had in the old days. In some way being pregnant had changed all that for her. The incident with Giulio would have only confused things.

Don wanted them all to stay at the house but Carlo insisted on going back to Rome that evening. It clearly frightened him even to remain for the night in a place where Tuccio and his people had been. Don drove back with them. All the way in the car Eva was thinking that she would ask for the divorce immediately they were alone; but in the event when they got to the flat she was overcome with nervousness and decided to wait until their 'quiet period'. And so began a routine of procrastination which she tried day after day to break with. Time and time again she watched herself, as if hypnotized, lie down on the bed in a state of nerves as Carlo got the Adam and Eve box out of the drawer in the magot chinois, knowing she could speak any minute, but deciding to wait until they'd smoked the first pipe, and then the second . . . In contrast with what she'd been led to believe about opium, it didn't muddle her brain in the slightest. On the contrary, she could see even more clearly, as through a newly cleaned window, that it was her will-power, not her intelligence, which was eroded by the drug. It was like Rosa Agambo had said. The will was corruptible, like a liver or a tooth. She could see that quite clearly.

As the months went by, her life settled into a rhythm. She got up late and dawdled around the apartment. They had lunch around two, cooked by Graziella. After lunch there was a little siesta, and then she went to the paper shop on the Piazza di Spagna where the English papers were reserved for her. She started piano lessons in the afternoons: she had a vague idea that she could make a record with people she knew in England, when she got divorced. Sometimes she had tea with a friend. Then at about seven she and Carlo retired to their room for their 'quiet period'. Nobody was allowed to disturb them here: at the far end of the corridor which led to their bedroom the tall double doors were closed and locked. In summer the light was at its most beautiful outside the window. The roofs and cupolas of the city were spread out before them: the trees of the Pincio gardens, the twin domes of the Piazza del Popolo, the brick campanile of San Giacomo. As evening came on, the pine trees went almost black and the red tiles looked soft and mottled beneath a forest of television aerials; above them the swallows dove and swooped and the bats flitted nervously. Their friends and guests sometimes laughed and hinted delicately about the cloistered joys of married life: some of them probably believed it. For Eva the whole succession of such evenings merged into one single occasion in her memory; and of even that one time she had only the most fleeting recall, like those sensations of the past which can be conjured by a piece of music: a long-stemmed pipe with a silver bowl, heavenly elation, and a sense of growing intimacy as the light closed down around them. She had no idea what had been spoken, if anything was said at all. And just as the light of that single unified evening closed gradually down, so did the light of the year become gradually darker, and at some stage – though she had no recollection of exactly when – a candle was lit, and then another and another, until they were sitting down to smoke surrounded by candles with the smell of chestnuts bought from a street brazier lingering in the still and perfumed air of the oriental bedroom, and the heavy red velvet curtains hanging in deep folds to the floor. The only things she could remember about taking opium were the times when they didn't have it. Apart from that, a year seemed like a day to Eva, just as an hour seemed like a year.

Time passed. She lost confidence. Since her miscarriage she shunned the endless streams of people who formerly visited the apartment. When Rosa's film was being shot a little of her confidence had come back because when she was working there were things that had to be done, people that had to be seen, there was a structure to her life. When Carlo gave a dinner party at the flat she even enjoyed herself, almost like in the old days. But when the shooting was over she retreated again, turning the flat into an island of quiet. And when the film came out it was even worse because she realized she wasn't good in it. She read all day on the balcony in her dressing-gown, putting off from one meal to the next the moment to start practising the piano. She had her first hallucinations. At Fernia, coming into the shuttered bedroom, she switched on the light and saw a silver girl lying on the bed who looked like herself. She stared at it and the apparition faded. At the time she thought it was the effect of the changes of light on her sluggish eyes – the glare of the garden, the gloom of the corridors, the dim yellow lamps of the bedroom; but other hallucinations followed in the ensuing months. They always went away if she stared at them.

What frightened her more were the premonitions. The first time she could remember it happening was in a church in Trastevere where she had stepped in to get out of the rain. On the wall there was a fresco of St John the Divine, pointing towards a riband floating in the air, on which a Latin text identified itself as REV.XX:XV. Her curiosity aroused, she made her way to the lectern and opened the Bible at the end. As she read, she felt her heart begin to race and her skin to prickle unpleasantly: 'AND

WHOSOEVER WAS NOT FOUND WRITTEN IN THE BOOK OF
LIFE WAS CAST INTO THE LAKE OF FIRE.'

As soon as she got home Carlo said, 'Eva, I have some bad news
for you. Your mother rang to say that your dog died yesterday.'

Johnson! That day she had the first of her attacks of shaking.
Carlo took care of her, putting her to bed and making up a little
pipe of opium for her to smoke. He soothed her and sat with her
until the shakes began to subside. He was very good to her. He
was always very good to her.

One day Maria Beckman rang up. She wanted Eva to join her
in Venice for the Carnival. 'Dog's not coming,' she said, 'we're
separated now. There are going to be lots of men but I'm afraid
they'll all be gay. Still, Venice is always heaven. I'm getting my
costume from the theatre shop. They don't allow you to hire from
them normally if you aren't stage but Scrope set it up for me. Do
you think I should be Cleopatra or Marilyn Monroe? Scrope sends
his love.' And Eva thought: I'll go on my own. Then when I come
back I'll tell Carlo I want the divorce.

Under normal circumstances it might have been difficult to
prevent Carlo from coming with her, but this time luck was on
her side. The planning application to re-zone the abattoir land
was going to have its final hearing and he would certainly have
to remain in Rome. Since Don had disappeared back to the States
Carlo had become quite an expert on the technicalities of planning.
He was more and more obsessed by the scheme.

'Yes, of course, go to Venice,' he said, 'and by the time you get
back I hope I'll have good news for you.'

It had become more important than ever that this should be
so, because contrary to what Don had told them, the site itself
appeared to be worth only a fraction of what they had paid for it.
In fact, in his gloomier moments, Carlo wondered if they would
be able to sell it at all.

Venice was cold. Carnival figures wandered aimlessly around the
streets in Wellington boots. In St Mark's, duckboards had been
laid down to make walkways. Eva and Maria stayed with American
friends of Maria's parents on the Grand Canal. A private boat took
them to landing stages decked with lanterns from which ancient
stairways led up to frescoed ballrooms.

Maria had changed. She had given up drugs and dyed her hair
blond. She looked older. And how fat she had become! When she

was slim Maria had been cute and pert; now she was buxom she looked much coarser. But she hadn't lost all her old fire. She sat with Eva in their shared bedroom and gossiped about London, her split-up with Dog, and the people they were staying with.

'I'm on the look-out for a new beau,' she said. 'Not a man so much as a pretty boy. I find I prefer them very young these days. I suppose it's a sign of age. I was having an affair with Hugo Cram's younger brother Crispin. He's only eighteen, absolutely divine, but his father sent him to Australia. It was all a bit of a secret because I wasn't supposed to have a boyfriend at that time – it's part of the programme, you know. But doesn't that just make it all the more exciting? I suppose I'm rather immature really, what do you think? By the way, I saw Scrope the other day and he told me about Johnson being shot. It must have been a terrible shock for you.'

'What do you mean shot?'

'My God, didn't you know? The new gamekeeper shot him in the swimming pool. He must have thought Johnson was a stray or something.'

They were having dinner in a house on the Grand Canal. Eva couldn't remember who their host was, though she remembered Maria saying to someone when they arrived, 'I like your house. But couldn't you get a motor for that boat in the hall?' Inside, the house seemed to be exactly like several others they'd been to that evening; unless it was the same one they kept coming back to each time. Maria was dressed as Marilyn Monroe. She had on a low-cut dress out of *Gentlemen Prefer Blondes*. Her bosom, pushed up by a special brassière, certainly had a Fifties' look, but her waist was too thick, and her tiny mouth, even with lipstick, didn't approximate to the wide smile of the actress. She was still as self-obsessed as she used to be, only now the obsession took the form of analysis, with her interlocutor cast in the role of analyst. 'Of course, all the time I was taking smack I didn't remember a damn thing about what I'd said or done. I mean, people keep coming up to me and saying that I've got so much nicer but honestly I can't remember being horrible to anyone. It's such a self-destructive thing that you do all these awful things without hardly even knowing it. It's only when other people at Broadway start saying about what they did that you sort of remember, or at least realize, what a burden you've been to everyone all along. I don't see Dog, of course. It would be impossible. In any case, he has to realize for himself that he needs help. I don't want to enable him to go on the way he is. We've got to split up now, you see. When you're junkies and you get married you don't really know each other at all; I mean, smack's the thing, that's all. But then when you stop taking it you might find you really don't have anything else at all in common.' Eva had heard all this in their bedroom when she arrived and she was hearing it again now across the table. Maria's voice was as strident as ever. It almost drowned out the young man on Eva's right who was trying to talk to her about a new museum in Venice – a topic of conversation she had been through so many times since her arrival that she was already sick of it. What hell this all was. She hated this carnival which sought only to imitate its own past. She hated Maria for being such a bore. And she resented her because it seemed she had succeeded in some way where Eva had failed. In what way had she succeeded? Yes, that was it: she had stepped out of her marriage. But wasn't Eva going to do the same thing when she got back to Rome?

The young man on Eva's right had moved on to the Venice Film Festival; at least, Eva assumed it was the Venice one, though she hadn't really been listening. 'You're in Rosa Agambo's new film, aren't you?' he was saying. 'I've heard a lot about that. Apparently it's very original.'

Eva knew that when she left Carlo she couldn't go back to her parents. Her pride wouldn't let her do that. In fact it would be better if she stayed out of England altogether from that point of view. She would have to get a job here in Italy. But what sort of job could she get? And who would help her? She knew no one here who wasn't more Carlo's friend than her own. In the old days she could have fended for herself, like she had when she ran away from school to the South of France. But she was not sure she could still do that. In Rome she was often afraid to leave the apartment. 'As a matter of fact I'm on the board,' the young man was saying. Was he talking about the film festival or was he back on the museum again? And in virtue of what was he on the board of either? He looked too young and ineffective to be a director. She had a vague idea his family owned some huge corporation: she had heard Maria talking about a young man of incredible wealth whom everyone was worried about because he was a junkie. Perhaps she should ask him for some heroin . . . on the other hand, he didn't look like a junkie.

'It's an attempt to document and conserve the history of documentation and conservation,' the young man was saying. 'A museum of museums. Naturally Venice presents itself as the ideal location, but it concerns all Europe, really . . .' If he was the one she was thinking of she remembered somebody saying he had been put in the charge of a priest who specialized in drug addicts, known as Padre Pica. 'A power greater than ourselves.' Maria had said they got off junk by believing in that. Was it a question of replacing one's own rotted will with the will of God? It seemed too like a conjuring trick to be real. The difficult thing was to change oneself, to make decisions and enact them, to create one's own destiny. None of that seemed to amount to a 'power greater than ourselves', as God seemed to be known familiarly these days. Across the table, Maria's companion was showing her how to eat a persimmon, and Maria had managed to turn the whole performance into a flirtation. As usual with her, it was hard to tell how much she really wanted to go to bed with him, and how much was just for histrionic effect.

Eventually their hostess stood up and led them through into the main salon for coffee. It was a long room, slightly austere, with painted panels and rather poor chandeliers, and a marble floor. The party seemed diminished by its spaciousness, and perhaps to compensate for this they all sat down at one end, by the windows looking on to the canal. The curtains and shutters were open and one could make out through their bottleglass panes, slightly distorted, the floodlit façades of the palaces across the way, and their reflections in the black water, intermittently embroiled by water taxis and vaporetti. Maria was on the sofa with her dinner companion. She said to Eva, 'By the way, guess who Polly Fort's new amour is? An old flame of yours.' Eva knew at once what this meant, but she said, 'Which old flame?'

'Son-of-a-preacher-man Larry. They hold hands at dinner. It's adorable.'

Eva took her coffee and went to the far end of the room, pretending to look at the pictures. She knew there would be a ball to go to later that night. But even the prospect of a change of cast didn't really excite her, because she felt she knew already the people she was going to meet and the sort of conversation she was likely to have, and these were the same as she would find any night of the week in Rome. She observed the scene at the far end of the room. Everyone was lying back in their sofas and chairs, replete with food and drink. They were all older than her, at that comfortable age, late 30s, early 40s. *Nel mezzo del cammin*. Dante had been 35 when he wrote that. She remembered Larry struggling through it by the swimming pool, writing his neat marginalia with the thick Mont Blanc propelling pencil with its white star on top. How easy everything seemed then! How little importance they had attached to anything! And now, only two years on, she was married and Maria had become a teetotaller and Larry was fucking Polly Fort! Couldn't he at least have found somebody new? There was something terribly second-hand about his taking up with Polly, as if he couldn't be bothered to look any further than the old circle. Would they all end up marrying each other? She felt old, like the people around her. They were all too full and comfortable to move, and the women were no longer all that attractive to the men. Beyond them, in the bottleglass window, a patch of colour flared. Fireworks? She went over to the drinks tray and poured a big shot of J & B. She could hear the others talking about a ball, the words, '*Sala da ballo stupenda, del settecento, proprio da impazzire, con la Contessa Branalozzi in maschera da Medusa . . .*' were followed by a hail of laughter. Yes, they would talk about the ball now, and in a few years the house and garden. Still clutching her glass, Eva slipped out of the room. She was in the small sitting room at the top of the stairway now and she could still see the others through the tall doorway, whose double doors stood open. An old woman servant carrying a tray went through to the long room, and returned with the coffee pot and cups. She said to Eva, 'Is there anything you want?'

'I'd like my coat please,' Eva said. 'I want to step outside for a minute and get some air.'

'Certainly, signorina.' The woman returned with her coat.

'Are you feeling all right?' she asked. Eva realized she was shivering.

'Just a little chilly. But it's all right. Please don't disturb anyone on my account. It sometimes comes over me. Fresh air will take it away.'

She went down the dark stairway with her whisky in hand into a courtyard with trees in tubs and a statue of a bearded man. The statue had a ghostly appearance in the half-darkness, its features leprous with exposure to the salt air of the lagoon. Suddenly it turned crimson and a mass of curls detached themselves around its head: a rocket burst overhead and a huge red flare burned foggily in the sky, drifting away on its parachute, and coming clear as it did so of the cloud banks. The sky returned to blackness. But as if the firework had lit some chemical reaction, big flakes began to fall, singly at first, but gradually becoming more numerous, settling like white moths all round her in the trees, and on the pavings and the statue, sugaring the ground where the light fell through the windows, silently and heavily, till the air began to be thick with it. For a moment she stood and watched, the flakes falling on her head as they fell on the statue's; then she pushed open the gate and slipped into the street. At uneven intervals along it, bracketed street lamps lit up whirling globes of snowflakes like glass blizzards. From a house nearby the bass line of some pop music emanated from another party. Presently a gaggle of figures emerged and began to walk in her direction. In the pools of light she could distinguish details of the group: a cat mask, with a body stocking and a long tail which it carried in its hand, a youth of about 20, astonishingly handsome, carrying a trident and wearing Wellington boots, a girl dressed as the Queen of Hearts, with a crown on her head and a huge painted playing card strapped to her front. She wore a red mask over her eyes. Beside her two great birds stood out above the rest of the group, resplendent with iridescent feathers and trembling crests. One had a bill like a parrot, the other a long spiky beak like a marsh bird, though Eva didn't recognize either of them as belonging to any species. As they approached she could see their faces looking out from holes in their necks; but when they turned to look at her she found her gaze inexorably drawn upward to their long beaks and their eyes made from sequins. She felt a little afraid, as though the costumes were telling her something. Further down the street a rocket veered downwards across the rooftops with a whirling sound and disappeared.

'Eva.' She heard a voice behind her and turned around. Maria was standing in the doorway. 'Wait a minute, the others are on their way down.'

'I don't want to go with them.'

'But we're going to the ball, you said you wanted to go to the ball.'

'I don't any more. I just want . . .' She saw that the group of revellers was at the end of the street, about to go out of sight round the corner.

'Yes, Eva? What do you want?'

'Oh, I don't know!' she shouted, throwing her glass down on the ground so that it shattered. The whisky made black holes in the snow. From the hallway, the clack of heels on marble and sounds of boisterous laughter preceded the plume-breathing guests into the garden.

'*Eva! Eccola! State scappando, voi due?*'

'*Ahi! Aiuto!*'

One of the ladies was standing on the threshold like someone on the bank of a swift-flowing river, unwilling to venture her white satin shoes and the bottom of her dress across the snow-wet surface of the paving stones; a bevy of men alternatively exhorted her to walk and offered to carry her; someone put up an umbrella to protect her head and it became jammed in the doorway. Eva ran out of the gate, skidded and fell. Among a chorus of shouts people dashed towards her as she picked herself up off the snow, wet, shocked and smarting from the fall. She hobbled away down the street saying, 'Leave me alone!' Inwardly, she cursed the pain in her right knee which prevented her from going faster. Her heart was beating hard and she was trembling. At the end of the street she saw the carnivaliers on the landing stage of the vaporetto, and the boat arriving at the quay. She hastened towards them, and shouted for them to wait, but the thick snowfall and the noise of the engine drowned out her voice. The boatman didn't see her as he loosened the rope from the capstan, and when she got there the vessel had already pulled away, though it was still almost stationary. She could see the cat man pass a bottle to the Queen of Hearts. The handsome boy with the trident saw her and waved, and the others all waved and blew kisses, and the boat took them away into the darkness, laughing and drinking out of their bottle.

The room where she and Maria slept must have been a maid's room at one time. It was at the top of the house, at the back, and it contained a wardrobe, a wooden table and two beds with painted bedheads. Through the window she could see the snowflakes and up in the sky the fireworks going off. The display seemed to originate from a point not far away from her. Surely the damn things would be over soon, she thought. She was still trembling, whether from cold or fear she didn't know. She had a pain in her chest.

She knew she had brought them with her but they weren't in her sponge-bag. She looked in her handbag and then in the pockets of the clothes she had hung in the cupboard. Eventually she found them in the side pocket of her travelling case: painkillers which she'd taken from Carlo's medicine cupboard before she left. She shook out two and swallowed them with a glass of water and drew the light cotton curtains across the window. Then she got into bed and pulled the covers up to her chin. Larry and Polly Fort. Johnson in the swimming pool. The fireworks flashed and flared against the flimsy cotton curtain. She had tried to close the shutters of her room but the hinges were all rusted up. Now she was unable to sleep. She was still trembling and she didn't know why. Dear God, let it not be one of her trembling fits. The explosions outside were as loud as guns. She remembered November the fifth at Clermont, her father crouched down beside the fuses in the blackness, his hawk-like face with its jutting brow lit up ghoulishly from below by the taper he shielded in his hand. She remembered being a child, the terrifying noise of the detonations, running and stumbling on the tussocky park, her knees and hands wet and muddy, picking herself up, her short legs struggling across the great expanse, the boom of the rockets, the steps, tugging at the big door handle above her head, her dash to the library door and then the couple on the sofa, her mother's face, Alexei Menelov on top of her with his trousers down: Alexei Menelov, her mother's lover and her own father.

The next morning she woke late. Her head felt terrible and she was so weak she could hardly stand up. Maria put her back into bed and fetched a thermometer. She had 40 degrees of fever. She stayed four days in bed before she was well enough to go back to Rome.

At Palazzo Spinelli her little yellow car was in the courtyard. It had been broken down for months now and the garage said it was not worth the price of a new engine. That was one thing she wouldn't be taking back to London. In fact, there was nothing she wanted to take back with her. The Jaguar was parked almost opposite. That didn't necessarily mean Carlo was in, but she steeled herself in any case. The lift took her up.

He was sitting in the kitchen with his elbows on the table. There was music playing on the radio so he didn't hear her come in. His head was in his hands and he was staring blankly at the empty formica surface in front of him. She switched off the music and he looked up. His expression was so forlorn it was as if he knew already what she was about to say to him. Eva hesitated. Perhaps if she put it off till they had their quiet period it would be easier for him, and in addition she would have the clarity of mind which came with opium.

He said, 'How are you?'

'Fine, really fine. It must have been some bug that's all over Venice.'

'Did the Bartons look after you?'

'Wonderfully. And Maria stayed on specially. She was very kind.'

'I was worried about you.'

'There was no need to be.'

They were talking like strangers. He must know. She had never seen him so phlegmatic and grave. She said, 'Shall I make coffee?' One of the things she was going to give up when she divorced Carlo was coffee, but there was no point in starting now. There would be plenty of time for that when all this was over.

Carlo nodded. She got a handful of beans out of the jar and let them run out of the side of her hand into the grinder. She lit the gas. Apart from anything else it was unusual to find him sitting in the kitchen. Suddenly he said, 'Eva, I have some bad news for you. The zoning permission. We've been refused.'

'Refused altogether?'

'That's right.'

'But why?'

'They didn't say. Just turned it down flat. No appeal. Apparently they don't have to give reasons.' He seemed completely broken by this setback.

Eva said, 'There must be something it can be used for. Even if it can't be developed it still must be useful for something. It's only a question of finding out what.'

It was one of Carlo's most irrational as well as one of his most touching characteristics that a few simple words of encouragement could make him quite optimistic for no real reason at all. He was like a child in this way. It was sufficient to divert his attention from whatever was making him unhappy and, in a matter of minutes, he could become quite gay and cheerful again. When she said this, about finding another use for the land, he cheered up enormously, as though she'd brought him a piece of good news, or as if she somehow had a better grasp of the situation than he did himself.

'Do you really think so, Eva?'

'Why not? I mean, we haven't even looked yet. Probably once we begin we'll find something right away.'

'Really? Well, perhaps you're right: perhaps we can sell the thing in any case and pay off the debt to Tuccio and then we can go to Fernia for the summer! Of course! In a month or so we may have forgotten the whole thing!' He stood up and began to pace up and down the kitchen. His whole demeanour had changed and she knew he would be quite cheerful in a minute. She also knew that in reality it would not be so easy. They were bound to have problems selling the abattoir now the zoning had been refused. And even if they did manage to arrange this and hand over the whole of the money to Tuccio, they wouldn't be going to Fernia together, because she was going to leave him. It didn't seem right to tell him that now, though. His vulnerability was pathetic and in a way sympathetic: she considered how hurt he had been by Annette and Martina. People said even the dancing girl in India had treated him badly.

She went into the bedroom. After a few moments he came and sat down on the end of the bed, smoking a cigarette and looking out of the window. Beside her on the brass tray lay the box with Adam and Eve on the lid and the ivory-stemmed pipe.

'Ah, Eva,' he said. 'What would I do without you, my precious, my jewel?'

Larry was looking at her. She realized she had told him none of this, though she would have liked him to know. But there was a look of alarm on his face. He took his jacket off the back of his chair and said, 'You're shivering. Here, put that around you.'

— 15 —

When the bill came Larry took it and put it together with a 100,000 lire note on the little dish; but Eva snatched it up.

'They haven't put on the tax.'

Larry was not paying attention. He was wondering about the conference tomorrow, and whether he would cover it after all, or whether he would spend the day with Eva.

The waiter came to take the money. Just as he was about to pick it up, Eva slapped her hand down hard on the dish.

'One minute,' she said. 'Where's the tax?' The waiter took the bill and began to explain that among the indecipherable items listed there was a charge to VAT.

'It's not true,' Eva said. They were beginning to attract attention.

The waiter said, 'Signora, I'll go and verify it immediately.'

'This isn't a *ricevuta fiscale*!' Eva insisted. 'I want a proper *ricevuta* with the tax marked clearly on it. Now take this away and bring me a real one.'

The waiter fled into the kitchen.

'Well,' said Larry. 'What was all that about?'

'They're trying to trick us.'

'What do you mean?'

'In this country they have inspectors outside the restaurants.'

'But Eva, if we get caught without a *ricevuta* it's the restaurant that gets the rap, not us.'

'No. They already planted money on Carlo. They're after us.'

'Who are?'

'The tax people.'

'Listen, Eva. Just relax, OK? This is my bill and I'm the one who's going to get into trouble if anybody does. In any case, you know them here, don't you?'

'I'm sorry. I don't know what's come over me.' She was flushed, and in spite of his jacket about her shoulders she was still shivering. He wondered if she had a fever.

The bill came and he paid it. He took her arm and they began to walk back to her flat. Whatever was on Eva's mind now, she was finding it hard to explain to him. Probably she didn't quite know what it was herself. If Spinelli wasn't back tomorrow he would skip the conference and spend the day with her and talk it all over, try to find out what was the matter. They reached the big coach door of her building. Eva said, 'Come to Fernia with me. Please.'

'What do you mean?'

'Right now. I have to go there now!'

'But why on earth?'

'Please come with me. You can stay in the spare room. We can even come back tonight if you want.'

'Come back tonight? But why?'

'I'm afraid to stay in the flat on my own. An awful thing happened to me here.'

'What awful thing?'

'I'll tell you about it when we get to Fernia. Please come with me, Lily. I'm so afraid.'

It was strange that she used that name after all this time, and yet it didn't sound strange. Larry took the keys of the Jaguar from her and they got in.

It was his confidence, Eva thought, that kept him safe. Bad luck smelt out fear like an animal. Yes, and like a school of sharks disasters smelt out death. Hence Johnson in the swimming pool; and the miscarriage. God knows, if Larry wasn't with her now she would be afraid; but at his side she felt safer, as if his confidence and luck protected her. They left the autostrada and the car span across the coastal plain on narrow country roads, the headlamps picking up the green verges. Outside their beam the grass and rushes looked grey under the moonlight.

'ATTENTI AL CANE!'

The signs were newly painted with a picture of a dog's head on them, and the headlights picked them out at intervals along the fence. The fence itself was a forbidding affair, five metres high with spiralling barbed wire on top. They pulled up at the gate.

'Christ!' he said. 'Is this it?'

'This is it.'

'It looks like a prison.'

'It's meant to be automatic, but they haven't connected that yet. So I have to unlock it.'

She got out of the car and fitted a key into the lock. When Larry drove through he noticed that she locked it again after him. In front of him in the beam of the headlights he could see the square façade of the yellow house with its green shutters. Cypresses and pines clustered on either side. Eva got back in and slammed the door. The drive was full of potholes and the car bumped slowly towards the house.

'Where's the dog?' Larry said.

'There isn't one. I just put the signs up to scare people off. I'd like to have one. The trouble is, if anyone is going to break in they usually poison the dogs first. So in a way it seems cruel to have them at all. Especially when you know there are people after you.'

Larry stopped the car outside the front door. He said, 'But nobody is after you, Eva. It's all in your imagination. And there's been no money planted on Carlo. I think you must know that really, in your heart of hearts. Because it's quite clear, even to me, that the money he was caught with at the frontier was the money your trusts paid for the two houses. You're upset. Maybe you should take a couple of weeks off, go and stay with Scrope, think things over. I think you need a rest.'

Eva suddenly felt calmer. Of course he was right. She should have known it wasn't a plant all along. It was obvious if you thought about it. But why then had Carlo told her it was? She said, 'You're probably right. But they really are after us, I'm not imagining that. Listen, will you have a drink with me? There's something I want to tell you.'

They went inside and Eva got a bottle of Russian vodka out of the fridge and a couple of glasses.

'You take these into the garden,' she said. 'I'm just going upstairs for a minute.'

Larry found his way through the house and opened the shutters of the garden door. Above him the night was starry and clear. The sawing noise of cicadas filled the darkness, and behind that he could discern the faint swishing of the sea. On his left he saw the pool with the summer-house beside it. As he approached, a frog dropped invisibly into the water and a faint ripple flickered across its surface. He watched as it regained its composure, and the wobbly stars reappeared, infinitely distant, the great highway of stars which stretched across the sky and which was our own galaxy: us, the sun and a hundred thousand million other stars, all revolving about their galactic centre.

He didn't see her as she came towards him from the house. He was still looking down into the pool with his hands in his pockets, and although she couldn't see his face at all well she could infer from his whole stance its brooding expression. He was a little heavier than when she had last known him, and a little thicker in the chest, but it made him look strong and she thought it suited him. There was a certain roughness about him which had to do with his slightly unkempt manner of dressing and his unselfconsciousness. It was very un-Italian.

'Ah, Eva, there you are.'

'What are you brooding about?'

'I was looking at the stars.'

She remembered how he used to know all the names of the constellations. He had learnt them from his father in Africa. She said, 'Tell me what they are.'

Larry looked up into the sky and pointed to the broad arc of the Milky Way.

'It's our galaxy. Try to think of it as a saucer which you're looking at end on. Of course, there are billions of other galaxies.'

'No, Lily, I mean the constellations.'

'It's full of constellations. Look. There's Cepheus, Cassiopeia, Perseus . . .'

'I can never see them unless you go slowly. Come and sit down.'

They went to the table in the summer-house and he put down the bottle and glasses on the table. There was a candle here in a glass protective jar and Eva lit it.

'What have you got there, Eva?'

'It's Carlo's pipe. Very occasionally I have a smoke of this stuff. Shouldn't really. I'm supposed to have given it up.'

She held a spill in the flame of the candle and lit the pipe from it. The flame leapt up and down in front of her face, illuminating in bursts her long nose, her fine brows and slanting eyes. How beautiful she was! At one time it had seemed to him there was nothing in the world more important than this wide mouth with its heavy lips, those slightly crooked teeth. And yet now that he was here Larry did not feel impelled to become involved with her again. He saw she was in trouble, but he saw too that she had always made trouble for herself and always would, and it would be foolish to pretend otherwise. At one time that had seemed almost like a challenge, but now it was only pitiable.

She finished the pipe and made another. He thought that with all this opium and the enormous amount of vodka she had drunk she would probably soon fall asleep, but that night there was something keeping both of them awake. And as though a tap had been turned on, she suddenly began to talk.

'Carlo was away and I was sitting in the bedroom. It was about seven in the evening, the time when we usually have a bit of a rest. Carlo smokes opium then; not me, I've given it up. Still, as it happened that day, being alone and feeling lonely, I had smoked some, in fact I'd had a lot. I was lying there dreaming, when it seemed that I heard men's voices speaking in the sitting room at the end of the corridor. At first I think I must have assumed it was Carlo. I don't think it occurred to me that Carlo was away – but anyway I didn't care in the least who it was. The doors at the end of the corridor were locked as they always were during our quiet period: at this time of day nobody came to the bedroom. Then, still from the direction of the sitting room, I heard a crack like a shot, and like a shot it seemed to enter into me, and reverberate there. It was actually the sound of the door splintering as the men kicked it in. Next thing they were in the room. There were two of them. One was fat and ungainly, a piggy man with a big mouth; the other was of medium height and looked like a weasel. They seemed taken aback to see me lying on the bed. I didn't move. I wasn't sure at first if they were real or imaginary. They were so like animals, it was like seeing Beatrix Potter characters in a violent movie. But I wasn't afraid. I was waiting to see if they would change into something else, or disappear, or what. Then one of them said, "It's his woman." And the other one said to me, "Stand up." They put a blind over my eyes and tied me up and laid me back down on the bed. I thought they were going to rape me, but in fact they just left me there. I was there all night until Graziella came in the morning. I suppose I was lucky, really. Apparently those sort of people don't mistreat women. But you can imagine how scared I was. As soon as the blind was on I went down into hell. I saw the souls of the dead sitting round like birds, and the colonies of bats, and the tortures of the damned. It seemed like I was there for eternity. In fact, I thought I had died. When Graziella came in the morning she cut me loose, but I couldn't explain to her what had happened. I guess I was a bit incoherent. Then I went into the bathroom. Lady Macbeth was lying in the tub with her throat cut. They'd written stuff on the walls in blood, about how Carlo had to pay his debts. You can't imagine how horrible it was.

'My first idea was to get out of that apartment. I told Graziella to go home and not to say a word to anyone about what had happened. The poor thing was as frightened as I was. It's not surprising she went back to her mother. Then I took the car and drove up here to Fernia to try and sort out in my head what I ought to do next. But I was too hysterical to think very clearly. When I got here I was afraid to go in the house. I kept thinking somebody would be dead. I kept imagining dead people in all the rooms of the house, with writing in blood on the walls. And in my head I kept on hearing again and again the crack which the door had made when they kicked it in. So I didn't go inside. I was crazy. I drove to the village and bought a bathing costume and a beach towel and a paperback and then I drove to the beach and parked the car at the camping ground, where the day-trippers go. I just pretended I'd come to the beach for the day. I didn't want anyone to think I was connected with the house. I stretched out my towel on the sand and lay down in the sun. The only trouble was there were two guys hanging around who realized I was on my own. First they stayed a little way off. I noticed they were looking at me but I pretended to read my book. It took them a while to get up the courage to come and talk to me. I was just reading my book, or pretending to, and I thought I'd pretend I didn't understand them. But then I realized I couldn't do this because the book I was reading was in Italian and they were bound to notice. Sure enough, the first thing they said was, "What are you reading?" They sat down on either side of me. You know, it's a funny thing, but I think if they'd sat down on the same side of me I could have got rid of them in the usual way, but when they sat down on both sides of me like that I was suddenly struck by the idea that they had come to take me to the house and tie me up there. I don't know why I did it, I started screaming like crazy about anything that came into my head, and I sat up and started to wave my arms around. I didn't know what I was saying. Anyway, I put the wind up the two boys – they slipped away like they didn't know who I was and I went on screaming because I couldn't stop now, and then in a bit I started crying. I didn't want anyone to come over and start asking me what the matter was, so I managed to get into the sea and wade out till I was up to my shoulders in the water. I felt less conspicuous here and I got control of myself again. It was good to be able to swim. If you swim for long enough your fingers go crinkly and there isn't a scrap of dirt left on you anywhere, not a dirty nail. I felt clean. I knew I was just keyed up about Lady Macbeth and the men coming into my room, but I didn't feel like hanging around on the beach now everybody had seen me screaming and carrying on so hysterically. So I went back to the car park and took off inland towards the hills. I knew where there was a pretty nice restaurant where you could sit outside under the trees. I thought I'd go there and have lunch and then maybe drive around a bit till it was time to go back to Rome. I knew Carlo was going to be back some time that day.

'When I got to the restaurant I was too frightened to get out of the car. I tried telling myself that nobody could possibly know I was here, but it was no use. And I kept hearing the crack of the door breaking in my head. The only thing to do, I thought, is to drive back to Rome and get my gun. So I went back to the flat. I didn't dare go in the bathroom. I locked the door on the bedroom side and lay on the bed with the gun. I'd hardly been there ten minutes when there was a noise of somebody inside the flat. The first time I thought I heard sounds coming from the hall. Then I definitely heard steps in the corridor. I put the safety catch off the gun and fired two shots into the bedroom door. I screamed for them to get out of the flat or I'd shoot them dead this time. Then I heard Carlo's voice saying, "Eva, it's me, Carlo." I was crying so uncontrollably I couldn't explain to him what had happened, but he was very sweet to me. He took the gun away and sat on the bed with me until I'd calmed down. Then after he'd heard the whole story he said, "This is all my fault. And the worst part of it is that you're the one who's been hurt by it. For this I can never forgive myself. From now on I'm going to look after you completely, you've got nothing to worry about."

'That evening he insisted I share his opium pipe with him. We sat on the bedroom floor and smoked, and I must say it made me feel calm and happy for the first time. Whenever I smoked with him it always seemed as though things could be worked out between us.

He said, "It's all because of the abattoir. I expect you've guessed that by now. Tuccio wants us to pay back the money he lent us."

'I could hardly have failed to gather that much for myself. I nodded, and he went on.

'"We always planned to sell the abattoir if everything went wrong. I've been trying for months now, and I can't. The fact is that it's worthless, and Don knew that all along. He tricked us into buying it, there's no question about that. He was clever, because he sold us the idea before he even suggested there was a possibility we might come in on it. Do you remember how he used to go around saying making money was easy? He got us into the frame of mind where if we'd been asked to name a beautifully simple, hugely profitable enterprise, his abattoir scheme would have sprung immediately to mind. Only then did he suggest that we might be able to buy it ourselves. Anyway, there's nothing we can do about it now. Our problem is to pay back Tuccio's loan. Now what I suggest is this. The house at Fernia is worth a lot of money in today's market, and the flat in Rome is probably even more valuable. By selling both of them we could have almost all the money we need straight away. The only problem is that we wouldn't have anywhere to live. Now your trustees have refused to advance you a large sum of money, and from their point of view that's quite defensible. But would they refuse to buy you a house if you had nowhere to live? That would be much more difficult. So I say, why don't you ask your trustees to buy you the house, and even the flat as well? That way we still have somewhere to live and we can pay these gangsters their money."

'He looked at me and drummed his rings on the rim of the brass tray. I noticed how hollow his eyes were, and how his quick, bird-like movements were the twitching of a man haunted by death.'

Yes, and for a moment she imagined she saw the angel of death standing behind him, a tall man with a sword in his hand and long curling hair made out of bronze; but the vision disappeared as quickly as a thought. Of course, they were both going to die now, their life together had been nothing but a preparation for this. Their child had died first: that had been a kind of preparation. Then there was the opium-smoking, which removed you little by little from real life into eternity. These incredibly ugly and dangerous men, it was entirely natural that they should have broken into the flat and tied her up. Death attracts such people and draws them near. It was perfectly probable if her trustees really did have that much money that they would buy the houses for her and the mobsters would take the money and leave them alone; but this was only one incident. There would be more. Death was inside them already, and they attracted death from every corner, like a mink vixen drawing in her foxes across scores of miles of surrounding country.

Eva gave a little shiver. She raised the glass of vodka to her lips and drank it off.

'I said I didn't know if my trustees would have enough money, and Carlo said, "That's just about exactly what they do have." I suppose he'd spoken to my father at some stage, or maybe to Scrope. Anyway, he seemed to know. And he had to have it all now or he was a dead man. Of course, that was fine by me. I'd been just as fooled by Don as he had, and just as convinced about the abattoir; and though it's true I'd probably never have embarked on something like that on my own I certainly didn't blame it all on Carlo. I called my pa and asked him if it could be arranged with the trustees to buy the house and the flat. To my surprise there didn't seem to be any problem about this. Perhaps he was pleased to get it invested in this way because then I wouldn't be able to spend it. So the sale went through. The only hitch was to get the money to Switzerland where we'd agreed to pay it back. Unfortunately, because Carlo's an Italian citizen we couldn't have the trustees send the money there: the authorities over here would have considered it an export of currency, and that's not allowed because of exchange controls. So the money had to come to Italy, and we decided to smuggle it into Switzerland ourselves. So we went to the bank and got the whole lot out at once, in cash.

'The scene at the bank was grotesque. While we were waiting for them to bring the notes up out of the vaults Carlo and the bank manager sat there making social chit-chat about Capri as if nothing unusual was going on. Of course, large amounts of cash almost always signify something illegal somewhere along the line, and the bank manager knew it perfectly well, but we sat round chatting like we'd dropped in for tea while the wads of money were brought in and Carlo stashed them away in a brand new case he'd bought specially. I kept wanting to burst out laughing. The whole business made me feel light-headed, it was so silly. But I was happy too about the way things were turning out.'

She broke off and reached for the bottle of vodka. Her hand was not very steady and she didn't want Larry to see it, so she rested the neck of the bottle on the edge of her glass to make it easier to pour without spilling it on the table.

'The truth is,' she went on, 'that for a long time I've been wanting to split up with Carlo. And giving him my money made this seem much easier. I wanted him to keep the house too. I wanted him to have it all. The truth is that I never loved Carlo. It was a terrible mistake that I ever started an affair with him, worse than a mistake, because it wasn't even a wrong decision, but rather a lack of decision, I didn't ever intend to go to bed with him. I wasn't even attracted to him – physically, I mean; of course, everyone finds him attractive as a personality. But I just slid into it. We slept together a couple of times, then I was pregnant. I didn't want to get married even then, but he persuaded me to, and my parents persuaded me to, just for the sake of the baby. We were going to get divorced right away after the baby was born, it was understood. But then I could never bring myself to do it. The truth is that it's far more difficult to get yourself out of that kind of thing than to get yourself into it. For instance, how could I tell him I was walking out on him when his life was in danger? For one reason or another you have to keep putting these things off. I never had any intention of staying married to Carlo as long as I have; just as I never had any intention of marrying him in the first place; just as I never had any intention of having an affair with him. They say the road to hell is paved with good intentions, but it's not true: the road to hell is paved with no intentions at all. The worst of it all is that I know it's not Carlo who's to blame for any of this, but myself. In love the wicked person is often the one that's weak, like I've been. The truth is that weakness can cause as much suffering as strength. That's why I feel so guilty toward Carlo, and why it's been so hard to tell him that I want a divorce.

'I can see it all quite clearly now, and I have made my decision at last. I am going to leave Carlo. I can tell you this now because I'm going to tell him as soon as he gets back.

'I feel free again. It's an odd sensation. I feel like I've gone back three years in time to where I was when I started. Even with you nothing feels any different, it's all exactly the same, just as it was. The truth is . . .'

What was she saying? She realized she had said nothing, that only an instant had elapsed, that she still held the bottle of vodka over the glass in front of her on the table, about to pour.

'Well?' said Larry. 'The truth is what?'

'I can't remember,' Eva said. 'I can't remember what I was meant to be talking about.'

She poured, and the colourless liquid spilled over on to the table.

'You were saying you were happy about the way things were turning out.'

'That's right. He can have the money. I'm going to leave him. I'm really longing for it to be over. God, you can't imagine how I long for it. You can't imagine.'

She got up and walked over to the pool, glass in hand, and stepped on to the diving board. When she looked up the stars were turning unsteadily, the sky was sliding . . . she blinked, trying to make them stand still. Cepheus, Cassiopeia . . .

'Eva!' He jumped to his feet when he heard the splash, and ran across to the side of the pool.

'Are you all right?'

'Oh, hello, Lil. Are you coming in?'

He could see her moving around darkly in the water. Her shirt had billowed up palely behind her head. He said, 'Did you jump or fall?'

'I kind of slipped in off the board, I was watching the stars go round.'

She detached herself from the shirt which remained on the surface, held up by its air bubble. As she swam he could see her dark head moving across the rippled water, and occasional flashes of her white body underneath, like when a fish turns over in the river.

He took off his watch and slipped out of his trousers. He pulled at his shirt and the buttons came undone and he heard one tick on the pavings underfoot. In a moment he was naked, pushing out from the steps into the warm water. Suddenly everything had gone very quiet. He heard the gentle swish as she moved away from the shallow end towards him. Getting into the pool with her felt a bit like getting into bed. But of course they weren't getting into bed. They weren't doing anything at all except swimming about the pool quite separately. And yet it felt as though they were doing something very important, so important he found it difficult to breathe.

— 16 —

Eva always hated waking up in the morning. If Carlo was still in bed with her she would pretend to be asleep so he didn't try to make love; she detested this more than ever when she had just woken up. She was frightened of pregnancy too: her worst dreams were of waking up in the spare room and going into the lavatory and being sick. The best days were the days when the bed beside her was empty and Carlo already gone.

She looked at her watch. It was still only seven o'clock. She got out of bed and went into the bathroom. How many days had begun with the smell of coal-tar soap and the noise of a seashell in the lather on her hair? But this morning was different. It was different because for the first time in months – perhaps even in a year – she felt exhilarated at the thought of the day ahead.

She stepped out of the shower and took a big towel off the rail and dried herself. Then she wrapped it about her and combed her dark hair back so that it lay close to her head. She dropped her Alkaseltzers into a glass and ran some water on them. Out of the window the brick walls and the greenery of the garden still had pastel colours in the early light. It was relatively cool. The seltzer stopped its hiss and she drank it back. She cleaned her teeth. When she went back in the bedroom Larry was still asleep. Let him sleep now, she thought; she lifted the sheet and slipped in beside him.

They had coffee by the pool. They sat in the garden-house because by that time it was hot in the sun. Larry ate toast with apricot jam. Eva smoked a cigarette. The opium pipe and the little piece of opium were still lying on the table and when she finished her cigarette she made up the pipe and lit it. Larry said, 'D'you smoke that stuff all day?'

'Don't be silly. I hardly ever do. Anyway, this is nothing. You don't get high off one pipe in the morning. And it's organic, you know.'

'I know.'

'That's why I can take it or leave it. Do you know, it's much harder to give up coffee than this stuff.'

Larry said, 'When Maria Beckman came out of the clinic coffee was all she could have. She was so desperate for it she used to make it with warm water straight out of the tap. She couldn't even wait for the water to boil.'

'They're so boring, those people who've done the programme.'

'Oh, I don't know,' Larry said. 'They're not so bad as all that. Maria's become positively human.' He got up, and stepped out into the sunlight beside the pool. Eva's clothes from the night before lay on the bottom. He recalled the pool at Clermont the first time he'd seen it, through the ironwork gate of the garden, floodlit, with all the heads bobbing around in it and Dog sitting in a chair by the poolside because he couldn't swim. Then in November he had proposed to her there.

Eva said, 'Do you really think Papa will pay them?'

'He isn't stupid.'

'D'you think he can afford it?'

'Let's hope so.'

'He always says he'd never give money to blackmailers or kidnappers.'

'Luckily, this is a debt.' On the bottom of the pool he could see the glass she had been holding when she fell in. It was lying on its side, transparent and insubstantial.

Eva said, 'I have to talk to Carlo before I go.' That wasn't going to be easy. But it made her feel competent to be taking even an unpleasant decision.

Larry said, 'Yes, I suppose so.'

When they left the workmen were at the front of the house, putting the finishing touches to the automatic gate and the new surveillance installations. None of this would keep out Tuccio's people for very long, Larry reflected, but that didn't matter if her father paid them the money.

All across Rome the traffic crawled. Vendors walked down the lines of cars selling coloured cigarette lighters and paper handkerchiefs. Eva sat in the passenger seat with her feet on the dashboard. When she thought of taking her clothes off with Larry she got a constricted feeling in her throat. She looked at his arms and legs and immediately she wanted to touch him right here, in the car. The thought of it almost choked her.

In the flat the shutters were closed, the room seemed unusually cool. It was clear that Carlo had arrived, because his suitcase lay on the sofa in the sitting room, but there was no other sign of him. Eva went through into the bedroom and took the Adam and Eve box from the drawer in the belly of the magot. There was nothing in it; and the pain in her chest, dull and indistinct until now, welled up again suddenly. She returned to the suitcase and began to go through it, but she found nothing except a box from the chocolatier in Florence which he knew she liked. She put everything back and shut the case and lit a cigarette. She realized she was shaking. She could feel a wave of panic growing inside her. She inhaled deeply on the cigarette and felt a twinge of pain inside her lungs. It felt cold in here. She opened the door on to the balcony and threw back the shutters.

She knew immediately that it was a hallucination. Large birds of bluish black had gathered on the roof of the house opposite. Some had their heads turned to one side, and you could see their curved beaks; others sat face on, passive and unblinking as owls. A faint mephitis hung in the air, making her feel slightly nauseous. She thought she could make out pieces of carrion in their claws and hanging from their beaks. Behind them the sky to the east had filled with grey and was smudged with traces of blackening cloud like half-erased pencilling. She watched as the birds started to dissolve into zoophytic smudges resembling the clouds, and then became black spots in her vision. Suddenly she felt very faint. She went inside to the ice-box, got out the frosted bottle of vodka, unscrewed the top with a spin and gulped down the icy syrup as the cap bounced and danced on the floor like a spinning top. She steadied herself. The vodka burned its way into her stomach and chest. A stiffness in her neck and shoulders, which she had hardly been aware of before, relaxed itself. She upended the bottle again. The extreme cold of the frosted glass made her hand ache, but she held on to it tight, to stop the shaking.

After the drink the pain relapsed to a dull ache. But her confidence had gone. The hallucination, typical enough in itself, brought back all her anguish and uncertainty. Although Larry was only a few blocks down the road at his hotel, he suddenly seemed on a different planet, the past day spent with him like something outside her life, almost as remote as the time of their affair. She went into the spare room and got the letters out of the desk drawer and sat down on the bed.

. . . that I cannot bring myself to believe I said goodbye to you on the station only two months ago. It doesn't seem possible that you could have fallen in love with him so immediately afterwards; but if it is true, so be it. There is not a thing either of us could do about that. The only thing I beg of you – and I do it on my bended knees – is not to marry him out of weakness. You must realize that it is not easy for me to plead with you, since you have rejected me. But Eva, is it really Spinelli that you want? How long ago is it since we decided to live at the old mill at Castagna, the day you fell through the floorboards? How long since Santa Maria dell'Orto? Why don't you write?

She stuffed the letter back in its envelope and was about to return it with the others to the drawer when she changed her mind and put them into her handbag instead. Her hand was shaking again and she felt hot and flushed. She pulled off her T-shirt and stepped out of her skirt and went into the bathroom. The shower motor whirred and hiccuped. She stepped into the water and adjusted the temperature to cool.

She dried herself and put on a clean dress but she still felt shaky so she went into the kitchen and made herself a vodka martini. Where was Carlo? She decided to pack a suitcase, went into the box room and got a big blue one and brought it into the bedroom. She threw in clothes from all the drawers and cupboards, and when it was full she realized she didn't want any of these things and put them all back, crumpled and unfolded. Then she took the case back to the box room. Thank God Carlo hadn't come in and found her in the middle of that! And yet, in a way, wouldn't it have made it easier to broach the subject? She remembered the half-finished martini in the kitchen and went back to it and sat at the table looking at the paper. The headline was about the big demonstration planned for the next day, to coincide with the conference on nuclear power. The newsprint danced in front of her eyes. She knew that Carlo would make a scene and she knew that she wouldn't be able to stand it for very long and she would have to leave him then, or else stay married to him for ever. She wished she had left him before, when she got back from Venice. Even if it had only been for one or two nights that would have been better than nothing. At least it would have prepared the way. She thought to herself: was there really any point in going through with it all now? The scene was going to last for hours, she could see that; and it wouldn't really be settled in Carlo's mind for weeks, even months. Couldn't she just walk out and leave a note on the table? Was there any point in behaving 'well' when you were behaving badly? Wouldn't it make it quicker and easier to break it off if she did it in the worst possible way? Wasn't Carlo going to hate her anyway? The idea brought a sense of relief and was swiftly followed by another: it was certain that Carlo would find another girlfriend almost straight away. Like he had found Martina, Annette, Eva herself. It was like when she told him not to worry because things were certain to turn out all right: he soon forgot his troubles. He had a talent for rewriting his past as he went along. She thought of the plethora of stories about him; the iguana, the Black Masses on Capri.

When he arrived she was watching TV in the sitting room. He came in and kissed her and said, 'Home at last.'

'Are you OK, Carlo?'

'Fine. Prison wasn't that bad. In fact they were splendid to me. I got special treatment.'

He looked absurdly pleased by this, nodding vigorously. Eva said, 'Did you go to Florence on the way back?'

'Sure.'

'You got some?'

'Of course.' He patted his breast pocket. Eva immediately went into the bedroom and got the brass tray and the pipe and brought them back. He handed her a little lump wrapped in silver foil and she started to make up the pipe.

She smoked first. The pain in her chest went away, the air in the room settled to a comfortable temperature, she no longer was troubled by sweat or shivering. But more than any of this her confidence returned. Reflecting calmly on their situation she could see with the utmost clarity how things stood: she didn't love Carlo, she did, and always had loved Larry. There was really nothing to it except that. There could be no question of her staying with Carlo because it would do none of them any good. She would never be in love with him. The fact of her marriage was completely irrelevant.

She didn't have to die because she had married the wrong person. That was a mistake, not a death sentence. And Larry hadn't come here as a harbinger of death, but to deliver her.

Carlo said, 'We have to face it. Things don't look very good.'

'Carlo, why did you tell me the money had been planted on you? That was our money, wasn't it?'

'Don't be angry, my darling. I didn't want you to be frightened while I was in prison.'

'I'm not the least bit frightened. I've spoken to Larry and he says it can all be sorted out.'

'Larry says so?'

'Yes.' Suddenly she blushed deeply, and began to fiddle with the ashtray beside her. 'He says . . . I don't know. He's going to talk to Scrope.'

'You mean your family . . . ?'

'Yes. I mean, I don't know. I think maybe he can work something out.'

Carlo nodded encouragingly. 'That's good. That's very good. By the way, where is Larry?'

'He's in a hotel . . .'

'Why isn't he having dinner with us? Do you want me to call him?'

'Not now. He's probably eaten.'

'Really? Ah, well . . . in any case we can see him tomorrow.'

It seemed odd to Eva that they were both so confident that Larry could get them out of their predicament. After all, there was little he could do which they couldn't have done themselves. Once again she was thrown back on the idea of his confidence as a kind of protection. It was all a question of confidence, of keeping one's nerve.

The light faded in the flat. Outside, the storm broke which had been building up all evening. Between long silences great claps of thunder went off like bombs falling on the city. Carlo was preoccupied. As he made up the silver pipe he spoke a little about the arrest, and prison, but for the most part he was silent, unusually for him. She thought he looked old. The skin under his chin was slack, like an old man's.

It was midnight. They began to get ready for bed. Carlo had a bath with an evil-smelling homoeopathic essence. When he came out wrapped in a towel he was surprised to find her still fully dressed on the bed. He sat down beside her and began to undo the buttons on her shirt. She had to say it to him now.

At four in the morning, without a suitcase, her eyes swollen and on the verge of hysteria, she arrived at Larry's hotel. There was a farcical scene in which the night porter thought she was a prostitute and wouldn't let her upstairs. In the end Larry came down and gave the man some money and they went to his room.

'There are no seats on this evening's flight, signore. Do you want me to put you on the waiting list?'

'Yes please. And reserve two seats on the flight after that. When will that be?'

The girl tapped the keys of her terminal and peered at the screen. She had glasses with very thick lenses through which her eyes appeared shrunken to the size of little blue marbles. She said, 'Tomorrow at ten-thirty. Smoking or non-smoking?'

'Smoking.'

'What is the name of the person travelling with you?'

'S, P, I, N, E, double L, I.'

'First name?'

'Eva.'

Larry paid for her ticket and went out on to the hot street. He was wondering if he wasn't mad to be doing this, after everything he'd gone through to get her out of his system, and after all the times before when he'd taken her back only to see her slip away from him . . . What was it that drew him to Eva? She had always been fickle, destructive, addicted to instant gratification. She had taken everything from him and what had she given him in return? Polly had been loyal, generous, good-humoured – indeed, she had almost every good quality. Yet he had not been happy with her. If he didn't at least try to work things out now with Eva he felt he would spend his whole life sleeping with women he didn't love and not sleeping with the women he loved. He wondered if she was all right at the hotel. She had looked so vulnerable this morning as she stood naked at the end of the bed, holding a bottle of beer with her thin arm. Now he knew she was in real danger she seemed more fragile than ever, yet he didn't see what harm she could come to provided she stayed put and didn't try to go back to the flat. She wasn't even registered in the hotel room. And they would be gone soon, very soon if they managed to get on this evening's flight. In London they would go to his flat; it would be better not to go to Capilano Place. It was a good thing that apartment was going to be sold. Now they would have to make a completely fresh start.

Larry walked up to the top of the Via Veneto. The traffic was jammed solid in every direction. He crossed between the stationary cars and walked through the garden of the Villa Borghese. He became aware of a crowd chanting ahead of him to the left, and he realized it was the demonstration. The bridge into the Pincio was cordoned off by police, but he showed his press card and they let him through. The garden was crawling with police and there were four ambulances parked in a row at the back of the Casina Valadier. At the end of the garden by the parapet there was a huddle of press. He went over.

Beneath them the piazza was full of people. The crowd was a little thinner on the opposite side, but all in all it was a big turnout. From where the press were standing you looked right down on the stage from behind; some of the photographers were discussing how they could get down there again. Apart from this one shot there wasn't much action up here, and the back view of the stage would make it useless when the speeches began. Larry took some general shots of the scene.

Soon the chanting stopped and one of the speakers came forward to the microphone and received a long ovation. Then his voice began to boom out, very distorted by the amplification. Some youths had clambered up on to the base of the obelisk in the centre of the piazza and Larry took some shots of that. There was nothing much to it so far, but his professional reflexes were aroused in a mildly agreeable way. He smoked a cigarette with a man from *Repubblica* that he used to know in London. 'It is essential that we take control of our destiny,' the amplified voice rang out. 'The battle is not won or lost yet, the issue is still hanging in the balance. It is on your decision and your will that the future of your children depends. Nobody can say, "Nuclear escalation is inevitable." Nobody can say, "Nuclear war is inevitable".' The crowd broke into cheering and the chanting started up again.

— 17 —

'Vodka martini,' said Eva.

'Good evening, signora,' said the barman mournfully. 'And how's the Principe?'

'He's . . .' Dear God, what was she doing here when Larry had told her not to go out at all? They all knew her at this place, not only Settimio here and Paolo, the younger barman, but many of the customers as well . . . in fact it was one of the first places anyone might look for her. If she needed a drink she should at least have stayed away from her old haunts. And when Settimio asked after Carlo, was there a barely concealed mockery behind that impassive, jowled expression? She felt for Carlo's sake she must put a brave face on it.

'He's very well,' she said. 'He got back last night.' She had hoped that by being open and authoritative she would put an end to whatever insinuation Settimio's original enquiry had contained, but he added, 'It isn't going to finish badly, I hope.' Again, Eva couldn't make out what layers of meaning this outwardly bland statement might comprise. Was he alluding to their problems with the Mob? Did he mean their marriage? In a small place like Rome everybody knew everyone else's business. Many of the people in this bar cast sidelong glances at her, she thought, and looked at her from time to time. She couldn't understand why of all bars she had come to this one.

Settimio stirred impassively with a little glass rod and poured the cocktail through a strainer into the conical glass. He put the glass on the bar, squeezed a lemon peel above the surface and pushed it towards her. She took a swallow. The drink was perfect, the way only this bar out of all the city made them. Ah, Larry could wait while she had this one. The ache in her neck eased off. She had no pain in her chest today but there was an unpleasant knot in the pit of her stomach. Soon that would go away too. When she got back to London she would have herself checked over for cancer or ulcers or whatever it was. Her nerves were calming now, and she could see that Settimio had expressed nothing hostile or accusatory: on the contrary, his expression carried as it always did a hint of that spectral humour which was the hallmark of his conversation. Probably he hadn't even heard about her split-up with Carlo. After all, she hadn't told anyone except Larry. She twisted the little goblet by its stem on the glass counter. Beneath it, as in an aquarium, were ranged plates of little canapés: shrimps on mayonnaise, asparagus tips, lumpfish eggs, smoked salmon.

'Settimio,' she said, 'have you any pizza left?'

'Certainly.' He brought out a plate from the other end of the bar. 'Shall I warm it up for you?'

'Yes please.'

He picked a little slice off the plate with a pair of tongs and slotted it deftly between the walls of the toaster. Behind the impassiveness of his jowled face he sometimes gave the impression of thinking about higher things. But as if he had long ago submitted to the impossibility of conveying these to his customers, his conversation trundled along mundane, well-defined tramways. He said, 'Another martini, to accompany the pizza?'

'*Va bene.* Another martini.' There was easily time for this. It would have a calming effect on her. It was important that she thought clearly during the next twenty-four hours. Otherwise she was sure to ruin everything. She looked at her watch. Half past seven already! No wonder the bar was crowded with people! With a pang she thought of her quiet period at the flat, the oriental hangings and brass tray, the light fading outside the window. It was better not to think about that.

'Settimio,' she said. 'Can you sell me a quarter of vodka? You know, one of those little bottles.'

'Signora Principessa, you know we don't sell bottles.' He looked faintly amused at such a suggestion.

'But just this once. For me, as a favour. And if you don't sell them, lend me one.'

'But we don't have small bottles. We only have ordinary-sized ones.'

'An ordinary one then.'

'I have to get it from our store in the back. First I must serve these customers.'

'You're an angel, Settimio.'

While she was waiting for him to get the bottle she went to the pay-phone at the street end of the bar. She rang the hotel and asked to be put through to Larry. It had just begun to ring when to her horror Rosa Agambo walked into the bar. She put down the phone.

'Hi, Rosa. I'm looking for Carlo. Have you seen him?'

Rosa, a little startled, said, 'Carlo? I thought he was out of town. So he's back already is he? Why don't you both come over for a drink later on?' Incredibly, it seemed she hadn't even heard of the arrest.

'No, I don't think so. I'm rather off the booze at the moment. Getting serious about things at last. In fact I'm going to England.'

'Really! When do you leave?'

'Any minute. At least tomorrow. I'm not sure. A lot's happened which I can't tell you now.'

'Is it an audition?'

'Yes. Well, not exactly.'

The waiter came back with the bottle of vodka wrapped in tissue paper. Eva got out her purse and spilt a sheaf of banknotes on the floor. She knew she was blushing about the vodka, and the sight of the notes brought back the vision of the briefcase in the bank manager's office, which increased her confusion. She stooped to pick them up, trying to hide her face. She said to the waiter, 'Keep the change.'

'And when are you coming back?' Rosa said.

'I'm not coming back,' Eva said with relief. 'I'm going to London for good!'

'Have you had a row with Carlo?'

'Yes – that is, no. Listen, Rosa, will you promise not to say anything?'

'About what?'

'About having seen me here. About anything. Will you?'

'All right. But I don't really understand.'

'It's important for me that I don't mess this up. I've been letting things slide rather, you see, in the last few years. It started with losing the baby really. Or maybe even before that. I've got a real chance now to sort out my life so it's important I don't miss it, you understand? I have to leave immediately.'

'Brava. Keep in touch with me.'

Out on the street Eva broke into a run. She ran down the block and at the corner she cannoned into a man who came out from behind the building. The bottle flew out of her hand and hit the ground with a crack like a gun, like the sound of a door breaking. Liquor and broken glass went everywhere, a woman shrieked. The man was on his hands and knees. Eva ran. She ran straight into the Corso under the wheels of an oncoming car which swerved violently, missed her by inches, and slammed into a shop-front in a cascade of smashed glass. People were screaming. Eva ran.

It seemed she'd never run so swiftly. She didn't tire, she wasn't out of breath. In the distance she could hear a siren. She stayed in the narrow streets because she wanted to lose herself, to become inconspicuous. Outside a cinema a crowd of people stared suspiciously, and she quickened her pace, hoping to God no one recognized her. A little further on she saw a church door and ducked inside.

There was a service going on, and she knelt down at the back next to a wax statue of the Virgin, shaking all over. The Virgin was robed in dirty white. She had a blue sash falling from her joined hands and she was strung about with blue and transparent necklaces with crosses hanging from them. She had a very peaceful, serene expression. About her head stood a ring of twelve stars lit from the inside, some of them rather faint, and in front of her two real lilies stood in a Murano vase. Lilies are for death. It had been only a matter of inches, just now. Next time would surely be the one. She wondered about the plane journey, and imagined the aircraft spinning like a silver boomerang out over the celestial blue Mediterranean: in the cabin, coffee cups flying, screams, she and Larry sitting beside each other. But they might go even sooner than that. If only she could believe in the Virgin now, how strong she would feel. Like the Marxists. As long as you could face death with some kind of conviction. Beside her was a row of electric candles, red and white, with switches to turn them on and off. A little plaque said, 'Offerte L. 200'. She got a coin out of her bag and dropped it in the slot underneath and switched one of them on. But it meant nothing to her. She noticed for the first time that at each corner of the altar a tall pole projected into the air to a height of ten feet or so, and that on top of these poles were gilt carvings of the ox, the lion, the eagle and the man, symbolizing the evangelists. The eagle stirred under her gaze. She looked away quickly. The priest announced a hymn and the organ began to lead the congregation through a slow, raggedy first verse. The meagre light inside the building gave the priest's features a metallic tinge, as though they had been sprayed with silver paint. Eva began to worry that this image was beginning to wobble as well. She looked away. The whole church appeared vaguely threatening now, as she felt her heart begin to race. The wax statue of the Virgin seemed to be filled with power, like a voodoo object. She looked up. The evangelists had gone. The four poles were surmounted by small inconspicuous spheres. For a moment she was rooted to the spot. Then she turned and ran to the door, tripped in the darkness on a wooden kneeler and went sprawling on the marble floor, picked herself up and burst through the swing door into the street.

She crossed the hall to the lift and pressed the button. She was sweating and her legs felt like they might give way underneath her. At the top she hesitated for a moment outside before putting her key in the lock. She turned it as quietly as she could and then pushed the door gingerly ajar. The kitchen light was on. Through the window, from the music school, came the sound of someone frenziedly practising Stockhausen. There was mail addressed to her on the kitchen table. She ignored this, and went straight through to the bedroom and pulled open the drawer in the magot chinois. It was empty.

'I thought you might come back sooner or later.'

Carlo! She turned round and he was standing at the bathroom door. He must have heard her come into the flat and waited in there to surprise her. She said, 'Where have you put it?'

'At Fernia.'

'At Fernia?' A wave of nausea passed through her. It couldn't be true. She said, 'You're lying.'

'Why should I lie? I went out there today to think things over. I feel a lot calmer about it all now. I want to apologize for making a scene last night. I was wrong to try to stop you, if you really want to go to London with Larry. I don't want to keep you here against your will. I don't want you to think of me as a tyrant, whom you have to escape.'

'I don't think of you like that, Carlo.'

'Thank God. At least I have that consolation. Can you try to think of me with, if not love, then at least ordinary affection?'

'Of course. I do.'

'I wonder.'

'I promise I do.'

'Will you do something for me? No, on second thoughts, maybe I shouldn't ask you. I don't want it to seem like a demand.'

'What is it?'

'I'm not going to be upset if you say no, it's just that I'd like to talk things over a bit together. I'm not going to ask you to stay, that's a promise. I won't make another scene, either. We could go out to Fernia, and talk for an hour or two, and then I'll drive you back to town. We don't even have to discuss your going away if you don't want. Please. It would make me feel that at least there was some kind of affection between us, some kind of mutual trust.'

Under the plane trees on the Lungotevere cars were already showing lights. On hot summer nights like this people want to get out of their apartments and the traffic builds up in the streets of the city. By the time they got on to the *raccordo anulare* the day was fading. Then it was dark, and the broad swinging curves of the highway were delineated only by the streams of white headlamps coming towards them, and red tail-lights going away. From time to time the winking lanterns of a big jet passed overhead. They had missed the evening flight by now, she thought.

At the gate Carlo got a buzzer out of the glove compartment and punched in a code. It was the first time she had seen it work. Carlo was absurdly pleased. He parked in front of the house and got out. The crickets were deafening. A sliver of new moon hung in the sky.

Eva went upstairs to the bedroom and got the opium and the pipe. In the sitting room Carlo had put the vodka on the table by the sofa with a little glass beside it. She poured herself one and drank it while he made up the pipe. When they had smoked, a lot of the tension between them disappeared and it felt almost like old times again.

Carlo said, 'I know you've made up your mind to go off with Larry and I'm not trying to stop you. Have your fling, do whatever it is you want to do. But don't say you're leaving me. When you've got it out of your system, come back to me, Eva. Come back to me because I love you, because I'm your husband. At least say you'll consider it. At least say it's not out of the question.'

It seemed so generous and loving that for a moment she was

overcome. She wanted to say yes, she would at least consider it. Perhaps he was right after all and once you were married to one person there was really no point in going off and getting married to someone else. But she had made up her mind to be tough and she reminded herself that tomorrow it would all be over, and she would be in London with Larry. The one thing she must not do is give Carlo a lot of false hopes about her coming back. She said, 'You'll soon have another girl, Carlo. Probably younger and more beautiful than me.'

'Never. I'll never love anyone as much as I love you.'

'I'm sure you said that to Annette and Martina.'

'I'm different now. I'm not like the person I was then.'

Yes, and he'd change again, she thought. It was in his nature. Like a snake, he had plenty more lives ahead of him, sloughing his skin and starting over again. But she couldn't do that. She was growing old like everyone else. She sucked and held in the perfumed smoke and thought of Larry, how he looked a little bit older than before. The handsome mouth, the hair slightly receding. Yes, they had changed, it was true, and so had the world. Maria was a Christian, Polly was married. And Carlo? They say junk keeps you young. Was he embalmed in opium like a fly in honey, hermetically sealed? Perhaps those things which happen to everyone in life, and which make it impossible for one to be quite the same from then on, perhaps those things simply didn't penetrate inside him? He said he had been hurt when Martina left him, but had he really been? She wondered if she too was a little embalmed by the drug. Would she suddenly look older when she stopped smoking it? Would she come back from Paradise, like Gilgamesh, 'with the face of one who has taken a long journey'?

'I know that things haven't been right between us for some time now,' he was saying. 'I should have spoken to you about it before – don't say anything, I know it's my fault. The thing is, I've been so preoccupied with this damned abattoir and all its ramifications that I've neglected a lot of things which were very important. I know you're dissatisfied with the way we live. I know the social life here doesn't interest you much. I know you're basically quite bored. And I know how much it upset your confidence when we lost the child. But I thought we could work these things out. Honestly, I'm prepared to make changes and concessions. We can spend more time in England, for example, and we can try to have another child.

The doctor only said to wait for another year or so. There's no reason it should happen again. We'll see the best specialists this time, in Harley Street, in America, wherever they are. And we'll see some new, younger people – I don't mind, in fact I prefer it. I'm fed up with the same old crowd we always see here.

'I know you're determined to go off now with Larry and though I don't agree with it, I can't stop you. In some ways I'm pleased you're going to be out of the country because I think you may be safer in London. But I don't think it means everything's over between us. OK, so you're not in love with me the way you used to be, maybe some of the first freshness and excitement has gone out of it. Well, you can't be on honeymoon for ever. Do you remember when we were first together?'

'Of course I do.'

'Nobody can be in love like that all the time. That's what you have to realize.'

Eva thought of the time when she had first been with Carlo. Normally she would have been irritated beyond endurance by such a claim, but now the opium was making her very calm and very lucid. She realized that he simply had no inkling of her deepest feelings and that he never had. There was no point in being angry with him about that. She knocked the dead ash from the pipe and began to fill it up again. Ought she to phone Larry and tell him she was on her way? He must have expected her hours ago. The phone lay on the table in front of her, but she couldn't very easily call him now while Carlo was in the room. She wished she had at least left a message at the hotel before going out. Why hadn't she spoken to him from Settimio's? Eva thought of the hundreds of days she had longed to be out of this house, to leave Carlo, to be rid of this whole life she had somehow slipped into, without even wanting it. Well, now she was going. All she had to do was walk out of the door and get in the car and – already she could feel the marble staircase of the hotel beneath her feet – she would be standing at Larry's door. He would still be there: where else should he be? It struck her that the impasse she had reached in her life would have been disastrous, insoluble, without him. She was fortunate indeed to be able to hold out her hand and have him help her up, as easily and swiftly as if he'd been helping her out of a chair.

Carlo said, 'Marriage isn't just about being in love. The whole point of being married is that you agree to make an effort to work things out. There's no sense in breaking it off just because you have a misgiving: who are you going to find that you don't have some kind of misgivings about? In any case, this is the first time we've even mentioned having a problem. Once you've loved each other like we have, what's the point in trying to start all over again with someone else?'

Like someone watching a child playing with a jigsaw, Eva could see with the greatest of ease that this piece, which didn't fit their marriage at all, was exactly what filled the gap in her love affair with Larry. Suddenly she couldn't bear it any more. It was too hypocritical to sit here listening to him tell her how much they had loved one another when she hadn't ever loved him at all, when in fact most of the time he filled her only with pity or disgust. She jumped to her feet and went into the kitchen. The strip-lights flickered as she snapped them on, illuminating in lightning flashes a man standing by the sink, facing her: a pig-like man, with a snout and little eyes set close. She blinked, waiting for the vision to fade, but instead the man came towards her and grabbed her roughly by the arm. He said, 'Don't try to struggle.'

She was lying on the bed upstairs. Through the window she could see the tops of the cypresses like a row of blackened halberds, and the falcate moon shining above them. Footsteps sounded about the house. A little earlier she had heard them bring Carlo up to the spare room, and his muted cries. Because the window was closed there was no sound of the crickets outside, just these steps in a silent house. The moon seemed very close, bathing everything in its faint, silvery light. She felt completely in its power, like the tides of the ocean and like the lobsters that walk under the sea. A silvery woman tied down to the bed. Andromeda. She could see it all with perfect clarity: not just what was happening now, but the endless succession of weaknesses which had bound her down gradually over the years. Outside in the passage the sound of splashing water came to her ears, the voice of the sea, a heady perfume – was it of seaweed, or the engines of ocean-going liners? It was the perfume of petrol.

— 18 —

It was one of those summer days in England when the weather never settles for more than a few minutes: a strong, gusty wind blew dark clouds across the sky, running their shadows over the fields and downs. Sometimes a few spots of rain fell and people put up their umbrellas; but the next moment a swathe of blue sky would open up and a cold bright sun appeared out of nowhere. Larry had driven down with his grandmother. As the car rattled over the cattle-grid the sun came out again and the drive shone black after the rain. They passed through the iron gate and pulled up in front of the house. There were a lot of cars here already. Larry recognized Polly's red Mini and Scrope's Volkswagen. Dog's Bentley had a crumpled wing and the paintwork was covered in pigeon droppings. Larry remembered the cars jumping in the flash of the exploding fireworks; he had peered into the darkness, looking for the yellow Renault. And after the display he had waited by the empty place at dinner – when had he not waited for her? He had waited when she was with Ricky, he had waited when she was with Gawain.

A group of people, among whom he recognized Hugo and Suki Brett, were making their way along the path which led down to the chapel. Larry and his grandmother got out of the car and walked behind them. The far end of the park was overcast, but where they were walking and on the chapel itself was a hazy sunlight. The wind in the tops of the trees was making them roll like ships. You could see it gusting on the surface of the lake.

He had waited for her at the hotel. It was cool in there after the heat of the afternoon and it seemed almost unnaturally quiet after the demonstration. When he went up to his room and saw she wasn't there, he thought, damn Eva. He could never rely on that girl.

Her bag was on the dressing table. He took her cigarettes out, and as he did so a letter caught his eye, addressed in his own handwriting: 'Eva Clermont, Villa Patrizia, Fernia, Lazio'. The postmark was three years old. Why on earth was she carrying this around with her? It was written on the notepaper of Polly's house in Rutland Gate. He recalled the scene: it was before he had begun his liaison with Polly. He had been at a party there, and he was very drunk. The letter itself suggested this, replete with arrows and crossings out, written in slanting lines squeezed in at the end, without margins, rambling and allusive . . . 'My darling,' he read:

What hell this all is, which would have been bad enough if you had been here, but which without you seems impossible – so unlikely and hellish that one could almost doubt its reality, and certainly would, were it a film or a play. Let me explain, darling. We both agreed that the Gawain and Ricky episodes were forgiven and forgotten, so perhaps I shouldn't raise sleeping dogs. There is a song they've been playing tonight, I don't know if you know it, about murdered Delia who tries to get up out of her grave – and, well, that's how I can't help feeling about these episodes. I'm sure you never could conceive the appalling pain of my imaginings where your infidelity was concerned. But Eva, all that is song and dancing compared to the tortures of the damned in hell that I am living through now without you. It is as though you were dead. How can you ever hope to live happily with someone else if you couldn't live happily with me? I see you everywhere since you have gone; on the street, in the bus, even at the office. The air is full of your ghosts . . .

Larry turned on the television. On the news there were pictures of the demonstration. A politician was saying that Europe must take its own destiny in hand. A priest was interviewed about the apocalypse, a mother about children. He thought of Eva losing her baby, her sense of doom, her premonitions of death. He thought of the day at Castagna when he'd waited for her, playing cards with Dog and Maria while the wind banged the loose shutters round the house. Why was he even thinking about that? In any case, she had come to the station.

She would be all right now. She was in little danger on the streets provided she came back here and didn't go to Carlo's flat. Probably she had gone to get a paper, or simply for a walk, and she would soon be back where she had stood this morning, with a beer in her hand beside the fridge, her tapering legs, her funny slanting eyes. The phone rang. When he picked it up he could hear a hubbub of voices for a moment, the sound of a crowded room, and then the other person hung up. Was that Eva? And if so, why had she hung up? He wondered if it had been Carlo, expecting Eva to answer.

He turned on the taps in the bathroom. From the red and white striped sponge-bag on the shelf he took a canister of shaving foam and spread it over his face and neck. He ran the hot tap over the razor, and then he paused. The bath taps were drumming so loudly he thought he wouldn't hear the telephone so he went and fetched it as far as the wire would reach, between the end of the bed and the bathroom door. On the television a doctor and a biologist were arguing the effects of nuclear winter in terms of hundreds of millions of dead. When he went back to the basin the mirror was all steamed up from the hot tap. He wiped it off with his hand and his reflection appeared, white-bearded like an old man. He began to shave himself.

The phone rang while he was in the bath. He leapt out and crouched beside it on the floor. 'Hello? Eva?' But it was Potocki calling from London. 'Larry, hello! At last! Where the hell have you been? I thought you'd disappeared completely . . . What happened? Didn't you get my message? . . . Jesus, why didn't you call in? We've been going nuts over here, trying to get hold of you. Listen, we want you to go down to Tripoli tomorrow to get some action on this big deal new hijack . . . what hijack? Christ, Larry, are we on the same planet? . . . Yeah, a PIA 727 on some military airfield outside of Tripoli . . .'

As he was speaking Larry could see the pictures going up on the TV in front of him. He said, 'Listen, Danny, I can't go down there, I've got something important to do here in Rome.'

'What d'you mean you can't go down? What the hell's going on in Rome, have they shot the Pope?'

'Listen, Danny. I've got some good shots of the demo here. But I can't go to Tripoli tomorrow. I have to bring my fiancée back to England.'

'I don't care what your fiancée's doing. I need you to get down there. What fiancée?'

The congregation got to their feet as the priest came in at the door of the chapel. Behind the priest walked Lady Clermont, as white as a ghost, supported on either side by her husband and Scrope. They took their places.

The priest said, 'We are gathered together today, not to mourn, but to give thanks to God . . .'

Everyone mumbled the amens. They sang 'Abide with me'. Whenever the sun came out the stained-glass windows scattered little flakes of coloured light on the stone flags of the nave. On the walls there were plaques commemorating the Clermonts of former ages. Generation after generation they had gone up, like photographs in an album. The altar was choked with lilies, the air heavy with their fragrance.

'*As soon as thou scatterest them, they are even as asleep: and fade away suddenly like the grass.*

'*In the morning it is green, and groweth up: but in the evening it is cut down, dried up and withered.*'

When he'd arrived the ruins of the villa were smouldering under the glare of the firemen's floodlamps. They had already put out the blaze by this time, though you could smell the particular bitter smell of the fire from as far away as the village, so different from woodsmoke or coalsmoke or any other kind of smoke. Most of the roof had fallen in, the windows were empty. Thick black smoke billowed out of one corner only, where a helmeted figure stood directing the jet from a thick hose. It looked like something from one of those bombed-out cities – Dresden or Hamburg – of which he had seen pictures. Where the parking shelter had been stood a burnt-out chassis. Most of the firemen had gathered by the engines, their tasks completed. Against the trees a blue light was flashing from the roof of a police car. He saw the firemen point him out and then the policemen came over.

There were two of them, a fat middle-aged subordinate and a young one with wavy hair who seemed more intelligent. The middle-aged one took out a set of handcuffs but the young man told him to put them away. Larry got in the back of their car.

'. . . *I saw a new heaven and a new earth: for the first heaven and the first earth were passed away; and there was no more sea.*

'*And I John saw the holy city, new Jerusalem, coming down from God out of heaven, prepared as a bride adorned for her husband . . .*'

'Mr Hudson, how well did you know Mrs Spinelli?'

'I would say I knew her well.'

'Very well?'

'Yes, I think you could say that.'

'You don't seem very sure.'

Larry didn't reply. He drew in a lungful of smoke and looked out at the clouds of insects which swarmed into the firemen's lamps. It must be two or three in the morning now. Inside the car an air freshener overlaid the bitter smell of the burnt villa. The windows were all down, he could hear the monotonous crunching of the waves down on the beach. He wondered if they would let him go or if he'd have to spend the night in a cell.

'Mr Hudson, did you see Mrs Spinelli regularly?'

'No. I saw her about three years ago. And then yesterday.'

'And Mr Spinelli?'

'I only met him once.'

'Why did you come to the villa tonight?'

'It was an impulse. In view of what happened perhaps one should say an instinct.'

'I see. Mr Hudson, when I first saw you you were taking a photograph of the burnt villa. Why were you doing that?'

'I'm a photographer. It's natural to me. I do it without thinking.'

The organ began to play. The priest walked slowly away from the altar, holding the cross in front of him, and the Clermonts fell in behind. Once they had left the other pews began to empty, row by row. Larry took his grandmother by the arm and went out into the park. In front of them a thin file of black-clad figures was making its way across the lush grass in the direction of the house. After the mustiness of the chapel and the cloying scent of the lilies it was a relief to smell the rain-drenched pasture again. They reached the gravel at the front of the house. His grandmother said, 'Do you want to go in?'

'Just for a minute, Grandma.'

'Then remember to introduce me to Lord and Lady Clermont.'

'Of course, Grandma.'

On the table under the tapestry of Cronos, Mrs Gramercy left her coat and umbrella. They went up the polished wooden stairway and along the gallery into the library. There was quite a hubbub in here. They said hullo to the Clermonts. Maria was standing by the window with little Suki Brett. Already these two had become plump and matronly; dressed in their black it was not hard to imagine them as widowed crones. He joined Ricky Berlin and Patrick Lynch.

— 242 —

'It came as a terrible shock to me,' Ricky was saying. 'I hadn't seen her since before she was married. In fact I don't think anybody had. She never got in touch from Italy – but then that was typical of Eva. She always lived for the moment.'

'It's only three years ago she was married right here,' said Patrick. 'I wasn't asked. I don't think anyone was. Maria might have gone, and Dog. Did you ever see her, Larry?'

'Only a couple of times.'

He felt a hand tighten about his wrist and turned round. Maria drew him aside. She said, 'Scrope told me you were going to bring her back when it happened.'

'That's right, Maria.'

'Is it true what they're saying, that it might not have been an accident? You know, about the Mafia . . .'

'I don't know, Maria.'

'I'm sorry. I didn't want to be a gossip. It's just, well . . . it's so horrible. I could tell something was the matter when I saw her in Venice. It was like she wasn't there, she was so absent, distracted. She got sick there, quite delirious. She mentioned your name.'

'What did she say?'

'I don't know, she was delirious. But she was talking about you. Did she ask you to go down there?'

'It was coincidence, really. I was covering a conference down there, on nuclear power. There was a big demonstration.'

'Poor Eva. Everything went wrong for her, didn't it?'

He found Polly at the far end of the room standing by the celestial globe. He said, 'I thought you were on honeymoon somewhere on the other side of the world.'

'We couldn't go away. Or at least the doctors said it would be better if we didn't. You see, I'm three months' pregnant.'

Now that he looked at her he saw she had become a little thick-waisted. He thought she looked paler, or perhaps it was only her black dress and her red hair tied back which made her appear so. Anyone could see that she was happy. She said, 'By the way, your photos are wonderful. You're the best. Thanks.' She kissed him on the cheek.

He couldn't find his grandmother now.

Thinking she must have gone downstairs he went and looked for her in the hall and at the front of the house but she was not there either. He began to climb the terraces towards the gardens, but when he got to the iron gate he didn't go in, but put his face between the bars and looked in on the swimming pool with its bathing hut behind and the white plastic chairs. A gardener was fishing out leaves with a net on a long bamboo, depositing them on the tiled surround at the edge of the pool. He remembered Dog sitting there while the others swam, his elegant black clothes strangely at odds with his surroundings. And he thought of Johnson's bark echoing against the brick walls.

Larry turned away. From where he stood he could see the brick house below him surrounded by its smooth zebra-striped lawns, and beyond that the park dotted with cows and pollard oaks. Black rainclouds were moving across the far end of it, darkening the waters of the lake. If the wind dropped it would surely rain. All along the far shore the young beeches tossed their bright leaves like the manes of young foals; and beyond them he could see the rectangular pens for the flamingos and the roof of the aviary. He remembered the sick bird lying in Lord Clermont's shirt at lunch and the cooing noises he made in his throat when they went to see the tragopans. He had said then that one day he would return them to the wilderness. For a moment in his mind's eye he saw a vision of Lord Clermont standing among the deodars, loosing his tragopans into the air like carrier pigeons.

He began to walk back down the terraces towards the gravel in front of the house. Some people were beginning to leave now. He could see his grandmother waving to him from the car.